26/7 £1.⁵⁰

GW00542359

October 1993

When two unlikely members of the movement are sent on a mission to take out the breakaway commander of the Fifth Brigade in London, they find themselves inside a web of mayhem which their target has spun around himself. Their mission involves collaboration with the British authorities from the local police station to Downing Street, but the outcome is more than the protagonists had ever intended.

The Lethal Link

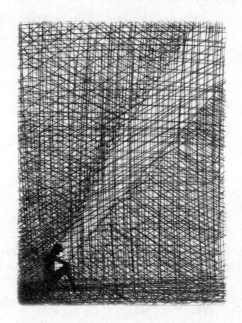

James McCauley

RED LION PRESS

First published in 2002
[At The Sign of The Lovely Lilac]
by
Red Lion Press, Great Oak, Callan, Co. Kilkenny, Ireland.
Phone   (00353) 056-25162
e mail: redlionpress@elivefree.net

Cover Design: by   FRESH01.com
Illustration: by   Kurt Ozficici

Editing and Format: by   Jim McAuley

Printing: by   Modern Printers, Kilkenny
                    Phone   (00353) 056-21739

ISBN   0-9535769-3-0

This novel is a work of fiction. The characters, names, incidents, dialogue and plot are the products of the the author's imagination or are used fictitiously.
Any resemblance to actual persons, companies, or events is purely coincidental.

All rights reserved. No part of this publication may be copied, reproduced or transmitted in any form or by any means without the permission of the publishers and copyright holder.

James McCauley

Acknowledgements

There is no doubt in my mind that this book would never have materialised, if it wasn't for the dedication, support and patience from my uncle, Jim McAuley. Above all, it was his willingness to help me fulfil a lifetime's wish. To tell a story.

When the hour-long telephone conversations were taking place between Brighton, England, and Kilkenny in the Republic of Ireland, I often wondered to myself how I ever would have achieved what I have, without the priceless help of this man. I strongly believe that there is no man I know that has a better understanding of the English language and how it should be used. I also believe that he has an open mind that knows no boundaries. He has been more than a mentor for me, he has been the right foot my backside always needed. Although it's my name that is shown on the binder of this book, to me, Jim, it will always be our book, our project, our headache and our dream. And the fact that you, dear reader, are reading this acknowledgement before going through the door to *The Lethal Link* proves one thing. The dream has come true.

I remember, at Granny McAuley's ninetieth birthday, my uncle Jim remarking in his speech that almost every person on earth believes he or she has the greatest parents. Well, in my case, I have an added bonus when it comes to this. My friends tell me that I have the greatest parents. If I phoned my father tonight and said, "Dad, I want to become the best international tiddlywinks player there is!", I know his first reaction would be, "Son, is there anything your mother and I can do to help?" As always, the love and support of my parents and my brother, Eamonn, in this project has meant everything to me. I hope I do them proud.

The help and guidance from Úna Ó Murchú, a member of the Arts Council of Ireland on this project has been incredible. By reading the successive drafts of this book she has played an essential part in 'guiding this ship into port'.

A great big thank you to Kurt Ozficici for the fantastic design, photograph and art work of the book's cover. You are a good friend, Kurt. Your advice always has been and always will be heeded — you know damn right!

But my greatest thanks must go to my best friend in the world, my wife, Linda. She was my greatest inspiration in this project. If you remember, Linda, back in Horley five years ago, when I first spoke about writing this book, you were the first person who told me to 'go for it'. My God! If only you knew then what you know now. Your patience has been tested to its maximum. You have had to live with the various sacrifices that have come with my imagination.

I will never forget that.
I will love you forever.

James McCauley
Christmas 2001

DEDICATION

To my dear children,
Mia Rose and Toby James.

To my sister Maria.

Pull up a cloud,
Sit down and have a read,
Tell me what you think..........

Once my heart has stopped beating,
My voice will keep on singing.
Once my body's done with burning,
My old 45s will keep on turning.

Zakk Zombie. 1974

1

DEATH ON THE SMALL SPEAKER

The Chinese restaurant was very busy that Friday night. It was now 11.20 p.m. and everyone had just left the two local pubs. Taking up almost a third of the restaurant was a group of young men out celebrating a stag night. They were very drunk and loud but harmless to the other people and young couples who were scattered around the restaurant, trying to ignore them.

A Reluctance To Leave

Seated there in the middle of the restaurant were two quiet and lonely bodies, a young boy of about twelve years and a man who looked to be in his mid twenties. The older man had a black ponytail of about 7 inches, a silver earring in his right ear, an unshaven, yet clean looking handsome face, dark denim jeans, desert boots and a red paisley designed shirt. The young boy was wearing bright blue jeans, a white T shirt and faded white running shoes.

'It's still raining, Billy', said the man, looking across the stag party to the window. 'It's still raining', he repeated. The boy raised his head slowly.

'Yes, I know', he spoke, trying to fight back tears.

'You don't like the rain, Billy?' The boy just shook his head.

'And you can't stay here all night', the man continued.

'I know', replied the boy. A tear ran down his face. 'I can't go without you', he pleaded.

'You have to, Billy. I'll be with you in a week or so.'

The boy looked at the man's face, looking for belief. Somehow he found it and said reassuringly, 'Okay.'

No one was taking any notice of them at all. It was their little private conversation, their little world, protected by the noise of the crowd.

'It's still raining, Billy', the man spoke with a certain quizzical tone. The boy now looked through the stag party to the window, which was now impossible to see through with the rain crashing against it.

'Billy, what are you going to do?' the man asked.

The boy suddenly realised something significant to his situation. His tears had stopped and a smile grew across his face.

'I'm going to.......' He looked around the restaurant and saw couples romancing and minding their own business. His smile grew bigger until it became cheeky.

'I'm going to blow my brains out, right here, right now.'
The man was looking at him with an even bigger smile.

'Good', he said. A minute passed in silence.

'I've got to go, Billy', the man informed him. The boy sat there just looking into space with a big grin on his face.

'Billy', the man spoke, catching his attention. 'Tell Mary I love her and I will see her soon.'

'Okay', the boy whispered.
With that the man left the table with his jacket and headed out the door into the rain. The boy just watched him leave with a feeling of reassurance.

A few moments later a waiter approached the table with a concerned look on his face. In his very poor English he fired a question at the boy.

'Everything okay with meal?'
The boy just looked at him with that same big cheeky grin on his face. The waiter was curious to know why this boy had been left to pay the bill.

'Are ready to pay bill?' he enquired with a slightly quizzical voice.

'No', the boy replied as he reached down to the small rucksack sitting beside his feet and pulled out of it what seemed to be a small handgun. Holding it in his right hand, he placed the barrel of the gun neatly under his chin and looked straight into the eyes of the waiter. No one else in the restaurant had noticed this new situation yet. The waiter froze as Billy spoke:

'I'm off to see Mary.'

Behind the restaurant was a train station where a sudden ghostly gun shot echoed through the night.

Suicide on The Ceiling

It was a good thirty five minutes before Detective Warwick arrived at the restaurant. A man in his late thirties, of medium height, with a good physique apart from a stomach born from self abuse and a face marked with lines of worry, supporting the aged bags under his eyes. This was only his third week back on the Police Force after six months' paid leave. He had taken time off to recover from the emotional shock of losing both his wife and son in a freak car accident. Not a day went by where many moments of loss weren't felt for his wife, Helen, and his son, Jonathan.

Warwick was met in the doorway by Detective Williams, a young face in the force who got on great with Warwick on the surface, but inside, Williams would be far happier if he never set eyes on Warwick again. By returning to duty Warwick had just demoted Williams from his temporary position as Head of C.I.D. As far as Williams was concerned, Warwick didn't have what it took any more. He didn't dislike Warwick one bit, but he was young and ambitious. Feelings had no place in his plan to get back to that position again.

'Alright, Tom?' Williams greeted.

'Cut the bollocks, Dave! What the fuck have I got out of bed for now?' Warwick demanded.

'Apparently a suicide case, and we're together on this one.'

'What is the point? Suicide is an open and shut case, isn't it?' said Warwick before wiping the sleep from his eyes and yawning.

Not this one', Williams informed him. Warwick was just ready to make his way in when Williams held his arm to prevent him.

'The boy was only twelve years old', Williams spoke sympathetically.

Warwick froze for a minute, then made his way past eight uniformed officers surrounding the scene. Two officers could be heard getting violently sick in the background.

Warwick stood absolutely still in front of the boy's body. He was stunned. The small body lay on the floor with a white blanket covering what was left of the boy's head. An officer from forensics was on a step ladder about three feet from the body. He was examining the ceiling.

'Jesus Christ!' Warwick whispered.

'Tom!' the man on the step ladder called to him. 'Good to see you back again!'

'Stan! What can you tell me?' Warwick reached out his hand to greet him.

'He was pretty confident about what he was going to do, as far as I can gather.' He looked up to the part of the ceiling he was examining. 'I'm pretty confident that this lad didn't even hesitate.'

'Will you call me the minute you have more information, Stan?' Warwick asked him.

'You can count on me, Tom', Stan assured him.
Warwick admired him and knew he was one of the few people he could rely on.

'You're a good man, Stan', Warwick said as he walked over to where Williams was interviewing the waiter. Williams was just finishing his interview as Warwick approached.

'There was a man sitting with him all night, Tom. He left about two minutes before it happened.'
Warwick's eyes pierced into him as he relayed this information. Warwick nodded for more.

'The boy's name was Billy Hopkirk. He had a rucksack with him, with school books, a pencil case, music magazines and a sweat shirt inside. We've just run his name through the computer. He's not on the missing list and there's no answer at his home address', Williams informed him. He could see

Warwick thinking as he looked back at the boy's body on the floor behind him.

'This man that was with him - did he settle the bill?' Warwick asked.

Williams looked confused as to why Warwick asked him this.

'No, he didn't.'

'Sir!' a uniformed officer approached Warwick. 'There's someone outside I think you should talk to.'

The two men left the restaurant and went into the rainy night. Warwick stopped half way across the green verge to light a cigarette when the lady in question approached him. She was small and fairly plump with a face that read years of worry upon it.

'Excuse me, sir', she asked, 'what happened here tonight?' Warwick couldn't stand people being nosy when he was in this sort of mood.

'That is confidential', he snapped. 'Why do you ask anyway, what is it to you?'

She explained in a very innocent apologetic voice: 'Well, you see, I was to pick up my son here but I was a bit late. You may have questioned him about something. His name is Billy Hopkirk.'

Shock for A Sore Head

It was 9.40 a.m. next morning and Church Street, Enfield, was getting prepared for the usual Saturday shopping spree. Decorated shop fronts displaying sales that seem to go on for months. Market stalls were sitting like targets waiting to be attacked by the ever growing religious cult, "The Bargain Hunters", and banks were open doing their Saturday morning shift. It was like any other Saturday morning on Church Street.

Martin Harman was sitting in his office in the bank thinking to himself why he goes out with his friends on a Friday night, getting drunk beyond words, when he's got work on a Saturday morning. His office was absolutely silent, when suddenly the door opened and his friend was standing there with two cups of coffee.

'You look like ten tons of shit, mate', he told Martin.

'Ken, close the door, Whiley thinks I'm snowed under in paper work.'

Ken closed the door with his feet.

'So how did you get on with that bird?' Ken asked him.

Martin went pale with shock, 'What bird?'

Ken looked shocked, but just couldn't help but begin to laugh.

'Oh, shit', he whispered, 'please tell me it wasn't the one in the Enfield Arms the other night!'

'Yes, that bird', Ken informed him.

'Oh, shit, she's a maniac. Why can't I remember what happened?'

Martin suddenly felt disappointed at the loss of what could have been a great memory. Suddenly the phone rang and interrupted his train of thought. He answered the phone on the principle that the ringing was away too loud this early in the morning.

'Hello', he answered.

'Martin, I know you told me that you're not in today, but this guy won't take No for an answer.'

'Okay, Carol, put him on line one..... Hello! Martin speaking, how can I help you?'

'You make one mistake in the next ten minutes, Mr. Harman, then people will die because of you.'

The new voice he heard was strong to the point that he recognised it straight away. It was Northern Irish. Martin looked up at Ken and Ken knew something serious had happened.

'Tell your friend to sit down and don't you dare look out that fucking window!' the voice instructed him.

'Ken, sit down!' Martin whispered to him.

'Put me on the speaker, Mr. Harman. I want to speak to both of you', the voice instructed.

Martin leaned forward, pressed a button and put the phone

down. The voice now came from the small speaker next to the phone.

'Right, Mr. Harman and friend, I'm going to hand you over to someone who is going to give you some simple instructions. You ignore them. . . . then Church Street will be all over the lunch time news.'

'Oh shit', Martin whispered.

'Good morning, gentlemen.' This voice was in polite English.

'Our sloppy introduction this morning has reduced our time to nine minutes and three seconds, so let's not try and be heroic. Otherwise there will be an explosion so loud that people on Mars will be asking 'What the fuck was that?'

'Oh shit', Martin whispered.

'Right, Harman's friend, go to the cupboard behind you, find the small spare phone speaker and plug it into line two on the phone set.'

Ken got straight up and proceeded to do so.

'Harman, dial this number on line two and then switch it to speaker two.'

As the voice was relaying the number to Martin, Ken got the speaker prepared on line two.

'Okay, what now?' Martin asked.

'We wait. Oh, by the way, Harman's friend, you look out that window again then I'll shoot your fucking face off, the voice instructed.

'Oh shit!' Martin whispered.

The number could now be heard ringing on the new speaker. Suddenly the ringing was answered.

'Good morning, Sergeant Davis speaking.'

'Code 5471. Eight minutes and sixteen seconds left on the clock of Barclays Bank on Church Street. How are you this fine morning, Sergeant Davis?'

There was a brief fifteen seconds of silence.

'Who am I speaking to?' this Davis character asked, but his tone was almost indicating that he knew full well who he was talking to.

'Commander of the Fifth Brigade, serving for the Provisional Irish Republican Army', the voice on line one replied.

'Oh shit!', Martin whispered.

2

THE POWER OF PARALYSIS

The clock on the wall showed 9.35 a.m. but the room gave the impression that it was the night time as four bodies sat around the large varnished table. Only a telephone set with a small speaker, two fairly packed ash trays, four cups of coffee, one top secret sealed file - freshly opened - and four note pads with adjoining pens lay upon this antique piece of furniture.

Four Men Waiting

One sat upright in his chair displaying his uniform proudly. He was George Taylor, head of R.U.C. in Northern Ireland. To his right was Peter Allan, head of Section 13. On file he answered to Sir John Primark, Director of Security Services. In reality he answered to the Prime Minister only. He was slumped in his chair smoking a cigarette which was one of many smoked at this gathering, as was evident from the cloud of smoke hanging over the heads at the table. To his right was John Hayward, Prime Minister of England. Like Peter Allan, his jacket was hanging around the frame at the back of his chair. His top button was undone, giving space to loosen his tie to allow air to his panicking nervous body, brought on by his present uncomfortable situation. To his right was Sir Patrick Maynard, Secretary for Northern Ireland. He also sat jacketless but his head and eyes were transfixed on the phone and its speaker at the centre of the table.

'I hope you're wrong about this phone call, Paddy', Hayward spoke in Sir Patrick's direction.

'So do I', he replied.

'We've been sitting here for five hours waiting for this mysterious phone call', Taylor spoke. 'With all due respect,

Prime Minister, I think we're wasting our time.'

'With all due respect, George, I'd like to settle the killing of innocent people', Hayward replied in an accusing tone.

Taylor sat silently looking in the direction of the Prime Minister, his eyes filled with hate.

'The people before me in my position gave your people plenty of opportunity to sort this mess out', Hayward continued. 'I feel the tax payers of this country have financed your little game for far too long now, George', he concluded.

The room fell silent for a few moments. Everybody sat motionless looking at the phone speaker. Everybody jumped in sequence as the telephone came to life and filled the room like an evil spirit. Sir Patrick leaned forward and pressed a button on the telephone set and a voice then spoke through the speaker immediately.

'Code 5471. Seven minutes and twenty four seconds and counting at a High Street Bank in a built up area, Sergeant Davis speaking.'

'What's the demand?' Peter Allan inquired.

'Same as last time, release of political prisoners serving time at the H-Blocks in Long Kesh, Northern Ireland', the voice replied.

Allan turned in the direction of Sir Patrick and the Prime Minister, looking for a reaction

'They'll do it just to add a chapter to their book', Allan told them.

'You can't do a deal with them', Taylor intruded.

'Shut up, George!' Hayward instructed him. 'Paddy?'

Sir Patrick sat there motionless, knowing he had to decide between the people of London and the people of Belfast.

'What about extra time?' he asked the speaker.

'That demand is for extra time', he replied.

That confirmed Sir Patrick's decision. Church Street was about to become the subject of conversation all over the nation.

Three Files and A Note Pad

Detective Warwick was sitting at his desk studying the three files that had been placed there at 7.27 a.m. that morning, five minutes before he first opened them. It was now 9.28 a.m. The first file was on the interviews carried out the previous night at the restaurant. The second was a file on young Billy Hopkirk and the third was on Billy's father, William. His note pad which accompanied the files contained Warwick's interview with Mrs. Hopkirk last night.

The file covering William Hopkirk, was basically about the suicide he committed three years earlier. Pictures were on display around the top of the desk, showing a body slumped across a table somewhere, a bottle of whiskey in one hand, an empty pill bottle in the other.

Name:	*William Hopkirk*
Age:	*38*
Sex:	*Male*
Nationality:	*British*
Religion:	*None*

That was one of many things that did not make sense to him.

Religion:	*None*

The waiter claimed that the boy had said: "I'm off to see Mary" just before he killed himself. Warwick, who had been brought up as Catholic, thought if someone just said "I'm off to see Mary" before they were about to kill themselves, he would have linked it to what he believed to be the Mother of God. He was obviously wrong on this occasion. Another thing that defied his powers of deduction was why this man who had been sitting with Billy Hopkirk all night and didn't pay the bill before he left.

Detective Williams walked into the office holding out a piece of paper to give to Warwick.

11

'Here you go. The name of the guy who was with the boy last night at the restaurant', he said.

'This incident happened at 11.20 p.m. last night. I left you to finish the interview with Mrs. Hopkirk at 12.35 a.m.', Warwick informed him.

'Yes, and....?' Williams couldn't understand where Warwick was going with this.

'What has taken you so fucking long to get this bloke's name?' Warwick asked quietly, looking Williams straight in the eye.

'Sergeant had me sorting out paper work all morning for an old case', Williams answered.

'I thought you were meant to be helping out on this case. Well, since you're not........., fuck off', Warwick informed him, remaining calm.

Warwick grabbed his jacket from the coat hanger beside the door and headed down the corridor towards the Sergeant's office.

Problems of Personality

It was 9.37 a.m. when Warwick flung open the door of the Sergeant's office to find him seated behind his desk, completely unmoved by this sudden, unannounced intrusion. Warwick stood just inside the doorway.

'The next time you decide to take someone off a case that I'm working on, at least have the fucking decency to tell me!' Warwick shouted at him and with that he slammed the door behind him as he headed back down the corridor. He had walked up ten steps when he heard the same door reopen.

'Warwick, get back in here!' the voice called after him.

Warwick didn't even hesitate. He turned around and headed straight back to the Sergeant's office, avoiding eye contact with him.

'What's your problem, Warwick?' the Sergeant asked as he closed the door behind him.

'I've been sitting on my arse since seven thirty this

morning, waiting for Williams to get me some very important information on the suicide case last night. Unknown to me, you have decided to put him back on some old case without bringing it to my attention.'

By this time the Sergeant had made his way back to his seat, still without eye contact from Warwick.

'Do you need Williams on this case? Because, as far as I can tell, you have a killer and you have a victim. All I need from you is the finished paperwork', the Sergeant informed him.

'Firstly, I didn't need or want Williams on this case. He's a cock-sucking little shit and you know it. So stop pairing him up with me. Secondly, I want to interview a Mr. Jacobs, who sat with the victim all night until approximately two minutes before the incident happened', said Warwick.

There was a minute's silence. Warwick knew that the Sergeant was waiting for eye contact, and he had to give in and look at him.

'Okay', the Sergeant told him as he started to get back to his paperwork. Warwick looked confused.

'What? That's it? No argument?'

'That's it. No argument', he answered.

Warwick didn't understand. He knew the Sergeant didn't like his people wasting too much time on a case like this. He was right, there was a victim, a killer and there was a restaurant full of witnesses. So why was he letting him off so easy?

'Why?' Warwick asked him calmly.

The Sergeant looked back up at him and put his pen down on his desk. He let out a small sigh and gave him a look that could almost pass as friendly.

'No one here can begin to understand what you've been through in this last year', he began. 'And, as far as I can tell, I don't think you can either, and that worries me, Tom — for your sake more than anyone else's."

'Let's cut this 'Tom' shit for a start', Warwick spat back at him.

'Okay, then. Here it is. As you may have heard, there has been some serious financial cutbacks on the force lately, and the thought of having to pension you off early made the Board shit their pants. They couldn't believe their luck when they heard you wanted to come back. So don't be getting any heroic ideas in your head about the Police Force wanting you back because of your years of experience or your great record of cases solved because, as you know, there aint that many, is there, Warwick?'

Warwick had a look on his face that showed his hate for the Sergeant.

'Why didn't you accept the pay-off, Warwick?' the Sergeant asked.

'Why don't you fuck off and mind your own business?' The anger was building up inside Warwick. He wasn't ready for this sort of confrontation but the Sergeant just wanted to break Warwick down at the earliest opportunity. For some unexplainable reason the Sergeant had made it perfectly clear on Warwick's return to the force that he was totally uncomfortable with the situation.

'Can you please refrain from using that sort of language when you're discussing something with me!' the Sergeant informed him. 'You so much as put a foot wrong under me, Warwick, and I'll have you off this Force quicker than you can possibly imagine.'

'Go fuck yourself!' Warwick answered back.

The Sergeant completely ignored this comment.

'I'm going to give you one whole week to get this case wrapped up and, as you know, that is plenty of time. So I suggest you use some of the time to think about re-applying for that pay-off, Warwick.'

The office was completely silent as the two men looked at each other with nothing but pure hatred. The silence was broken by the telephone and the Sergeant answered it after only one ring.

'Good morning, Sergeant Davis speaking.'

Upon hearing the reply, he put his hand over the phone to silence his talking to Warwick.

'That's it, can you leave!' he informed him

On leaving, Warwick heard the Sergeant speaking on the telephone.

'Who am I speaking to?'

Relentless Ticking of Time

Peter Allan was on the telephone in the small room, just to one side of the meeting room where he had just sat with the P.M. and other members of the secret meeting called that morning at No. 10 Downing Street. It was 9.46 a.m. and he had just been put through to the T.S.S. (Telecommunication Secret Service).

'Hey, Ted', he spoke into the phone, 'we've got three minutes and forty three seconds on the clock. The address is Barclays Bank, Church Street, Enfield, EN1."

Allan then put the phone down, reached into his shirt pocket and took out his cigarettes and lighter. He quickly lit one and drew in a well wanted breath of smoke to calm his nerves. He knew that all he could do was wait for the P.M.s decision and act on it without question. As he entered the meeting again there was a raging argument going on between the three other members of the meeting.

'We are sick and tired of having to clear your mess up off the streets. Now you have to deal with some of the consequences, you can deal with some of the mess!' George Taylor was shouting across the table to the man he was shaking his finger at, the Prime Minister. John Hayward was fuming.

'Whatever the consequences are today, George, I'll make sure that at twelve o'clock, midday today, every house in West Belfast is turned upside down. You are going to be in for a very long day and night. I suggest you get back to base as soon as possible.'

With that George Taylor stood up, removed his hat from

the table and headed towards the door.

'Good day to you, gentlemen', he farewelled them.

As the door closed behind him, John Hayward buried his head in his hands and let out an unnerving sigh. There was a minute's silence.

Martin Harman sat staring at the speakers in his office in Enfield.

'What now?' he asked.

'We wait for an answer', the voice on speaker one answered.

'Come on, Davis! We're waiting for an answer', Martin shouted into speaker two.

'Keep your voice down, Harman! Otherwise you won't live to hear the answer!' speaker one ordered him.

Twelve minutes to ten! 'We only have two minutes, Prime Minister!' Peter informed him. Hayward sat there in a trance, staring at the phone set. He felt hopelessly trapped. What could he do. Does he try to bargain with people who know no limit of demands, or does he impose the deadly silence upon them that will surely spell death for the innocent of Church Street.

'We can't deal with terrorists, he finally announced, 'no matter what the situation.'

He then turned to look at Allan.

'Peter?' he asked, motioning his left hand towards the phone set.

Allan leaned forward in his chair and pressed the button that broke the contact with Sergeant Davis. As he did so, he knew his action would start the ball of terror rolling.

At eleven minutes to ten Davis heard the dialling tone cut in on line two. He leaned forward and pressed the button that broke his contact with Church Street.

On hearing the dialling tone cut on line two, Harman jumped out of his seat and was just about to scream out when the walls around him suddenly sprung to life. As he felt the first grains of dust touch his finger tips an incredible force lifted him up and threw him clean through the wall behind him. This was the last chapter of his life complete.

A Tired Emptiness

John Hayward re-entered the room to find Allan and Maynard in deep conversation about a meeting that had taken place with Sinn Féin earlier in the week.

'When is the next meeting arranged to take place?' he asked them.

'Monday', Maynard answered.

Hayward sat there staring at an empty glass on the table.

'I'm tired', he almost whispered.

'It's been a long night', Maynard agreed.

'I don't mean now, I mean in general. I'm tired of dealing with people who won't go outside the boundaries of their own belief to try and help the bigger picture', he said, looking directly at the chair where George Taylor had sat earlier. Then he stared back at the empty glass before continuing:

'I'm tired of lying to my own country. I'm tired about the facts of meetings we're having with people we know are our country's worst enemy and, on top of that, if anyone knew we were talking to these.... bastards! I would shoot the leader of this country myself, if I were in the shoes of another man.... I lead a party who I know will not win a General Election for a very long time and they don't even know it yet....."

He looked as if he was going to continue but suddenly realised he was heading down a road he wanted to travel on his own. His present company had heard him speak like this a lot lately but never spoke to anyone else about it. They knew they were the only people the Prime Minister could trust with this information.

The Prime Minister looked very tired. Over the previous months John Hayward had taken on a great amount of pressure both personally and publicly. Publicly, Northern Ireland was further away form peace than ever. Britain was in the middle of its worst economic state and his cabinet had become something that resembled a pack of savage dogs, tearing the government to pieces in the eyes of the public with their sleaze and corruption.

John Hayward no longer looked like a leader. He looked like a tired man who was being dictated to from the wings. Too many times he palmed the blame off onto other politicians for things that were clearly his responsibility as a leader. Too many times he stood by and let members of his cabinet be drawn into tabloid stories of sleaze. Too many times he looked like a "has-been" at Prime Minister's question time as the young Andy Blayre with good a looking confident face tore the government to pieces with ease and confidence.

Privately the stress his body was undergoing with this public shambles was starting to take its toll. His personal doctor had ordered him to take two days' rest from public duty to let his heart and nerves relax. That meant no meetings with the pack of savage dogs or other members of his party. Obviously, his doctor knew nothing of this secret stressful meeting and the one he had arranged with his cabinet for this afternoon. This afternoon's meeting was meant to be based on the weak communications this government now had with what is regarded as Britain's greatest friend, America. But John Hayward knew only too well he'd be getting a phone call from President Clinton today pushing for a plan for peace in Northern Ireland.

His head began to pound as all the thoughts in his mind seemed to be crashing into each other like wild buffalos running for freedom on dusty ground.

'Can I speak openly for a moment?' Peter asked him.

'Please!' Hayward replied with some relief.

'Let's leave him out of the picture for the moment', he said, looking at Taylor's empty seat. 'He won't say a thing to anyone at the moment because he knows that not one of his men will complain about what's going to happen when we start turning over the Nationalist parts of Northern Ireland today. They will simply rub their hands together at all the overtime that's in store for them. He won't say anything because he knows that while these people bomb this country, it makes his job safer and even more secure. The benefits in store for him are more than he can ask for.

'What we have to do, as hard as it is, is to keep going forward. Even if you lose your power here in office, Prime Minister, at least people will know that you were the one that got the ball rolling. And only you will know how much hard work that really took.'

Hayward just sat there looking at the empty glass.

'Get the best man available for this job, whatever the cost', he told Peter.

3

REELING AGAINST THE ROPES

A young couple were just pulling up at 10.30 a.m. outside what was to be their second home. With them was their eight year old son, Kevin, an active little boy. The house was semi-detached with a garage. It sat neatly on Tenniswood Road at the bottom of Enfield Town. As they approached the house they were greeted by the previous owner, a Mr. Jacobs. A very handsome looking man with a ponytail and a silver earring in his right ear.

'Mr. and Mrs. Casey?' he asked.

'Yes, that's right', replied the lady with a smile at being greeted so warmly.

'Come inside', he instructed, letting them walk in first.

An Original Rocking Horse

As Mr. Jacobs closed the front door behind him he patted Kevin on the head.

'Who's this little fellow, then?' he asked happily.

'Kevin', the boy shouted with a laugh in his voice.

'Hey, Kevin, how are you?' he laughed.

'Okay', again he shouted.

Mr. Jacobs handed the keys to Mr. Casey and then led them around their new house. It was a neat little three-bedroomed house with a loft conversion that seemed to be a play area for a young child. Kevin's eyes lit up when he saw an original rocking horse sitting nearly in the middle of the room.

'Wow!' he shouted with excitement as he ran towards it.

'Kevin, don't! It looks very expensive' Mr Casey happily demanded.

'Yes, it's an original. Ever been on an original rocking horse, Kevin?'

Kevin shook his head with his ever innocent smile.

'Go on, have a go!' Jacobs invited.

'Mr. Jacobs, is this horse staying here?' Kevin loudly inquired.

Mr Casey was just going to say something when Mr. Jacobs quickly replied: 'Yes, of course it will, Kevin.'

Mr. Casey interrupted 'Mr. Jacobs, you can't!'

Mr. Jacobs raised his hand.

'Please! It used to belong to my young niece. She is no longer with us in this world.'

The room fell silent. All that could be heard was the horse rocking backward and forward.

'I'd like to see it go to a good owner', Jacobs added.

They all made their way downstairs to the hallway as the Caseys were explaining how they had to get back to their old address to see how the removal men were getting on. All of Mr. Jacobs's belongings had left early that morning with another removal firm, apart from a table, two chairs and a rocking horse. Just as the young family was leaving, a man was approaching the front door.

'Can I help you?'

'Mr. Jacobs?' the man asked.

'Yes.'

'I'm Detective Warwick. May I come inside?

'Yes, of course', Jacobs replied, looking very confused.

Mr. Jacobs brought him into the kitchen and offered him a cup of tea and a seat at the table. Warwick noticed the house being empty as he came through.

'Moving in?' he asked.

'Moving out, actually. You've just caught me. I leave for Scotland tonight. What seems to be the problem, Detective.....?'

'Warwick. You were with young Billy Hopkirk last night at the Oakwood Palace, Mr. Jacobs — is that correct?'

'Yes, I was. Is he Okay? Is he in trouble or something?' Jacobs asked with genuine concern.

'Sit down, please!' Warwick asked. He kept his eyes on Jacobs as he reached into his pocket to get his cigarettes and lighter. He pulled one from the packet and offered one to Jacobs.

'Thank you!' he said as he accepted.

Warwick took a long hard puff and exhaled a new formed cloud of smoke into the silent air.

'About two minutes after you left the restaurant last night.... Billy committed suicide. He shot himself with a small hand gun.'

Jacobs just froze to the spot. He turned to Warwick to see the truth written all over his face.

'What time do you leave for Scotland?' Warwick asked.

'Not until tonight. 9.30 flight", Jacobs replied trying to find himself.

'I'll need you to come down to the station - not for interrogation, I assure you. I just need to get as much information as I can about Billy and about last night before I can close the case. I'll make sure I can get you back here within the next few hours.'

'Okay', Jacobs replied, still in shock, 'just give me a few minutes to get myself together.'

'I'll wait in my car', Warwick replied.

Warwick stood up and walked towards the kitchen door, then stopped and turned once more to Jacobs.

'Mr. Jacobs, are you religious at all?'

Jacobs didn't react. He just sat there staring into space and then looked up at Warwick, suddenly realising he had missed a question.

'Sorry?'

Warwick just raised his hand.

'It's Okay. I'll wait outside.'

Jacobs sat there waiting for the sound of the front door to close behind the Detective. When that sound had made itself known, Jacobs broke into a small laugh.

'You did it, Billy, you bloody well did it!'

As Warwick sat in his car looking at his notebook while smoking his cigarette, he started to wonder about Mr. Jacobs and his reaction to the news of Billy Hopkirk's suicide. He didn't give Jacobs much time to take the information in before he fired another question at him. That was the thing that was bugging Warwick. Jacobs had answered the question immediately.

Warwick then looked at the four words he had written in his notepad: *"SHOCK? Or something else?"*

Why didn't Jacobs try to understand what he was being told instead of informing Warwick of his flight to Scotland?

'Why?' Warwick asked himself. 'Shock can be a weird fucking thing!' he concluded as he killed his cigarette in the car's ashtray.

He then turned a few pages back in his book to the other question that was puzzling him.

'Why didn't Jacobs settle the bill in the restaurant before he left?' he asked aloud.

Warwick looked up from his notebook as he saw Jacobs making his way over to the car. He quickly placed the notebook back in his pocket, not wanting to look hard faced in what he knew to be a delicate situation. Jacobs let himself in on the passenger side, carrying with him a rucksack. He placed the sack on the floor in front of him, turned to close the door beside him, turned to face Warwick and then asked him one simple question:

'Are you a religious man, Detective Warwick?'

Immediately after asking he grabbed Warwick by the back of the head with his right hand and grabbed his stomach clothing with his left and slammed his head on to the steering wheel with great force. As he pulled Warwick's head back up with the same speed, a trail of blood from the top of Warwick's nose sprang in a line from the wheel up the windscreen, across the roof of the car and behind him on to the back seat. Jacobs then proceeded to punch him with two full left handed blows into the stomach and then repeated his first action, again just catching the roof of Warwick's nose in the slam. Warwick was conscious but felt completely lifeless as he fell limp across Jacobs's lap.

'Fuck off!' Jacobs said in disgust as he threw him back across to his own side.

Jacobs then pulled a towel out from his rucksack and proceeded to wipe the blood from his lap, only to make the stain even worse. Warwick's eyes were already puffed up from the two heavy slams to his nose but he could just about focus on Jacobs though his body still felt completely lifeless. His head was resting against the driver's window. Jacobs then pulled a small hand gun from his pocket and sat the barrel on the end of Warwick's bloody nose. Warwick could not even find the energy to flinch. Jacobs's look of disgust had now changed to a look of satisfaction with results from his earlier actions.

'There is a Heaven', he happily informed Warwick, 'and there is a great comfort to be had from knowing it — especially knowing that Helen and Jonathan might be there.'

Warwick slowly began to lift his arms and move the top part of his body forward, but by the time he could fall forward Jacobs had departed from the car at top speed. Again Warwick just fell limp across the passenger seat and fell unconscious.

Visible Work of An Invisible Enemy

Four blue Transit vans with '*O'CONNEL*' written on their sides could be seen right in the heart of the debris, aiding the ambulance and firemen trying to locate any remaining bodies. There was an almost silent, ghostly chill around the place. Both ends of Church Street were blocked off — no photographers, no cameramen, no reporters and no members of the public were allowed anywhere near the heart of the town.

Sergeant Davis made his way to the middle of the debris where a tent had been set up. As he got closer to the tent he could hear the small generators running which were feeding the small flood lights surrounding the tent. Blankets were lying on the ground all around him with the shapes of people underneath, people who only a couple of hours earlier had been going about their normal business — banking cheques, paying bills, worrying if cheques would clear, demanding to know why cheques hadn't cleared, applying for overdrafts, wishing they could find a miracle to wipe out their mortgages. All this was now so irrelevant.

As he came to the entrance of the tent he met a man in plastic overalls coming out.

'Sergeant Davis', he informed the man.

'Arthur Reynolds, we spoke earlier.'

Davis could see three men inside the tent. One was holding up what seemed to be a circuit board. Another seemed to be spraying the board with something, while the third had a small computer sitting on his lap with two leads running off the circuit board.

'Any luck with the bomb?' Davis asked.

'They're setting up another tent over the North end of the site where we've just located it. This here is the telephone exchange box. The phone call made to the Bank was not from a public phone. There were no beeps. It came from a private or business line. We've got a slim chance of finding these evil fuckers. I'd make sure you have about twenty bodies to move at a moment's notice. These guys will have an address for you in the next five minutes."

'Okay, no problem', Davis replied.

As he turned away to move back to his car, he suddenly realised the strong smell he had been breathing in since he arrived. A mixture of dust, gas, burning plastic, burning flesh, smoke and diesel from the generators. This was nothing short of a battlefield where an innocent army had been wiped out by an enemy that didn't even have to show up for the battle.

Davis was suddenly stopped in his tracks by one of the builders, a man who just walked out in front of him and stared him straight in the face. Davis looked at him completely unmoved. He knew this man and this man knew him.

'Go about your business!!' Davis whispered with demanding coldness.

The man looked around him at the blankets on the ground and then looked back at Davis with a small smile on his face, only noticeable by the squint in his eye, and with a slight Irish accent he replied:

'You've certainly been going about yours by the looks of things.'

Davis swung to look around him to see if anyone could hear the conversation.

'Go fuck yourself!' he quietly spat back.

'Let's go!' Reynolds could be heard shouting from the tent.

A Not So Simple Suicide

As Warwick came around he felt a pain in his head like never before. He raised both hands, one to each side of his head, quickly trying to give the strain of his skull some relief through small movements of massage. He rubbed his eyes with his left hand, noticing that they were swelling already. It was when he moved his hand further down his face that he became aware of the open cut at the roof of his nose.

'Oh shit!' he cried out at the pain that was stronger than the one he came around in. He sat still for about thirty seconds until this greater sense of pain was replaced by the one of his throbbing head. It was then that he reached into his jacket pocket and pulled out his cigarettes and lighter. He opened his packet of Marlboro Lights and noticed straight away — seventeen to choose from. Warwick could tell by the three missing gaps at the front. Unlike the current trends of Government warnings, anti-social finger-pointing, people keeping fit and wanting to live until they were 150, Warwick absolutely loved to smoke. He loved the surge sensation of the instant rush to his head, the exhalation of smoke from his nostrils that he saw James Dean, Robert de Niro and even

Mel Gibson do in the films, the quality time of your own thoughts like the married man who visits the toilet of his own house with a newspaper after a hard day's work.

As he smoked his cigarette, he noticed his own blood all over the interior of the car, all over his clothes and all over the dashboard where he suddenly noticed a white envelope. He stared at the envelope without touching it until he finished his cigarette. He leaned across and picked it up with his bloody hand. No writing on the envelope and not even stuck down at the back. He opened it up and pulled from it what seemed to be a note paper folded in half. He opened it up and read the writing, written in blue felt-tip.

"Stansted 21.30   BA 4132"

Warwick sat thinking about what Jacobs had said to him earlier about Helen and Jonathan and how Jacobs had openly invited him to track him down at the airport. Warwick felt confused at how such a simple case as suicide had turned so complicated. He felt tortured at how a stranger could mention the names of his deceased wife and son in a way he had not thought about them. He felt curious as to how this stranger knew about them. He felt betrayed by his own inability to do his job as he used to do, as he wouldn't be stuck with a simple suicide case, and he felt foolish at the bloody and painful state in which this stranger had left him.

He reached back into his jacket pocket and once again pulled out his pack of Marlboro Lights. Sixteen to choose from. As he removed the chosen cigarette, the road leaped into life with loud sirens and flashing blue lights. Two Transit police vans packed with bodies, three police cars and one unmarked police car. Warwick's immediate reaction was to jump out of the car and let himself be known for any assistance required, until he realised where they were heading, straight to Jacobs's house. He stayed in his car and watched from across the road. The back doors of the vans sprung open and ten policemen from each van ran straight to the front door, fully armed and ready. They broke the front door open and ten policemen from each van ran straight to the front door, fully armed and ready. Warwick could tell by the formation they used to enter the house that they would have it entirely scanned within ninety seconds. This was the basic break-in drill. One of the police cars blocked the bottom of Tenniswood Road and the other drove straight past Warwick to block the top.

All Warwick could think about was getting away from the area, getting himself medically cleaned up and getting to the airport for 9.30 that night to confront Jacobs again about his knowledge of Helen and Jonathan. Nothing was to stand in his way. He looked in his wing mirror and saw an empty drive behind him. He started the car up, slammed it in reverse and manoeuvred the vehicle on to the drive. Just as he slammed it into first gear, he glanced again at Jacobs's house and suddenly noticed Sergeant Davis standing to one side of the unmarked police car, staring straight into the eyes of Warwick. Warwick paused for a moment, looking straight back into the eyes of Davis. All Warwick could think about was getting to the airport and with that in mind he drove at a normal speed from the driveway to the top of the road.

As Warwick approached the top of the road he was flagged down by one of the policemen. The policeman with a bullet-proof vest, baseball police cap and a loaded gun-belt took one look at Warwick and the bloody mess inside the car, then went straight for his gun, pointed it at Warwick and shouted his panic-struck instruction:

'Out, Now!'

He was a young rookie, obviously on training experience as Warwick could tell by two things. Firstly, by the way the second policeman stood a few yards behind him, overlooking the situation, casting his experienced eye over the young rookie. And secondly, on how the young rookie didn't at all look comfortable. As he flagged the car down, Warwick could see the rookie's mouth open as he breathed in the brisk air of the night. A face of confidence is one with a closed mouth. Simple but true.

'Hold it a second!' Warwick tried to reason as he went to reach for his badge from his inside pocket.

'Make one more move and I'll shoot your fucking face off!' The Policeman was panicking now, Warwick could see the gun shaking in his hand.

'I'm Police! If you let me slowly get my badge, I'll prove it. Otherwise, shoot me!'

'What?' the policeman quizzed.

'Shoot me!' Warwick calmly informed him.

Before he knew it, Warwick had quickly pulled out his badge and was holding it through the window, ready for inspection. The policeman cautiously received it from Warwick but didn't take his eye off him and passed it slowly to the other policeman behind him.

'It's clear', the second policeman informed him.

'Call it through', the first policeman instructed.

With that the second policeman spoke into his radio:

'Sergeant Davis?'

'Receiving."

'We have a Detective Warwick here. You *did* say that no one was to leave the area.'

Warwick could see Davis in his wing mirror. He looked as though he hadn't moved a muscle since they eye-balled each other a few minutes earlier. Warwick could feel himself beginning to panic inside, he had to get to the airport. He reached into his side pocket to feel the cold metal of the Smith PK automatic pistol touch the sweaty palm of his hand. What had he got himself into? Here he was, ready to shoot a fellow policeman for reasons he could hardly bring himself to understand.

'It's Okay, leave him through!' Davis informed them via the radio.

Familiar Frustration

Peter Allan was seated in a small room on the first floor of 10 Downing Street, known as the P.M.s "thinking room". A small fire place with an armchair on either side, a small side cabinet with various bottles of whiskeys and brandies, a shelf full of Jack Higgins novels, all of which had been read, as was obvious from the creases on the sides, and a table covered with the notes that Allan had brought with him. The walls were lined with pictures of cricket matches, batsmen, bowlers and two single cricket bats hung like trophies each side of the cabinet.

John Hayward entered the room looking stressed out from the meeting he just had with the Cabinet. He removed his jacket and flung it over the back of the vacant armchair. He undid his top button and loosened his tie.

'Jamesons?' he asked Allan.

'Please!' Allan acknowledged.

As Hayward poured the drinks he played the meeting he'd just had with his Cabinet, over in his mind. He decided to avoid the American issue in the current state of events and ordered his Cabinet to try and pull together on the Northern Ireland issues in these darkest hours. He told them of his plans to talk to the IRA's vocal political party, Sinn Féin. He told them of a peace deal that he and Sir Patrick Maynard were putting together. He spoke of his party building an everlasting road to peace in Northern Ireland and of being the first British Government to put a stop to the mayhem and violence that had reigned in Northern Ireland for over thirty years. But he didn't want the pack of savage dogs to screw it up. He didn't want his ministers mouthing off to the press about what they think should be done with the IRA and how this country should get behind the British people of Northern Ireland to fight the disease of terrorism. Now was a time for silence and a call for peace. Not a time for political game playing. He ordered his Cabinet to behave over the next forty eight hours or they would be out of the party indefinitely.

He brought the drinks to the small table in front of the fire and slumped into the chair looking into the eye of the fire. He sat up and took a sip of the whiskey. The bite to the back of the throat, the taste buds coming to life through confusion and the fume that finds its way to the roof of the nose — he felt the better for it.

'Bring me up to date! I hear we have an address', Hayward enquired as he took another sip from the glass.

'No joy. The house was rented and the rent was paid in cash on the first Friday of every month without fail.'

'There must be a name?' Hayward asked.

'Jacobs. No fingerprints anywhere in the house, no records, no pictures, no nothing. A professional vacation of the house', Allan informed him as he reached for his drink.

'This sounds so familiar', Hayward added.

'Your thoughts are right, I'm afraid.'

Hayward stared into space as he spoke.

"Dwyer", he whispered.

'That's right, Tony Dwyer.' Allan could see the fear in Hayward's eyes. The fear of more blood on the streets of London.

'I remember!' Allan started, "being seated in this very room, in this very same chair and your predecessor sat where you are now! I told her what I knew then of Tony Dwyer and his history. The very next morning she had men at each end of the street building the famous security gates. She had 126 people arrested for stopping their cars on Whitehall the following week. You know I was very close to Maggie Thornbird. Even today I have nothing but respect and gratitude for what she did for my country and me. For all her great achievements and victories, she couldn't get to Dwyer but, by Christ, she tried.'

Hayward sat in silence for a moment thinking about the great Iron Lady, and then found himself asking that question he had asked so many of his fellow aides:

'Do you think she would have followed the path that we

now find ourselves walking along?'

'No, definitely not', Allan was certain as he continued, 'but then again she never got to Dwyer. She never even came close.'

'Okay!' Hayward was feeling positive again. 'I hear Sinn Féin have been in touch.'

'They've convinced the I.R.A. to give us two men. One to go out into the fields with our man, and one to stay in London where I can keep up to date with him concerning all field movements.'

Allan then pulled out a photo from his files and passed it to the P.M.

'Brooks. Martin Brooks. Section 13's best Field Agent ever.' Hayward looked at the photograph. A man getting out of a car, mid thirties, black hair with grey bits at the sides, medium build and well dressed. Allan passed another photo to the Prime Minister. It was almost identical to the first, only a little closer. It was close enough for Hayward to notice the distinct feature of this man, his piercing blue eyes.

'Any information on him?' Hayward asked.

'No', Allan flatly answered, 'Dwyer was responsible for the deaths of three S13 Field Agents two years ago. Even went as far as Russia to have one of them killed. Brooks was adamant from day one not to have a file kept on him. It turned out Dwyer had an informant at the Ministry of Defence, in the printing office.'

Allan took the pictures from the PM and threw them into the fire.

4

COOLNESS IN PURSUIT

Warwick made his way to the bar opposite McDonalds at Stansted Airport and ordered himself a pint of John Smiths. He then made his way to one of the tables outside the bar that overlooked the "City Flyer" desk that Jacobs would have to check into. The hands of the large Airport clock were exactly on 8 o'clock. Warwick pulled out his packet of Marlboro Lights, nine to choose from. He checked the roof of his nose where he had applied a plaster earlier, to make sure no blood was dripping from the sides.

Meeting Friends, Old and New
He was just about to choose a cigarette when a packet of Marlboro Lights was thrown on to his table from behind him. Warwick kept his eyes on the packet and waited for the provider's introduction. The man sat to his right, placed two sports bags on the floor between them and then proceeded to open the packet of cigarettes, removed one for himself and then offered one to Warwick. Short grey cropped hair, in his mid forties, clean shaven, but instantly recognisable. Warwick looked at him in confusion.

'Jacobs?' he asked.

'I worked at the Dominion Theatre three years ago', Jacobs happily informed him, 'make-up department and, in case you're wondering, this is the real me.'

Warwick was in shock. Jacobs' appearance seemed to have naturally aged nearly twenty years since he last saw him only hours ago. How had he not noticed the make-up when he met him earlier? How had he not noticed that Jacobs' hair didn't change a bit when he gave Warwick a beating in the car? Had Warwick's vision not been so blurred after Jacobs' first punch, surely he would have worked out that it was a wig.

'Jesus Christ! I don't fucking believe it!' Warwick announced, totally shocked by this new revelation.

'How demoralising!' he thought as he rubbed his nose wound, checking for any bleeding. 'Getting beaten up by a man in make-up!'

Jacobs looked at Warwick's nose and apologised:

'Sorry about your nose but, as you could tell, I couldn't hang around for the visitors.'

Jacobs looked over to the "City Flyer" desk and nodded to a Jamaican man with shoulder length dreadlocks, then turned back to face Warwick.

'Now you know what I really look like, okay? I'll be in touch.'

'Hold it!' Warwick demanded, 'who are you?'

'Who am I!' Jacobs laughed and then became dead serious. 'I am the one who ruined your life. I am the one who is going to become your worst fucking nightmare.'

Jacobs was now nose to nose with Warwick but was unaware of two things. One, Warwick had managed to slip his foot through one of the handles of one of the sports bags and two, there were two armed airport policemen about sixty yards away from them walking in their direction.

'What do you mean you ruined my life?' Warwick demanded.

Jacobs quickly glanced at the Jamaican who was nodding in the direction of the oncoming police. Jacobs turned to see the policemen were only twenty yards away.

'Good evening, Detective Warwick. Like I said, I'll be in touch.'

He went to grab the two bags only to notice that Warwick had his leg inside one of the handles.

'Don't be a fucking smart-arse!' Jacobs demanded.

Warwick peered over Jacobs's shoulder and noticed the policemen were now only a few yards away.

'What do you mean, you ruined my life?' Warwick again

demanded.

Jacobs turned around and noticed the policemen walking straight towards them. With that he calmly walked away leaving the bag behind.

'I'll be in touch', he parted.

'Tom?' one of the policemen asked, looking at Jacobs walking towards the check-in and then back to Warwick.

'Everything Okay?' he asked.

Warwick looked at the policeman, a man in his late thirties and looking well for it.

'David? David Linsey?' he asked.

'Tom Warwick! How the devil are you?' the policeman asked.

Warwick and Linsey had done their training together nearly twenty years ago.

'Not too bad, David', Warwick answered.

'You look like shit, Tom! Do you realise you're bleeding?'

Warwick put his hand to his cheek and felt a trickle of blood.

'Who's the fella?' Linsey asked.

'Just wanted a light', Warwick lied. He realised he had something of importance belonging to Jacobs and didn't want Linsey to get involved. He needed to know what Jacobs meant and he knew he couldn't find out in a police interview. He'd have to find out in person.

'I was meant to meet someone here but it doesn't look like they'll show. You wouldn't happen to be walking towards the car park, would you, only this injury is making me feel a bit sick', Warwick asked.

'You can tell me how to avoid getting a beating like that, Tom', Linsey acknowledged.

With that Warwick picked up the bag and walked with the two policemen across the main area towards the Exit. Jacobs was watching from the check-in. He turned to his Jamaican friend:

'Follow Warwick, get the bag back, but don't waste him.

That's three simple instructions - any problems?'

'No problem!' the Jamaican, looking friendly, answered in a Birmingham accent, then proceeded to follow Warwick and the two policemen.

The Confidence of An Expert

The lift doors opened at 23.00 hours and a handsome man walked out into the empty reception area two floors below ground level in the Ministry of Defence. 5' 11", black short hair with grey sides, dressed in dark blue evening suit, light blue shirt and matching tie, shoes that shone as bright as the day they left their box, a rain coat carried over his left arm while his right hand carried a black shiny briefcase. Yet the most distinctive feature this man held was his piercing blue eyes.

He made his way to the desk and placed his coat and briefcase on the vacant chair, then made his way to a monitor screen and keypad on the wall to the left of the desk. He placed his hand on the screen and a bright white line ran across it. The words *"SWIPE CARD AND ENTER CODE"* appeared on the screen.

'Come on through, Martin!' Peter's voice could be heard through the speaker. Just then the two big doors to his right opened revealing a long corridor.

'The long corridor to another mission', he said to himself as he picked up his coat and briefcase and headed through the doors.

Peter Allan was seated at the top of a large table in a room lit only by three table lamps and six small lights - a relaxing setting for important talks. Seated with him was Sir John Primark, Director General of Security Services and James Moore, Allan's right hand man.

'Brooks knows why we are here?' Sir John asked Allan.

'I faxed him a scrambled message this morning.'

'Martin's had me gathering information for him all day', James added. Sir John turned back to Allan:

'Do you think he can get this bastard?'

'If he can't, I don't know who can!' Allan responded.

Just then the door opened and Martin walked in, placed his case and coat on the chair next to Moore and made his way straight over to Sir John, hand extended to grasp his.

'So good to see you again, Sir! How are you keeping?'

'Not too bad, Brooks!' Sir John always warmed to Martin.

'How is the lovely Mrs. Primark?' Martin asked.

'Lovely?' Sir John laughed. 'If I had any sense left in me, I would divorce the moaning, ugly, old bag!'

'Peter!' Brooks shook his hand before making his way over to Moore who had now started to tap the keyboard of the computer in front of him. A large screen came to light, filling the far wall of the room. Brooks standing behind Moore, placed his hands on Moore's shoulders and began a small massage.

'James, how did you get on with gathering that info for me?' Brooks asked.

'No problems', Moore told him.

'Right, Let's begin. You will have to bear with us as James and myself haven't had time to prepare', Brooks said to Peter and Sir John. Just then the whole screen was illuminated with a picture of Church Street taken before the bombing. Martin stood looking at the picture, studying every detail.

'Let's have a look at the market next to the Bank', he ordered.

James moved his mouse across the pad and clicked the cursor over the market. The whole room was silent, you could almost hear Martin's head investigating as he walked closer to the screen and pointed to a street camera on the opposite side of the market.

'There!', he pointed, 'let's have a view of the Bank from that camera.'

James tapped instructions on to the keyboard and then once again made use of the mouse. The screen changed to a view of market stalls, part of the street and an entrance to the Bank from the side.

'Bingo! Can we get the film from this camera for the hours of this morning?' he asked Peter.

'Yes. But what is it you're looking for?'

'Two things', Martin said as he walked over to his case, opened it and pulled out a file. He sat down and arranged his paperwork in front of him. The anticipation in the room was electric. What had Martin come up with? It was obviously something that had been overlooked as his confidence was so enjoyable to watch.

'First', he began, 'the explosion damaged the market, the King's Head public house, the main shops of the opposite side of Church Street, four shops to the right hand side of the Bank and the Bank itself.'

He looked up at the other three men for a response. No one could see it yet. James sat with his arms folded. Peter looked at the big screen and Sir John looked at Martin with confusion and then spoke.

'I'm sorry, Martin, we're not with you.'

'The people who made this device', he responded, "knew the actual physical impact of this bomb." He stood, walked over to the screen and picked up a long ruler from under the screen as an indicator. He pointed the ruler at a litter bin right outside the Bank, and continued his explanation.

'So why not put the bomb in there? Why not put the bomb next to one of the stalls, or in the toilet of the pub, or in this cemetery behind the Bank? They killed twenty two people this morning. They knew there would be victims, so it didn't matter where the bomb was placed. Yet they decided to place it in the basement of a high security building. Why?'

Again there was no response, but he continued as he went back over to his paperwork and took a sheet in his hand as he faced the other three, like a lawyer facing his jury. He paused for a moment as he looked at them before speaking.

'I phoned the Bank's Head Office today to see what transactions were made out of the Bank this morning. Due to the explosion, they have to go through all their main computers which they won't have completed for another twenty four hours. But what they *could* tell me, answered my suspicions. All transactions into Church Street go via a computer at a main London branch.'

He held a sheet of paper up and then read from it.

'This sheet of paper shows thirty six requests for transactions between 9.40 a.m. and 9.49 a.m. this morning. Not one of those requests were answered.' He looked up at them before delivering his punchline.

'Barclays Bank in Church Street did nothing for nine minutes this morning because it was being robbed.'

The room was completely silent from this fresh revelation. Martin sat back down and let his colleagues take the information in. Sir John hit the table with the palm of his hand and stood up before shouting his instructions.

'James, get that camera film sorted, A.S.A. fucking P.! Peter, fill in Martin on our plans.' He walked over to Martin to shake his hand.

'Get this bastard, Martin!'

'Hold it a second', interrupted Peter. 'You said there were two things?'

'That's right. If we're not keeping you from something, Sir John, I'd like to hear the telephone conversation that took place prior to the explosion', Martin asked.

'You're only keeping me from an ugly woman', Sir John said, as he sat back down. Martin turned to James, 'Roll the tape.'

James pressed the play button on the tape machine next to his keyboard and the voice filled the room:

"YOU MAKE ONE MISTAKE IN THE NEXT TEN MINUTES, Mr HARMAN, THEN PEOPLE WILL DIE BECAUSE OF YOU"

Martin had a small smile on his face as he turned to ask Peter something.

'Is there any phone conversation the T.S.S. don't have on tape?'

Peter let out a small laugh, 'That's Security for you!'

'Security for Democracy!' Martin answered.

Appraisal and Assessment

Warwick was driving anti-clockwise along the M25, aware of the car following him about four vehicles back. He would wait until he got to Enfield before he would take action. He placed his left hand on the sports bag in the passenger seat, thinking over everything that had happened in the last twenty four hours, first, the discovery of Billy Hopkirk's body, minus a head, at a Chinese restaurant, meeting Billy's mother and having to break the awful news to her. The confrontation with Sergeant Davis, the news that the Force wanted to be rid of him and the fact that Davis had given him a week for the Billy Hopkirk case, more than enough time. Meeting Jacobs, disguised as a private tutor in his late twenties, taking a beating like never before and then the police turning up to raid Jacobs's house. Jacobs telling him that Helen and Jonathan were in heaven.

'How the fuck do you know my family?' Warwick said to the driving rain in front of him. How did Jacobs know his family, because the death of his wife and son was kept from the press. The Police knew but no one outside the force would know, apart from maybe the small talk that the lads from the station would have had down at the pub.

'How the hell do you know them?'

Why were the police raiding Jacobs' house? He could now start to feel his head hurting again. Stress and tiredness weren't helping the situation. He reached over to the left hand side of the dashboard and took a cassette, placed it in the stereo and then lit a cigarette. The music suddenly took him away from his thoughts as the singer's voice drowned out the driving rain.

> *Smashing down the school halls and their freak shows,*
> *Spitting on the Queeen of England's nose.*

The sound of Zakk Zombie. The music his wife never liked. The reason why his car was full of Zakk Zombie tapes. Zakk Zombie was not only one of the most successful Glam Rock singers of the seventies, he was the musical hero of Tom Warwick. Zombie was the brainchild of sixties folk singer Toby James. Toby James decided that instead of tampering with the sound of pop, as other folk singers were doing very badly around the start of the seventies, he made the decision that he would change his musical sound, appearance and name completely for an eight year period. He unashamedly would become an out and out punk, Glam hero. With a distorted guitar as his weapon, he shouted about the uprising of the working class against the establishment.

In fact the message in the music of the Zakk Zombie years was no different to the folk music of his Toby James years. Instead of the singer armed with only his acoustic guitar to deliver his single voiced message, it was delivered by a man in a glittered silver jump suit, bright silver face paint, long blue dreadlocks in his hair, black nail varnish, white platform boots and an attitude to match.

> *They say,*
> *Do as I say, not as I do,*
> *I say,*
> *Who gives a shit at all about you!*

Warwick came off the M25 at junction 25 keeping a steady pace, allowing the red Vauxhall Cavalier to follow him until he decided it was time to do something about it.

A Small Blue Object

Back at the Ministry of Defence they were still listening to the cassette. After the cassette had finished, Brooks made his way over to the screen which was now displaying the original picture of Church Street.

'Harmen's office is at the South side of the building, overlooking the cemetery', he began, looking in James's direction. 'Check all routes out of the cemetery, there are three schools behind it, so there has to be a camera there.' He then made his way back over to the cassette machine, pressed REWIND until the number gauge displayed 0036 and then he pressed PLAY.

"Oh, by the way, Harman's Friend, you look out that window again, then I'll shoot your fucking face off."

'The phone call was traced to Tenniswood Road, half a mile away', Peter spoke, excited that he was on the same track as Brooks.

'That's right', Brooks acknowledged. 'The caller was in touch with someone watching Harman's office.'
Brooks could not take his eyes off the screen.

'Next picture', he instructed.
The next picture showed the aftermath of the Church Street bomb. Clouds of smoke floating above a broken ground, a ground that looked as if it had a building thrown upon it from above the floating clouds. Although the picture was in colour, the two most distinctive colours were dark grey and red. Bodies lay amongst the rubble like abandoned dolls on a skip. Dolls that looked like they had been terrorised by a young scoundrel, a boy who had pulled arms and legs off some, broken others in half and beaten the remainder with a heavy object. To look at such a picture and understand and accept the reality of it defied all belief.

Peter Allan had his mouth open in shock; James had his hand over his mouth, eyes wide open; Sir John looked as if he would begin to cry. Brooks walked over to James and took control of the mouse, moved the cursor across the screen to a small blue object. He made a small square around it and then the whole screen focussed in on what was the small blue object.

'Oh, Jesus Christ!' Sir John muttered.

'Oh, shit! No! James moaned with his hand now on his head.
A baby's pram. The nearest comparison, a pram that had been hit by a bus, and then thrown on the skip. It was a picture that reached inside you and made you feel as if someone was

trying to tear your heart out.

'I am absolutely positive, Gentlemen', Brooks declared, 'we are looking at the work of Tony Dwyer, the sickest and most effective terrorist our shores have ever known.'

Familiar Territory.

Warwick turned right at the first set of traffic lights off the M25 and headed towards a road he knew like the back of his hand, Whitewebbs Lane. This road ran a length of two and half miles, with six street lamps at either end of it, barely enough room for two cars in certain places and more bends than Warwick cared to remember, but he knew every one of them.

When Warwick was seventeen, he and his friends would race down Whitewebbs Lane in the dark, without lights and against the clock. This was his territory.

As Warwick's car entered the Lane, he turned off his lights and stereo and pushed the accelerator to the floor. The first hundred yards of the road were dead straight and, as Warwick sped off, the red Cavalier kept up with him, at some points only inches away from his bumper. Warwick drove towards the heart of the first bend at seventy five miles per hour and, just as he could feel himself coming into the bend, he pulled up the handbrake very sharp and spun the steering wheel to the left, allowing the back half of the car to swing to the right. This movement forced the red Cavalier to drive to the right to avoid hitting Warwick at full speed, and ended up half buried in the bushes.

Before Warwick allowed his car to become stationary, he slammed the gear stick into second gear and drove out of the bend like a true professional. He drove past the next two bends before he switched his lights back on. The third bend of the road was the highest point of Whitewebbs Lane and it was here that Warwick stopped and looked in the rear-view mirror and saw the red Cavalier had now made its way back on to the road and was driving out of the first bend.

Warwick's heart was pounding so fast and hard he could almost hear it when his mouth opened in shock at seeing the Cavalier back on the road. He turned his lights off and drove off in search of the lay-by he knew was after the fifth bend.

5

DANGER AND DISTRUST

Peter Allan and Martin Brooks were now on their own in the room at the Ministry of Defence. The screen was no longer on the wall. In its place were various pictures of battle scenes from World War Two. The air now had a cloud of smoke drifting through it as Peter Allan was on his second cigarette since Sir John Primark and James Moore had left earlier. A freshly opened bottle of Johnnie Walker Red Label sat on the table accompanied by two small glasses.

'This will be the most unusual mission you've ever encountered, Martin, and this is a mission you can not fail to complete.'

'Who will be aware of my movements?' Martin asked.

'You, myself and the Prime Minister. If anyone catches up with you, then you are on your own.'

'Charming!' Martin mused as he necked his glass.

Stalking The Prey

Warwick pulled in to the lay-by and reversed along it until he was out of view from the road. He took out the Smith PK from his side pocket and got out of the car. He walked around to the passenger side and opened the door and took out the sports bag and made his way into the bushes, waiting for the red Cavalier to drive past. He could feel his heart beating, from his chin down to his stomach. He took out his cigarettes, opened the packet but quickly declined as he could hear the car heading towards the fifth bend. His arms seemed to shake in time with his beating heart.

'Calm down, for fuck's sake!' he said to himself.

The road in front of him was now completely lit by the red Cavalier's lights as it drove out of the fifth bend and past the lay-by. Just as it seemed to be near the end of the lay-by the car slammed on its brakes and came to a complete stop.

'Oh, my God! Oh, shit!' he thought to himself.

The red Cavalier reversed into the lay-by. What had the driver spotted? Warwick looked over to his own car and couldn't believe what a stupid mistake he had just made. When he pulled the sports bag out of the passenger side, he mustn't have closed the door correctly, and the interior light was still on. It was only on faintly, but just enough for the hunting eye to see.

All Warwick could now hear was his own heart beating, it was beating so hard, he almost felt it was hurting. He saw the dreadlocked Jamaican make his way out of his car and around to his boot. As he opened his boot, Warwick stepped out of the bushes at the same time so that the rustle of leaves could be camouflaged by the opening of the Cavalier's boot. Warwick was about six feet behind the Jamaican. Regardless of being a cold night, Warwick could feel the sweat dripping from his forehead and down around his eyes, and for those brief few seconds he stood there. He once again tried to make some sense of this bizarre situation. He moved slowly towards the Jamaican until he was right behind him. Warwick raised the P.K. until its barrel was only inches away from the dreadlocks of the man. He unclicked the safety catch, indicating to the Jamaican that he was right behind him, and then moved the barrel of the gun until it rested on the back of his head.

'Make one more fucking move, and I swear to Christ I'll kill you.' Warwick's voice was full of panic and the Jamaican was aware of it.

In a split second the Jamaican swung around to face him and Warwick could see in the light of the moon that he had a gun in his hand at waist height.

The gunshot caused the bush to come alive with the sound of frightened crows as they took flight across the fields.

The M.o.D.'s Mission of Distrust

Peter Allan lit up his third cigarette as he began to tell Brooks the details behind the mission. As much as he trusted Brooks, he still felt nervous about some of the details involved. He wasn't sure how Brooks would react to the fact that the present Government had been holding secret meetings with Sinn Féin. Worse still, how would he react to the fact that Allan had been to two meetings with Sinn Féin where the heads of the Southern Division of the Irish Republican Army were present. With Section 13 working under the strict orders of the British Prime Minister, who was absolutely determined to get some sort of peace agreement started in Northern Ireland, Allan found himself sitting opposite men whom he really should have shot in the face, let alone sit down and listen to the problems they were having with one of their own divisions.

'What sort of problems?' Brooks asked very matter of fact. Brooks was one of those people in life who either had no opinions or just had a great gift of being able to put them to one side. Allan believed it was the latter, and believed it was a great gift. Allan had watched many people confuse passion with stupidity, people standing by their beliefs and opinions, but Brooks seemed to hide his own and use the important bits of everyone else's to get what was needed out of life — success.

'Six years ago when we made some major steps in security', Allan began, stopping briefly to enjoy a puff of his cigarette, 'the I.R.A. reacted by making the London Division, known as the Fifth Brigade, totally independent of the rest of the movement. They raised their own funds, bought their own weapons and explosives, planned their own missions and not once in six years have they taken any orders from West Belfast, Dublin or anywhere else for that matter.'

'A great idea to avoid the National Security System, but a dangerous one if the leadership falls into the wrong hands', Brooks said as he leaned forward to fill the two glasses with healthy measurements of Johnnie Walker.

'Exactly, which is where our friend Tony Dwyer comes into it. A one time free lance terrorist, who carried out contracts for the I.R.A. on the British mainland. The heads of West Belfast were so impressed by his actions that they made the sick bastard the commander of their London Brigade in late '87', Peter told him as he reached forward for some whiskey before continuing.

'As you know, Martin, Dwyer is one of the few people in the world aware of Section 13. He killed, or had killed, three of your fellow field agents with the help of an informant within our security.'

'And he has always covered his tracks. We don't even know what Dwyer looks like.' Brooks spoke as if speaking to himself. He wanted Dwyer's blood so much, he could almost taste it. If it wasn't for the fact that Brooks was adamant that no files were to be kept on him, then he too would be nothing more than a name plate in the ground.

'The I.R.A. want us to work with two of their men to find Dwyer and kill him and then, and only then, they will call a ceasefire. Otherwise London will be broken down, brick by brick', Allan said as if he had dirt in his mouth. He couldn't believe what he was telling Brooks, that they, two men from the Ministry of Defence, would be working side by side with two men from the Irish Republican Army. It made him feel disposable. The Prime Minister and his predecessor had always maintained that Section 13 officially did not exist and the facts of this mission proved it.

'So the I.R.A. want our help to find Dwyer', Brooks said with a slight laugh in in his voice.

'Remember, Martin, if we work with them on this, they promise they can give John Hayward a ceasefire and, with Section 13 being officially non-existent, we can do this without making the Prime Minister look like he's got egg on his face if it backfires', Allan told him as he was extinguishing his cigarette. He then sat forward to face Brooks, looking at him straight in the eye, before asking the question that had been bugging him for the last three weeks.

'The thing is, Martin, can we trust these bastards?'

'No. the thing is, can these bastards trust us. Because when I find Dwyer, I'll kill him along with our two freedom fighters', Brooks said as he raised his glass in a toast.

A Midnight Meeting

A blue ford Escort was travelling at great speed along the N76 away from Kilkenny towards Clonmel, South Tipperary. Its driver, Dermot O'Shea, was concerned and worried about the meeting he was on his way to in Kilsheelan, a meeting with the heads of the Southern Division of the Provisional I.R.A.

Dermot O'Shea was at one time a highly respected body within the movement of the I.R.A. He had spent sixteen years as the Southern Division's Training/Recruitment Officer. He had trained some of the most skillful snipers working the streets and flat-tops of West Belfast. Every mission he had worked with, went off with Republican success. He along with Tommy McMahon of the South Armagh Unit, planned and organised the assassination of Earl Mountbatten in August 1979. He trained the two I.R.A. scouts who obtained all the necessary drawings and information of the Grand Hotel in Brighton which almost led to a wipe-out of the British Government in 1984. But his involvement with the movement came to a stop in November 1987 when he approached Sinn Féin, and called for them to publicly condemn the Border Units for the bombing of Enniskillen.

The Enniskillen bombing was one that had the hardest of Republican and IRA sympathisers questioning their own beliefs. The IRA detonated a 30lb bomb witout warning upon a Remembrance Day service. The building where the bomb was located collapsed burying men, women, old age pensioners and children underneath a heap of rubble. Eleven people died and sixty three were injured. Shouts of condemnation could be heard from all four corners of the globe and the words of one survivor, Gordon Wilson, echoed the pain of the situation as he described the last moments he had with his daughter who was killed from the blast.

"'Daddy, I love you very much". These were the exact words she spoke to me and those were the last words I heard her say. .... I have lost my daughter but I bear no ill will, I bear no grudge.'

O'Shea had for a long time expressed his concern for the publicity surrounding the I.R.A. He had always said in training, "Take out your target, and any victims that get in your way." But the bombings at this time, especially on the British mainland, seemed to be taking victims, with no important targets. He believed, like everyone else in the movement, that you had to instil fear and terror into the British, to make them sit up and listen. But O'Shea also believed that there was a thin line between fear and strength. If you put enough fear into something, then after some time, that fear will turn to strength, a strength that could overturn all the fear it has ever endured. This was fact and the British people were proof of this. They were proof of it in World War Two, and they were proof of it now.

As he drove through the sleepy town of Callan, he opened his packet of Carrolls cigarettes.

What did the movement want with him now after six years of silence? They knew that he'd condemn the bombing that had taken place in Church Street, London, that morning, and he was absolutely positive it had to be something to do with that. Earlier that day when O'Shea had popped into town in Carlow, where he now lived, someone had been to his house and left an envelope in his letter-box.

"O'Leary's, Kilsheelan, Midnight."

Three simple words written on a plain simple piece of paper. A reaction, not an action. It also proved something else to him. The I.R.A. must have been watching his movements, but why? It would have been cheaper and safer to have him shot but, for some reason, this never happened. Maybe they knew that it was much worse for O'Shea to spend six years constantly looking over his shoulder. Maybe that was the punishment for trying to publicly condemn their cause.

O'Shea drove the lifeless, wet and silent N76 through different patches of mist drifting across the road from the fields until he came to the Stores in Seskin and then took a left down the R706. He drove until he came to the railway track at the back of Kilsheelan and then parked up his car. He would walk the last hundred yards, which would give him a chance to survey the area first. As he got out of the car, he threw his cigarette out into the road, then put on his Trilby hat over his silver hair, and walked his five foot ten inch body towards Kilsheelan. When he came to the side of O'Leary's pub, he noticed three cars parked out on the N24. He made his way over to the nearest, a Volkswagen Polo. He placed his hand on the bonnet, still warm. He walked over to the Post Office and stood inside the shadows. He still had five minutes, time enough for a cigarette.

Scraping The Hunter off His Face
Warwick's body was laid out on the gravel of the lay-by on Whitewebbs Lane. Blood covered the hair and face; the shirt which was once white was completely blood covered; one hand held the Smith PK and the other held the sports bag. The engine of the red Cavalier was still running and the light from the moon had become even brighter.

Warwick suddenly started coughing and immediately sat upright. He threw the bag and the gun to each side of him to allow his hands to clear the liquid from his eyes. He looked down at his chest and saw his blood soaked shirt. In a panic he tore the shirt open looking for where he'd been shot. He first checked the area of his heart, as that was the area that was immediately hurting. Nothing. He ran both his hands all over the top part of his body checking for where he'd been shot. Nothing. He stood up to check his legs but, from the fact he could stand up, he knew there were no gun wounds down there. That was when the light of the moon lit up the Jamaican man's body in front of him, and Warwick was immediately sick. He had never shot anything or anyone with his Smith PK before but on this night he learned how powerful it really was, for the Jamaican man was now lying on his back with only half his head intact, the other half was what Warwick had cleared away from his eyes only moments earlier. Warwick's body now had the tingling feeling of pins and needles all over. His nervous system was going into overdrive from all the excitement earlier, to passing out after the gun shot, and then to the feeling of sickness from the revelation that his face was covered with the blood and remains of another man. Warwick didn't waste another second as he grabbed the gun and the bag and threw them into the car and drove away from the scene at top speed.

Breaking The Silence

Dermott O'Shea opened the front door and walked into the empty front bar of O'Leary's pub. He could hear the rattling of pool balls coming from the bar at the back. As he headed around to the doorway, he could hear the voices of the young O'Leary boys, Paul and Danny. They were giving a running commentary on what you would imagine was the deciding match of the World Pool Tournament. He stood inside the doorway and saw Bill O'Leary and his wife, Maggie, sitting at a table next to the fire. Their daughter, Marion, was sitting on a separate table, reading a magazine on all the best bands and good looking actors, the sort of magazine any twelve year old girl would be reading. The bar fell silent when they noticed O'Shea standing there. Bill looked at O'Shea from head to toe and back up again, before speaking with complete coldness.

'In the kitchen.'

'Okay', O'Shea answered softly and shortly.

He felt awful at the sight of the O'Learys waiting in their own back bar. Their living quarters had been taken over by the I.R.A. for a meeting, and Bill O'Leary had no choice but to hand it over. Bill O'Leary was a man of huge stature with mean eyes and a beard. His appearance alone would send a shiver through you, but even he wouldn't stand in the way of the movement. He, along with O'Shea and 7000 other refugees of Northern Ireland, moved to the Republic for safety from the British on August 11th, 1971. As O'Shea stood there looking at Bill O'Leary, it made him think about how Bill may have run away from the troubles, but the troubles hadn't run away from him.

O'Shea walked into the smoke filled kitchen. Three men were seated at the table. On the left was Tom Hill, a big shape of man in his forties with messy hair, the sort of hair that had accompanied a body on a hard day's work. He was the man that had replaced O'Shea as the Southern Division's Training/Recruitment Officer. On the right was the Officer of Divisional Intelligence, a man in his late sixties, well dressed in a suit and tie with his hat sitting on his knee. Séamus Kelly, a wise old man, a man that O'Shea had served with on many missions. Seated in the middle was John Fitzpatrick, Southern Chief of Staff. A man, like O'Shea, in his early fifties John was also a refugee of August '71. After seeing the British soldiers and R.U.C. torturing some of his friends and two of his brothers in the early hours of August 9th, '71 in his home town of Ballymurphy, he took off for the Republic and set up the Southern Division with Séamus Kelly.

'Good to see you, Dermott, have a seat', Fitzpatrick greeted him.

'No, it's ok. I'll stand because I'm not staying long.'

'Why?' Fitzpatrick asked.

'I'm only here out of curiosity, to see what it is that's made you break six years of fucking silence.' O'Shea almost spat the last of the words out as his eyes pierced into Fitzpatrick.

'Dermott, sit down, please', Kelly urged.

O'Shea did so just to try and annoy Fitzpatrick with the fact that he would listen to Kelly, but not to him.

'Let's cut the bullshit and tell me why I'm here. It's obviously something to do with the bomb that took place over in England this morning', O'Shea said as he pulled out the cigarettes.

It was Séamus Kelly that did all the talking. He told O'Shea of the meetings that they, along with Sinn Féin, had been having with representatives of the British Government to try and strike up some sort of peace deal. He told him all about Tony Dwyer, a one-time mission subcontractor who was now running the Fifth Brigade in London to his own satisfaction.

'Jesus Christ!' O'Shea whispered. 'Tony Dwyer, a mad bollocks of a man, and you made him commander of the Fifth Brigade!'

'You know him?' Fitzpatrick asked.

'We were going to use him in '84 for the Brighton job but I wasn't impressed by his handiwork on the Harrods bomb the Christmas beforehand. Five innocent people killed, eighty people injured and not one worthwhile fucking target in sight', O'Shea said as he lit his cigarette.

'We need you to find him, Dermott, and put a stop to him', Kelly explained. 'Otherwise he'll continue a meaningless bloodshed which is out of our hands. He somehow has his own finances, has his own team of our men and claims responsibility for his actions on our behalf.'

O'Shea was staring into space, almost looking as if his mind was somewhere else. He leaned forward and put his cigarette out in the ashtray, stood up, placed his hat on his head and then spoke as he turned to leave the kitchen.

"Well, I'll be seeing you.'

'Where are you going?' Fitzpatrick asked. 'You've not been dismissed.'

O'Shea spun around and slammed both hands on the table and came face to face with Fitzpatrick before shouting,

'Don't you dare for one fucking moment think that you've

got any control over me. Dismiss me? You fucking prick!'
O'Shea then felt the coldness of a barrel on his temple, the
barrel of a Browning automatic. Tom Hill had pulled it out at
the same moment as O'Shea hit the table. O'Shea let out a
little laugh before speaking.

'Oh, go on, Tom. Don't let me stop you', he said before
turning to face him, forcing the Browning's barrel to rest on
his own forehead, 'Go on, Tom, be a hero. Shoot me down in
cold blood, a one time fellow soldier who did more for this
movement with my piss than you could do with your whole
life.'

'Tom, put the gun away!' Kelly instructed him and Tom did
so without question.

As Present Becomes Past. . . .

As Warwick drove out of Whitewebbs Lane, the rain started to
pour down for the second time that night. He couldn't
remember a time before when he had felt such panic. His
hands were constantly shaking, the cigarette he instantly lit
as he drove away from the lay-by had to be held by his lips,
but the smoke was now irritating his left eye and the rain
that had just started was making his vision of the road in
front of him very poor. All he wanted to do was pull the car
over and get his head together, but he knew it was important
to get as far away from Whitewebbs Lane as possible.

He could not even begin to understand how he had got
himself involved in the activity that had just taken place. If
there was ever a time when he wanted to turn the clock back
twenty four hours, it was surely now. Sitting at home,
drinking a glass of draught Guinness, smoking a Marlboro
Light whilst listening to Zakk Zombie sing about the day a
young girl walked out of her School master's office with a gun
in her hand. Was there any way on earth of turning that clock
back. If there was a way, he would surely turn it back six
months, and prevent his wife and son from making that fatal
car journey.

Warwick's head was once again hurting. He really had to get his thoughts together as to what his next move was going to be. One thing was for sure, he was not, under any circumstances, to head home. If he was ever linked to tonight's activity, he knew that in his present careless state he would leave a trail of clues around the house. He always kept a change of clothing in the boot of his car in case of an unannounced stake out, so all he had to do for the moment was keep driving. Just drive until he was far away from Whitewebbs Lane, away from the body with half a head, away from the red Cavalier and far away from the bullet he had carelessly forgot to retrieve from the scene of the crime.

6

LAYING THE CHESSBOARD

As O'Shea was making his way across the floor of the front bar of O'Leary's pub, Kelly called out from behind him.

'Hang fire there Dermott!'

'Is that an order or a request?' O'Shea asked mockingly.

'A request', Kelly answered.

With that, O'Shea turned around to see Kelly make his way over to a bar stool with a bottle of Jamesons in one hand and two glasses in the other.

The Art of Persuasion

'Come on you hard bastard, sit down', Kelly asked of him, and he did.

'What's your problem with Fitzpatrick?' Kelly continued.

'As Southern Chief of Staff, he made the decision to begin the silence with me six years ago, but now he wants me to go and work with those British bastards to find Dwyer and kill him.'

'It's not that simple Dermott', Kelly explained as he poured out two full glasses of Whiskey before continuing. 'The whole movement is in a right mess at the moment. The British have got the whole of West Belfast under camera, tape and satellite right now. None of our boys can even take a shit without the R.U.C. being aware of how many sheets of paper he's going to use to wipe his own arse. The main committee haven't been able to have a meeting for the last three weeks because they know that every fart they produce is being smelt before it even leaves their own under pants."

'That's technology for you Séamus, the movement has to move with the times', O'Shea interrupted.

'Exactly, which is why we need this mission to work.

57

Firstly, we can't have this Dwyer fella doing whatever the hell he wishes in London because, as you know yourself, that isn't the best publicity for the movement. Most importantly Dermott, like you've said yourself, technology is what the movement needs, but technology takes time.'

'I don't follow', O'Shea told him.

'The only chance we have of being able to compete with those bastards, is to equal them. We've equalled them before. For every man of ours that they've put on the ground, we've taken two of their scum. For every volunteer's wife that they've widowed, we've taken their children's protected future. It has been down to our pure terror, that the British have entertained the unpalatable prospect of sitting down and talking with us. We have to make sure that the terror never ever goes away, but we need time to get to grips with the technology.'

O'Shea began to smile as he became aware of what Kelly was trying to tell him. He took a swig of Jamesons before acknowledging this to Kelly.

'And a cease-fire is the only way of making time to get to grips with the technology needed.'

'Bingo', Kelly confirmed.

'But why do we need the English to help us to get to Dwyer?'

'West Belfast deployed two of their best men to go after Dwyer three months ago, but they got lifted as soon as they stepped off the plane at Heathrow. So they now want us down here to have a crack at it', Kelly told him as O'Shea was lighting up one of his cigarettes.

'Why don't we approach the Americans, surely they'd help us.'

'We did, but as much as they would love to help us, their relationship with the British forbids them from active service on the British mainland. So to prevent any of our men from being lifted again we need to make it look to the British like we're working with them.'

O'Shea was staring at himself in the Guinness mirror behind the bar. How he had aged in the last six years, six years of worry, six years of guessing how his time with the movement would once more be played out. Would it be as a victim, or as an activist? Surely with the news of them wanting him to play a key role in this mission, he should have felt relieved, but he just could not feel further away from that, if he had tried. To go to England and work with the British, to find the man who was carrying out the killings in London just didn't sound right. If he were the brains behind this, how would he plan it.

'Does West Belfast know what you're asking me to do, work with the British?' he asked Kelly.

'No. This is strictly a Southern Division mission. Sinn Féin are aware of it, but they'll say nothing because, if this works, it's in their favour more than anyone else's."

I.R.A. head quarters didn't know, but Sinn Féin did. That sounded a bit messy. How would anyone prevent the head quarters in West Belfast from finding out? If the mission went wrong, it wouldn't matter because the agents in the field couldn't make it back to tell anyone about it. But if it didn't go wrong, if they got to Dwyer, Headquarters would start investigating. They'd want to know how he succeeded.

'So when the job is done', O'Shea began, 'at what stage will you have me shot. Straight away, or will I at least be given a chance to run?'

Kelly's facial expression didn't change, but he did go a little red with embarrassment. He gave himself a little smile as he took another swig of whiskey. It had just dawned on him how O'Shea's brain must have been thinking the whole mission over to come up with such a question so quickly.

'You'll be working with another representative of the movement on this mission, someone to do the field work for you. That person won't get a chance to run, but I give you my word, Dermott, we'll give you twelve hours after the mission's complete before we come looking for you. So get as far away as you can. You'll be paid well, and you'll be paid before you leave.'

As unfair as that statement sounded, O'Shea recognised it for what it truly was, a lifeline. A chance to see out the rest of his days somewhere else in the world, a place where he could relax without having to look over his shoulder every time he left his house. Although Kelly told him they'd come looking for him, he knew that after a week, they'd stop, otherwise West Belfast would become suspicious with men on missions during this planned-to-be cease-fire.

'Who will I be working with?'

'Dillon.'

O'Shea threw a sharp look at Kelly from hearing that name mentioned.

'Sinéad Dillon?' he shot.

'The very one. Any problems with that?'

'No, no problem', he lied.

. . . . As Past Becomes Present

Warwick drove until he arrived at the service station in South Mimms. He sat opposite the entrance until he felt it was safe to go into the toilet, which was just to the left inside the entrance.

When he did enter, it was 2.30 am. He walked to the far end of the toilet and immediately filled the sink with warm soapy water. He removed his top bloody clothing and washed all the blood from his hair, all the bits of dried bloody skin he found around the front part of his neck and behind his ears. He dropped his trousers to reveal a partly blood covered underpants. Once he had washed the red areas at the top of his legs, he made his way to one of the cubicles to change into his clothing.

When he opened the bag of clothes, he had one of the most sensational feelings he had felt for quite a while. It was a short sensation, but a sensation all the same. He could smell the perfume of his wife as soon as he opened the bag, for she had packed this bag for him a good seven months earlier. 'Aromatics' perfume. That smell was made for Helen as far as he was concerned. It was the smell that reminded him of their time together in Orlando. A smell that reminded him of an untouched beautiful richness. Whenever he made love to Helen, he could smell it along the skin of her neck, along the rose of her cheek and in the sweat of his own upper lip. It reminded him of the time they were nearly arrested in Orlando, for being caught having sex in an outdoor swimming pool in the early hours of the morning, and then heading straight back to their hotel room to carry on, like nothing in this world was going to stop them from making love in the early hours. In those days they didn't care where they made love, for when that feeling came, it had to be fulfilled, no matter what. Through all those times, she wore 'Aromatics', and she still wore it seven months ago when she packed Warwick's bag for an announced stake out. Warwick could suddenly hear Jacob's voice in his head.

'There is a heaven, and there is a great comfort to be had from knowing it, especially knowing that Helen and Jonathan might be there.'

It was then, for the first time ever, that Warwick started to wonder if there was some sort of after life. If Helen could see the mess he was in right now. She had always teased him for how he would get himself into awkward situations, going home and discussing these situations with her, while she would pour him a glass of Guinness before rubbing his shoulders with a smooth and day saving massage.

He buried his head into the bag to try and smell some more of her odour, but to no avail. It was gone, as gone as she was and as gone as Jonathan was, and there he sat in his underpants, in South Mimms service station toilets, dwelling on the memories of the past.

What One Doesn't Know.......

Peter Allan sat behind his desk looking out at the morning view of Whitehall. He was enjoying his first cigarette of the day and thinking about all the information he had passed on to Brooks the night before.

He was one of the first people into work that morning and had left his door slightly ajar. He could now hear the sound of the weekend overtime workers typing out memos and letters on their computers. Workers that were only down the hallway, but might as well have been a thousand miles away. How would any of them react to the fact that his department was about to work side by side with the Provisional I.R.A. How would he react if he knew this of the departments either up or downstairs. He remembered the pictures that they had looked at the night before in the conference room. The pictures of the bombing, the pictures of the bodies lying among the concrete rubble and the picture of the pushchair that only moments before the bomb had exploded, was the safe small cocoon for a six month old baby girl.

His stomach started to rumble from the lack of breakfast, but his brain was not interested in acknowledging this, for it was busy thinking over every step that would be taken on this mission.

As soon as he finished his cigarette, he opened his pack, took another one out and lit it immediately.

'Thank Christ I won't be relying on you to cover my back in the field. At the rate you're smoking, you're not going to be much use to anyone around here.'

Allan looked up to see Martin Brooks standing inside the doorway.

'Ha, fucking Ha', Allan replied

'What's new?' Brooks asked.

'Well our two new friends are flying into Stansted this morning', Allan answered

'Does the Prime Minister know I'm on board for this mission yet?' Brooks enquired as he walked over to the window to take in the great morning view.

'Oh yes. He knew before we even asked you', Allan told him as he extinguished his cigarette and walked over to grab his coat before instructing an astonished Brooks.

'Come on, we've got a plane to meet.'

A Specious Sauciness

Dermott O'Shea was sitting next to Séamus Kelly in the lounge bar of 'The Fox' bar, which was located just off the R415 outside Kildare. There were a few Americans at the tables enjoying a full Irish Breakfast complete with both white and black puddings. O'Shea watched one of them closely, as they ate everything on their plate apart from the puddings. He then turned to Kelly who was also watching the American.

'Claim to have Irish blood in them, but can't stomach a bit of pudding. What sort of bollocks is that?' O'Shea asked, clearly agitated from waiting for their guest to arrive.

'Can I ask you something Dermott?' Kelly spoke as he took a sip from his cup of tea. 'There's something you're not telling me.'

'What do you mean?' O'Shea asked, genuinely confused.

'Sinéad Dillon. Your reaction to knowing that she was the one you're going to work with on this mission.'

'It was just the fact that I'm going to work with a woman on this that kind of threw me a little, you know', O'Shea told him, feeling a little uneasy with his own answer.

'I've known you a long time Dermott but do you know something? I'd rather you'd not give me an answer than bloody lie to me.'

O'Shea felt embarrassed but knew that Kelly was right. He shouldn't lie to him.

'I'm sorry Séamus, but it's none of your business.'

'OK, that's fair enough', Kelly answered, 'but I've got this mission to think of.'

'It won't interfere with this mission I promise you.'

'No offence, Dermott', Kelly said before leaning forward to

face O'Shea, 'but if it does, I'll kill the pair of you. So whatever your problem is with her, now is your chance to say something, otherwise, like I said, I'll kill the pair of you.'

'Séamus, there's no problem', O'Shea lied once again, only this time more convincing.

Just then, the door to the front bar opened and in walked the figure of Sinéad Dillon, a figure that stopped the loud Americans from talking what O'Shea always referred to as their 'loud meaningless horseshit.'

A slim figure of about five foot six, brown short messy hair that would almost pass as a style and a face so pretty it would defy belief to understand what sort of activities she had carried out for the movement. There she stood, in a black baseball styled jacket, light blue jeans, working boots and a plain white T-shirt that outlined her small firm breasts. She was a woman that just seemed to be at the stage in her life, where any clothing, any hair style and any doorway she stood in, made her twenty seven year old features a picture.

'Jesus Christ, if I were only half my age, I would go on this mission myself', Kelly told O'Shea, eyeing Dillon over from head to toe.

O'Shea ignored Kelly's comment, as he opened his packet of Carrols and helped himself to a cigarette. He didn't look at Dillon as she walked across the floor to their table and sat down opposite them. He could smell the body odour of her, it wasn't a bad smell of body odour but it wasn't a perfumed one either, it was just the natural smell of a clean women.

'Good to see you again Dermott', her beautifully light tuned, west coast voice acknowledged.

'Yeah', O'Shea replied.

'Any chance of a smoke?' she asked him.

He gave her a frowned look, before becoming aware of Kelly's presence again.

'Help yourself', he told her.

She took the packet and removed a cigarette, placed it in her mouth in what seemed to be slow motion to the onlookers in the bar, lit the cigarette with O'Shea's 'Jack Daniels' lighter and exhaled the cloud of smoke like a mating call to all the eyes fixed on her.

'Is there something of fucking interest to you here lads?' O'Shea asked the onlooking Americans. They all looked clearly embarrassed as they stared back at their finished breakfast plates like something of interest had jumped onto them.

'Nice to see you haven't lost your touch', she told O'Shea as he was still staring at the now uncomfortable Americans.

'So how come you got picked for this mission?' he asked her, still looking at his prey.

'Sinéad is the only other person we can trust for this. Kelly answered.

'In other words, I'm the only other person who doesn't know of the new locations for the I.R.A.'s training grounds and store areas, since they were all moved ten days ago', Dillon told O'Shea.

O'Shea took his eyes off the now departing Americans and fixed them straight on the green eyes of Dillon before asking of her: 'What do you mean?'

'I know that all the locations that I was aware of, were moved ten days ago and no one made me aware of where they've moved to. You don't know where they've been for the last six years. So we are the only two people that won't give anything away to the British if this all backfires.'

'This won't backfire', O'Shea replied to her.

'That's the spirit Dermott', Kelly approved.

'How can you be so sure this won't go wrong?' Dillon asked O'Shea.

'Because I won't allow it to go wrong', he replied leaning forward coming much closer to her face before continuing, 'this may just seem like another mission to you, with two expendable agents working on it, but to me, this could be the most important mission the south division has carried out since the Brighton bombing.'

Dillon gave a smile that was an introduction to a laugh, but seemed to stop just short of it.

'The most important mission? Jesus Christ, Dermott, catch yourself on, will you', she spat at him before stopping briefly to take a drag from her cigarette before continuing. 'You've been away from the movement for six years. You have not got the slightest fucking idea or notion of the missions I've been involved in since you've been scratching your fucking arse out in Carlow. Brighton bombing?' The beauty of Sinéad Dillon seemed to be even richer in her moment of anger. Even the swear words she was spitting across the table at O'Shea had an air about them. 'The Brighton fucking bombing? You didn't even scratch that miserable dog's arse of a whore Thornbird!'

'Come on Sinéad, take it easy', Kelly interrupted.

'Fuck off Séamus!' she said, still keeping her eyes fixed on O'Shea who was absolutely caught off guard by this verbal attack. 'Everyone in the Southern Division knows', she took her attack even further, ' that six years ago, you approached Sinn Féin, to condemn the Border units for the bombing in Enniskillen. Do you think for one moment that anyone in England condemned their government for the blatant murder of Bobby Sands? Do you think for one moment that anyone in England condemned their soldiers for changing a child's view of the streets in West Belfast by walking around armed to the fucking teeth past school gates, past working mothers, past unemployed fathers of the wrong religion, past people denied of their civil fucking rights in life and you wanted our own political wing to condemn the soldiers that fight for these peoples freedom? Enniskillen was a mistake, one bloody bad mistake, but under no circumstances do we ever condemn our own people, never.'

Her face was red with veins appearing around her bright green eyes.

'Yet you have no problems in going after Dwyer and putting a stop to him', O'Shea asked her.

'Dwyer's not Irish, he's not one of ours, he's not fighting for

the same reasons as the rest of us, he's fighting for money.'
Kelly and O'Shea both looked at Dillon, intrigued by her last comment concerning the fighting for money. What did she know that they didn't?

'And at the end of the day', she continued, 'it's all about the money, isn't it, Dermott.'
She obviously knew about the pay off O'Shea was going to receive, or at least she had worked it out for herself. O'Shea's plans to win over the confidence of Sinéad Dillon were in tatters. He still believed that his actions six years ago were the right ones, but he could not ignore the words that were coming from the lips of Sinéad Dillon.

'Do us all a favour, Dermott', she spat at him as she stood up from her chair. 'Help me find this Dwyer in London, even if it means working with the English. But after that, just fuck off somewhere in the world where we don't have to listen to your old views and bullshit ways!'
Of all the verbal abuse and opinions that she threw at him in those last few minutes, that was the quote that made him feel empty. That was the quote that would stick with him. That was the quote that would make him feel sad at a moment that he would later have to himself.
If only she knew why!

7

SABBATICAL AGENDA

Warwick woke up from the six hours sleep he managed to grab in the driver's seat of his car. He took a look at his watch, 9.20am. As he viewed the South Mimms carpark around him the memories of the previous night's activity were with him. As soon as he got his head together, the panic started to set in. He hadn't made it to his office that morning. If ever he was linked to the killing last night, surely his absence this morning would confirm it. Then he suddenly remembered the time he had been given by Sergeant Davis to get the Billy Hopkirk case closed up - a week.

Refreshment and Rally

He looked across the car park to the inviting cafe. He decided that he would have to make short notes of everything that had taken place up to the killing last night, so he could somehow make some sense of it all, and what better way of doing it but over a cup of coffee and some toast, which was about all he would be able to stomach under the current situation. He checked his top pocket for his toothpaste and traveller's toothbrush, both of which were packed in with his change of clothes. He decided that he could fit in a cigarette between here and the toilets, before heading for his breakfast. As he was just about to close the driver's door, after a small stretch and yawning session, he checked behind his seat for the sports bag he had taken from Jacobs at the airport. After his breakfast, he would finally check the contents of the bag.

Books Behind Schedule

John Hewitt sat at the meeting that was taking place that morning, on the third floor of the building site that was to become the new book shop and headquarters for *BOOKS Inc*.

He had been at home the previous night, going over every thing that had gone wrong with this job. Going over every detail that had led him to be sitting at this table this morning opposite five other men, drinking coffee and looking more uncomfortable for having to attend a meeting on a Sunday morning themselves than he was.

The meeting was being chaired by a fat man with glasses, a beard and a patch of hair at each side of his head. His voice was very quiet for a man so large, as if he didn't have enough energy left in him to give his words more volume. He was the leading architect, Dave Lamb, airing his concern at the pace and quality of the work taking place on site.

His listeners were the Project manager of O'Connel Builders, the Mechanical and Electrical foremen from Roger & Ruspers and their Construction Manager and John Hewitt himself, the Construction Administrator.

'As you can tell, the fact that we are here for a site meeting on a Sunday morning does in itself express the urgency of resolving the problem at hand.' Lamb's voice could be heard, softly across the paper and note filled table. 'Roger & Ruspers have issued thirty five R.F.I.s (request for information) to O'Connel Builders concerning routes and requirements for electrical and mechanical services within the building. Not one of those R.F.I.s have been answered.'

At this stage, Tony Letts, the Project Manager for O'Connel Builders was looking and feeling clearly embarrassed.

'This has led to the construction and building work falling behind by three weeks and, as you know, we are due to re-open this shop on Thursday.'

At this stage John Hewitt decided to intervene. He knew that if he wasn't successful in getting the book shop open for Thursday, he would be in grave danger of receiving the blame and accusations through lack of knowledge for his position. He knew he was partly to blame for not keeping a closer eye on the job, but it was the lack of site co-ordination by O'Connel Builders that had landed him in this mess. As far as he was concerned, they were going to pay for it.

'I've been in talks with the financial and labour departments of Roger & Ruspers and they assure me that they can get the manpower needed down here for the next three days to get this job completed. I've also been assured by Dave here that he can get two more draftsmen down here working round the clock to get the necessary drawings together to get this bloody job finished.'

He stood up and walked around the table until he came opposite to Tony Letts before continuing. 'The question is, is your company going to foot the bill for this, considering it's your company's actions on this site, or should I say, lack of action, that has landed us all in this mess?'

Never in John Hewitt's twenty three years in the building trade had he witnessed such a farce as O'Connel Builders. He was going to make them suffer for their stupidity of acting in such a fashion on one of his jobs.

'I need to speak to our Director', Tony Letts replied.

'You do that', Hewitt said to him, before leaning forward on the table to come even closer to Letts before continuing. 'And don't forget to remind him, that if he doesn't play ball with me, I'll make sure the Evening Standard spells his name right when they want to enquire who's behind this almighty cock up.'

'Okay. Give me ten minutes to go and speak to him on the phone downstairs, then I'll come back to you', Letts almost pleaded, just to get out of the room. The sweat was pouring from his forehead at an embarrassing rate. He looked like he was going to pass out, but Hewitt was not going to let up. He stayed leaning across the desk looking into the eyes of Letts.

'If you're not back here within ten minutes, then I swear to God, I'll get another building company in here to finish this job, and I'll put a block on every contract O'Connels ever try to obtain.' He leaned even closer towards Letts before finishing, 'I'll make it my fucking vocation in life!'

'Okay!' Letts spoke, clearly nervous with the whole

situation. 'I'll be back in ten.'

With that, he made his way out of the room at a quick pace, whilst everyone else looked at each other, clearly impressed with what they had just witnessed at what was usually a boring and indecisive meeting.

Breakfast at McDonalds

Central London's Denmark Street may be world famous for its guitar shops, but the only interested person on this dry cold morning, looking at the guitars on display, was a Mick Jennings, walking along with his six year old daughter, Louise. She was clearly bored and agitated at having to look at these guitars again, like she had the Sunday before, and the Sunday before that. Every Sunday morning, he would drive from his house in Brixton, park his car in Soho Square, walk over to and up and down Denmark Street before treating himself and Louise to breakfast at McDonalds on Tottenham Court Road. It was a routine they followed weekly to allow Mrs Jennings a good morning's sleep after her night shift, nursing at St Thomas' Hospital.

'Come on Daddy, come on', Louise pleaded, as she pulled at the sleeve of his jacket.

'Just be patient, otherwise there'll be no McDonalds at all', he answered, trying to be firm, but he almost began to laugh himself.

'Oh yeah, as if you'd miss out on a McDonalds yourself Dad', she fired back, still pulling at his sleeve.

'Louise, how many times do I have to tell you? It's not yeah, it's yes.'

'Oh yeah I forgot', she laughed at him.

'Louise!'

A 'Cuppa' Cut Short

Hewitt was in the middle of telling the other members of the meeting what was really going to happen in the week that was to approach them.

'The other builders will be here first thing in the morning. They are fully aware of our situation here, so they will not only fall into the scheme of things, they'll bend over backwards to impress me as they're after every one of my jobs that O'Connels are working on at the moment.'

'Jesus Christ, this will sink O'Connels!' Dave Lamb spoke, staring out of the window across the table, almost amazed at how this whole mess had come about.

'Ah fuck 'em, Dave. They let us down, that's all there is to it. You can't afford to act the way they did on this job, not with how political the whole building trade is these days. Fair enough, O'Connels were the best builders at one time, but now they've lost it, so fuck 'em, that's life.'

With that, he made his way over to the coffee trolley that was just on the left hand side of the doorway. He picked up a paper cup before asking the other members of the meeting.

'Anyone for a cuppa?'

Then it happened.

All of a sudden there was a decompression effect from the doorway. All of the paperwork and paper cups flew out of the doorway as if a gigantic hoover was pulling them in an attempt to clean out the whole room. Then a second later, it stopped.

Everyone in the room was silent and motionless until John Hewitt's voice broke the silence.

'What the fuck?'

Then it really happened.

An amazing gigantic blast of air came flying through the doorway with such an almighty force, it sent John Hewitt's brain into a daze. The kind of daze people experience when they are involved in a car crash, or when they receive a blow to the head. It's the kind of daze a drug user receives when he either injects heroin or takes L.S.D. It sends the brain into a sensation of slow motion, where a second can feel like twenty.

John Hewitt turned around to face the already shattered

window to see Dave Lamb, still sitting in his chair, with his elbows on the desk in front of him, fifty feet in the air above Charing Cross Road.

One of the foremen from Roger & Ruspers was spinning across the skyway until he crashed against the wall of the opposite building like a paintball off the stomach of a weekend soldier.

John Hewitt could see steel site boxes that must have weighed up to half a ton when filled to the brim with tool boxes and drills, fly across the airway above Charing Cross Road like empty shoe boxes on a windy day.

Just then, he could feel himself fall to his right hand side. He was falling, but had no feeling of control whatsoever. He looked down to see that his right arm had been torn away from his shoulder in the blast. Even though he was on the third floor of the building, he had a clear view of the ground floor through the enormous hole he was standing over, the hole his body weight was pulling him towards.

As he fell through the hole, he could see all the cable drums, step-ladders, plaster boards and timbers flying towards the main road from the floors below. It was at that moment that his brain regained the sense of realisation. It was at that moment that he began to scream, but before his vocal chords had a chance to do the job they were being asked to do, the ground floor rose to meet him at top speed.

Fifteen minutes later, a woman would be heard screaming from the steps of the London Astoria, one hundred and fifty yards down the road, where the complete arm of John Hewitt was discovered.

Beneath A Dusty Curtain

Mick Jennings awoke beneath a rubble of bricks and dust, holding on to his daughter, Louise.

When he'd heard that first rush of wind go through the building of *BOOKS Inc.*, he knew something was wrong. All the rubbish on the street, swept in the direction of the

BOOKS Inc. doorway in a completely unnatural manner. He didn't know why, but he just knew that something wasn't right and his first reaction was to pick up Louise and run like mad towards Tower Point. He had no idea what he should be running from or what he was running for, but he knew that he had to run like their lives depended on it.

Just as he went to pick Louise up, the explosion happened. Luckily Louise was shielded by the body framework of her father, but he was not going to have such luck.

Mick Jennings could feel a stinging sensation around his waist the moment he awoke, but his first reaction was to check that Louise was okay. She was coughing and spluttering into his jacket, which indicated that his immediate worries and concerns were allayed, but he couldn't ignore that stinging pain around his waist. He shook the rubble from the top part of his body before turning on his side to give himself a clear view of his waist.

'Oh Jesus no!' he gasped, completely horrified.

The question of the stinging sensation was answered by the unbelievable horrific view below his waist. He could see a trail of veins, human tissue, blood clots and bloody bits of skin lying on the pavement where the bottom half of his body should have been. As he could feel his heart skip a beat from the shock of what he saw, he noticed the flow of blood increase across the pavement. As he lay there holding on to his daughter to protect her, he accepted the facts there and then, his time was up.

He didn't want her to see the mess below his waist, so he pulled the curtain that happened to be lying beside him, over his waist to cover up the ever increasing flow of blood. God only knows where that curtain had come from, from which building it had been blown out, but it was the one thing that was going to give him his last piece of dignity in front of his own daughter.

'Daddy, what happened?' Louise cried.

What ever life he had left in him, was going to be spent on

saving his daughter from being mentally scarred for the rest of her life, from seeing what was under the dusty curtain that lay upon an area where his legs should have been.

'It's okay babe, it's just some sort of explosion, are you okay?'

'Yeah, come on dad lets get out of here!'

Just then, he could hear the siren of the Police car pulling into the top of Denmark Street. He held his hand up so they could see where he and Louise were lying.

'Are you alright?' one of the policemen's voices could be heard shouting out to them.

'Yes, but would you please help my daughter?'

'Daddy, I'm okay, now come on!' she instructed him as she reached out to move the curtain, thinking that it was obstructing him from moving.

'NO!' he shouted at her, 'Just head towards the Police car, I'll be right behind you.'

He was feeling colder by the second. He could barely feel his arms, his vision was becoming so weak he could only see the outline of Louise as the unfamiliar uniformed figure picked her up and ran towards the top of the road.

'Daddy?' He heard her voice cry out to him, one last time.

'It's okay...........babe...........I'm right..........behind .... you."

Mick Jenning's vision of Denmark Street, blended into a peaceful shade of darkness until he took his first steps of eternally uninterrupted sleep.

8

STEPPING TENTATIVELY

The sound of The London Symphony Orchestra playing the 'Wasps Overture' at 10.30 a.m. on the M10 to Stansted was rudely interrupted by Peter Allan's mobile phone ringing. Martin Brooks was glad of the interruption for he couldn't stand classical music. He could handle the smooth pieces of music, but the fast confusing movements like the 'Wasps Overture' was too much for him. To him it just sounded like a complete and utter pompous mess that clever people made out they could understand just to impress others. He would never complain, because at the end of the day, Peter Allan was his boss, who absolutely loved classical music and nothing but, so he just had to put up with it when he was in his company.

Peter answered the phone, clearly agitated from having his mental vision of the Wasps moving around their nest in an almost hypnotic pattern, interrupted.

'Yes?' he snapped.

Overture Aborted

It was obvious that Allan was clearly shocked at the news he was receiving. He was completely stone faced for the next minute as the voice on the other end of the phone was relaying the information to him.

'I want a full report on my desk in two hours. I want everyone down there on it straight away. Anyone clocking off from the night shift can fucking well forget about it', he shouted down the line, and with that, he closed the receiver of his phone before throwing it on the dash board.

'Fucking bastards!' Allan shouted at the road in front of him. 'Dirty fucking bastards!'

'What is it?'

'Looks like the Fifth Brigade have been busy this morning. They've just taken a big chunk out of the Charing Cross Road in London. Killed six people in the blast, one was a man walking past the target with his six year old daughter.'

'Did they phone it in yet?'

'Yes. Said there would be another bomb in twenty four hours time if we don't start releasing political prisoners serving time in Long Kesh.'

Brooks said nothing. He just stared at the road in front of him, thinking over the facts he had just been given before speaking.

'What about the girl, the victim's daughter?'

'Survived, thanks to her Dad shielding her in the blast.'

Brooks kept his eyes fixed on the quiet road in front of them for the next whole two minutes before speaking again. 'What a lovely mental scar she'll grow up with.'

Allan's voice was much quieter than before. 'Dirty bastards.'

Haunting Questions

Sergeant Davis stood at the window of his office looking out over the quiet Sunday morning view of Silver Street, Enfield. Two things were playing on his mind. Firstly it was Warwick. What in God's name was he doing in Tenniswood Road yesterday when they raided the house from where the phone call was made to Church Street? Secondly, the confrontation with the builder at the bomb site on Church Street. That second thought was making him feel more agitated as it filled his mind.

'Bloody O'Connels', he said to himself, regretting the day he ever got involved with them.

'Bloody Irish gypsies.'

Warwick had two bites from a slice of toast in the South Mimms cafe before pushing the plate away and settling for a cup of coffee. He stared at the notepad in front of him that bore his handwriting.

Billy Hopkirk, suicide
Meeting Jacobs in disguise.
Police raid on Jacobs' house, two vans, three cars.
Meeting with the real Jacobs at Stansted.
The sports bag ?
Whitewebbs Lane.

When he tried to focus on one thing he could feel himself drifting to another. Nothing seemed to have any pattern to it. He should have been concentrating on young Billy Hopkirk, but Jacobs was the main thing on his mind at the moment. He couldn't get it out of his mind, the things that Jacobs had said to him regarding his deceased family. He found himself asking that same question that had been going through his mind again and again when he thought about Jacobs.

'How in shit's name do you know my family?'
The same man that sat with a young boy who committed suicide in a restaurant somehow knew his family and claimed to have ruined Warwick's life.

Warwick needed answers and he needed them quick. He stared at his notepad and looked at the words that may have well said to him 'door to your answer.'

The sports bag.
He finished his cup of coffee before heading back to his car to finally investigate the contents of the sports bag.

Tightening Tension

Sinéad Dillon and Dermott O'Shea stepped off the shuttle inside the airport and made their way down to passport control. They hadn't said a word to each other since parking up O'Shea's Escort in the car park of Cork Airport, as Dillon was grabbing her suitcase out of the boot she had casually asked him,

'Have you been paid up front yet?'
O'Shea felt shocked and embarrassed but he didn't and couldn't lie to her.

'Yes. Séamus settled up with me this morning.'

'Good, then that's one less thing to worry about', she replied to him in disgust. Not one word was spoken between them since that.

O'Shea was starting to feel a little nervous at the sight of the passport control desks ahead of them. Stansted was well known in the movement for pulling people in for a forty eight hour investigation. This was an action the Police were allowed to carry out under the 'Prevention Of Terrorism' Act. Dillon seemed to be completely unmoved by the sight ahead of her. O'Shea started to sweat around the collar as he played with his tie and loosened his top button.

'Jesus I could murder a cigarette!'

'It wouldn't be the first thing you've murdered Dermott," she replied to him with laughter. He looked at her completely stone faced which made her laugh even more.

'How the fuck can you laugh at a time like this?' he demanded.

'Oh yes I forgot', she was now laughing uncontrollably, 'this is the most important mission ever.'

'Jesus Christ Sinéad get a grip, girl!'

'Oh Dermott, what a time to start feeling kinky, come on then, get your bollocks out and I'll give 'em a grip.'

O'Shea stood there looking at her in astonishment. How could she be acting so giddy at a time like this, at a time when they were now moving behind enemy lines on a mission and a very important one at that? How could any of this be in the slightest bit funny, how could any of this stress and worry bring a smile to your face let alone a laugh to your stomach? When he looked into those eyes of hers, the reason became clear.

'You stupid fucking bitch, you're stoned aren't you', he said, grabbing her chin with his left hand to examine her eyes before continuing, 'still smoking that marijuana shit? Jesus Christ, you pick your fucking moments, Sinéad, you really do.'

Sinéad turned totally serious in the blink of an eye. As she raised her right arm at great speed to push away his hand, the rest of her body didn't seem to move an inch. As she still faced Dermott, he could see her eyes were a little blood shot. She must have smoked a quick joint back in Cork before they checked in, that would explain for her being totally relaxed and quiet throughout their trip so far.

'Don't you dare fucking lecture me. Look at you, sweating like a dog on heat, as twitchy as a tout and me as calm as you like and you have the fucking nerve to lecture me.' She came even closer to him before continuing. 'Let me guess', she said looking down at his duty free bag, ' A bottle of Black Label and two hundred Carols. I'm right aren't I. You've got your vices, so fuck off and let me have mine.'

O'Shea knew he'd just have to let it drop and come back to it later, but he wasn't comfortable with her going into a situation like this feeling a bit stoned. If it was anyone else, he would make sure that at some point later on, he would put a bullet in their head and dump them. But this was Sinéad Dillon, he had his reasons for letting it drop, and they were good ones.

'Fair enough, I'll let it go this time, but don't forget who's the fucking boss on this mission', he told her.

When they both turned around to face the passport desk, they realised their argument may have been a little bit too public. Everyone was looking at them, including the two uniformed and armed Policemen.

'Well done Dermott, you prick, I think you've just landed us in it.'

One of the Policemen approached them as they tried to regain their composure.

'I think', he began, 'that you two should come with me.'

Examining The Contents

Warwick unzipped the sports bag with the caution that his job had bred into him. He noticed straight away the smell from inside, one of stale sweat and smelly feet. After glancing across the South Mimms carpark, he slowly removed the first item, a small black book and placed it beside the bag. He decided that it would be best to remove everything from the bag first before examining any of its contents. Apart from the book, the only other major items of interest were, twenty five neatly wrapped bunches of brand new fifty pound notes and a .357 Smith & Wesson hand gun, with spare cartridges. The rest of the contents being a pair of old torn Nike running shoes and a well soiled sweatshirt were quickly placed back in the bag. The twenty five wrapped bunches of fifty pound notes were obviously from a robbery or were forgery. Warwick was able to tell this by two things. One, there wasn't a crease mark anywhere to be seen around the sides of the notes and two, the numbers seemed to run in a numerical order. He then turned his attention to the gun and came to the conclusion that it was brand new and had never once been used. He unclipped the barrel to see it was unloaded and the chambers were still covered with the protective grease that new guns have to keep them prepared for action. But the item that would prove to be the must important was that little black book. As he flipped through the pages of the book he discovered that the first two pages were the only ones with any writing on them.

He looked out across the car park, checking that his privacy was still safe, before lighting a cigarette as he started from the first page.

Sunday, 4.00, Moon Under Water, Chase Side, Enfield.

Written in big letters covering the entire three inch by six inch note paper. He took a puff of his cigarette before turning the page over.

Mr Davis,   4k cash.
Fifth,   65k cash.
O'Connels Building Contractors Ltd.,   25k deposit
Midland Bank, Southgate. (622558 3758964521 05)

He turned his attention back to the twenty pound notes and had a rough count of the first batch. There were approximately eighty notes in each batch, which made four thousand pounds. He turned his attention back to the second page of the book, then to the first and then back to the four thousand pounds sitting on the passenger seat of his car.

'Stand up, Mr Davis, your time is up. As of four o'clock today, your arse is mine.'

He then reached over to the dashboard to pick up the piece of paper that had been left in his car the previous day with the words *'Stansted 21.30 BA 4132'* written on it. He held it next to the note book to compare the handwriting.

'And so is yours, Jacobs, you piece of shit!'

Diffident Despondency

John Hayward was standing in the Churchill room of Downing Street facing the two seated figures in front of him.

'Where in God's name is Peter this morning?' he asked, clearly agitated with the current situation he found himself in.

'With all due respect, Prime Minister, you've had more dealings with Peter Allan in these last few months than anyone else. Surely I should be asking you the very same question', Sir John Primark replied.

'OK John, don't go getting all defence on me!' John Hayward fired back at him.

'Prime Minister, you have called me here for a reason, of which you have not told me', Sir John said, feeling clearly on edge at being in the presence of the Prime Minister.

Peter Allan and many of Sir John's other colleagues, felt privileged to be working along side the current Prime Minister, but he didn't. He felt that he couldn't trust him. Sir John much preferred John Hayward's predecessor, Maggie Thornbird. He watched John Hayward very carefully and came to the conclusion that the P.M. didn't have the guts of the Iron Lady. He didn't have the front to make a harsh decision and stand by it no matter what the consequences might be. He didn't have the front to face the public head on and argue a case that they couldn't see the good in and he didn't have the front to tell the unemployed and the homeless to get on their bikes and look for work elsewhere in the country. He couldn't put the fear of God into the foreign nations of this world, especially Northern Ireland, as only the great Iron Lady could. You had to be able to do this sort of things without regret to become a great leader and in his eyes John Hayward couldn't. John Hayward would never be able to fill the high heeled shoes of Lady Thornbird.

John Hayward had his back to the two men now as he stared out of the window overlooking Downing Street's back garden. Sir Patrick Maynard, the other person in the room, finally spoke up.

'I don't mean to be disrespectful to you, Sir John', he said in Sir John's direction before turning his attention to the P.M., 'but do you think he's maybe doing the job you've asked him to do.'

Sir John wouldn't know any details of the mission that Peter Allan was on, only the people he was after. Even though he was Peter's boss on paper, he always had to leave the room when Peter discussed the specific details with Martin Brooks or any of the other field agents working for Section 13. That was how it worked, that was how Lady Thornbird had set it up and that was the way it had stayed. Section 13 answered to the P.M. and the P.M. only.

'What do you think Paddy?' he asked, with a hint of helplessness in his voice.

'I think the mission has started already.'

The Prime Minister was still looking out of the window as he spoke.

'Sir John, I wish you to leave us now, just let me know when Peter calls in.'

'No problem', Sir John answered, glad to be getting out of the room.

The Prime Minister still faced the back garden as he listened to Sir John gather his coat and case before leaving the room. When he knew it was just himself and Sir Patrick that were in the room, he let out a sigh of relief before making his way over to the table to join his friend and colleague.

'I'm starting to wonder about this mission Paddy, I'm starting to wonder about the people we're dealing with.'

'Look, it's just the shock of what's happened this morning', Sir Patrick replied.

'You mean the shock of knowing that six innocent people have spilled their blood on my streets. The street's only three miles from where I was born and only one mile from where we are now sitting. The shock of wondering where this is all going to end.'

There was a tremble in the P.M.'s voice.

'Like you've said yourself, it is just shock. What has happened this morning is nothing short of tragic, but we have to stay focused. We have to focus on ending this war because that's what this is, it's war. It's not a national war, we believe that this is the war of one man and he has to be stopped.'

'In Northern Ireland, it takes a lot of work, patience and time for the R.U.C. to make a member of the I.R.A. turn on his own people. It can sometimes fall to pieces when one of their members won't go in the witness box after pleading for immunity. The R.U.C. are promised names of the I.R.A. brigade staff, training grounds and weapons storage, but they come up with nothing because that person is too frightened to tell on his own people. Yet here we are, being promised by Sinn Féin that the Southern I.R.A. are going to help us find this Dwyer, and we just seem to take their word for it.'

'So what else are we supposed to do?' Sir Patrick quizzed, feeling frustrated by listening to the Prime Minister's negative train of thought. 'This might be an almighty set up by the I.R.A., but then again this might be our only chance.' He leaned forward on his elbows on the table before continuing.' This is a chance we can not afford to ignore.'

John Hayward always felt more comfortable talking to Peter Allan about such issues, but he knew his friend, Sir Patrick, was right. He turned away from Sir Patrick and looked out the window with a face of deep thought. His mind was one of constant worry about so many issues and Northern Ireland was only one of them. He turned back to his friend and spoke of a different subject altogether.

'Did you know, that the night before Richard Nixon gave up his post as President of The United States, he was witnessed talking to a picture of John F. Kennedy in the Whitehouse. Allegedly, he said: 'When people look at you, they see what they want to be. When they look at me, they see what they are.'

He took off his glasses and placed them on the table. Sir Patrick noticed the marks the glasses had left around the bridge of the P.M.'s nose and around the outside of his eyes. They were like cuts and wounds where the frame of the glasses had dug its way into the pumping worried face. John Hayward rubbed his tired eyes before continuing.

'At every Prime Minister's question time, I look across the house at a young handsome face that has a smile that could hide a thousand lies. I see a face that the unpolitically minded person would find trust in. I see a face that is ready to tear this government apart, to succeed in removing me from this office. I see a face that doesn't fear failure and I don't think it will ever experience failure.'

He seemed to be transfixed by his own thoughts.

'What I fear every night when I lay my head on my pillow is, I know a day will come when I will think of my opposition, Mr Blayre, the way Nixon thought of Kennedy.'

Sir Patrick was absolutely stunned from hearing the P.M. speak in this way, but deep down he felt the same about the man that had replaced the deceased John Smith in opposition. He too, knew that this Andy Blayre had the main key thing to become a great leader. It wasn't policy, it was looks. As he looked at the marked face of John Hayward, he realised that it wasn't the issues of Northern Ireland that was haunting the P.M.'s mind, but it was the looks of Andy Blayre. Sir Patrick knew that it would be from this angle that he could make the Prime Minister see sense about the mission.

'Prime Minister, we have to continue with this mission. Otherwise, his is the taking and ours will be the failure.'

'Very well', John Hayward acknowledged as he placed his glasses back on. 'But I will call time on this mission if I see fit.'

There was a knock at the door before a young man thrust his head through the open door. 'The press conference is ready for you now, Prime Minister.'

'Thank you David, I'm on my way', Hayward responded before speaking to Sir Patrick once more.

'I need to speak to Peter. I want to know that this mission is water tight. I don't need Mr Blayre's spin doctors seeing this thing land on Downing Street's doorstep if it all goes wrong.'

As he stood up he straightened his tie and brushed his hand through his hair.

'I know deep down, if this mission goes right, then we could leave this office with our heads held high knowing that we have done the right thing by the people of Northern Ireland and the people we've prevented from becoming victims because of the troubles. But if it goes wrong, I would be in for a leave of office, much worse than that experienced by Richard Nixon, and I refuse to let that happen.'

He placed his hand on the shoulder of Sir Patrick before leaving.

'Get some rest, Paddy, before heading back to Stormont, you look like you could do with it.'

Face-to-face Antipathy

Peter Allan and Martin Brooks sat behind the plain white table, staring at the closed door in front of them. They were both thinking over the news that they had received on their journey up to Stansted concerning the bombing that had taken place this morning. Brooks broke the silence by turning around to face Allan.

'Look, we have to forget about what's happened this morning and just concentrate on the job in hand. If we want to win the trust of these people, we have to give a little trust to them.'

A frown grew across the face of Allan, a frown of confusion.

'Last night you spoke about killing these people once the mission is complete. Now you want to trust them on the day a bomb has taken six lives in their name.'

'Look, firstly, *you* asked *me* on this mission, remember', Brooks adamantly told him before continuing. 'Secondly, we have to at least make them feel like we trust them or this is not going to work.'

Just then, there was a knock at the door.

'Come in!' Allan instructed.

Brooks turned away from Allan clearly frustrated from being cut off in the middle of a conversation.

'P.C.Linsey', the policeman introduced himself before continuing. 'We have the two subjects for you outside. Do you wish to see them now?'

'Give us one minute, please', Brooks asked of him.

He waited for Linsey to close the door before facing Allan again.

'I mean it, Peter, they have to think that we trust them. Otherwise let's just arrest them, lock them up and forget about this mission and let this Dwyer chap bomb his way through London, shall we?'

'Don't fucking patronise me Martin!'

'They have to think we trust them', Brooks replied, clearly wanting to state his case.

'Don't worry Martin, I've lied to you enough in the past and you haven't noticed.'

Brooks suddenly felt a bit thrown on hearing this information, but saw the needed relevance in it for the current situation. Still his face grew into a frown of confusion as he delivered his reply to the comment.

'I don't know why, but I somehow find that reassuring to hear.'

The door suddenly opened and in walked the thin tall figure of O'Shea followed by Dillon. The door slowly creaked before it closed behind them. The room was so silent it was hard to tell if anyone present was actually breathing. O'Shea kept his eyes on the two figures seated behind the table as he slowly made his way over to one of the chairs on the other side, whilst Dillon seemed to be admiring the decor of the room as she totally ignored the three men.

Both Allan and Brooks looked straight past O'Shea at Dillon and both silently agreed on her beautiful features and slim figure, but let it pass for professional reasons. They all made use of the silence to eye each other up. O'Shea knew that they had the immediate advantage because of Dillon's beauty and he was the first to break the silence as he reached out his open hand to Allan.

'Dermott O'Shea, serving on behalf of The Provisional Irish Republican Army.'

Peter Allan reached out his hand before O'Shea had spoken, but pulled it back on this announcement. Brooks stood up and reached his hand out to O'Shea's and spoke.

'Martin Brooks, serving on behalf of Her Majesty The Queen.'

O'Shea's hand clenched into a fist for a moment and then unfolded again. Then their hands clenched tightly together, most probably, the first time ever in history that a hand representing Her Majesty The Queen, shook a hand from the I.R.A., and their hands stayed clenched for about thirty seconds before Dillon's voice broke the momentous occasion.

'So how the fuck are you British scum going to help us then?'

O'Shea seemed totally embarrassed as he tried to introduce her into the equation.

'This is Sinéad Dillon, my second in command for this planned mission.'

Allan looked clearly annoyed by her sudden outburst, but Brooks seemed to suddenly have it all clearly under control.

'Well what is it you want from us?'

'We want full co-operation from your government to try and track down this English scum bag who has been bombing London on our behalf and taking money from donators that belongs to us.'

O'Shea was annoyed at Dillon's behaviour. To him it seemed totally unprofessional, for he couldn't see what she was playing at. She wanted to be cocky and mouthy with them from the outset to test their patience. She wanted to see if one of them, or both of them would call this mission off before it had even started. She wanted to give them the feeling that she was a loose cannon, to see if they had the bottle to see this mission out with her on board. It had always played on her mind that the British only entertained the fact of talking to the I.R.A. because they actually feared them and their actions. She wanted to keep that feeling in the air, so she was going to speak to these men as if they were dirt. Yet because she and O'Shea hadn't spoken on this journey so far, he didn't know what she was playing at. He wanted to throw her a dirty look or say something to her, but he knew that it would also be unprofessional of him to display a show of conflict with her in front of the enemy. He knew that he would have to let it drop until later, along with the fact that she was stoned.

Peter Allan couldn't find it so easy to let it drop, he didn't have that sort of patience.

'Who in fuck's name do you think you are?'

'Oh dear, did I hit a nerve?' she replied in the hope of continuing to annoy him.

'This mission is not to retrieve your fucking donation blood money my sweetheart, I assure you. Secondly, I didn't hear that wanker, Garry Addams, condemn the bombing this morning or the Church Street bombing yesterday that was carried out in your movement's name, did you?'

'I didn't hear that wanker, John Hayward, condemn the midday raids that took place in West Belfast and South Armagh yesterday that broke the community spirit on what he calls the Queen's Highways, did you?'

Brooks was clearly impressed by this beautiful woman he saw before him, standing her ground better than the person she was arguing with. Allan was fuming. As far as he was concerned, he could see right through her beauty. To him she was a member of the I.R.A. that happened to have a pretty face, but it wasn't pretty enough for him. He continued by ignoring her comments.

'We've arranged a car for you. You can follow us out of the airport to a place where we can talk in private. Maybe you could use that time in the car, Mr. O'Shea, to put some fucking manners on your second in command.'

Dillon was just about to say something when O'Shea beat her to it.

'How we deal with our people has never been and never will be any of your business. I suggest you get a fucking grasp of that very quickly, otherwise gentlemen I'm afraid we're wasting our time.'

The room went silent once again. Dillon was impressed with the way O'Shea spoke to Allan. Brooks knew that this was a stumbling block and was hoping that Allan was going to reply in the correct manner, otherwise this mission was over before it had even begun.

'I do apologise.' It was hard to tell if Allan was being sarcastic or not, but after a moment of staring at Allan in the eye, O'Shea replied.

'Very well, apology accepted.'

9

THE COMPLEXITY OF DISTRUST

P.C.Linsey was just ten minutes away from clocking off from a sixteen hour shift. His usual hours for a shift were eight, but due to the two bombings that had happened within the last twenty seven hours, everyone was doing a double shift and not one person complained, because overtime hours were few and far between.

A Weird Encounter

He made his way over to his locker and pulled out his diary. The officer that trained him up when he was a junior nearly twenty years ago, always stressed how important it was, that you write an entry into your diary about every shift you undertake. Even when you think there is nothing of importance to enter into your diary, you must look for things to fill the eight lines allocated to that date. For the little bits of information that you may think are of no importance, could be the information that you may rely on one day to save your own skin or the skin of someone else. P.C.Linsey wrote about his meeting with Warwick at the start of his shift, and about the two suspects whom he had met that 'Intelligence' had come down to interview. "Two Irish people," he wrote, "one man and one woman. Here to meet 'Intelligence' within Twenty Seven hours of two I.R.A. bombings."

'Two arguing Paddies', he said to himself, as he stared into space, 'Here to meet Intelligence! Jesus Christ, that's a weird one.'

Conflict of Principles

The Czechoslovak Radio Symphony Orchestra were playing 'Mars' from Holst's 'Planets', much to the annoyance of Brooks as they approached the junction of the M25 and the M4. He sat sideways in the passenger seat of Allan's car, trying to watch the road in front of him, as well as occasionally watching the car that was following them, as well as trying to read the mood of the quiet Peter Allan beside him. Allan had his window slightly open, letting the smoke out from his third cigarette since leaving Stansted Airport an hour ago.

'What's playing on your mind?' Brooks asked him.

'You shaking the hand of a bloody terrorist, that's what's playing on my mind.'

'But you were going to shake his hand until he announced his representation of the I.R.A.'

Allan moved his head in an awkward motion from having this pointed out to him. He took a last puff on the cigarette before throwing it out the window. Brooks looked behind him again at the car following them containing O'Shea and Dillon. He leaned forward and turned down the music that was really annoying him before speaking again.

'Look, this is a mission like no other - that I grant you. But we have to make this work, and with all due respect Sir, you letting your feelings interfere with this is only going to result in us failing.'

Allan looked at him sideways as he turned the radio's sound back up to his favoured volume. Brooks just stared at him with annoyance from being ignored. His face was filling up with a rage he hadn't felt in quite a while, and this 'bloody pompous music' as he referred to it, wasn't helping.

"You stubborn bloody fool!"

Thinking 'Out Loud'

Dillon was driving the car as O'Shea just kept his eyes fixed on the road in front of them. He hadn't said a word to her since they left Stansted an hour ago. She kept thinking about the way O'Shea had spoken to Peter Allan back in the interview room at the Airport. He'd surprised her. She just thought of him as an old fool, in this for his money, until he stood his ground, her ground and the ground of the movement with the way he had defended them both.

'A penny for your thoughts Dermott?'

O'Shea took his packet of cigarettes from his pocket and extracted two of them. He lit them both and passed one of them to Sinéad and rolled down his window a little.

'What do you think of them Sinéad?'

'Well that Allan seems no different to any other British prick I've met. He has his head clearly buried up his own arsehole.'

O'Shea smiled at her response, but then his face went serious again as he stared out at the road in front of him. He started to think about the meeting that had just taken place at the airport and the meeting that had taken place back in Kilsheelan.

'I'm starting to feel like a tout, like a fucking supergrass', he muttered quietly.

She looked at him surprised at his statement, but only found herself agreeing with him.

'I have to admit, I know what you mean. We might have to sink the entire Fifth Brigade trying to get hold of this Dwyer.'

O'Shea leaned forward, opened up the ashtray and broke away the first piece of ash before replying to Dillon's comments. He really hated the British, he couldn't believe that he was actually going to be working with them to try and catch Dwyer, but he also couldn't forget about his new life after this mission was complete. He couldn't forget about the fifty two thousand pounds that lay at the bottom of his bag in the boot. He had to stay focused on the job in hand.

'There's two things you've said to me that are bugging the bollocks off me', O'Shea said to her.

'What's that?'

'Yesterday you mentioned that Dwyer was only in this for the money and today you mentioned he was English.'

Dillon gave a little smile to herself as she knew it was only a matter of time before O'Shea would pull her up about these two issues. O'Shea couldn't see the smile on her face, so he felt he was going to have to work a lot harder at trying to get a response out of her.

'You're totally pissed off at me, because you know I've accepted money from the movement for my time on this mission and my time in the past', he stated. Her face went serious from hearing this, so he quickly proceeded.

'The movement has no control over missions being carried out in London, which is mighty fucking dangerous when you think about it. Every shooting or explosion has to perfectly coincide with the actions in Belfast, but at the moment that isn't happening.'

He stopped to take one last puff on his cigarette, before throwing it out of the window and then continued.

'From that train of thought alone, it is very simple to come to the assumption that there's money controlling the explosions in London. Money can speak louder than politics.'

'And you seem to be a grand example of that, hey Dermott?'

'It certainly fucking seems that way, doesn't it Sinéad?' he quickly retorted.

She was shocked at his honesty and the strong manner in which he delivered it, and he didn't stop there.

'So why don't you tell me how you came to the assumption that this fucker is English and stop pissing me about.'

She kept her eyes on the car in front as she sat for a moment's silence before answering O'Shea's question. She could sense the anticipation from O'Shea as she took another puff on her cigarette.

'I know he's English, because I've met him.'

'Where and when?' was O'Shea's immediate reaction.

'Eighteen months ago in London.'

'Why the fuck didn't you mention this before?' O'Shea was starting to feel a little annoyed at her consistent lack of co-operation.

'Look, I'm mentioning it now, okay? Southern Division sent me over before to collect some funds from the Fifth Brigade, but it didn't happen', she said before taking another puff from the cigarette before throwing some ash out of her open window.

'What do you mean it didn't happen?' O'Shea asked her.

'A meeting was set up between myself and Tim Holleran, an old friend of yours from the Southern Division, way back?'

'Tim Holleran! Jesus, I remember him, go on.'

'We arranged to meet at an old warehouse in Kings Cross, but Dwyer showed up instead. He gave me a little souvenir to take back to the Southern Division.' She lifted her shirt up with her left hand to reveal an eight inch scar along the skin covering the left of her rib cage.

'He made it clear, that the Fifth Brigade of the I.R.A. was to receive its own funds in London and the headquarters in Belfast could ram it up their arse for all he cared.'

'Jesus Christ! Why in God's name didn't Séamus tell me this?' O'Shea asked, still looking at the scar Dillon was still displaying.

'Why, what difference would it have made?' she asked him. To that he didn't answer, but started to think of something else more significant.

'The British don't know what Dwyer looks like.'

'How do you know?'

'They wouldn't need us if they knew.' He turned sideways slightly to face the road in front of them as he started to think out loud. 'Southern Division think they're being clever, by making the British think we trust them, just to put a stop to Dwyer, to buy some time. But the fact of the matter is, the British don't know what Dwyer looks like, so they're playing the same game.'

'And we're in the fucking middle.'

'Do you still know a few of the contacts within the Fifth Brigade?' he asked her.

'That's the only fucking reason I was picked for the mission', she replied

'Do you still know what Dwyer looks like?'

'Oh I remember. I remember that Brit fucker's face', she told him, with a slight smile on her face, as if she was looking forward to meeting him again.

'Well that's the first thing they'll need to know. What he looks like.'

Big News on A Small Page

Williams was standing in front of Sergeant Davis's desk in Enfield police station with his notepad in his right hand. As he turned the small pages with his left hand, he was finding it hard to conceal his excitement, with the news that he was delivering to the Sergeant.

'The bullet we found beside the car has a serial number on it', he informed him.

Davis looked at Williams with annoyance. He so desperately wanted to get his week's paperwork up to date, but he had to contend with Detective Williams telling him every last sordid detail of the shooting that happened in Whitewebbs Lane last night.

'Without seeming to be rude, would you please, for God's sake, get on with it', Davis instructed him.

'The bullet came from a special handgun, the Smith PK. Only twenty six people in this country own such a gun, and every bullet carries the same serial number as the gun.'

Davis was looking at him completely unmoved.

'Please get to the bloody point.'

Williams handed over an A4 sheet of paper.

'Here are the owners details.'

Davis looked at the paper, then he looked straight back at Williams.

'Are you absolutely sure about this?' Davis asked him, with some abruptness.

'One hundred percent', Williams replied.

'Sweet Jesus!' Davis whispered.

Protection and Trust

Warwick reached down into the side pocket of the door and rumbled his fingers around until he found an old packet of headache tablets. He reached under his own chair, whilst keeping an eye on the road, and pulled out a bottle of water he kept for filling up the engine. As he washed down the tablets, he wished he had a nice bottle of crystal clear cold water, instead of the warm cloudy liquid that now lay around his mouth. As he crossed the main Oakwood junction in north Enfield, he glanced over to the Chinese Restaurant where young Billy Hopkirk had taken his life the night before last. He pulled into the car park outside, parked his car and turned off the engine. As he did so he saw a man in his early thirties walking along with his two year old boy.

The protection a man has over his child is an amazing sight to watch if you understand what that protection is all about. As the man was leading the boy to the car he looked around him in every direction for cars pulling into the car park or cars pulling out of spaces whilst talking to the boy at the same time about the morning's fun they had just had at the park opposite.

Holding the hand to guide, looking around for danger and talking for stimulation. Everything the man did was based around the child. Protection against the big bad world. Warwick then looked back at the Chinese Restaurant and thought of what little protection Billy Hopkirk had had in this big bad world. His father gone before him in the same style his son was to adopt. He thought of his own son Jonathan, and what little his protection had meant in the end.

He looked back at the man who was now placing his son in the child-seat of his car. He noticed the way he made sure the seat belt was secure but not rubbing on the boy's neck, the way he lifted the boy's jumper to feel his chest to see if he was too hot and the way he checked that the child lock was working on the door.

'If only it was that simple', he said to himself, looking in the man's direction. 'If only you could always be there, it would be that fucking simple.'

As he opened a fresh packet of cigarettes before lighting one, he started to think about Jacobs. He thought of how he may have pretended to be the protection young Billy needed in this world, or how he made it look that way to gain the boy's trust.

'Who the hell is Mary?' he asked himself, feeling frustrated at knowing so little about Jacobs. Mrs Hopkirk had no idea who this Mary was, so it had to be something to do with Jacobs.

He looked at his watch before starting up the engine and heading towards the meeting point for Jacobs and this Mr.Davis.

Cautious Stepping

Dillon stayed close to the car in front, as they drove up a small side road to an old warehouse that appeared to be abandoned from the outside.

'If at any stage you can see yourself getting close to Dwyer, I want to shake these arseholes off us, OK?' O'Shea was instructing her.

'No problem.'

'And for fuck's sake, watch your back!' were his last words, as they pulled in through the gateway.

Allan drove towards the left hand side of the enormous building, across a ground that gave the impression that it had been abandoned for quite some time. The path to the building was made up of broken down weeds, bushes and big pieces of boarding to hold down all the wild growth. As the two cars got closer, the shutters to the building seemed to automatically open to allow the two cars to enter the building and, once inside, the shutter automatically closed.

On its closure, all the interior lights automatically came on revealing a fresh, clean, clear, white interior.

'I have to hand it to them, that was pretty cool', Dillon acknowledged.

O'Shea didn't seem to be impressed at all. As far as he was concerned they were out in the middle of nowhere, behind enemy lines. He could only think of what he would be doing, if he had a couple of Brits behind their enemy lines. In fact he knew full well what he would do. He'd torture them to within an inch of their lives.

The two cars drove along a wide passageway until they came into an open area equivalent to that of a major supermarket. Allan stopped his car about twenty feet short of the only visible feature in this huge white arena, some office screens. Dillon proceeded to do the same. Once the engines were switched off, Brooks and Allan got out of their car and waited for their guests to do the same. Dillon went to open the door as O'Shea spoke.

'Hold on Sinéad!'

O'Shea glanced around the open empty arena. All he could see in this vast wide open space was a little office set up in the middle. Four people sitting at four separate desks. They were typing into their computers and staring at the monitors, completely unmoved by the two cars that had just pulled up only twenty feet away from them. They didn't seem the slightest bit interested in who their new guests were. All that interested them at that moment in time were the monitors in front of them. Suspended on a small rig from the ceiling were seven more television monitors. These showed the surrounding areas of the warehouse. All he could think about was what would be happening if the roles were reversed.

'Like I said before, Sinéad, watch your fucking back!' he said as he opened his door and got out, followed by Dillon.

Brooks watched them as they seemed to take in their surroundings.

'If you'd like to follow us, please', Brooks then directed them.

'Where are we?' O'Shea asked before making any attempt to walk anywhere.

Allan couldn't help but feel agitated by their accents and

manner. The pair of them seemed to display some sort of cockiness as far as he was concerned.

'For obvious reasons, we can't take you anywhere that is covered by the 'Special Secrets Act', so we have set up this location, purely on a temporary basis, so we can discuss our progress when needed', Brooks explained to them.

'That's all fine and fucking dandy, but how do we find our way here again?' O'Shea asked him.

'Miss Dillon will be working with me from now on and you'll be staying here. We have some fine living quarters upstairs', Brooks replied.

'Bollocks. I'm not staying here!' O'Shea stated.

All that kept going through his mind was what would be happening if the roles were reversed and what would happen the minute Dwyer was found. The only way he would be leaving here then, would be in a body bag.

'So where do you plan on staying then?' Allan asked him, clearly getting annoyed with this whole issue.

'You can drop me off somewhere later when we've finished here', O'Shea said in Allan's direction.

'Very well, that's no problem', Brooks answered for Allan, who was returning a dirty look in his direction.

Whilst all the debating was going on, Dillon was scanning the area around them. She was trying to see if there were any other entrances or exits to this arena, which was hard to fathom out due to the floor, walls and ceiling all blending into one complete colour of white. If there were any other doors around, they were well camouflaged. It was also hard to work out just how big this area was.

She couldn't see what the four people were looking at on their computer monitors. If she could, she would have seen her own reflection looking back at her on one, the face of O'Shea talking on the other and the views from both left and right of the party on the others. They were trying to see if they had either O'Shea or Dillon on their records, or on record anywhere else. This computer system could compare them to any records in the world on their voice sound or face outline alone. The computer had also scanned them for weapons but found none.

To one side of the four desks there appeared to be an open office, similar to the one used at the M.o.D. A large meeting table, a drinks cabinet and six table chairs, accompanied by two similar armchairs to those in Allan's office. Brooks gave a little smile in Allan's direction at the sight of this little set up. As they made their way over to the office set up, James Moore stood up from one of the desks and joined them.

'This is James, he's our informations man, and my right hand man', Allan said introducing him.

James didn't say anything, he just nodded acknowledgement in their direction as he led the party to the large meeting table. Dillon and O'Shea sat down in the nearest seats causing Allan and Brooks to go around to the other side. This just added to the list of things that were slowly building up inside Allan, but he decided to put these things to one side in his head, as he would try his best to get through this.

'Drink anyone?' James asked of them all.

Everyone declined apart from Dillon.

'I'll have a beer if there's any.'

'No problem', James replied as he took a bottle of Budweiser from the small fridge behind the drinks cabinet.

'Glass?'

'No I'll have it out of the bottle, thanks', she replied.

'What a lady', Allan tried to joke.

'Fuck off', she quickly shot in his direction, to which he looked a little embarrassed.

'Right, let's get straight down to business, shall we?' Brooks began as he received a piece of paper from James. 'Our computer system, as great as it is, doesn't have a clue who you are.'

O'Shea looked to his left to where the three other workers were sitting, only this time they were looking straight at him, three women. He looked at the floor and gave a little laugh to himself. No wonder they didn't look up from their screens on his arrival, he thought, they were watching him by camera all the time. How did he not think of that before? He felt that he was either getting old or he had been out of the game for too long.

'You have to understand that we are as apprehensive as you are about going into this, so you have to accept that every step we take will be a cautious one', Brooks said as he noticed O'Shea looking back at the workers.

O'Shea thought about Brooks' quick reaction to the fact that he wouldn't stay in the living quarters upstairs. Brooks was obviously trying to see things from their side as well. Or so that's how it seemed to O'Shea and, as much as he hated to admit it to himself, he was going to have to start seeing things from their point of view as well.

'Fair enough, we know we're clean as far as your records go, that's the main reason why we were picked for this mission', he replied to Brooks, still looking in the direction of the three women before continuing, 'but can we have some privacy?'

'I think we'll call it a day, ladies', James instructed them. With that they all quickly left their desks, walked past the two cars, down the ramp to the passageway where their high heels could be heard tapping along into the distance. While this was taking place no one said a word. O'Shea tried to describe this bizarre place to himself as he watched the three women walking off into the distance. It wasn't British and pompous with stupidity, as he would have loved to have described it. It wasn't intimidating either. He would have to think more on it later.

10

THE FOX MUST SLEEP SOMETIME

Warwick pulled into the carpark of The Moon Under Water and reversed his car into a spot where he could see most of the interior of the pub and the entrance of the carpark. He looked at his watch to see it was 3.40pm. He was unsure as to whether he should go into the pub or wait in the car park. As he laid his head back on the seat, he could feel the tiredness in his eyes and the pounding in his nose wound. He decided he would wait in the carpark.

Retrospection and Reflection
He closed his eyes and thought about Jacobs. He thought about how Jacobs had intimidated him by somehow knowing about his wife Helen and his son Jonathan. That was the thing that not only bugged him, but it frightened him as well. As he closed his eyes, he thought about the night that he'd received the dreadful news of their accident.

He was busy on that rainy April evening, looking at some snap shots at the station. The case on which he was working at the time was a case involving a bank robbery at the Midland Bank in New Southgate, where two of the security guards were shot dead. Warwick was waiting for one of the snap shots he was looking at on the computer screen, to match up with the photograph he had on his desk.

At this time a rash of bank robberies had broken out across North London and Warwick's old friend, Mark Gerald, who was now working at the Police Station in Kilburn, North London, had a hunch from observing the pattern of these robberies, that they would be coming to either Barnet or New Southgate. Warwick was waiting.

None of his colleagues were willing to take a risk and help him out on this. None of them was willing to take a bit of his own time to cover one of the banks mentioned in Mark Gerald's list. Sergeant Davis wasn't interested in helping him out, due to the fact that nothing is worse, as far as paperwork goes, than a stakeout that produces nothing, that has been put together from a hunch. But Warwick was determined.

He observed the main bank that Mark Gerald had predicted. The Midland Bank in New Southgate. Warwick sat opposite the building with his camera, in his own leisure time, photographing and observing the comings and goings. He watched carefully, taking pictures of every suspicious character that entered the bank. Apart from the customers doing their Saturday morning business, the only other bodies moving around the entrance of the building, were the builders doing the renovation work to the pathway outside. Warwick sat in his car, drinking coffee from the flask that Helen had prepared for him that very morning. The voice of Zakk Zombie could be heard singing a heartfelt ballad on the radio-cassette player.

> *She sings hollow words of regret,*
> *She sings of times she can't forget.*
> *Holding her own,*
> *Because she's never been shown,*
> *The right way to bereave.*
> *She brings back things you can't retrieve.*

As the voice filled the inside of the car with it's beautiful melody and the fresh taste of coffee satisfied his taste buds, the only thing left to do was enjoy the moment with a Marlboro Light. He took one from his packet, leaving seventeen to last him through the day.

Nothing seemed out of the ordinary............. until he heard the two gun shots. He threw his new cigarette out of the open window and put his cup down on the dash board and when he turned around, after picking up his camera with his left hand, the doors of the bank flew open and Warwick's camera started flashing like mad.

> *She'll hold the things that we can't grip,*
> *She'll sink the last unsinkable ship.*

Four hooded men ran from the entrance of the bank to a car parked just a few metres along the pathway. Warwick's heart was beating like mad.

> *Standing her ground,*
> *As the troubles are bound,*

As the robbers were making their getaway one of the hooded men saw Warwick across the road in his car taking pictures.

> *She'd sooner die than admit defeat.*

The hooded man raised his shotgun in Warwick's direction but, for some unknown reason, one of the other hooded men stepped in front of him and flagged him in the direction of the getaway car, preventing him from shooting Warwick.

> *She'll catch the things you cannot see.*

As they drove away, they removed their hoods and Warwick got a clear picture of one of them. The picture he was now looking at on the computer screen.

As he clicked from picture to picture, smoking a cigarette and drinking a small glass of Jamesons from the bottle he kept stashed in the bottom of one of his drawers, little did he know that he was only three pictures away from a match before Sergeant Davis interrupted him with the news that was to change the rest of his life.

'Tom I'm afraid I've some bad news for you', Davis's voice echoed through Warwick's head.

Warwick sat there in the carpark of the 'Moon Under Water' playing the whole event over in his head until it sent him into a deserving deep sleep. Moments later, Sergeant Davis walked across the carpark, in his casual suede jacket, shirt and jeans, not noticing the sleeping Warwick in his car.

A Two-hour Nap

'Two bombs, within twenty seven hours of each other and the threat of a third tomorrow doesn't leave us much time to feel each other out for trust', Brooks said, breaking the uncomfortable silence that hung in the air since the three ladies had departed.

'So what's the plan?' O'Shea asked.

'The first thing we need to have is a description of this piece of shit', Allan answered.

O'Shea looked at Dillon with a smile on his face that she was returning in his direction.

'How long have we got?' O'Shea asked.

'Seventeen hours', Brooks answered.

'We need some rest, we've had little time to prepare for this mission and I could do with getting my head down for a couple of hours', O'Shea informed them whilst rubbing his eyes.

'We can't afford to waste a couple of hours', Allan informed him.

'I don't think you have much fucking choice, do you?' Dillon chipped in.

'Your quarters up stairs will do for me just to have a nap', O'Shea said in Brooks' direction, before turning to Dillon. 'Are you okay with that?'

'I'll stay down here, I'm okay for a while', she replied.

'Very well', Brooks concluded.

Rising to The Bait

Davis walked across the non-smoking part of The Moon Under Water into the main bar, stopping briefly to survey all the tables and chairs for the person he had arranged to meet. After coming to the conclusion that he wasn't here yet, he decided to get himself a pint of Fosters and wait in one of the seating cubicles until his associate would arrive.

As he sat there, sipping on his drink, he started to think about the day he got involved with O'Connels Builders, a day he had regretted ever since.

It was an ordinary Tuesday, no different to any other, when this small Irish man in his mid fifties walked into the foyer of the Enfield Police station, asking to speak to the resident Sergeant.

When Davis came down to the foyer, he was confronted by this 5' 2" Irish man with glasses.

'I'm Sergeant Davis, how can I help you?' he said, extending his hand to meet this small man

'Peter O'Connel, Director of O'Connel Building Contractors, working on the new leisure complex on Caterhatch Lane. Could I have a word in private?'

Davis invited him to an interview room so they could talk in private.

'So how can I help you?' Davis asked him.

'We've been doing various contracts throughout the surrounding areas of London in the last eighteen months. St Albans, Hatfield and Walthamstow, to name a few.' O'Connel stopped briefly, removing his glasses to rub one of his wise old looking eyes before continuing. 'The ground work stages of the contracts are the hardest, due to blocking the odd public highway for deliveries of concrete and waste collections. We've had a few problems in some other areas, but not in your constituency', he concluded.

'I don't follow you', Davis replied.

O'Connel gave a little laugh to himself before continuing.

'What I'm trying to say is, because the authorities of Enfield haven't bothered me with my contract on Caterhatch Lane, I've made a nice tidy profit on that job so far. I'd like to show my appreciation by making a donation to your Police fund.'

Davis sat there thinking carefully over what this small man was telling him, but also keeping his guard over the fact that money had just been mentioned.

'I appreciate the offer, but I don't think that will be necessary', Davis said as he tried to close the meeting.

'Look, hold on a second. I'm offering to make a donation to your Police fund, your Christmas collection or your favourite charity. I'm not a resident of Enfield, but I've other contracts coming up in the area.' O'Connel removed his glasses and moved his face a few inches closer to Davis before continuing. 'It would be nice to see a fund of some sort do well out of it all. I'm just asking for the odd delivery of concrete to take place on one of your highways.'

Davis said nothing, as he sat there thinking very carefully over this small man's offer. He started to think of how the Police Christmas fund could do with a boost, so he accepted O'Connel's offer. A mistake he regretted ever since.

It wasn't the blocking of public highways that became the headache of Sergeant Davis, it was his rising suspicion of their involvement in something much bigger that he couldn't quite put his finger on. The only problem was that when he discovered what it was they were involved in, it was too late to turn his back on it because he had received quite a substantial amount of money, on the behalf of funds and charities, from O'Connel Building Contractors Ltd..

Wriggling on The Hook

Warwick was still asleep in his car, when Jacobs walked across the carpark towards the pub. Looking clean shaved and wearing a black bomber jacket, he didn't notice Warwick, as he entered the pub through the non smoking section.

As Davis sat there in the cubicle, both hands wrapped around his pint glass, he started to wonder how he'd ever get himself out of this mess. The options running through his head were interrupted by a packet of Marlboro Lights cigarettes landing in front of him, having been thrown on the table from behind him.

Davis turned to see the man he had come to know as Tony Dwyer. Mid forties, grey cropped hair, clean shaved and wearing a black bomber jacket.

'Good evening my good Sergeant Davis. Glad to see you out on a night that your constituency is in a pretty piss poor way', Dwyer said as he sat opposite Davis, placing his pint of Guinness on the table and removing a cigarette from the packet and lighting it.

Davis looked around the pub to see if any one had noticed him sitting with this man that he had come to despise.

'So what news do you have for me today', Dwyer asked as he blew a stream of smoke into the air.

'Warwick shot your acquaintance on Whitewebbs Lane last night', he informed Dwyer.

Dwyer's eyes switched from looking at the drifting smoke from his own mouth to the eyes of his informer. His face lit up, showing all the facial veins around his temples. He broke out into a small laugh, not taking his eyes off those of Davis. His laugh became so loud it embarrassed Davis as a few people started to look in their direction. One voice from the bar was heard to say,

'Alright mate, calm down.'

Dwyer responded by jumping straight out of his seat and looking in the direction of the bar with a face that had turned from joy to hate in the blink of an eye.

'Oh yeah, why don't you just fuck right off', he shouted, 'I'll laugh as loud as it suits me, you fucking prick.'

There was a total silence at the bar and a total silence from all other areas of the pub. Dwyer's eyes were hidden beneath the watered pupils and red skin of hate. No one said a word.

There were men present, who were a fair size compared to Dwyer. But his face of hate was close to that of a face of madness, a face that even the strongest of men would be wary of.

'I'll laugh as loud as it suits me', he said in no one's direction as he sat back down in front of Davis who by now had his right hand up in front of his face, trying to hide himself from everyone in the pub. Dwyer slapped Davis's right hand away from his face, much to his annoyance.

'What the hell are you doing hiding your face, these are your people. You should tell them to have some fucking manners', Dwyer told him.

Davis could feel the sweat dripping down his back. He felt as if he was sitting with a mad man. He would give anything to be able to just stand up and walk out, but he knew the chances were he wouldn't make it to the gateway of the carpark. His left hand was gripping onto his glass. In his head he could picture himself smashing the glass of lager into the face of Dwyer. The blood of Dwyer and the lager fizzing into a foam on the table, would be the greatest picture in Davis's head for those passing seconds.

'What's playing on your mind Davis?' Dwyer broke his train of thought.

'What's playing on my bloody mind? Are you bloody serious?' Davis usually hated swearing, but his anger was starting to build. 'You nearly blew a fucking hole in the Earth yesterday in Enfield and you sit there and ask me what's playing on my mind!'

'Calm down, Davis, you'll get your cut of the money, just not tonight. OK?' Dwyer said casually with a little teasing smile on his face.

'Jesus Christ, it's not the money I'm bothered about', Davis spoke with panic in his voice.

'Right, that's enough of this bullshit.' Dwyer was firm, and Davis reacted sheepishly to this.

'Warwick, how do you know it was him that killed my

acquaintance?' Dwyer continued.

'The bullet had the same details as his gun records.'

'Was there a bag found at the scene of the shooting?' Dwyer prompted quickly.

'No, why?'

'How many people know that it was Warwick?' Dwyer continued, ignoring Davis' question.

'Just myself and a Detective Williams.' Davis felt like a suspect being interviewed in his own station.

Dwyer sat looking at Davis, thinking hard about the situation, thinking hard before he opened his mouth. He then leaned his elbows on the table to bring himself nearer to Davis before pointing his finger at him and speaking.

'If anything happens to Warwick, I'll kill you, plain and simple. Do you understand?'

Davis was confused by this demand, but nodded in acknowledgement.

'Do I need to take this Williams out of the equation, or will you?' Dwyer asked.

Davis stared at Dwyer, knowing how it would be useless to argue with him over this. Here was the man that had just killed twenty two people, only a mile up the road from where they were now seated. What would one more life mean to him. Davis knew the job would be safer with him, as he would make sure no else had to get hurt in the process.

'I'll take care of Williams', Davis said with a cold whisper.

Warwick was still asleep in his car, when Davis and Jacobs walked out of the pub at separate times, and neither had noticed him.

Sleep That Knits The Ravelled Brow......

Brooks walked back into the open area, having just shown O'Shea to the living quarters upstairs. James Moore had decided to take a couple of hours' break, so he headed off to get some food for himself. Dillon was sitting in the passenger seat of the car in which they had driven here and Allan was still seated at the main table. Brooks went and sat next to him.

'This is bloody ridiculous. Under seventeen hours to go and he wants to get his head down for a couple of hours', Allan said, quietly enough for Dillon not to hear him.

'We have to be patient. When he wakes up, we'll have fifteen hours before another IRA bomb goes off in our capital. I don't think we've ever had that much warning before, as well as PIRA wanting to help us', Brooks reasoned.

Allan was looking Brooks in the eye, as he thought the whole situation over.

'I hear what you're saying, but let's not forget our original plan. Once we find Dwyer, I want these two jokers out of the picture — permanently.'

'I couldn't agree with you more, Peter.'

'Good', Allan quickly responded as he stood up to leave. 'I better get in touch with the P.M. I'll be back in an hour and a half. Will you be okay?' he asked Brooks.

'Yes, I could do with the time to get to know her a bit better', he replied, looking in Dillon's direction.

With that, Allan picked up his cigarettes from the table and headed over to his car. As he walked, he kept eye contact with Dillon every step of the way. He felt like a betrayer to his own country. Everyone that worked for him had respect for the position he held and everyone he dealt with was envious of the personal relationship he had with the Prime Minister. Yet here he was, seventeen hours away from another bombing by the IRA, and he had the eyes of one of their people looking at him with loathing and disgust. If his own people only knew the dangerous game he was playing, maybe they would be delivering the same sort of look in his direction.

What Allan didn't realise was, that the only reason Dillon kept eye contact with him was because she was trying to roll herself a small cannabis joint without being caught. With O'Shea having disappeared upstairs for a quick nap, Moore popping out for a bite to eat and Allan now heading off somewhere, she thought she could have herself a quick smoke, get a nice little buzz going for an hour, with time enough to sit down and start talking business again. Allan was feeling wound up again by the looks he had received from Dillon, which is why he spun the wheels of the car as he pulled away at a sharp speed.

After Allan's car had disappeared down the tunnel from the main hall, Dillon cleared all the spilled tobacco and grumbles of green leaves from the dashboard into a small Golden Virginia tin she kept with her. She placed the tin in her pocket whilst holding the roll-up to her nose to smell the sweetness of its herbs. She then inspected the roll-up to make sure its paper was correctly secure and that there were no lumps or gaps in its contents. Once she was satisfied with her ritual inspection, she placed it between her lips. It was at this stage that she noticed Brooks walking over to the car.

'Bollocks', she said to herself.

Out came the Golden Virginia tin and away went the roll-up, for the time being. She noticed that O'Shea had left his packet of cigarettes in the side pocket of the passenger door, so she helped herself to one. A fine substitute, for the moment.

Embittered Lines of Beauty

As Brooks slowly walked over to the car he was thinking about how he was going to approach this situation. He had made a mental note about how she was responding and talking to Allan. She was able to overcome Allan with her passionate rage, which was most definitely her greatest asset. If someone contradicted her opinion or belief, then the chances were that she would react. As Brooks was once told in his training for Section 13.

'A person's greatest asset, can also be their greatest weakness.'

'Can I sit in? Brooks asked.

'It's a free country, or so I hear it is anyhow', she replied, much to his amusement.

'Well not in your part of the United Kingdom, I suppose.' he responded.

'Are you trying to fucking piss me off?'

'Sorry, I meant in Northern Ireland.'

To this she was still giving him a filthy stare.

'Okay, sorry, I meant in Ireland.'

Dillon just shook her head as she still looked at him with disgust.

'Is this whole thing just some sort of fucking joke to you, Mr Brooks? Is this just for the benefit of you and Mr dickhead to score some points with your own people?'

'Maybe it is', Brooks quickly responded. 'Is it the same for you?'

'What do you mean?' she demanded.

'Are you doing this to impress the IRA in West Belfast?' His question came quick, catching Dillon off guard.

'West Belfast would blow London clean out of the water if they knew this was. . . .'

She realised she had just said a little too much. She gave Brooks a little smile, acknowledging that he had caught her out fair and square.

'Well done! I better watch my back', she told him.

Brooks knew he had to be very careful not to make her too wary of him too early, otherwise it would only make his job harder in the long run.

'I'm not trying to catch you out, I'm just trying to find out who I'm going to be working with.'

Dillon looked across the open white area in front of her before responding.

'Okay, fair enough. What do you want to know?'

'The same thing any man would ask of you. How did someone as pretty as yourself get involved with the IRA.'

Dillon gave a little laugh to herself as she took another puff of her cigarette.

'And I suppose I'm meant to take that as a compliment, am I?'

'From where I see things, yes, it is a compliment', Brooks acknowledged.

'Well from where I see things, that's a pretty big fucking insult.'

'Hold on a second . . ', Brooks tried to reason, before she interrupted him.

'The British took the pretty looks away from the women of Northern Ireland. They replaced the lines of beauty with lines of worry. Worry, from waiting for their loved ones to be free of the Kesh. Worry, from waiting for their young ones to be free of the poverty enforced upon them. Worry, from being of the wrong religious background.' She took a last puff on the cigarette, before continuing down the road that Brooks had led her. She stared hard and long at the dashboard before speaking.

'My mother had the greatest looks a woman could ever ask for.'

'Had?' Brooks asked.

A short space of silence followed.

'She passed away some time ago', Dillon then responded. Silence now seemed to take the inside of the car over completely, as she still stared at the dashboard with Brooks staring at her.

Brooks let the short moment pass. He had to give Dillon the opportunity to continue talking, otherwise she could become protective of the revelations she was starting to tell. The moment was becoming longer, so he had to start leading her out of this silence.

'Is it your mother's looks that you carry with you now?' he asked with a warm sincere tone in his voice that didn't sound the least bit patronising, which of course it really was.

'Up to a little while back yes, until I cut the long flock of hair identical to hers', she replied, pulling on her cigarette once more.

'What made you cut it all off then?' he continued, amazed

at the luck he was having.

'People reminding me of how much I looked like her. There's nothing worse than knowing that you're constantly reminding people of a dead person.'

As she turned to face him, realisation had set back in, her surroundings had set back in and she became defensive.

'You fucking bollocks!' she spat at him.

'Hey hold on', Brooks tried to reason.

'Jesus, I have to hand it to you, your a fucking smart one.' Dillon was clearly annoyed at herself for letting her guard down like that. She decided to get out of the car and make her way over to the table.

'I'm sorry', Brooks said as she parted from the car. Anyone else would have followed her over to the table to continue their apology, but not Brooks. He decided that he had just obtained some important information from her, so he thought it would be best to leave her alone for a short while.

The Safety of Distrust

The room had no windows at all, as it was situated at a central point of the building. To think of this location as only a temporary one was strange, considering the detail of this room. The relaxing wall lights, the *en suite* bathroom, the writing desk, the television set, the arm chair with side table and the small oak mini bar. O'Shea straight away thought to himself that this was one hell of a false sense of security, as this was only meant for his accommodation. This was a fine example of his character, not to be misled by such a fine looking bait. This would explain why he was lying on the bed, still in his boots and fully clothed with his coat on.

He lay sideways, looking at the bag of money, the money he had just counted. Fifteen thousand in Irish punts. Not much really for his past, but at least he had his future back — when the mission was complete that is.

He also started to think about the conversation he had

with Séamus Kelly in the lounge bar of O'Leary's pub in Kilsheelan. He remembered how Kelly had said that Dillon would be hunted down by Southern Division after this mission was complete, to stop West Belfast knowing what had happened. As he thought about this, he stared at the bag of money again and thought of how he would let Dillon have access to it, if he couldn't survive this mission himself.

11

MOON MADNESS

Warwick opened his eyes and stared at the doors of The Moon Under Water. He sat there thinking over what he was going to say to Jacobs, once confronted by him again. With the physical damage that Jacobs had inflicted on him on their first meeting, he knew it was time to toughen things up a little. He pulled the Smith PK from his coat pocket and checked to make sure it was loaded. On completion of this, he ran both of his hands over his tired face and decided at this point that it would be best if he had a cigarette to keep himself awake. As he reached over the dashboard to pick up his cigarettes he noticed the time on the clock — 5.15pm.

'Oh fuck!' he shouted at himself, realising that he must have nodded off into a deep sleep and missed the four o'clock meeting. He jumped out of the car and headed towards the pub doors at top speed, without a second thought, with his gun at the ready in his right hand.

If only he had stopped for one second to think, he would have collected himself and put the gun back in his pocket, but his mind had become irrational with self annoyance.

A 'Smoking' Debate
In the non-smoking section of the pub, just inside the doorway, a small debate was taking place between two of the customers.

'Look! you stupid little fart, I'm smoking in the bloody smoking section', the bigger of the two men was explaining, with great aggression.

'But your smoke is drifting over here to the non smoking section across our table, where we're trying to eat our meal', the smaller man was explaining with great politeness, which seemed to annoy the bigger man even further.

'Oh fuck off you stupid little tosser!' The Big Man departed, after pushing the smaller to the floor with one casual push to his stomach.

He was known in the pub for pushing his weight around, and always on the smaller kind of man. As he walked away from the situation, he glanced at some ladies who were viewing the situation from their table in the smoking section. He gave a little smile to them.

'Okay Big Man', he said to himself. 'Let's show these fine ladies what's behind these good looks.'

By the look of his great physique, he was a man who had obviously spent a lot of his time in the gymnasium. He was clearly very proud of his physique, as he felt the need to display it on this cold day by only wearing his track suit bottoms and a vest. He turned with a little rhythm in his step, in the direction of his new admirers.

Dramatic Entrance

Just as he danced into his third step, the doors flung open with great force. The right hand door hit the Big Man with such a great force that the glass shattered straight into his face.

'Jacobs? Jacobs you piece of shit!' Warwick shouted, as he flew past the shattered door into the heart of the pub.

The ladies who had just been admiring the Big Man began to scream at the sight of the gun in Warwick's right hand. Warwick searched the non smoking section without a care for the gun he had on full display.

'Hey!' the manager shouted from behind the bar.

'Fuck off!' Warwick replied before running into the toilets that were situated at the edge of the non smoking section. There was one man at the urinals, another washing his hands but no one in the cubicles. Once Warwick was happy that Jacobs was not in the toilets, which took all of three seconds, he ran straight out and over to the smoking section, which took up two thirds of the pub. There were about forty people in this section.

'Hey Jesus Christ, calm down for Gods sake!' the manager shouted to him again.

'Look, fuck off!' Warwick replied, as he continued on his hunt around the pub, pulling people out of the way so he could get a good look at every corner.

Warwick's heart was pumping at a great pace due to the adrenaline that was running through him like an irrational bull in a field of red blankets.

All the men seemed to naturally back off out of his way, but the problem was, all the women seemed to scream at the same time.

'Look, you're scaring the hell out of my customers. Now please put that thing away and leave!'

Warwick now had enough of this guy's voice. He turned, like the bull heading for the clown that was tormenting him. He headed straight for where this voice was coming from, which was a whining high pitched annoyance as far as Warwick was concerned.

'Right, that's it, I'm calling the police', the voice whined in Warwick's direction once more.

Bingo! He had him in his sights. Warwick's brain automatically read a quick description of his target:

'Fat, glasses, bum fluffed facial hair, spots and a ponytail that's an extension of the greasy long hair that thatches his fat ugly fucking head.'

A Mad Moment

Warwick leaned across the bar and pulled the manager completely across to the drinking side by his ponytail. Everyone at the bar backed away from the situation. As with the Dwyer episode, that happened only an hour prior to this, there were a few big men there, who could have quite easily handled Warwick in a physical battle, but that gun changed everything.

The manager was shouting out in pain from this action. One of the barmaids reached for the phone but Warwick saw this and gave her a glance that was enough to prevent her from completing the task.

'Right you fucking dick-head!' Warwick shouted, as he unclicked the safety catch of the Smith PK and rested the gun's barrel on the forehead of the manager.

A chorus of women's screams greeted this action.

'Okay, Okay. Whatever you want.' The manager was crying at this stage. 'Take the money, whatever you want.'

He was so petrified that he started to sob like a frightened child.

Warwick stood there looking at him. Thoughts were running through his head as if the wild bull was on acid.

'I've missed Jacobs............ I had one great chance to get a little bit ahead of the game and I missed the opportunity................ because I'd fallen asleep .... Jesus! I think this poor bastard's going to piss himself.'

As the manager sat there on the floor at Warwick's feet, sobbing, with the barrel of the gun resting on his head, shouting options up at what he saw as his life's decision maker, Warwick started to realise the mess, the great big mess, he had just got himself into. He looked around at all the people staring at him. There were people gathered around the Big Man, who by now wore a bloody mess for a face due to the door that flew open on Warwick's entrance. Crowds were near the two exits, but no one made a move to leave as they were convinced that this man before them was mad.

He looked down at the Manager who was still looking up at him.

'How the fuck am I going to get myself out of this mess?'

12

UNCERTAINTIES

The journey between Hayes and Downing Street was approximately forty minutes, but Allan still managed to slip in six cigarettes on his travel. His smoking was getting worse and he knew it. As he opened the door of his car outside number ten, he made a pact with himself that, once he was rid of his Irish counterparts, he would quit once and for all.

A Downing Street Meeting

'Time for a mint', he said to himself as he approached the policeman outside number ten. He helped himself to a polo from the packet he had in his inside pocket, reserved for his meetings at number ten.

The doorman, known as Eddie, pointed towards the stairs as Allan walked in.

'The PM's expecting you, he's in the Churchill Room.'

'Cheers Ed, is he in a good mood?'

'No, he's superbly pissed off.'

'Jesus Eddie, you should be barred from talking to Clinton's bodyguards.'

Eddie was actually front house security. He was a well built man in his mid forties and looking very good for it. He had served under Thornbird before Hayward, chances were he'd serve under the next Prime Minister as well. He was the best at his job, but the funny thing was, he had no time for politics, only politicians.

John Hayward was seated at the main table in the Churchill Room, going over the details of the two bombings. Members of the cabinet had been phoning him all day, outraged at the actions of their country's attackers. Even Andy Blayre had the nerve to phone him up and ask when moves for peace would be made for the people of Northern Ireland and Great Britain as a whole. Imagine if Blayre knew what was really going on! Imagine if he knew the little scam that he and Peter Allan had going at the moment. A scam, that's how the opposition would see it, a dirty bloody scam. Working with a division of the IRA, whilst their capital was being targeted.

Of all of the phone calls and conversations that Hayward had today, it was the one with Blayre that really shook him. If Blayre knew what was going on he would expose the government for his own benefit, no one else's.

All of these thoughts were racing through his head at a rapid pace. He decided that a strong glass of Jamesons Whiskey was in order. Just as he was about to stand up and walk to the drinks cabinet, someone knocked at the door. He decided not to grab a drink, as he was very particular about who he drank with or in front of.

'Come!' he ordered to the door.

Allan stepped inside the room, to which the Prime Minister rose out of his chair and straight over to the drinks cabinet.

'Where the bloody hell have you been?' Hayward demanded of him, as he poured himself a very healthy measure of whiskey.

'With Brooks, and yes I'd love a drink', Allan replied just as Hayward was putting the cap back on the bottle after only pouring out one glass.

As he was pouring out a healthy measure for Allan he told him of the phone calls he'd been getting all day.

'Blayre phoned', he concluded.

'What for?' Allan inquired.

'Wants to know when I'm going to start getting a peace deal on the table at Stormont.'

'Well it won't be long now, will it', Allan said, referring to the mission, as he sat down in the chair at the top of the twelve seated royal oak table.

'What do you mean?' Hayward asked as he sat down a few

seats away from him.

Allan froze for a minute, looking at him, trying to read his thoughts. Then his face grew into a frown.

'What do you mean, what do I mean? You know full well what I mean.'

Allan was getting annoyed now. He had been listening to Brooks all day, who was trying to convince him that they were doing the right thing and now he was expected to go over the whole thing again with the man who asked him to do the job in the first place. He started to wonder about what Sir John Primark had said to him about the Prime Minister one night, as they cleaned off a bottle of Walker Black Label between them.

'If there's two people in this world that I like the least, it would have to be that fat fucking bitch of a wife of mine and John fucking Hayward.'

'What do you mean?' Allan asked as he entertained his taste buds with more Whiskey.

'Well, it has to be said that, as much as my wife resembles Jabba The Hut, I'd trust her more than I'd trust the Prime Minister. No one, in my estimation, can do a better job than Thornbird did and he knows it. The only way he'll make an impact is to take a few risks.'

Sir John looked at Allan with total seriousness before continuing. 'And anyone who has to take risks, Peter, can't be trusted.

Cold Feet

'I'm not too sure that we should go ahead with this plan of ours, it's getting too risky.' Hayward said, without being able to look Allan in the eye.

'Why?' Allan was now very stern.

'Why what?' Hayward answered with a weary quiver to his voice.

'Why the sudden worry for it being risky. We've always

known this was going to be risky, but no matter what, this will not land on your doorstep, you know that.'

'How can you be so sure?' Hayward asked, now looking Allan straight in the eye.

'Because Section 13 doesn't exist, remember. If it all goes wrong then it stops with myself and Brooks.'

'OK, fair enough, but I want to put the mission back a few weeks', Hayward replied as he stared at the glass of whiskey in front of him.

'Too late', Allan replied as he necked his glass.

'What do you mean?'

'Brooks is with our two Irish friends at this very moment.'
Hayward stared at Allan with disbelief in his eyes.

'You're joking?' he asked.

'Do I look like I'm bloody joking?' Allan replied.
Hayward then stood up, walked over to the window and looked over the back garden where the uplights had now come on to shine through the high trees and bushes as the early evening drew in. It was a sight he was very proud of, as he had designed the outlay of the back garden lighting himself. There was little comfort to be had from looking at it now, not in this mad moment.
Allan sat there thinking about O'Shea and Dillon. He had already decided that if Hayward was to ask him about the two Irish counterparts, he would have to lie about his opinion of them, otherwise Hayward would call the whole thing off there and then.

'What are they like, these Irish friends of ours?' Hayward asked of Allan.

'They're IRA, that's all we need to know.'
Hayward stood in silence, as he watched the Downing Street cat appear from the bushes, with a prize hanging from it's mouth. A small blackbird. A bird that must have flown into the back garden to collect some seeds that Nora, his wife, had thrown over the lawn. Hayward became transfixed for a moment, as he watched the cat walk to its little hideaway, by

the large oak tree at the far end of the garden, still with its prize clenched between its jaws.

'Section 13 answers to me and me only?' Hayward asked, for confirmation.

'That's correct. Even Sir John Primark hasn't the slightest idea of our mission', Allan answered, surprised at the question.

If only Nora knew, that her action in throwing the seed on the lawn resulted in the death of a blackbird. To say she would be upset would be an understatement

'If I'm in total command of Section 13, then you have to follow my orders without question', he reminded Allan.

'Without a doubt', Allan acknowledged.

Hayward decided it would be best to keep the news of the cat's prize to himself.

'Then this mission is aborted, indefinitely', he stated.

Allan felt his body go completely cold at the shock of hearing this.

'But Brooks is with them now.'

'Then get him out now. This issue is over, do you understand?'

Allan let twenty seconds pass in silence as he stared Hayward in his left eye without blinking.

'Do you understand?' Hayward again asked of him.

'Can I speak openly?' Allan asked.

'No.'

'Then yes, I understand.' With that, Allan slammed his glass down on the table before making his way over to the door. Hayward spoke just as he opened the door.

'Peter, it's nothing personal.'

Allan looked at the wall to his left hand side, and noticed for the first time ever, a picture of Maggie Thornbird shaking the hand of a Fireman with a patch over his left eye. Of all the times he had sat in this room before, in different meetings, he had never noticed this picture before.

'Sir it's nothing personal, but she had bigger bollocks than you have right now.' He then slammed the door behind him.

A Quiet Sunday Afternoon

Dillon sat at the table in the Hayes warehouse, thinking over the things she usually does with herself on a Sunday afternoon. Her Sundays usually consisted of the following: An eighth of squidgy hash, a large packet of red Rizla, her tin of Golden Virginia, a percolator of coffee and a packet of ginger nut biscuits. This was usually accompanied by the sound of Richie Blackmore's guitar ripping through riff after glorious riff, on top of David Coverdale's voice constantly telling his audience that everything was Rock and Roll, whilst Jon Lord's Hammond organ sounded as if it was playing to a pornographic film, all of which made up the classic sound of Deep Purple, Sinéad Dillon's favourite band.

It was the way she loved to see out the end of the week. Some people loved to see the tail end of a week out on a binge of alcohol, followed by hours of trying to piece together a conversation with a total stranger in a pub, whose landlord couldn't wait to see the back of the pair of them, no matter how much money they'd spent.

Dillon, on the other hand, loved to take the phone off the hook, light up and sing her heart out to songs like "Lady Double Dealer" and "Burn". This Sunday she was behind enemy lines, silent and sober. She agreed with herself that a bout of heavy smoking would be a great comfort at this time, so she helped herself to one of O'Shea's cigarettes, again.

Brooks started to make his way back over to her. This should have been annoying to Dillon, but it wasn't. As she watched him walk from the car to the table, she realised that he was the sort of bloke she would have taken a shine to under different circumstances. She noticed back at the airport, straight away upon meeting him, his eyes. Blue, pure ocean blue. She also had a thing for men who were going slightly grey. Distinguished was always a better word for it, a word that truly suited Brooks.

'Look I'm sorry for upsetting you like that back there!' Brooks said.

'Jesus, don't flatter yourself. It takes a shit load more than that to really upset this girl', she replied, with an air about her that Brooks hadn't experienced yet. It was as if she had forgotten the whole episode back at the car already.

'How do you usually spend your Sundays?' Brooks asked her, to which she responded with a look and a small amount of laughter.

'What? What's funny?' he asked.

'Don't ask', Dillon replied, before turning very serious without warning. 'So, cut the bullshit, what's the plan?'
This caught Brooks off guard, as he thought they were unwinding a little bit, but Dillon obviously was now playing her own game.

'Come on', she continued. 'What is it you need from us to put a stop to Dwyer?'

'The first thing I need', Brooks caught up very quick, 'is an address of one of his workers. It doesn't matter which one, it doesn't have to be an important player in the Fifth Brigade, but just one address will do.'

'So you lot can turn it over?'

'No, so you and I can turn it over, without them knowing', he told her as he walked over to the drinks cabinet. 'Another beer?'

'No, I only drank that last one to piss your fella off', she replied, referring to Peter Allan. 'I'll have a coffee instead, please.'
Brooks found her response very amusing as he filled the kettle with water from the tank beside the fridge.

'Who are you referring to as *them?*' she asked.

'My people', Brooks replied as he filled a mug with a teaspoon of coffee. 'Sugar?'

'One, please. So no one else gets involved?'

'Not unless I think it is totally necessary. Milk?'

'Just a little bit. How do you know when it is necessary?'

'I'll just know, you'll just have to trust me on it OK? Biscuit?'

'Okay, fair enough. Yes I'd love one', Dillon replied, as she put her cigarette out in the fairly packed ash tray in the middle of the table. As Brooks put the mug of coffee in front of her, he took the ash tray away and emptied it in the small waste paper bin beside the fridge.

'You obviously live alone', she observed, as she could sense that he was not a smoker. But he emptied the ash tray, wiped it clean with a tissue, placed it back on the table for her to use again and not once pulled a face of complaint.

'Yes, what about you?' he replied.

'Yes, it's a lot easier that way, especially in this line of business.'

'Most definitely.'

'Right, well I'll finish this and we'll make a move, OK', she said as she took her first sip of coffee from an Englishman.

'What about the others?'

'What about them, you've a mobile phone haven't you?'

'Yes, he acknowledged.

'And Mister Dickhead has your number, right?'

'Yes.' He couldn't help but smile at her attitude.

'Right, well that's that then.' She took a long sip of the coffee this time before standing up. 'Let's go!'

Unfinished Business

As Allan's car was pulling out on to Whitehall, Eddie was running down to the gates, trying to stop him, but his car sped away at top speed. He paused just in front of the big iron protectors as he watched Allan's car drive towards Trafalgar Square. As he turned to walk back towards Number Ten, he took a radio from his inside pocket and spoke into it.

'It's no good sir, I've missed him.'

Hayward put his radio down on the table, as he slumped into the chair, like a fighter who had been well and truly fought.

'Damn it!'

He picked up the radio and spoke into it again.

'Eddie, can you do something about that bloody cat!'

A Picture of Dreadlocks

As Brooks drove the car out of the big open area, O'Shea walked in from the far end of the Hayes warehouse. He thought for a second that he had been left on his own, until James Moore walked in off the ramp at the far end. O'Shea suddenly felt very alone. As much as Dillon had annoyed him about a few things on this mission already, he felt very alone without her. For some strange reason he felt very vulnerable.

'Cup of tea?' James asked of him.

'No thanks', O'Shea replied.

They both walked in silence to the big table, both feeling a little uncomfortable in each other's company. James was the first to break the uncomfortable silence.

'Can I show you a picture of someone?'

'Sure', O'Shea replied as he helped himself to the packet of cigarettes that Dillon had left on the table.

James talked as he walked over to his desk.

'Brooks asked me to get some pictures from a camera that was positioned at the back of the bank in Enfield, yesterday morning. He thinks that someone was watching the back of the bank.'

As he walked back over to O'Shea he asked 'I just wondered if you recognise the face?'

O'Shea took the picture from him and studied it. A Jamaican man with shoulder length dreadlocks.

'No, I'd remember a face like that all right. Have you not run it through your computer yet?' O'Shea asked as he lit his cigarette.

'No, but I think I'll do it now. Care to join me.'

O'Shea looked over to where the two cars were earlier.

'Well, it looks like I've got bugger all else to do.'

13

MAKING SENSE OF MADNESS

She held the cards that knew my feelings,
She wore a look that drove me wild.
As she tore the skin right off my shoulders,
She licked her lips and threw a smile.

Jesus Christ, I hate Zakk Zombie. Can you turn this shit off?' The manager whined, and with that, Warwick turned around and hit him between the eyes with the handle of his gun, but kept control of the car as it flew along at ninety five miles per hour.

The manager was out cold.

'Peace at last', Warwick said to himself as he turned the music up even louder.

Warwick hadn't noticed how much he had changed in the last twenty four hours. He never noticed what a beast this obsession with catching Jacobs was turning him into. Never before had he become so unfocused on his job in hand. Which was, to find out the truth about the suicide of Billy Hopkirk. Yet here he was, driving around the M25 at ninety five miles per hour with a manager of a pub that he'd just kidnapped.

'Crackerjack.' Warwick laughed to himself, just thinking about it.

Oh yeah, bang bang bang,
She shot me down.

Zakk Zombie's voice seemed to be his only avenue out of all of this chaos at the moment.

Bang bang bang,

The only thing that seemed to be able to clear his head, to help him try and think straight again.

131

Bang bang bang,
Come on babe!

Warwick couldn't remember hearing a police siren in *"Shoot your Love"* before. He leaned forward and turned the stereo off.

Still the siren wailed.

He looked in his rear-view mirror and then noticed the Police car that was pulling around in front of him.

'Shit!' he whispered.

Officer to Officer

Warwick stayed in his car as he watched the young policeman get out of the passenger side. An older policeman got out of the driver's side. He leaned forward and opened the glove compartment, then leaned forward a little more to open the secret hatch behind it, and placed his Smith PK in there. As he removed his hand from the front compartment, he took his ID badge from there as well. Then he sat back and watched the two officers approach the car very slowly.

'Would you like to step out of the car, Sir, please?' the younger officer asked, as the older one peered through the passenger window at the manager.

Standard procedure, Warwick thought to himself. The older one was breaking the younger one in.

'What's his problem?' the older policeman asked, as he noticed the bloody mess of the manager's face.

'I'm escorting him back to my station', Warwick said as he handed his ID badge over to the younger one. The policeman studied the badge and then studied Warwick.

'You seem to have some serious fresh injuries to the face sir.'

'Part of the job and it's all ahead of you.' Warwick smiled as he received his badge back.

'Okay Sir, no problem, but could you please watch your speed, as you'll end up getting pulled over again doing ninety five and your valuable time will have once more been wasted.'

'Standard procedure answer', Warwick thought to himself, 'for a young Rookie to give to a Plain Clothes.'

'Not so fast', the older officer said as he walked around the front of the car to Warwick.

'Let me see that badge?' he asked as he took the ID badge back from Warwick. 'Check the plates!' he ordered to the younger one.

'But he seems clean', the younger spoke out.

'Don't question me, just fucking check it', he shouted, keeping eye contact with Warwick.

'Okay Jack, Jesus', the younger replied, clearly used to this mannerism of his partner, as he walked back to the car to check the plates on their radio.

'A Could Have Been', Warwick thought to himself. 'An old policeman in uniform, who could have been a Plain Clothes, but either he wasn't good enough or he made some silly mistakes along the way. Yet here he was, maybe six or seven years away from retirement, still doing his shitty beat with the Rookies.'

'It says here on this badge that you're positioned at Enfield police station', he said to Warwick, with almost a glimmer of enjoyment in his left eye.

'So?' Warwick replied.

'So, how in God's name can you be driving back to your station, when you're driving in the opposite direction?'

Something Amiss

'What do you mean?' Warwick asked, now starting to feel a little agitated. He was concerned that the manager might wake up and start crying like a baby to this Judge Dredd wannabe.

'You know bloody well what I mean. Maybe I should wait for our friend in there to wake up and see what the chances are of him telling me that you're just driving around this motor way, beating the shit out of him.'

'Okay, let's do that shall we!' Warwick bluffed. 'But when he wakes up, you and your rookie can deal with him, because as you can see' - he paused to point at the cut at the top of his nose - 'I've had more than my fair share of his karate crap.'

'How did you knock him out then?'

'Just luck, I guess. I rammed his head into the dashboard.' The older policeman had noticed some blood on the dashboard when he looked in earlier. The policeman stood looking at the car, then back at Warwick and then at the manager in the front seat.

'Bullshit!' he replied. 'I don't buy it.'

Moon Under Water

Williams had only forty minutes of his shift left to do, when he was assigned to investigate the disturbance at the Public House in Chase Side in Enfield Town. He felt tired from the weekend's work he had just completed. He'd just done twelve days straight and wouldn't be having any time off again until next weekend. He was doing all the overtime that he could just to pay for the builders who were doing the work in his back garden. To top things off, he promised his wife that he wouldn't be late tonight, as she had arranged for a baby-sitter so they could go out for a meal this evening.

At the Pub, he was glad that he had some back up, just to calm the Big Man down alone. By this stage, he was going mad with the pain in his face. There was a three inch piece of glass in his right eye, that would be the cause of him never being able to see out of it again. Also, he would never be rid of the scars that scored both of his cheeks.

Williams had three other police men with him, but they were interviewing various members of staff. As he stood in the middle of the pub, taking in the chaos of the after effect, he noticed the video camera in the corner.

'Bingo.'

A 'Loony' Case

As Williams was walking around the till of the bar, one of the other policemen stopped him for a brief second.

'Sir, you're not going to believe this.'

Williams didn't say anything. He just stood there looking at this nervous young officer, waiting for more information.

'After pulling the manager across the bar, here.....', the young policeman stopped to point at the bar in front of him, 'this nut case then kidnapped the manager, but didn't take any of the money.'

'Fucking great', Williams remarked as he walked away. He was twenty minutes away from the end of his shift and he lands himself the case of a loony.

He found the television monitor in the manager's office. He opened the cabinet below it, to reveal two video recorders. The one on the left was still recording. He turned on the monitor to see that the camera was pointed at the front of the house where this loony was reported to have pulled the manager across the bar.

'Bingo', he remarked as he pressed the right hand video player to record. He stopped the one on the left and rewound it to 5.15pm. He helped himself to a packet of Cheese 'n' Onion crisps from one of the many boxes in the manager's office as he waited.

He had briefly thought about Warwick before, and what Davis was going to do about the shooting in Whitewebbs Lane. Williams had done what was asked of him and kept the details, of the handgun used, to himself but the suspense was killing him.

'Good job I've got something else to occupy my mind', he said to himself.

The video clicked to a halt as Williams removed his jacket, laid it on the spare chair and pressed play on the remote control as he sat in the big chair behind the manager's desk.

Looking for A 'Loony'

Williams sat with his eyes fixed on the monitor, watching the reactions of the people at the front of the house, as the loony must have been running around with the gun in his hand in the Non Smoking section.

'Oh, another packet of Cheese 'n' Onion would be lovely, thank you', he said to himself as he helped himself to another packet of crisps.

Williams was getting a little concerned because not once had the camera picked up this loony's face up to now. The video didn't pick up anything in audio, so he couldn't hear what the manager and the loony were shouting to each other. Then the loony could be seen going over to the bar and grabbing the fat manager by his ponytail. He places the gun on the manager's head, says something, looks around at all the people, all the women are screaming, that much is visually clear, then..................

'Jesus Christ!' Williams says in utter shock. He rewinds the tape a little to where the loony looks up at the crowd by the front house exit.

He presses pause.

The face is clear to see.

'Warwick?'

An Altercation

'You've been beating that poor bastard half to death and you know it', the policeman shouted at Warwick.

'Listen here, old timer, I'm going to make sure that you're doing fucking foot patrol in some council estate in Birmingham, if you don't fuck off out of my way', Warwick threatened him.

'You can't do anything to me, that hasn't already been done before, you bent piece of shit', he replied.

'Jack?' the younger one shouted from the car.

'What?' the older replied without taking his eyes off Warwick.

'I think you should listen to this.'

'Wait here', he said to Warwick, as he walked back to their car.

Warwick took this opportunity to get back in his car and

retrieve the Smith PK from his secret hatch in the glove compartment. He placed it in his left pocket and removed the safety hatch as he waited for the policeman to return.

'Jesus, this is all I need', Warwick whispered to himself.

Making The Report

'It was definitely him sir, I'm absolutely positive.'

'Okay, Williams', the voice of Sergeant Davis could be heard crackling through the receiver.' Meet me back at my office, at once.'

'I'll put out a call on Warwick, on one of our men's radios', Williams told him.

'No, I'll take care of that, just get back here now and bring that tape with you!' Davis ordered him.

Williams cursed the Sergeant as he put the receiver back down, as he knew there and then that he was going to be late tonight.

As soon as he put the phone down from Williams, Sergeant Davis picked up the phone again and pressed two digits on the keypad.

'He's just left The Moon Under Water in Chase Side. He'll be driving along Silver Street in about two minutes.' He spoke without introduction.

Free To Go

Warwick stood up out of the car as the older policeman approached him again.

'Go on, fuck off. It seems like this is your lucky night', he told Warwick.

Warwick stood there for a moment looking at the old policeman. His hand wanted to come out of his left pocket and shoot this old timer in the face for talking to him in such a fashion.

'You heard me', he said, walking a little closer to Warwick.

'I'll go when I'm good and fucking ready, old timer',

Warwick spat at him.

'Come on Jack!' the young voice shouted out to him as the engine of the police car started off again.

'Go on Jack!' Warwick mocked.

'Detective Thomas Warwick of Enfield police station. I won't forget you', the old policeman told him, as he turned and headed for the awaiting car.

Warwick stood and watched the police car drive off into the now rainy night. He took the gun from his pocket and unclicked the safety hatch. His face grew into a frown as he felt like he had just snapped out of some crazy phase. He looked at the gun. The gun had never been used until the incident in Whitewebbs Lane last night, let alone used to kidnap the manager of a pub, and then contemplate using it to shoot a uniformed policeman in the face.

What the hell was happening to him? How did he end up in such a stupid mess from investigating a simple suicide.

'Jacobs', he said to himself as he felt himself slipping into this crazy phase of his again.

As he got back into the car again his mind became focused once more, or unfocused. It was becoming hard to tell.

'Time to be rid of you, my friend', he said to the manager who was still slumped in the passenger seat.

14

WHEN IT RAINS, IT POURS

Davis sat in his office of Enfield police station, trying to block out of his mind any involvement he had with Dwyer and the actions that would be taken against Williams. He closed his eyes, allowing his left hand to play with one of the shiny detailed buttons of his uniform. He had changed into to his uniform twice today and that alone was making him feel uncomfortable.

Jenny At Her Desk

His thoughts now were with Warwick as a frown grew across his face. He picked up the phone and punched one of the memory keys at the side of the set.

A woman's voice answered.

'Warwick's phone, Jenny speaking.'

Jenny was new to CID and she was very keen to make a good impression. Davis had noticed that she had been in the office almost every day for the last week or so.

'Jenny, it's Sergeant Davis here. Why are you in the office again today.'

'Williams is taking me out on a new case tomorrow, so I just wanted to make sure that I've got everything ready. It's going to be my first case, Sir', she replied with her soft nervous voice.

On any other day, Davis would have been furious to learn that Jenny had spent so much time in the office before being thrown into her first case. But the mention of Williams had sent a cold shiver down his spine.

'Where's Warwick?' he demanded.

'I haven't seen him since yesterday, Sir.'

Davis didn't even say anything. No good-bye, no thank you, no anything. He just put the phone down.

'Wanker', Jenny observed, as she went back to her nice polished clean desk, the cleanest in the office.

An Earful of Fury

'Look I don't know, I'll be as quick as I can.' Williams was getting the third degree from his wife, Macie. He had been on the phone, in the manager's office for the last three minutes getting an absolute earful.

Williams had always loved the look of a black woman. The way the light would shine along a long black pair of legs would make him weak at the knees. The way the teeth would shine out, was a gift that other races could only yearn for. Afro hair, looking as cool as it was in the seventies, could only be naturally grown and look naturally good on black people.

Macie had natural green eyes which, against her tanned skin, made any man look at her for a third time. The only thing that tipped things out of her favour was that temper of hers. As hard as it was for Williams not to think about it (for fear of being classed as looking at black women from a typical stereotype point of view), she had a pure black woman's temper. No doubt about it. "Hell hath no fury like a woman scorned" Hell would be vacated by the devil himself, when a black woman is on a war path. Especially Macie Williams. She wore the trousers in their house. But that's one of the many things that appealed to Williams about her. It just didn't appeal right now.

'Oh don't bring the kids into this, Macie, for Christ's sake. And stop calling me shitty white trash!'
He was just about to say good-bye, when she gave him the clear threat, the threat that would really play on his mind.

'What do you mean you'll call Davis yourself? As if', he laughed.
What a mistake that was. The dialling tone cut in.
'Macie? Macie? You bitch!'
He pressed redial on the hand set..... Engaged.
This time he dialled the number again...... Engaged.

He dialled Sergeant Davis's number....... Engaged.
Again he pressed redial on the hand set....... Engaged.
  'Oh Jesus Christ', he said as he made for the door.

An Unwelcome Call

Davis sat looking at the view over Silver Street, still trying to block the whole Williams thing out of his mind. How would Dwyer deal with Williams? As much as he tried to erase the whole thing from his mind, it kept raising itself like a bad smell.

Suddenly the phone erupted into life. He could tell from the ring that it was an outside line. A frown grew across his face. Rarely would anyone call him on a Sunday, not direct to his desk.

'Hello, Sergeant Davis speaking.'

'I was just thinking, why should I clear up this mess on my own?'

'Jesus Christ, Dwyer. What the hell do you want?' Davis went absolutely pale with shock.

'Well, fuck it. This Williams should be your problem, yet I'm having to deal with it on my own.'

'Then I'll deal with it. Just don't call me here again, OK? I told you this before, you stupid idiot!'

He wanted to shout at Dwyer down the phone, but he knew that Jenny was only down the hall, so he had to shout in a whisper.

'Too late. We're in this together. I've started the job, now you can finish it', Dwyer told him.

'What do you mean?' Davis then noticed the red light flashing on his "CALL WAITING" sign.

'Hold on a second, I've got another caller', he told him.

'I wouldn't advise it. Time is slipping.'

'Just hold on a second!' Davis softly shouted as he pressed the change over key.

'Hello, Sergeant Davis speaking.'

'Hello Sergeant Davis, it's Macie Williams here.'

'Hello', Davis answered, completely stunned. He started to wonder if this was just a complete sick dream.

'I was just wondering at what time you're going to allow my husband to come home', she started softly.

'What?' Davis was convinced that this was a sick joke being played on him by the Devil.

'He's been working flat out all weekend and we had plans to go out tonight before you intervened.' She couldn't help but scream this down the phone at him like a raging bull.

'Mrs Williams.........Mrs Williams.....?'

He couldn't get a word in edgeways as her attack became a flurry of loud, fast and abrasive words. Her attack was now in full swing as Davis felt that there was no way of being heard from his end of the wire. It was no good. He was just going to have to hang up on her, or at least put her on hold for a moment. He pressed the change over key in the hope that she wouldn't notice just yet.

'Dwyer?' he asked, to check that he was still on the line.

'Look out of your window Davis!' Dwyer instructed.

Davis did so without question. 'Where am I looking?' he asked.

'The traffic lights on the corner. Outside Enfield Grammar School.'

Davis saw it straight away. The blue Ford Mondeo. The blue Ford Mondeo that belonged to Williams.

'What have you done? What have you started?' Davis asked. But he felt like he knew full well what Dwyer had done.

'Two metres of 1.5mm red cable, six MN1500 batteries, a receiver and, oh what was the other thing?' Dwyer seemed to ask himself. 'Oh yes I nearly forgot. Two small parcels of semtex, enough to just about burn the trees outside your station from where Williams is now.'

'You sick bastard!' Davis's anger was building up so much that he screamed this down the phone at full volume.

Jenny walked out of her office and looked down the hallway, to where the Sergeant's office was. She had been alerted by his shouting down the phone.

'Are you OK, Sir?' she shouted, as she walked towards his door.

Four For One

Williams was waiting at the lights, which were now changing to amber.

'Oh dear he's getting nearer', Davis sung down the phone.

'What do want from me?' He panicked as he leaned on the table to back away from the window. Little did he know that he had hit the change-over button on the phone.

'To let my husband come home, what in God's name do you think I want, you white honkie piece of shit?' Macie Williams shouted down the phone.

The blue Ford Mondeo which had pulled away from the lights very quickly, had already gained about seven metres before Davis knew what Dwyer wanted from him. He quickly hit the change-over key.

Jenny had knocked at the door twice before opening it. She was absolutely sure something was wrong in Sergeant Davis's office. She opened the door. As she stood there in the doorway she saw Davis running away from the window as he was screaming down the phone.

'NOW YOU SICK BASTARD, DO IT NOW!' Davis screamed down the phone as he dived over his desk, taking framed pictures and paperwork with him in the process. Just as he hit the floor, the windows exploded behind him as the flames blew across the ceiling, over to the open doorway to wrap itself around it's first victim. Jenny didn't make it to see her first case.

The reception of the station got the worst of the blast as three officers burnt to death in the explosion.

15

THE HEART AND SOUL OF IRISHNESS

Most of the outskirts of the city would be quiet at this point of the weekend, as Saturday night usually knocked the wind out of most of them. Yet Kilburn still had something on offer. Something that could be heard most of the way down the Kilburn High Road. Live Traditional Irish Music.

As far as the people in this part of London were concerned, it was still the weekend, and whilst everyone else was either tucked up in bed or sat watching the last of the weekend television with a cup of tea in their hands, many a musician could be heard putting his or her heart and soul into the music as only Irish musicians knew how to.

The Heartbeat of Irishness

Brooks drove along at a steady pace. He hadn't been through Kilburn at night time before; there was no reason why he would. Nothing from his past life or the missions he'd carried out, would have ever required him to be in Kilburn. Except maybe to drive through it on a journey to a destination elsewhere. None of his missions had ever taken him into the depths of an Irish community, especially one as strong as Kilburn's. He could sense how the people in this part of London must really miss their homeland. Irish cafes and Irish newsagents selling all the county newspapers of the homeland. Irish record shops, Irish butchers, Irish clubs, pubs and bars.

Brooks knew from trips he had been on before, that Kilburn High Road didn't resemble any road in Ireland. It was a road filled with people who still wanted to be there.

He had come across many ethnic communities in London before. The Blacks of Brixton, the Greeks of Harringay, the

Indians of Uxbridge and the Jews of Golders Green. While the racists of London claimed that these communities were a threat, Brooks believed that if it wasn't for these communities, places like Kilburn would just be dirty long roads with no life or community at all.

Maybe he was wrong, but deep down, he didn't think so, because he wouldn't want to live in a place like Kilburn. No way. He was far happier with his three bedroom luxury bachelor pad, on the Thames with a fantastic view of London Bridge. Breakfast on his first floor balcony every morning, reading *The Independent*. Fresh orange juice, water melon, cereal with strawberries and a cup of fresh ground coffee. How could he ever see himself sitting in an Irish cafe in Kilburn, reading *The Irish Post*, full Irish fry up and tea from a mug that had been used already by thousands of others. Brooks and this community were worlds apart.

A Heart Transplanted

Dillon was starting to feel a bit agitated, as her fingers were rubbing against the cold metal of the Golden Virginia tin in her pocket. The sights around her were reminding her of the people that had no choice but to come to this God-forsaken land for work and money alone. Working Monday to Friday to support themselves and sometimes their families back home in Ireland. How these people must have wished for jobs back home in the towns that they knew and loved so well.

Towns where their accents wouldn't get them into trouble. Towns where they were among their own. Towns where politics had no control over their every day life. Towns where they could leave a pub at night and take in the fresh country air that they had been accustomed to. Towns where they only talked about the smog that polluted the air of London, not wake up to it every morning.

The only escape that some of these people had from the suspicions of being a murderer, a bomber, a killer or just a simple "thick fucking Paddy", was to enjoy the weekend in its entirety, with music and drink. And why not? Kilburn, along with Camden Town and Brighton, was one of the few places in southern England where you could walk the streets at night with an 'Ireland' football top on, and not worry about being stabbed to death because of it.

'Left here!' she instructed Brooks, as they came to the entrance of the National Club.

'Where abouts?' Brooks asked as they pulled past the long steps of the club.

'Just pull in here next to this phone box!' she replied.

The National Club was closed on Sunday nights, but the sound of a good music session could be heard from the open doorway of the Black Lion on the corner.

'Which house is it?' Brooks asked, after looking up and down the road to see if anyone had noticed them. He was so caught up in the moment that he hadn't realised how obvious it had become to Dillon. She felt that for him, her thoughts were irrelevant to the situation. A situation where he was just plain hungry to turn over a house where the IRA were resting one of the Capital's campaign bombers.

'Which house is it?' he again asked, looking out of the window to the row of houses to their right.

'I don't know. Give me a moment to try and remember!' she lied.

'Who are we looking for? What's his name?' he prompted, still looking at the houses.

'Jesus Christ. Give us half a fucking chance, will ya?' she shouted as she opened the door of the car.

'Where are you going?' he asked.

'For some air.'

'I'll come with you', he replied.

'If you must', Dillon answered slamming the door.

As she made her way over to the bench beside the phonebox, she searched through her pockets looking for the packet of cigarettes she had pinched from O'Shea back at the warehouse in Hayes. Then it came to her. She had left them on the table.

'Bollocks!' she gave out to herself as she opened the Golden Virginia tin to reveal the cannabis joint that she had rolled earlier in the car. She really needed a smoke to calm her nerves, but the joint would only send her paranoid under the circumstances.

'What's up?' Brooks asked in reply to her cursing herself.

'I've left my cigarettes back at the meeting point.'

'You've got a roll up there, can't you smoke that to keep you going', he said looking at the tin in her hand, not noticing the block of hash amongst the tobacco.

'No I'd rather a B&H. I'll get some from the pub over there. Wait here!' she instructed him.

'Look.....' Brooks began, but he couldn't find the words to apologise for being so pushy.

'OK, fair enough', she started. 'You're desperate to get Dwyer. So are we, but you have to understand how fucking hard this is for me, OK?'

'I know, I'm sorry.' He sounded genuine. That much she acknowledged. But she was using her instincts. He only sounded genuine.

'Just easy it up a bit, Batman, OK!' she replied, as she made her way over to the entrance of the Black Lion.

As Dillon walked away from him, he noticed what a beautiful backside she possessed. The way it moved from side to side in perfect motion with her steps. It was making the hairs on his neck start to prickle.

'Martin, focus on the job!' he said to himself as he turned around and looked back over at the row of houses.

The Soul of Irishness

Dillon walked through the main entrance of the Black Lion and stopped just inside the doorway to take in the view. Four musicians were sitting around a table. No microphone, no speakers, no stage and no lights. Just a guitar player, a fiddle player a button accordion player and a banjo player. A crowd of about ninety people were all facing this small table, totally mesmerised by the music being produced. Dillon stood there for a moment and couldn't believe the great music she was hearing. Of all the places in the world she could hear this fast, soulful, Irish music, it had to be on a Sunday night in London. 'In fucking London of all places', she laughed to herself as she stood there in the doorway.

The button accordion player was obviously the ring leader of the gang. Just as they seemed to be coming to the end of a tune, he lifted his head up, which up to now had been hidden by the long hair that hung around his face, and simply shouted at the top of his voice,

'HUP!'

Then they tore off into a new tune, in a higher key, and somehow sent the majority of the crowd into a mad frenzy.

'Mick, you fucking little bollocks ya!' one voice shouted at the accordion player, amongst the cheers.

Dillon just shook her head and laughed as she made her way over to the cigarette machine through the crowd of people who were all swaying in time to the music.

As she stood at the machine, feeding her fifty pence pieces into the slot, she suddenly started to think about her surroundings and the situation she was in.......
Was she betraying the people around her? ...... Her people!
Surely she was........ She was showing the British to the front door of a member of the Fifth Brigade, the only active IRA movement in London at the moment!

She looked over at the accordion player. Somehow she had blocked the sound of his music out of her mind as she stayed focused on his face. His eyes were closed, as his head seemed to move from side to side, in motion with every note that he hit.

Was it the sound of the music that was making him lose himself within himself, or was it something much deeper?
Was it his Irishness?

On the plane journey today, Dillon had read an article in a

newspaper, on International football violence. It had stated that, England had the worst reputation of football hooligans in the world. It talked of men with British bull dogs tattooed on their forearms, who continue to beat supporters of other countries half to death, all in the name of patriotism. Spitting at other supporters, whilst waving the Union Jack for all to hate, all in the name of patriotism. Visiting quiet villages and towns of Europe to turn them into battle grounds, all in the name of patriotism.

Here was an accordion player who was displaying his patriotism by simply playing his heart out, to entertain himself and the people willing to listen to him.

She looked at the crowd of people around her. Was it the community of Irish people together in one room that filled them with joy, or was it something else.

'Go on, Mick, ya bollix!' a voice again screamed out.
Then again, maybe it was just the music that did it, pure and simple.

She collected her cigarettes from the tray at the bottom of the machine, and headed for the door with her eyes to the ground, as she knew that this was the last kind of place she should be in at this present moment. It was filling her head full of thoughts and feelings that would sway her in the direction of defect, as far as this mission was concerned.

16

WATCHING THE PREY

Peter Allan sat on the edge of the car's bonnet, tapping the buttons on his mobile phone, as he contemplated breaking the bad news to Brooks. As he held the phone to his ear, listening to the ringing tone begin it's first call of attention to Brooks at the other end of the line, he was considering the possibility of continuing with the mission without the permission of the Prime Minister. He knew if there was anyone with enough professionalism to do this on the quiet, then that person was Martin Brooks. It wouldn't be the first time Section 13 had carried out a mission without anyone else's knowledge at the M.o.D. or Downing Street.

This idea swam around his sea of thoughts before he dismissed it as crazy and ludicrous. The consequences were completely different. They were in partnership with terrorists.

Rattling Cages

'Come on Martin where are you?' Allan asked of the ringing tone.

'OK I'm coming!' Brooks said to no one in particular, as he made his way back over to the bench, after he had retrieved his phone from the car.

'Hello?' Brooks never answered the phone with his name, for security reasons.

'Martin, it's Peter. Are you still at Hayes?' He asked, as he took a sip from a plastic cup of tea that he had just obtained at the nearby Mobile Burger Bar.

'Kilburn! What the fuck are you doing in Kilburn?'

'Dillon's showing me an address of a member from the Fifth Brigade.'

Brooks stopped to think of how quickly this mission was moving. He held his bottom lip between the thumb and fore finger of his right hand, as he was thinking of how he could entice this Dwyer.

'I want to rattle this Dwyer's cage', he broke the silence. 'I want to bring him out of his hiding place.'

'How are you going to do that?' Allan asked, suddenly intrigued, forgetting why he had called Brooks in the first place.

'I'm going to carry out a Code Seven', Brooks answered, as he scrunched his nose in disgust at the smell of urine coming from the phone box nearby. He shook his head at the thought of how people must walk past this phone box, first thing in the morning, having to put up with the smell of someone else's human waste.

'Martin, I don't think we've got the right back up for a Code Seven at the moment', Allan replied, as he knew that carrying out a Code Seven could end up making this mission involve more people, and this mission was officially over.

'We can't afford a Code Seven, Martin. No way.'
Why couldn't he tell Brooks that it was all over.

Brooks stared at the pavement as he felt something wasn't right at the other end of this phone call.

'Martin? Martin?' Allan asked, as the sudden silence on the airwaves was making him feel uncomfortable.

'What did the PM have to say then?' Brooks calmly inquired.
Allan knew that Brooks must have sensed something in his voice.

As Brooks sat there on the bench waiting for a response from Allan, he watched Dillon walking back over to him from the pub's entrance. He suddenly noticed her small firm breasts, swinging from side to side.

'Surely they must be going in time with that arse?' Brooks said to himself, keeping his voice away from the mouthpiece of the phone.

Allan was wondering how he would respond to Brooks, when his phone gave a signal that someone else was trying to get through to him.

'Martin, I'll call you back. I've got someone on the other line', Allan said with inner relief.

'Who was that?' Dillon asked, as she sat down next to Brooks, pulling on one of her new B&H filter cigarettes.

'Allan. He wants to know what we're doing here', he replied, as he waited for Dillon to settle on the bench, before turning to face her.

Then he appeared.

Brooks began his job of trying to build a small bridge of trust between himself and Dillon.

She didn't hear a word of what he said, as she was looking at the man who had just walked down the steps of the National Club, and was now walking towards the row of houses in front of them. She turned to look at Brooks, but he was still talking away to her about something, problem was she didn't know what. She had, once again, managed to block any sound out of her mind, as she focused on the job at hand. Then she looked back over at the man.

Liam Hennessy. The man who lived at Number 42. A man in his late fifties, with long grey hair, five foot eight, quite thin and well dressed. The Watch Repairer, as he was known amongst the movement's Fith Brigade.

She turned back to Brooks, who now seemed to be asking her a question.

'So come on, what are we doing here?' Brooks had no idea that their target was only across the road from them now.

Dillon just stared at Brooks, into his deep blue ocean eyes, before turning back to look at the man across the road. The Watch Repairer hadn't looked at them yet, but she knew that he would, any second now. It was procedure. All Dillon wanted was just a few more seconds, because then they would be out of the light from the street lamp, and he wouldn't be able to get a proper view of their faces.

The Kiss of Crisis

On the sound of Brooks's mobile phone ringing, the Watch Repairer turned in their direction straight away. In a split second, Dillon's reaction was the only one that she could think of, that would rescue them from this situation. She grabbed Brooks, with both of her hands around his head. She pushed his face towards hers, and at the insertion of her tongue into his mouth, began the most seductive kiss Brooks ever had the pleasure to experience. The Watch Repairer just gave a little smile to himself, as the view of the two young lovers reminded him of his departed wife.

They used to meet on a bench on the outskirts of Derry, to avoid her father and brothers, who were opposed to his involvement in the movement. This was a rare thing, for a family to openly admit to their disgust at The Watch Repairer's involvement in the Cause. He could have easily organised a visit to her house from representatives of the movement, to shut the men of the house up. But he had decided to respect their wishes and see his loved one on the quiet, until they could afford to leave Ireland and move to London to get married, where he would become a focal point in the IRA.'s main land campaign.
He lost her three years ago, to cancer.

As Dillon kissed Brooks, she kept one eye on the Watch Repairer, waiting for him to be out of view of them. At first, Brooks tried to resist the kiss, but the natural sensation got the better of him. The barriers of wonder had been broken, as the gap between them, for this short moment, had been closed. His sense of smell had taken over his sense of reason, as the smell of Dillon was now just overwhelming. It wasn't a perfumed smell, it was a natural body odour. Not a bad body odour, just the natural smell of a clean woman.

Brooks had feared the day that something would overcome his defences on a mission. Yet here he was, face to face with someone who had just taken that guard from right under his nose, and he couldn't see it. Well not for those twenty seconds, while her mouth moved. And it moved him to a different place all together.

Dillon, on the other hand, was watching the Watch Repairer while she seduced Brooks. She carried out the task, like a hunter loading the gun whilst watching the prey. The task was the practical action, but the watching was the natural skill of a soldier, waiting for the right moment.

The kiss lasted just long enough for the Watch Repairer to be out of their range. Once Dillon had acknowledged this to herself, she stopped the kiss, like a writer putting the pen down. No emotion, no relief, no anything. Just stopping.

'Let's go. And answer that stupid fucking phone will ya!' She ordered as she took another cigarette from the new packet, after declining to pick up the one she'd thrown on the floor in the heat of the moment.

Brooks was absolutely stunned. He took the phone from his pocket, unaware that it had been ringing since before they had kissed. His head was usually a text book of movements and a defender of emotions. For this brief moment, his head was a mess.

'Hello?' He answered.

Dillon walked back over to the car, with the biggest smile on her face. A moment to herself, a moment to reflect on the kiss.

'Christ I enjoyed that!'

17

UNFORESEEN CIRCUMSTANCES

Warwick had parked on the outskirts of the South Mimms car park facing the entrance of the petrol station. He looked at the manager, who was still slumped in the passenger seat. He was now feeling a little concerned at how long the manager had been out cold, since he hit him with the handle of the gun nearly two hours ago. Warwick leaned across and placed his forefinger sideways under the manager's nose to feel for a small draft from his nostrils. Once he felt happy that he was still breathing, he started the car up, ready to drive over to the petrol station to fill up. He had been driving his car around all day with the needle on the red of his petrol gauge. Under the current circumstances, he knew he couldn't afford to break down.

To Be Inconspicuous

He was waiting for the station to empty out a little before making his way over. Considering the manager was a bloody mess, he didn't want the nosy Joe Public looking in his car window and getting suspicious.

He laid his head back for a brief moment as the questions spun around his mind.

'Who the fuck is Mary?' he asked himself.

He opened his eyes and noticed that there was only one man at his car filling up at the far right hand side of the garage. Warwick drove over and parked his car at the far left hand pump. Before getting out of the car, he placed the Smith PK back in the safe box behind the glove compartment. He sat for a moment watching the man from the right hand pump make his way over to the night counter outside the station shop.

Warwick reached inside his trouser pocket and extracted

eighteen pounds in various notes and silver. Ten pounds petrol would be sufficient. He looked back at the manager before opening the door to carry out the duty required. He once again checked for breathing with his fore finger before getting out.

Closing In

Brooks walked back over to the car in Kilburn after he had completed his conversation on the phone.

'Well?' Dillon asked.

'There's been another bomb.'

'Where?'

'Enfield again, outside the Police Station. Killed three officers and one detective in the station and one detective who was driving a car containing the bomb', Brooks answered, looking beaten by the news.

'Any real people killed?'

'What?' Brooks asked in disgust.

'Any civilians I mean?' she pointed out.

'No.'

A short moment passed in silence as they both sat there thinking about the news. The kiss was now something of the past.

'What now?' Dillon asked looking at Number 42.

Brooks turned to see that Dillon's eyes were transfixed on something. He followed her eyes' line of focus and found himself looking at the door of Number 42.

'We go in', he replied, turning to catch her reaction.

Dillon kept her focus on the door knowing full well that Brooks had looked at it as well.

'Okay', she acknowledged before breaking her focus to look at Brooks and continuing, 'and do what, exactly?'

'Together, we will carry out what is known as a Code Seven.'

'What the fuck is a Code Seven when it's at home?'

'You'll find out soon enough', Brooks informed her as he

took a gun from his pocket and handed it to her.
She took it from him, with a look of surprise on her face.

'Unloaded, I take it?' she asked.

'You can check the chamber yourself', Brooks informed
her, as he took another gun out from his side pocket, before
checking its load.

Dillon pushed out the gun's revolver to reveal eight shiny
bullets in the chamber.

'Now that's what I call trust', she said with an element of
shock.

'It's called being realistic', he replied as he looked back
across the street at Number 42. 'Don't cause me pages and
pages of paperwork by being trigger happy. Only use it if you
deem it to be totally necessary.'

'No problem', Dillon spoke as she placed the gun in her
inside pocket.

Reacting To An Attitude

Warwick opened the door of his car to look in on the pub
manager before paying for the petrol at South Mimms Service
Station. The manager did not look as if he had moved an inch.
Warwick leaned across the driver's seat and placed his fore
finger under the manager's nose again to feel for a draft. As
he felt a small amount of warm air travel down his finger and
across the back of his hand, he decided there and then that he
would drop the manager off at a hospital once he had paid for
the petrol.

Just as he walked about two meters across the forecourt
away from his car, a Ford Escort XR3i pulled into the garage
and up to the night counter.

Four teenage males, Warwick observed. The driver opened
the door and made his way around the car while giving
Warwick a look filled with self attitude. The young man in the
passenger seat also got out, while the other two waited in the
back of the car. The music from the Escort's stereo was still
playing at full volume. Dance music.

'Jesus, I hate this shit', Warwick thought to himself, as the bass of the music got even louder.

He turned back to his own car to check that the manager hadn't woken up.

The man working the night counter was an Indian, in his late thirties, who spoke very poor English. The driver was giving him instructions while pointing through the window.

'A Cornish pasty!' he shouted, as the night-counter man walked towards the fridge like a game show contestant following orders from his team mate.

He picked up pies and sandwiches until he had succeeded in picking up the pasty, much to the delight of the driver.

But then things started to agitate Warwick. He just wanted to pay his money and get on the road. He wanted to be rid of the Manager. He didn't want to be standing in a petrol station watching these "little shits" playing their stupid game.

'Wait a little bit!' The passenger whispered to the driver, as they watched the night-counter man walk past the "Two For One, Cream Eggs" shelf and towards the "Monster Munch Special Trial" stall, before shouting out the next instruction.

'And a Cheese and Onion Sandwich!' the driver shouted, pointing towards the fridge again. The passenger burst out into a fit of laughter as he turned away from the window.

Once again the night-counter man picked up about four items from the fridge, before successfully finding the correct sandwich. As he walked past the "Monster Munch Special Trial" stall, another instruction was shouted out at him, much to the amusement of the passenger.

'Oh and four Cream Eggs please!'

'Stop taking the piss!' The night-counter man shouted out the words, in one long tone. The passenger walked back towards the car, laughing uncontrollably.

Warwick looked back towards his own car checking the manager hadn't moved. He looked like he hadn't, but Warwick couldn't be too sure. As he turned back towards the counter, the driver was looking straight at him. He stared Warwick down, looking for trouble.

The music coming from the car was making Warwick feel angry. He just stared straight back at the Driver.

'What you fuckin looking at?' the driver asked.

'I'm looking at you, you stupid little fucking prick. What the fuck do you think I'm looking at?' Warwick answered the driver without hesitation.

The Driver wasn't sure if he'd actually finished his question before it was answered. He looked at his car, but none of his passengers were looking out at him. He looked back at Warwick.

'Want to try your luck?' Warwick asked. 'Want to try me out on my own? I'll kick your stupid little fucking head in and then set fire to that stupid pissing car with you and your stupid fucking mates in it!'

'I don't want any trouble here', the night-counter man said through the microphone.

'Fuck off!' Warwick shouted. 'Well?' He asked the driver, who looked at the car again, but the passengers hadn't heard what was going on due to the loud bass of the music.

'Look, I'm sorry, mate', he apologised.

'Sorry for what? Sorry for insulting that worker in there trying to do his job? Sorry for playing that loud fucking shit at a stupid fucking volume? Sorry that you've insulted me?' Warwick then stepped up a bit closer to the driver. 'Or sorry that you've met more than your fucking match?'

The Driver was shaking with fear. He looked through the back window of his own car, where his passengers were still unaware of the situation.

'I suggest you fuck off and take them other virgins with you!' Warwick instructed him.

'All right', the driver answered, with a tremble in his voice. 'You win.'

As the driver walked away from him, Warwick stared down at the ground thinking over this whole bizarre scenario.

He had a bloody mess of a pub manager in his car while offering to take on a teenager in a fight. What the hell was his world coming to. Where was his rational train of thinking these days. He looked up at his reflection staring back at him from the petrol station window. Where had his pride gone. He, too, was a bloody mess.

'Jesus Tom', he whispered to himself, 'get a fucking grip of things.'

18

USING RESOURCES

James Moore and O'Shea were sitting in the Hayes office, both looking at the computer screen.

'There's a match!' James shouted with excitement.

'Whoop de fucking do', O'Shea replied after sitting in silence for the past hour, watching James Moore going through all the files on the computer.

'Stansted airport.' James was finding it hard to contain his excitement, as he was fairly new to this computer system, and still couldn't get over the things it could do. His enthusiasm continued, 'It is truly amazing, how this system can link up to all the public surveillance cameras.'

The Value of Technology

O'Shea sat there for a moment in silence, thinking over the conversation he and Kelly had back in Kilsheelan, about how the Movement would have to get a grip on this new technology, if they were to win the war against the British. The screen suddenly showed the Jamaican man standing by the City Flyer desk of Stansted airport. The film only lasted about fifteen seconds and didn't really show anything revealing to James Moore.

'What about the sound', O'Shea quizzed.

'Can't get sound. Surveillance cameras only pick up in visual, not audio.'

'What's he looking at?' O'Shea asked.

'I don't know', James replied.

'Can you get an architect's drawing of the airport?'

'Yes', James replied, as he tapped the instruction onto the keyboard. The screen showed a construction layout of the main area.

'The Jamaican is looking north-east, which means he's

looking at the proposed Bar area', he informed O'Shea.

'Can you...'

'Yes I can get a picture of the bar area at that precise moment', James replied, feeling a little agitated at the way O'Shea kept firing instructions at him.

They both sat there looking at the bar area shown on the screen.

'You see the table with the two guys talking, there?' James asked as he pointed at the screen.

'Yes', O'Shea replied.

'Well that's the table he's looking at. Do you recognise either one of those guys?'

O'Shea watched carefully.

'Go back and pause the picture, where they both look over at the Jamaican!'

O'Shea studied the picture very hard before answering.

'No, definitely not.' He then extracted a cigarette from the packet before continuing.

'But I bet you a penny to a pinch of shit that one of those fuckers is Dwyer.'

'How can you be so sure?'

'Because the only way he would hold a meeting with someone outside of the movement, is to hold it in public. Believe it or not, it's safer that way. He'd know that his associate would be more wary of being caught talking to the IRA than he would of being rumbled.'

O'Shea brought his chair closer to the computer screen. He watched the two men at the table, talking away to each other.

'You said the Jamaican man is the man you think was relaying the picture to Dwyer from the window of the bank in Enfield?' he asked James.

'Yes.'

'Well the chances are, he's one of Dwyer's trusted right hand men. So he'd be the kind of guy Dwyer would take with him on a meeting.'

Which Is Which?

O'Shea sat back in his chair, and lit his cigarette before looking into space and thinking out loud.

'Rumour has it, in the movement that is', he pointed out, by looking at James for a brief second, before turning his head back to look at nothing again, 'that Dwyer is a man of many disguises. Apparently he served his time in a costume and make up department for a theatre company. He can make himself look twenty years older or younger, and you or I wouldn't know the difference. So when he pulls out a disguise, he doesn't need back up.'

James was starting to understand, as they both looked at the picture of the two men on the computer screen, as O'Shea broke the silence.

'If you can make out which one of those two is Dwyer, you'll have his real identity, I'm sure of it.'

James sat there listening to this wise old Irish man, wishing that Brooks was here to witness this old man's wisdom. He suddenly found himself hypnotised by his soft accent.

'If you watch the way they're talking to each other, they're getting through a lot of information in a hurry. One of them is definitely Dwyer, the other is not from the movement, but I'll be fucked if I know which is which', O'Shea said, as he thought of Dillon. She'd know which one was Dwyer, because she'd already met with him. He decided to keep that piece of information to himself, because what use would he be to them once they knew Dillon could identify him.

'But you can't be one hundred percent sure that one of them is Dwyer', James stated.

'Oh absolutely not', O'Shea acknowledged. 'But you can't be one hundred percent sure that one of them isn't.'

'Okay, fair enough', James agreed, 'But we need to pick one, so we can try to trace them somewhere else.'

O'Shea looked at the screen, trying to decide between them. 'Okay, go for the one with the messy face', he said, pointing at Warwick.

'Okay', James agreed, as he tapped the buttons on his keyboard

.*To Be A Bond Girl*

'Well, when do we do this Track Seven?' Dillon asked.

'Code Seven, it's Code Seven!' Brooks corrected her.

'Okay, Mr Bond', she mocked, 'when do we carry out this Code Seven?'

Brooks couldn't help but laugh at her sense of humour.

'What's funny?' Dillon asked him.

'You. You'd never make a good Bond girl', he stated.

'If I was to be a Bond girl, which one would you want me to be?' she asked.

Brooks stared into space, thinking about the question.

'Plenty O'Toole', he answered.

Dillon burst into laughter, before looking down at her own small firm breasts.

'Somehow, I don't think so, do you?' she laughed.

'Okay, fair enough', Brooks replied, before looking back over at number 42. His face became very serious again.

'We'll have to wait until the pub on the corner empties out, then we go in.'

'Do you think the latest bomb is the one Dwyer threatened?' Dillon asked.

'I don't know. Allan didn't mention anything about a coded warning', he informed her.

'I need a coffee', she said, lighting one of her B&H cigarettes.

'I saw a twenty four hour garage about a hundred yards down the High Street', Brooks told her

'Sugar?' Dillon asked as she opened the door.

'One please', he responded.

Manager In Charge

Warwick walked back over to his car, after paying the Indian man the ten pounds for his petrol. He opened the door and looked at the manager as he climbed in. He was feeling a little agitated by the whole incident with the teenager. He just felt that he wanted to distance himself between this garage and the real issues at hand.

He started up the engine and drove over to the exit of the station. As he stopped just before the exit, he leaned over and placed his fore finger under the nose of the manager to check the breathing again. After he was satisfied, he reached into the glove compartment to retrieve his Smith PK. It must have jolted forward with the driving, as he couldn't seem to retrieve it. He undone his seat belt so he could lean over a little further, but he still couldn't retrieve it.

The coldness of its barrel rested on his temple as the reason for not finding it became all so clear. Warwick thought back to that moment back in the garage, when he looked over to his car and knew that he couldn't be too sure if the manager had moved or not.

'RIGHT, YOU FUCKING ZAKK ZOMBIE WEIRDO, LET'S SEE HOW YOU FUCKING LIKE IT!' The manager was shouting with both excitement and nerves. The manager was close to a nervous breakdown, Warwick thought.

'Okay,Okay, calm down, mate OK?'

'DON'T TELL ME TO FUCKING CALM DOWN!'

'Okay, Okay, you're in charge now OK! Warwick stated.

'Yes I am', the manager whispered to him, and then leaned forward to bring himself closer to Warwick, before continuing. 'And don't I just fucking know it.'

19

MAKING ONE'S OWN LUCK

Peter Allan drove to the edge of the explosion scene in Silver Street, Enfield, to where the blue and white police tape was stretched across the road. He stopped the car to show his M.o.D. badge to the officer on the line.

'Okay, Sir, come on through', the young rookie instructed.

'Thanks', Allan replied after rolling down his window.

What's Different?

Then the smell hit him. It was the smell he was so used to. Burning flesh, mixed with the air of dust and burning wood from where the trees once stood outside the Police Station, and the smell of fumes from the wreckage of a car that was lying in the middle of the area squared off with tape. It was the remains of the car that had carried the bomb.

There were six people in white plastic removable overalls, trying to remove what was left of the burnt out body of a driver.

'Poor bastard', Allan said to himself as he watched one of the six people placing a burnt bloody arm with a tag on it, into a clear zip up bag. He could see the arm crumbling like charcoal. He knew that he wouldn't find anything different from this place tonight, than he'd found from the scene of the bank yesterday. It was just a check up, to see that all the right services were at the scene, doing their right job. Retrieving evidence.

He knew, the people working here tonight were the best you could get, but even the best needed time to reveal anything that could lead them to the bombers. No warning. Could this be the bomb Dwyer had threatened them with, or was it just a little taster? These were the thoughts running through his head.

The smell of the burning flesh was becoming too much, as he decided there and then that he was going to get back to base at Hayes and get his head down for the night. It had been an unhappy ending to an unhappy weekend.

Just as he turned around to get back into his car, he saw something up in the trees outside the school gates. A long shiny light reflected at him and then turned away again. Whatever it was, it kept repeating this little action as Allan knew he was onto something.

'Hey!' Allan shouted at one of the policemen in front of him.

'Yes Sir?' the rookie answered.

'Up there!' Allan pointed. 'In the trees.'

The rookie took his torch from his belt and shone it up at the trees.

'It's some kind of tape', he informed Allan.

'Well I'll tell you what. You get that some kind of tape out of that fucking tree and get it sent to this address in the next hour, or you'll find my boot meeting the inside of your rectum at top fucking speed. Have I made myself clear?' Allan told him, as he wrote the Hayes base address down on a piece of paper.

'Yes Sir, at once.'

A Wall For Refuge

'So what do you want to do then?' Warwick asked.

'Just shut the fuck up and let me think!' the manager answered.

'You mean you've been sitting there, getting yourself geared up for this moment and, now that it's here, you don't even know what to do.'

'It's not easy trying to get a plan together, when you're trying to act unconscious, and someone keeps sticking their fucking ashtray of a finger under your nose', the manager replied.

'Ah, well that explains', Warwick remarked, turning away to look out of his window, completely cool, considering the circumstances.

'Explains what?' the manager asked, clearly frustrated.

Warwick was looking out of the window, as if suddenly he wasn't listening. Little did the manager know that Warwick was just playing for time.

'What?' Warwick finally asked, looking back at the manager.

'EXPLAIN WHAT YOU MEAN, YOU DUMB PRICK!' he shouted at Warwick as he was getting very angry over the whole confusion. Warwick looked at him for a brief moment, with a confused look on his face, then gave the impression that he remembered what he had said in the first place.

'That explains. About the non smoking part of your pub. You obviously don't like the smell of smoke', Warwick explained.

'What?' The manager was gob smacked at this statement that had come out of nowhere. Warwick was waiting for the right moment to take his foot off the clutch and let the car drive into the small wall in front of them. The manager was unaware that when Warwick pulled the car over to retrieve his gun from the glove compartment, he hadn't actually taken the car out of gear, he had just rested his foot on the clutch as he didn't plan on it taking this long.

'Fuck it, I'm going to claim self defence. There's enough witnesses in the pub who saw you kidnap me, so fuck it', the manager decided as he unclipped the safety catch of the gun, in the way he saw Clint Eastwood do it in the Dirty Harry films, and levelled the gun with Warwick's head.

'You won't get away with this', Warwick lied.

'Do you know that when you said that, you scratched your right ear.' The manager was right, Warwick did scratch his ear.

'So fucking what?' Warwick answered.

The manager gave a little laugh to himself, before lowering the gun and explaining.

'Well, you see, when people lie, they either cross their arms, look away, blink heavily, swallow for no reason, cough, move their hands, change the tone of their voice, imitate an accent, stare into space for an answer, brush some imaginary dust from their leg, rub their eyes, blush, scratch their nose or scratch one of their ears.'

'Bullshit', Warwick answered

'Exactly. They talk bullshit.'

'What are you, a fucking psychologist?'

The manager once again raised the gun at eye level with Warwick, as he continued.

'No. I am just a simple guy, and you and your Zakk Zombie music has pissed me off.'

Just as he pulled on the trigger, the car shot forward and into the wall with a great bang. The driver's side window shattered from the bullet that had just missed the back of Warwick's head, as it smashed the glass of the Coca Cola poster panel that farewells drivers, as they leave the garage.

Due to the fact that Warwick had loosened his seat belt earlier, he hit the dashboard head on, with full force and was instantly knocked out cold. The wound at the roof of his nose, opened up once again, as his blood splashed across the dashboard. The windscreen smashed with the impact of the manager's body, as it flew through it, like a tennis ball departing from a racket. His body was thrown over the small wall and down the muddy banks of the long ditch on the other side, which led directly down onto the motor way.

As the manager's body rolled across the hard shoulder and onto the inside lane, a Ford Traffic Transit van was just pulling across from the middle lane, with little time to stop. The van didn't even come close to topping over, as it drove straight over the manager's body.

As the Indian night-counter man picked up the phone to dial the emergency services, Warwick lay slumped across the steering wheel of his car. The engine still roared, due to his left foot still pressing the clutch to the floor, as his right foot was doing the same with the accelerator.

20

SWEET AND SOUR

Dillon got back into the car, holding a bright red flask. Brooks was looking at her in confusion.

'Coffee with sugar. They were selling these for two pounds ninety nine. So I just filled it with six coffees from the vending machine. Jaffa cake?' She offered him as she held the open packet out.

A Kind of 'Bonding'

'Ah, thank you Miss Moneypenny', Brooks acknowledged, trying to keep the Bond theme alive.

'So come on then. What's your favourite Bond film?' Dillon asked him.

Brooks didn't even have to think about the answer as it came straight out. 'Doctor No. In my opinion, Seán Connery played the part of Bond in a way that even he himself could never better.'

'Mine would have to be Live And Let Die. To me, that was when Bond was really born. Cool theme tune, cool bad guys and a very cool Roger Moore. Again like Connery, he never played Bond as good as that again.'

'If it wasn't for Connery's "Scotland forever" tattoo on his forearm, that you can just about see under the makeup as he runs across the beach in Doctor No, then James Bond would have been my hero, no doubt about it', Brooks remarked.

As the two of them sat there thinking about Connery running across the beach with his infamous tattoo, Dillon gave a little laugh to herself, as her next question arose.

'Heroes. Have you got any real heroes?' she asked.

Brooks was enjoying the fact that they were chatting away like a couple of normal real people. No politics, no differences and no tactics. But suddenly he didn't feel like Dillon was revealing enough of herself to him.

'You first!' he said.

'Okay.' Dillon sat there, looking through the window, having to think about it. Brooks admired that. People who don't have heroes, can be truly great individuals, as they don't measure themselves against anyone. They're too busy living their own life.

'Bobby Sands. Heard of him?' Dillon asked with a slight mock in her voice.

The silence had an edge to it. All the talk of James Bond, was talk of happy memories and a fictional character. This new subject would either make the night ahead an uncomfortable one, or Brooks could come up with the required answer to ease them through the night. You can make agreements and disagreements about fiction, but not fact.

'Bobby Sands', he started. 'Born in Newtownabbey, nineteen fifty four. Although a Catholic, he was born and grew up in a Protestant area of Belfast. Joined the IRA in 1972, probably caused by his family being intimidated out of their home by the Protestants when he was of a young age.'

Dillon sat there listening, absolutely stunned by the words coming from the mouth of Brooks. A member of the enemy, a member of the British establishment, talking about Bobby Sands with facts, not opinions. She was just about to congratulate him on his knowledge when he unexpectedly carried on.

'As a known activist of the IRA, he was picked up by the authorities in Autumn '72, and sentenced to the H Blocks of Long Kesh, I can't remember for how long.

'Went on hunger strike in Eighty One, I think it was Eighty One, demanding human rights for prisoners from both sides of the struggle. Whilst in prison, he won an election, which earned him a seat in the British Houses of Parliament.' Brooks looked at the dashboard as if looking at a book. He was trying to look for a piece of information in his mind. It came to him.

'Around thirty thousand people voted for him, I'm sure it was around thirty thousand, maybe more.'

He was glad he found it in his head, tucked away with his other trivial information.

'After sixty six days of the hunger strike he died', he concluded.

'Almost', Dillon pointed out.

Brooks smiled as he looked at her. 'Okay, which bit was wrong?' he asked.

'The end. He didn't die, he was murdered by that whore Thornbird.'

A Souring Thornbirdism

Brooks never showed his true feelings, opinions or emotions to anyone. But little did he know that his subconscious had put a little trust in Dillon since they kissed earlier, and he gave a response that, under normal circumstances, he would not have even given a second thought, to respond to the statement given.

'Maggie Thornbird was the best leader this country ever had. She took this country to levels that no one had ever dreamt possible. She took us through a war, and took no shit from anyone.'

Brooks quickly realised that he was heading for a serious back lash of opinion from Dillon. Why didn't he just nod and agree with her and keep his big mouth shut.

'I don't think we'll realise, until maybe ten or fifteen years from now, what an evil fucking bitch she really was. She was constantly on a fucking period. Bobby Sands wasn't just focusing on the soldiers from both sides of the struggle. The main thing that got him started on the hunger strike was the fact that there were lads in the Kesh of seventeen and eighteen years of age, who were completely innocent.'

Her face was red with anger. It became evident now why she was in the IRA. She was passionate about what she was fighting for and Brooks could see it in her eyes. He was glad now he had said what he had said. Now he could see what she really felt.

'People over here were shocked at the imprisonment of the Birmingham six and the Guilford four? Jesus Christ, there's thousands of them in the Kesh. Fellas were signing confessions who couldn't even read or fucking write for God's sake.'

She grabbed the packet of cigarettes from the dashboard and extracted one very quickly and lit it.

'Them bastards in the Kesh tortured the likes of Bobby Sands when all he was doing was torturing himself for the sake of human rights. Do you know what that whore said when Bobby Sands died, do you?'

'No', Brooks quietly answered.

'She said, "By God we have taught them a lesson! We've broken their morale." What a bitch!'

Dillon took a long hard pull on her cigarette before continuing.

'She killed innocent people in Northern Ireland. She killed people who were fighting for something they believed in, their future.

'You know, in all the harm she did to basic human rights, she only ever cried once, and do you know when that was?'

'No', Brooks quietly answered.

'The day she was fucked off out of her job by her own people. That was the first time anyone saw her cry.' Dillon looked into space thinking about the Iron Lady. 'The only time she ever cried was for herself.'

Brooks sat there thinking about what Dillon was saying.

'You say that she took no shit. She wasn't even prepared to sit down and talk to people about their human fucking rights. You and I are going after this Dwyer for different reasons. You need to stop him bombing and we need to stop him so we can get control of our organisation again. A day will come when the British will have to sit down and make a deal with the IRA whether you like it or not. When that day comes, just think about this. Maybe if she had listened to us back in the early eighties, a lot of people wouldn't have had to die for the conflict of Northern Ireland. She may not have taken much shit, but she played a key role in those bombs going off. I'll give you a quote', Dillon continued.

You have to be prepared to defend the things in which you believe and be prepared to use force to secure the future of liberty and self determination.

'From Michael Collins?' Brooks asked.

'Nope. From Maggie Thornbird', Dillon informed him.

Dillon smoked her cigarette for the next two minutes as they both sat in silence, thinking about the debate that had just taken place. Brooks broke the silence.

'So what would you class as the best Bond theme tune then?'

Dillon was looking out of the passenger window, which made it hard for Brooks to see if she was listening or not. But she answered.

'"Nobody Does It Better", by Carly Simon from The Spy Who Loved Me. Yours?'

'It has to be "Diamonds Are Forever" by that Welsh lass Shirley Bassey.'

They both gave a little laugh, before Dillon turned sideways and shut her eyes so she could go to sleep.

21

GETTING TO THE HEART OF THINGS

Allan drove back into the main arena of the warehouse to see O'Shea and James Moore seated at one of the desks looking into one of the computer screens.

'James?' Allan shouted over as he got out of the car.

'Sir?' James replied.

'There's a package coming to you in the next twenty minutes. It contains some sort of tape. I'm sure it's a video tape. Make sure you give it top priority, you hear?'

'No problem', James replied.

'I'm going to get my head down for a quick nap. Wake me when you've examined the tape!' Allan instructed him, as he made his way over to the door at the far end of the room.

'Oh, I'm fine, thanks for asking', O'Shea remarked with a degree of sarcasm.

'Piss off!' Allan replied under his breath.

Confusion

Warwick could feel himself coming around, as the sound of an engine awoke him. Then the sound of the siren brought him sharply back to life. What he couldn't work out was why he was lying down. As he went to open his eyes, realisation quickly set in. His left eye's vision was completely shut off by the skin under his eye being swollen from the impact he had on the dashboard when he hit the wall. He could only open the right one slightly, as he had to focus through his eyelashes to establish his vision.

'Are you Okay?' a female voice asked.

He was in the back of an ambulance. He could make that much out by the blue uniform of the lady leaning over him.

'He won't be all right when I've finished with him', a

familiar voice said.

'He's to undergo all the necessary medical treatment he requires before you get near him', the female voice replied.

'Don't bet on it, love', the familiar one replied.

'Oh bollocks!' Warwick said to himself. It's the old timer who stopped him earlier tonight. The Judge Dredd wannabie.

Warwick lay there for a moment thinking of how lucky he was to still be alive. But he couldn't get Jacobs out of his head.

'That bastard knows something, he knows something about my family', Warwick said out loud, as his emotions seemed to be overtaking the pain and bruising that covered his body.

'Sorry, love?' the nurse asked.

'I'll make the bastard sorry', the old timer added from behind her.

A Rude Awakening

Brooks shook Dillon's right shoulder.

'What?' Dillon asked as she opened her eyes.

'We go in in twenty minutes. Have a cigarette and a cup of coffee, as it's going to be a bit of a shock for you', Brooks ordered.

'Yeah right', Dillon answered with an air of sarcasm. She wasn't the slightest bit worried about what they were going to do. She'd visited supergrasses of the IRA in her time, and tortured them herself. With her own bare hands. As far as she was concerned, this was just a walk in the park.

Brooks paid no attention to her sarcasm, as he really felt, and knew, she was in for a shock.

'What time have you got?' she asked, looking at her watch.

'Eleven twenty', he replied.

'What! Is the pub empty already?' Dillon asked, as she turned around to see police loading the musicians into the back of their van.

'Well it is now, yes', Brooks said with an air of

achievement. He'd obviously reported the pub for after hours drinking to clear the way for his code seven.

'Right this is how we're going to play this, OK?' Brooks started, as he probed Dillon for a little more information on their target, before he told her the game plan.

Technology

O'Shea sat in silence, smoking another cigarette in the stark whiteness of the warehouse, as James Moore fed the tape that had been delivered to him from the latest explosion scene, into the tracking machine. As the machine was winding the tape into order, James began to set up the video monitor with his computer by connecting the commanding leads between his PC and the tracking machine.

O'Shea had to admit to himself that he was truly impressed by what he was witnessing.

Silent Entry

Brooks slowly stepped along the smelly sidewalk of number 42. He placed his micro pocket torch in his back pocket, as he knew he wouldn't need it. The full moon which was shining on the rear of the house, gave sufficient light for him to see where he was walking. When he got to the small open toilet window, he paused to try and hear if there was any activity going on downstairs. The whole house seemed to be in darkness, so he was half satisfied that the occupant might be in bed. At the end of the alley was a half beaten, half hanging gate. He moved it very slightly, as he noticed a track in the ground where the gate had been opened and closed many times before.

Brooks just couldn't understand how people could live like this. It would take twenty minutes at the most to fix this gate, but here it was hanging, waiting to make a big screeching noise with the ground when it opened. He had to give a little smile to himself as it all became clear. This must be one of the warning signs, an intruder warning. He noticed the gate to the next door garden already open, so he walked through it and jumped over the back wall into the garden of 42, with his gun at the ready. He looked down at his watch to see he had three minutes left before Dillon would take her position. He quickly glanced around the garden to check for any surprises. No cats or dogs to creep up on him unexpected. He went to the back door and shone his micro pocket torch along the lock to see the door had been locked. He pressed against the door and noticed that there was no play in the door moving back or forward. He would have to be careful when he unlocked it, as it would just fly open and make a noise. Another intruder warning. He took a small four inch squared black case from his pocket, and removed what is known as the "expansion key".

The expansion key was an invention that came to the attention of the M.o.D. nearly ten years ago. If the normal house burglar ever got hold of it, he would have the bed sheets off the Queen Mother's bed before she could say 'Gin and Tonic.' It could open a door in under two minutes, but it could do it in complete silence.

Brooks placed the long metal strip into the lock, and waited for the key to do its work. He looked at his watch. It would be two minutes and fifteen seconds before Dillon would be in position. The expansion key takes one minute to place its expanding arms around the shape of the lock, then it takes a further forty seconds for the metallic liquid to link the arms together, and a further twenty seconds for the liquid to set. This would only leave him fifteen seconds to take up his position. There was nothing he could do about that now as he watched the red digits on the end of the expansion key counting down its two minutes until it had made the perfect fit of a key inside the lock, without making any noise whatsoever.

Dillon took a last puff of her cigarette and threw it across the open road, as she slowly walked onto the pavement and through the gateway of number 42.

Brooks looked through the window of the back door before looking back down at the tiny display screen at the rear of the key. Twenty seconds until the expansion key has made the fit, and thirty five seconds until Dillon is in place.

Dillon checked that the palm and fingers of her right hand were comfortable in her pocket clutching the hand gun. As she got to the door step, she looked at her watch. Twenty seconds until Brooks would be in place.

Brooks counted the last five seconds down as he put his weight against the back door. The only problem with the expansion key under circumstances like these is that it automatically unlocks the door as soon as it's made the fit.

The door opened like a dream. No noise. Brooks stepped inside the greasy smell of a kitchen and quietly closed and locked the door behind him with the expansion key. In the last three remaining seconds that he had, he placed the silencer onto his hand gun. He stood in the middle of the kitchen looking down the hallway, waiting for Dillon to do her part.

Dillon counted down the last two seconds on her watch, and then rang the doorbell.

Job Satisfaction

'Right', James Moore said, as he tapped some instructions into the keyboard of the PC. The screen showed a very poor view of a bar area. The bottom half of the screen was fuzzy, which indicated to James that he should stop the tracking machine. He walked around the machine to where the tape was fed into to the machine's wheels, and poured some gel onto the wheels.

'Believe it or not, I need to stretch the tape a little', James said. As he distanced the wheels from each other a little. O'Shea sat there thinking of how James was enjoying the fact that he had someone to explain all this to.

The Watch Maker's Welcome

Brooks started to shake a little, not from nerves but from adrenaline. He stood there, with his right arm outstretched and the barrel of the silencer pointing down the corridor in the direction of the front door. His head was tilted slightly, with his left ear listening for the amount of foot steps he would hear from upstairs, and the shape of the body that would appear at the bottom of the stairs. Would it match up to the description of that given to him by Dillon.

The bell rang again for a second time. Then the sound of one pair of feet could be heard moving to the front left hand side of the house. By the quick surveillance that Brooks had done of the house from the outside, that would be the master bedroom. That meant that there was a good chance that the person behind the pair of feet was on his own.

Finally, a thin figure appeared at the bottom of the stairs. The hall light came on, and there stood a thin man in his late fifties with long grey hair, carrying a hand gun as he walked to the front door.

'Who is it?' he asked.

'An old friend who wants to come in out of the cold', Dillon replied from the other side of the door.

'Who the hell is it?' he again asked. There was a bit of a pause before Dillon answered once again.

'It's Sinéad Dillon, from the Southern D.'

The Watch Maker paused for a moment, thinking about what he should do. He released the safety catch from the chamber of his hand gun and opened the front door.

As the front door opened, Dillon tried to release the safety catch from the chamber of her hand gun, but it seemed to be jammed. The first thing to greet her from the open door was the barrel of a hand gun with the Watch Maker on the end of it.

'What do you want? Say what you've got to say, and then leave please', the Watch Maker demanded.

Dillon could see the outline of Brooks in the background from the corner of her eye.

'I need to speak with Dwyer', she replied.

'Why?' the Watch Maker asked.

'Southern Division have some information for him, which needs to be delivered in person.'

Dillon quickly walked into the house, catching him off guard and forcing the Watch Maker to step backwards into his own hallway. When through the door way, she kicked the door shut behind her. She thought this would surprise and throw the Watch Maker.

She was wrong. He stood there smiling at her action. As far as he was concerned, she'd just made his job easier. She was out of the road and into his hallway. Now he could shoot her and not have to worry about any witnesses.

Still she tried to release the safety catch from the gun's chamber, but couldn't believe her misfortune in the fact that it was jammed.

The Watch Maker placed the barrel of his gun on Dillon's head, as she raised her hands in the air.

'I thought we told you before, Dillon. Was that slice across your ribs that we gave you on your last visit, not deep enough for you?'

He came closer to her as he pulled the hand gun from her pocket. He held it up and examined it.

'Your safety catch hasn't opened!'

He had a confused look on his face. He wondered why she hadn't released it. Surely she must have known the kind of reception she'd receive.

'No wonder', he said. 'Someone has jammed the safety catch in place.' He turned it sideways for her to see. 'Someone has actually gone to the trouble of welding it shut.'

Dillon turned sideways to face the kitchen, and looked at Brooks with disgust.

'Why would someone do that, Dillon, why?' he asked.

The Watch Maker was still unaware of Brooks, but Dillon changed all of that when the anger spilled up from inside her.

'You stupid English bastard', she shouted.

The Watch Maker turned to look at the kitchen, but he didn't make it in time, as Brooks pulled on his trigger twice, shooting the Watch Maker in the head.

'Damn!' Brooks said to himself, as he felt annoyed at all the hard work he had gone to, to get into this filthy house. He now felt it was wasted.

Or maybe it wasn't. Not if the Code Seven was carried out to his request.

22

UNPLEASANT SURPRISES

The phone next to the bed interrupted Allan's much needed rest in the sleeping quarters of the Hayes warehouse.

'What!' he shouted down the phone.

'I think you should take a look at this sir.' It was James.

He sat up in the bed. 'Give me five', he replied before placing the phone back on the receiver and heading for the shower.

Nothing Personal

'Why?' Dillon shouted down the corridor of Number 42 to Brooks, who hadn't moved an inch since he shot the Watch Maker.

'Like I said before, it's called being realistic. It was nothing personal.'

'When someone has got a gun pointing at your fucking head, and there's nothing you can do, because some stupid British wanker has tampered with your gun, it feels pretty fucking personal.'

Brooks walked down the corridor, completely ignoring her, and bent down to check that his target was dead. Then, he was just about to make his way upstairs to check for anyone else, but before he took the first step he turned to Dillon.

'Like I said, it was nothing personal, so let it go. Get a bloody grip!'

She stood there watching his figure disappear up the stairs, before turning to walk into the front room.

'Fucking prick', she said to herself.

She switched on the lights. Nothing. No television, no seats, no wall paper, no shelves or pictures, just nothing. The windows were covered by red curtains that were drawn shut. As Dillon walked towards the front window she noticed that the floor had a settled pattern of dust. It had two shapes, or bare patches, where furniture would have once sat. It had obviously been bare for some time.

'Weird!' she said to herself as she reached the front window. 'Bloody weird!'

Before she touched the curtain she turned behind her to notice that her feet had made patterns in the dusty floor. No one had walked to this front window in recent times. This room must have sat bare for some time. As she rubbed her left hand against the dusty cold fabric of the curtain, she could hear Brooks' footsteps upstairs as he was obviously moving from room to room. Dillon moved forward to smell the red cloth. It smelt damp. Dillon knew that the Watchmaker had lived here for some time, and yet he had no use for this huge front room which had been knocked through to the back lounge in building renovation work.

'A man ready to move at a moment's notice!' she concluded as she could hear Brooks making his way back downstairs again. She lifted the bottom of the right hand curtain and pulled it up towards her and then let it fall back against the ledge of the window. As it did so, it left a trail of dust in its wake.

'Just like life', Dillon said as she admired the dust falling into the air. She then walked towards the centre of the room and stopped to take her cigarettes from her pocket.

Brooks walked into the room behind her.

'Nothing upstairs.'

He took the mobile phone from his pocket, pressed two numbers on the keypad and then waited for an answer.

'Yes, it's Martin Brooks. Clearance code, double seven three six five. I need a code seven, right away.'

Dillon took a cigarette from her pocket as Brooks recited the address before detailing his requirements.

Fitting The Pieces

Allan sat down at the table with a cup of coffee.

'This better be fucking good, James, as I am fucking knackered.'

'Oh it's good sir, it's bloody good.'

'Where's the old fella?' Allan asked as he noticed that O'Shea wasn't in the room.

'He's gone outside for some air.'

James began by typing some instructions into the computer keyboard.

'I still have no name for this fella, so let's call him Mr. Jamaica, Ok?'

'Okay.'

'Mr. Jamaica was first spotted at the rear of the Bank on Saturday, prior to the explosion. We think he was watching Martin Harman through the back window and relaying the movements to Dwyer. Next thing we know, he turns up at Stansted airport on Saturday night.'

James once again types the instructions into the computer's keyboard.

'He's acting as a look out for this meeting here.'

A picture of Dwyer and Warwick chatting at the table in the bar area comes on to the screen.

'One of them is Dwyer?' Allan asked.

'Yep', James confirmed.

'Which one?'

'Hold on a second, hear me out', James said as he typed some more information into the keyboard.

'I've studied the tape you found at the third explosion. Watch this.'

The screen was slightly distorted but you could clearly see Davis and Dwyer chatting at the table.

'The tape is from a security video of a pub. We don't know which one yet. This fella here is Sergeant Davis of the Enfield police station. He was in tonight's explosion. He's at Chase Farm hospital at the moment, trying to recover from some serious burns.'

Allan was absolutely spellbound from the information James was giving him.

'And the other?' Allan asked.

185

'Tony Dwyer. The other fella at the airport is a Detective Thomas Warwick of the Enfield police service.'

'Jesus Christ', Allan whispered. The police are somehow involved with Dwyer, which means they are involved with the Fifth Brigade, directly or indirectly.

'Oh it gets better yet, watch this. Detective Warwick turned up at the pub later.'

They both watched the screen, showing Warwick on his war path in the pub.

Waiting On The Code

Dillon filled up the kettle in the kitchen as Brooks walked in.

'Don't worry about me for coffee', Brooks said as the smell of the kitchen wasn't to his satisfaction.

'I wasn't', Dillon replied.

As Brooks washed his hands, which Dillon noticed were covered in blood, she walked to the kitchen door and saw that Brooks had turned the Watch Maker's body around.

'What happens now on this Code fucking Seven of yours?'

'We wait.'

'Wait for what?' Dillon asked.

'We wait for our back up.'

Disturbing News

Allan walked back into the open area after being in the toilet. O'Shea had come back in from outside. James stood up from his desk and walked over to Allan who was just about to say something to O'Shea.

'Sir! I've some disturbing news.'

'Go on!' Allan instructed him.

'It seems that Mr. Jamaica was killed on Saturday night. He was killed at close range, shot to the face, on Whitewebbs Lane in Enfield.'

Allan let out a long sigh of frustration.

'What about this detective fella?' he asked.

'I've still no location on Detective Warwick.' James paused for a moment before continuing. 'The victim from the third bombing attack, the one driving the car I mean, was also a detective.'

Allan closed his eyes, as he thought once more about the Prime Minister and the fact that this mission should be over. Should he phone Sir John Primark? Sir John was the only person Allan would ever turn to if he really needed help.

When he opened his eyes, the first thing he saw was O'Shea.

He was the last person he wanted to see. He turned to face James.

'The driver was a Detective David Williams', James concluded.

Allan took his cigarettes from his pocket and lit one. He felt, now more than ever, that he would never kick his habit, not with news like this.

'So let me get this straight. We've been after this Tony Dwyer and his bombing army for as long as I care to remember, and the one chance we had was a Detective from Enfield, who's appeared out of nowhere?'

'That's right', James informed him.

'And now he's dead from a bloody car bomb?'

'Yes', James once again confirmed.

Allan walked over to the large oak table and poured himself a double Jack with ice. He rested his cigarette in the ash tray for a moment, as he looked down into the glass before raising it to smell the sour mash of the whiskey. It was these little moments of solitude that always made him think a lot clearer. But it didn't take much thinking to work this problem out. Even if Davis, Warwick or Williams were working for Dwyer indirectly, one of them must be working directly for him.

'That means, someone else from within Her Majesty's Service is helping the IRA.', he concluded.

O'Shea said nothing, as he knew his Irish accent wouldn't be welcomed at this time. He knew, because of what he symbolised, that his opinion wouldn't count for much.

Allan sat in one of the chairs and started to think about the events that unfolded themselves over the last forty eight hours.

23

PUTTING DEVICES IN PLACE

Sir John Primark was seated at his desk in M.o.D. headquarters when the phone call came through. The voice on the other end of the line was nervous. To be dealing with Sir John directly in Peter Allan's absence could be very nerve racking, especially when asking for a code clearance, because that involved computer work, and Sir John hated computer work.

'Well what's the bloody code clearance number?' he asked out of impatience.

Clearing Code Seven

He wrote the number down on a piece of paper, before speaking once more.

'Right, hold on a minute!' he instructed as he typed the numbers 7 7 3 6 5 very slowly on the keyboard in front of him. As he typed each number in he had to say each number out loud as well. He squinted through his glasses to check the number on the screen with the one on his piece of paper before pressing enter. He quietly cursed Peter Allan under his breath for his absence. Then the screen responded to his request.

Brooks, Martin: Section 13.
Clearance accepted

'It's clear. What is it he wants anyway?' Sir John asked out of interest.

He removed his glasses when the answer was given to him.

'A Code Seven? Where?'

He didn't say good-bye or anything. He simply put the phone down and let out a wind of worry.

'What the hell are you playing at Martin? A Code Seven in Kilburn!'

Tracking Devices

Allan was in Hayes and had the phone in his hand, but was holding back from calling Sir John. What could he say to him? What could he ask of him? Sir John might react in the worst possible way when he found out that they'd been working with two of the IRA to find Dwyer. He placed the phone back on the receiver as he decided to deal with this himself.

'Sir, I've located Warwick', James shouted to him from behind his computer screen.

'Where the hell is he?' Allan asked.

'Same hospital as Davis, but he wasn't in the explosion. Seems like he has been involved in some kind of a car accident.'

'Fuck me! This is all getting a little too coincidental for my liking. I'll get over there straight away', Allan responded.

'Can you drop me off somewhere on the way? I want to book into a hotel somewhere', O'Shea asked.

'Why can't you just stay upstairs?' Allan asked clearly frustrated at this Irish man's stubbornness.

'Look I want to stay somewhere else, OK?'
James walked over to where they were and interrupted.

'Here's a mobile phone, your cigarette lighter and don't forget your coat.'
The coat was still lying across the back of one of the chairs at the table.

As he handed O'Shea the mobile phone, he added:

'Just destroy the phone when the mission is complete, we'll foot the bill, so you can phone whoever you want.'

'I don't think so somehow do you? You'll be tracking every fucking call I make.'

'Okay, fair enough', James laughed in agreement. 'But we'll want to be able to locate you whenever you're needed. There is only one number stored on there, and that number puts you through directly to me, OK?'

'Sound', O'Shea acknowledged as he placed the phone in his inside pocket.

Little did he know that all three items that James had mentioned to him, had a tracking device on them. He wasn't going anywhere without their knowing.

Effecting Code Seven

As the two sat in silence in the Kilburn kitchen, the sound of sirens could be heard in the distance, much to the delight of Brooks.

'Excellent', he said.

'Oh fuck!' Dillon responded.

Brooks turned to Dillon as the sirens got closer. He stopped for a brief moment before he said anything because he knew that whatever trust she had for him before, it would now be gone, thanks to the duff gun he supplied her with.

'Look, I made a mistake with the gun, OK?'

Dillon didn't reply.

'Look, when these people turn up, I want you to say nothing. Just let me do all the talking, OK?'

'What are you afraid of? That they'll hear my accent?' she asked, to which he promptly responded.

'Yes, that's exactly what I'm afraid of.'

Dillon sat there thinking about the situation she was in. She had to hand it to Brooks, he was being directly honest with her. She agreed with him.

'Fair enough, I won't say shit.'

The mobile phone in his pocket began to ring. He looked at her for a moment before answering.

'I made a mistake, I am sorry.'

Dillon said nothing for a moment as she looked deep into his blue eyes.

'I don't expect you to trust me, but give me a little credit, will you', she reasoned.

'I hear you', he acknowledged.

He pressed the answer button on the phone and held it to his ear, and said nothing as he listened to the instructions. He turned away from her and walked down the corridor to the front door, and opened it. A soldier in a green uniform walked through the front door and gave a salute to Brooks.

'Officer Gerald, of the 16th regiment, reporting for duty, Sir.'

'At ease Gerald', Brooks told him as he closed the front door.

'Right, listen carefully. I want two shots fired through the front door of this house on my signal. My signal will be the switching on of the hall light, ten seconds after I've opened the front door, OK?'

'Clear so far sir', Gerald acknowledged.

'After that, I want the media to be informed straight away that you have shot down the leader of the latest bombing campaign by the IRA. After they arrive, I want you to cover myself and my colleague here with a blanket', he said pointing at Dillon before continuing, 'and take us away from the premises under arrest. Any questions?'

Gerald looked a little shocked by the last instruction, but didn't want Brooks to repeat it, as it would make him look a little foolish.

'Do you want me to repeat the last part, Gerald?' Brooks asked, as he knew that this was an unusual request. But at the end of the day, he was running the show.

'Please, sir', Gerald asked.

'Once you know the media are here', he began slowly, 'I want you to arrest myself and my colleague, cover us up with a blanket and escort us from the house.'

Gerald gave a little smile to himself, as he now started to understand how this would look to the media.

'Very well, sir', Gerald said as he gave a farewell salute to Brooks before departing through the front door.

When Brooks walked back down to the kitchen to Dillon, she also had a smile on her face, as she understood what Brooks was playing at.

'Pretty fucking good, Brooks, pretty fucking good!'

24

SUBDUED FRUSTRATION

Chase Farm hospital lay on the outskirts of Enfield, just two miles from the M25 motorway. It was situated in a peaceful area of Enfield, away from the hassle and madness of London. The endless view of fields could be seen from the window of Warwick's room which was at the back of the hospital. The room where he was resting his injuries. The room where he was trapped.

Time To Think

As he turned sideways in his bed he let out a little curse from the pain coming from his ribs.

'Shit!'

It was a stabbing pain which separated the rest of his body from above his rib cage. It was where his upper body had slammed across the steering wheel.

He had been awake for ten minutes now, thinking of how he could get himself back out on the road again looking for Jacobs.

'You fucking idiot', he whispered to himself as he placed his hand over his eyes.

There would be no visitors for him. No Helen, no Jonathan, and no friends. Warwick had no friends. As far as he was ever concerned, friends were a burden and a complete waste of time. They were people who came to visit you at your home so they could compare the inside of their house to yours. Compare their lifestyle to yours. Friends were just people who didn't want you to do as well as them. As far as Warwick was concerned, that was fact.

'Fuck 'em', he whispered as he thought of all the people he knew when Helen was alive and the little he knew since she'd died. Helen was the warm one of the two and he loved that. He never had to worry about other people's birthdays, anniversaries and events that were so important to these so-called friends. Helen would take care of all that 'Bullshit', as Warwick always referred to it. He always admired the way Jonathan had a great number of school friends, unlike he himself had when he was that age. He was so grateful that Jonathan had taken after Helen, and not followed his own morbid outlook on life. Warwick was a loner. He is a loner. He is Warwick.

He lay there thinking of his own stupidity. Hindsight is such an amazing thing. He'd played the last twenty four hours in his head, completely different. He wasn't concerned about the Jamaican man on Whitewebbs Lane. As far as he was concerned, that was self defence. It was the point where he burst into the "Moon Under Water" waving his gun around like a looney. If he had played that moment in his life a little different, then who knows?

'Who knows?' Warwick said to himself as the pain killers once again kicked in to help him drift off to sleep.

The tune of Zakk Zombie's *'Things She Catches'* entered his head as he started to hum the tune. Then he stopped.

'Who knows, Billy Hopkirk?'

An Irksome 'Chip'

The M25 policeman, Jack, was seated on a chair in the corridor, facing Warwick's door. Unless Warwick wanted to run the risk of jumping sixty eight feet out of the window, then he wasn't going anywhere.

Jack was on his own. He didn't report back to his station at the end of his shift and he hadn't reported in yet to say he was still working. Worse still, he hadn't rung home to tell his wife, who by now would be going nuts due to his dinner being ready in about twenty minutes. His young rookie partner had reported back in half an hour ago because their shift was complete. Jack couldn't be sure if the young partner would report this incident to the station Sergeant, or keep his mouth shut about the whole thing. Jack had told him to say nothing. It was Jack's responsibility to report on what had happened, not the Rookie. He was just to do as he was told. If only it was that simple! Jack sat there thinking over the argument he had with his partner before he left.

'Jack this is crazy. The guy's a fucking detective for Christ's sake', the Rookie stated as their argument was drawing to a close.

'Meaning?' Jack prompted him.

'Meaning, whatever happened out there tonight, this Warwick guy is gonna have his arse covered. Maybe he doesn't need to cover his arse, maybe he's got nothing to hide. We're police, not detectives. This isn't our concern.'

'One man is dead and I want to know why. If you don't want to stay, then fuck off. I don't trust that son of a bitch in there. If he's responsible for killing an innocent member of the public because he has abused his position of power, then I want to be here to wipe that fucking grin of his face. If you're not interested, then like I said before, fuck off!'

The Rookie grabbed his hat and jacket, stood up and walked down the corridor. Before he walked through the double doors at the end of the passageway, he turned and walked backwards through them as he shouted back down to his partner.

'You're a stupid old prick, Jack. You should have reported this in. The guy lying on that bed in there isn't responsible for you still being on the beat at an old age. That's your problem, don't make it his!

Jack opened his mouth to shout back but it stayed open as he found himself stunned by his partner's comment. He paused a moment longer.

'Fuck off!' He shouted back at what now was a lifeless corridor and closed double doors.

Here he was looking at Warwick's door, thinking about his partner's parting comments. Maybe he was right. Was it the disappointment in himself that was driving all his anger in Warwick's direction?

His wife always asked him why he had never been promoted in his thirty five years in the service. Although he could never give her an answer, he knew the answer. He didn't have what it took. His manner was too aggressive and he knew it. It made him feel ashamed of himself, as he had seen so many rookies asking him one day where the mess room was, and the next thing he knew, he'd be taking official orders from them. He couldn't handle it but he didn't know how to do anything else.

Catch 22.

If he was suspicious of Warwick, then he should have handed this whole thing over to his headquarters who would have taken care of it straight away, no questions asked. But something was driving him to deal with this himself. An attempt to do something right on his own.

The parting of the double doors at the far end of the corridor quickly brought him back to reality.

'I'm looking for a Detective Thomas Warwick', Peter Allan said to Jack.

'He's in there', Jack replied before standing up to prevent Allan from going into the room.

'And who the fuck are you?' he asked Allan.

Allan took his badge from his inside pocket and showed it to Jack.

'Peter Allan, M.o.D. Here on a private matter with Detective Warwick. Who the fuck are you?'

'I'm the guy who's going to deal with Warwick first. I don't give a flying fart who you are, he's mine.'

Allan gave a little smile to himself, then he looked at Jack.

'Explain!' he ordered him.

Jack, with a great deal of reluctance at first, told Allan of the events that had taken place tonight. He told him of the state of the man in the passenger seat of Warwick's car, which had made him suspicious of Warwick in the first place. He told him of the incident that had been reported to him, about the showdown with the teenager in the garage. They went to the scene straight away, as Jack knew that the description he had received was that of Warwick. This was when they found Warwick half dead in his car and his passenger on the motorway below, having been run over by a transit van.

'Do you have an ID on the body?' Allan asked.

'Steve Hardwick, manager of the Moon Under Water pub in Enfield.'

Allan gave another smile to himself, as another problem of the puzzle was solved.

Belittled Again

'I'll make sure you are mentioned in my report. Thank you for your time, officer, you've been of great assistance', Allan said as he walked around a stunned Jack.

'Hold on!' Jack demanded.

'I'd also like to remind you that I will do my best to try and forget your terrible mannerism when I do fill out my report', Allan told him, to which Jack's rage wanted to scream out at him. 'I'm also going to forget about the fact that you were suspicious of a fellow officer and did nothing about it. Because of that, we have a dead man on our hands. My God, if I put something like that in my report, you'll be seeing out the rest of your days as carpark attendant, if you're lucky.'

'You bastard.'

'Yes, I like to think so', Allan told him as he walked through the door into Warwick's room.

Jack found himself looking at the doors leading into Warwick's room again. Only this time it was a different feeling he had inside. Only this time he had lost control of the whole situation. Only this time would be the last time. He would have to face his rookie partner tomorrow with the humiliation of the fact that he was right. Jack should have left the situation alone.

He stood up and walked over to the public phone to phone a taxi to take him home. As he dialled the number he, like Warwick, played the game of hindsight.

As Allan stood inside the door looking at a sleeping Warwick, he took his mobile phone from his pocket to call James. Before he pressed any buttons he waited a moment as he studied Warwick's face. How different it looked to the picture James had tracked down of him, when he first joined the force. A young, healthy, good looking man was now a slightly fat ugly bloody mess. What light could this bloody mess shine on the hunt for Tony Dwyer?

'This journey had better be fucking worth it for your sake, pal!' Allan said to the bloody mess of Warwick as he tapped the keypad of his phone.

He walked back outside the room once James had answered.

'James, it's Peter. Get the bedroom ready. I've got Warwick. He's coming back to Hayes tonight.'

Just then, Jack tapped Allan on the shoulder.

'By the way, this was found in the back of his car.'

Jack handed over the sports bag. He hoped this would get him some brownie points, as he didn't help himself to any of the cash inside. Allan unzipped it, looked inside, showed no emotions, zipped it back up and then turned to Jack.

'Thanks.'

Again no emotion. Jack could tell that it wasn't genuine. Then Allan turned away from him as he caught the attention of one of the doctors and walked away from Jack, leaving him to go home.

He would have to get his wife to pay for the taxi, as he had no cash at all on him now.

25

A FEELING OF HELPLESSNESS

Peter O'Connel was seated at the large table in the dining room of his Hampstead Heath house. He was eating his breakfast and thinking over the events that happened over the weekend. He was looking at the *Daily Mail* in front of him, looking at the pictures of the events that had unfolded over the weekend, but he really wasn't taking much of it in mentally. He heard his wife open the front door when his guest arrived.

A 'Working' Breakfast

Tony Dwyer walked into the room, around the table and sat down opposite O'Connel. He was dressed exactly the same as the night before, when he met Davis in the "Moon Under Water". The only difference was the fresh facial stubble and the tired bags appearing under his eyes.

'Morning', O'Connel greeted him.

'I've got a busy day ahead of me, what is it you want?' Dwyer asked of him, as he poured himself a cup of coffee.

Dwyer's voice had the early morning deepness about it. O'Connel always demanded respect from anyone he dealt with, but he knew he was never to receive any from the man who had helped his business do so well over the past few years. He was also, like many others, quite frightened of Dwyer and his madness.

'I think we should give it a rest for a couple of weeks', O'Connel started. 'An explosion on Saturday morning, an explosion on Sunday morning, a car bomb last night. I think we're pushing our luck', O'Connel told him as he took a sip from his orange juice.

Dwyer had a frown on his face.

'What do you think you're doing?' he asked O'Connel, calmly. 'What do you mean?'

'Don't you fucking dare tell me when or when not to do something', Dwyer shouted at him. 'You certainly didn't mind me carrying out the contract on the book shop, did you. No. Saved you a fucking fortune there, didn't I. And what about all the refurbishment work you'll be getting in Enfield, hey?'

'Look, I just think we're pushing it a bit', O'Connel started as he explained that he was grateful for Dwyer's help, but he felt that things were getting out of control.

The Morning News

Dwyer didn't hear anything of what O'Connel said as he started to focus on the news broadcast coming from the television, as did O'Connel when he realised he was being ignored.

The lady newscaster began to outline the morning's headlines.

Here are the headlines.

The main story this morning, is that an IRA bomber has been shot down on his door step in the early hours of this morning by police. Scotland Yard had been tipped off yesterday lunch time of the whereabouts of Liam Hennessy, a suspected leader of the IRA's latest bombing campaign in London, which has seen three explosions this weekend alone.

'Police tried to make an arrest this morning at his house in Kilburn, but Liam Hennessy opened fire on them, leaving the police no option but to shoot him down on his doorstep.

Two arrests were made of, what seemed to be at the time, fellow terrorists at Hennessy's house in Kilburn, but have since been released without charge.

The picture on the television changed to a picture of

Hennessy's house. A policeman was issuing a statement.

We waited until the early hours of this morning to make the arrest, but Hennessy shot at the police as they made their way up the path, so we were left with no option but to retaliate.
We also arrested two suspects that were in the house with Hennessy, but have since released them without charge, as we are satisfied that they played no part in the latest bombing campaign in London, or have ever played a part in terrorism at any time.
We are pleased that a successful operation has struck back at the terrorists that have inflicted such terror on the streets of this capital.

As the officer stood there before the cameras, so proud of what his force had achieved, little did he know that the next question was going to cause such a stir over the next twenty four hours.

'Sir, who were the two suspects that you arrested?' The reporter asked.
'That's confidential', the officer replied with confidence.
'But don't you think it is strange that you say that this has been a successful operation by the police, when really all you have done is shot a man and let two suspects go. If this was the ring leader or one of the ring leaders of the IRA, surely those two suspects could have had some vital information.'
The officer looked thrown off course for a moment.
'We have all the information we require.'
'You've obtained all the information to break down the IRA in the last six hours, have you? You've got everything there is to know about Liam Hennessy and the IRA in the last six hours?' The reporter was very calm in his questioning, but the nature of the questions

was one of anger.

The officer made the worst mistake possible, he caved in.

'I have nothing more to say', he stated as he departed from the group of reporters and cameras.

The reporter turned to the camera to close off his report.

'This is Tom Barker, for the BBC, reporting from Kilburn, where Liam Hennessy of the IRA has been shot by the police. Two other suspects were arrested, but have since been released without charge.'

Madness In Control

Dwyer pulled a gun from his pocket and fired six shots into the wide screen television set, causing the glass to shatter all over O'Connel. The shots were so loud within the breakfast room, that O'Connel's first reaction was to cover his ears, leaving his eyes exposed to the gas from the television tube. It was only seconds before the tears appeared in O'Connel's eyes.

As the remains of the television set fell from the edge of the table, Dwyer stood up and kicked the chair away from behind him.

'Who stayed at Hennessy's house with him?' he demanded.

'I didn't think anyone did. I thought he lived alone', O'Connel shouted, as he shook the glass from the front of his dressing gown with one hand, while rubbing his eyes with the other.

Dwyer placed the gun back in his pocket.

'May I suggest you find out where all of the Fifth Brigade were last night. If there's any suspicions, bring them to the Hackney warehouse by eleven o'clock this morning, do you understand me?' He instructed O'Connel who was still rubbing his eyes.

'I might be fucking blind, for fuck sake!' The pain was turning to anger.

Dwyer leaned across the table and pulled O'Connel across by

his hair. O'Connel screamed out from the pain.

'I don't give a shit. Eleven o'clock sharp. OK.?' Dwyer calmly told him, with a slight twinkle of a laugh in his voice.

'Okay', O'Connel agreed.

As Dwyer parted from the front door, O'Connel fell back into his chair. He, like everyone else around him, was in over his head with Dwyer. He was dealing with a man that was out of control.

His wife walked into the room. She had tears in her eyes. Her face was a collection of lines from the worry her husband's business had brought into their home on many occasions.

'I can't take much more of this Peter', she said as she slumped into the chair at the end of the table.

Although his vision was slowly coming back, he still couldn't see her, but he knew only too well from the sound of her voice that there was a familiar look on her face to accompany it. O'Connel had a look of shame on his face. Shame from bringing the woman he loved into this world of madness and violence that he had got himself wrapped up in. All because of his greed.

26

ADJUSTMENT OF STRATEGY

Séamus Kelly was feeling even more nervous now as he knew he was only a couple of miles away from his destination, "Tough Murray's Farm Complex". It was a farm that sat neatly on the border at Ballinaby, with one half in the republic and the other in northern Ireland. Its owner was Timothy 'Tough' Murray. He was the greatest smuggler on both sides of the border. The authorities knew full well what he was up to, but just couldn't make the evidence stick to him. Helicopters had watched him drive tankers of oil up to the northern side of the complex and pump the oil into tankers on the republic side for a clear profit. Whenever the authorities caught up with him, he would claim that he was paying tax to the opposite side of the border, or his work wasn't taking place in their country. He gave the same story to both sides of the border. No one could do a thing about it.

He would drive a lorry load of pigs from the republic into the north, then drive to Newry and claim for a subsidy of up to £8.00 a pig at the UK customs post. Then he would drive back to the complex, walk them to the south side and do it all over again. He was cute enough to know that there was money to be made from the border being there. While the RUC and the Army knew he was doing this, thinking he was just a small time smuggler without a bank account to his name, little did they know that he was actually the leader of the most feared and loyal section of the IRA movement, the South Armagh Brigade. He was also the assistant to Kevin McManus, the IRA Chief of Staff. Murray was the most respected man in Crossmaglen, South Armagh, and yet he was one of the most feared men outside of it.

A Meeting of Heads

Séamus Kelly had been informed of the meeting that morning by his leader, John Fitzpatrick. Fitzpatrick couldn't go as the Gardaí (Irish Police) were still hunting him down for a robbery he'd masterminded a few months back in Carlow, that went terribly wrong. Four members of the public were killed by one of the gunmen who had watched too many Quentin Tarantino films in his time.

Kelly knew full well what this meeting was going to be about. Three bombs in London within forty eight hours of each other. One of the Fifth Brigade had been gunned down on his doorstep, another two had been lifted by mainland police whilst another was found dumped on a layby with only half his head intact.

This was a meeting that would be attended by the main heads of the IRA's Army Council.

'Jesus Christ!' he said out loud to himself, as he started to think about the secret operation that was being carried out in London with the British. If the council had any idea that this was going on, there would be blood spilled for it, that you could be sure of. Maybe even his.

As he drove a further two miles along the Monog Road, he saw two men standing in the ditch of the road side, on the opposite side of the entrance to the complex. One was looking north as the other looked at a sheet of paper in front of him (a list of registration numbers), and then he looked up and motioned Kelly through the gate. Kelly noticed the earpiece he was wearing. He had obviously been receiving information from the scouts Murray had placed along Kelly's route. The man driving the blue tractor in Hackballscross and the sign writer in southern Louth. Kelly could see from his rearview mirror the man burning the piece of paper as he drove across the courtyard.

Voices Only

Tim Murray was standing in the middle of the old cow house looking at the floor. His body was facing the milking sections, where three cubicles were occupied. Each occupied cubicle had one man seated in a chair, with his second in command standing behind him. No person could see who was in the next cubicle.

The seated men were leaders of the most active sections of the IRA. They were the main heads of the IRA's Army Council. They had known each other's voices for years, but they had never set eyes on each other. Not once.

Between them they had organized what they would deem as incredibly successful operations. Many lives had been affected by these three men, in one way or another. Their organisation and planning was proof of their intelligence. If any one of them was ever picked up, there was no way they could inform the British on the other two. In fact, the council would have to be built from scratch, as Tim Murray would expel himself from the Council along with the other two. It would be down to McManus to reorganise the whole structure again. If he couldn't do it, then Murray would step in, but only to appoint a new Chief Of Staff.

It was "Brit Proof".

The only three people who knew the faces of the IRA's Army Council were Tim Murray and Kevin McManus and Murray's second in command, known only as "The Undertaker". He stood at the entrance of the barn, bearing an American 3.56 SMG (Sub Machine Gun). He knew that if any one of the Army council ever got arrested or lifted at a border check, his life would be taken. In his position it was impossible not to have seen the three faces of the Army Council. The Undertaker accepted this fact. It came with the job.

The tense air of waiting was broken by the man seated in the middle milking section.

'This is a fucking downright scandal, Tim, a dirty fucking scandal and someone has to pay!'

Murray looked across at the speaker, still keeping his head tilted down.

'I'll deal with it', he quietly confirmed, and then turned his head back to where he was looking before. 'I'll deal with it.' Murray had no choice but to deal with the problem at hand, and what a delicate problem it really was, for the Chief of Staff, Kevin McManus, was away in America on business. IRA business.

Murray knew that this was his greatest challenge yet. As they all waited for their guest to arrive, Murray thought back to the meeting that he'd had today with the Sinn Féin leader. The talk that had caused alarm for the IRA Army Council to meet.

Meeting The Head of Heads

The Undertaker cleared the pathway as Murray made his way through the empty public bar and into the back room to meet the man who had got in contact with him only an hour ago. As he opened the door, his contact stood up and greeted him with such warmth and genuine friendliness that the fact there was only the two of them there, proved that it wasn't false. For at the end of the day, it was the Sinn Féin leader who had asked to meet with him in person, not the other way around, as it usually was.

'Tim, how the hell are you?'

'Not too bad Garry, yourself?'

'Well, I've had to get some new glasses again, as my eyesight just seems to be getting worse every year', Mr Addams replied, making the two of them feel relaxed, which they did.

'Well you're the one who wants to write books, what do you expect?' Murray stated as the two shook hands.

'True enough Tim, true enough', Addams replied as they sat down in their chairs by the small dining table.

Murray had a lot of time for the Sinn Féin leader. He knew that this man could one day be recognised for the great coordinator and leader that he truly was. The movement had always been a little wary of the political wing, but Garry

Addams changed all of that. He always stood his ground behind closed doors with the IRA and always stood his ground with the British by not condemning the actions of the movement. Whenever a bomb or a killing took place, the media would hunt Garry Addams down more quickly than the British could hunt down those responsible, just to put a camera in his face and a microphone under his nose, and ask him if he condemned the violence and killings carried out by the IRA. Not once did he condemn the acts of the movement, and not once had he backed down in an argument face to face with the IRA's Army Council. But this was a strange meeting to hold. Just himself and Tim 'Tough' Murray.

'Jesus Christ, Garry, this must be very serious for you to call a meeting like this, behind the Council's back', Murray stated, as he helped himself to a glass of water from the jug of iced mineral on the table.

'Tim, thank you so much for meeting me at such short notice, but I think you'll understand why it was so important that you did, when you hear what I've got to say.'
Addams leaned forward in his chair using his elbows on the chair's arms to do so. Murray saw this as two things. Respect and trust. Or was it?

Addams allowed Murray to feel the stronger of the two as Murray was just sitting upright in his chair, looking down on Addams. But he was cute enough to know that if he was feeling the better of the two, it would be because Addams wanted it that way, as Addams never performed any piece of body language without a good reason. Murray looked at him for a moment, then sank the whole contents of the glass into his mouth, before pouring himself another glassful, and leaving it sitting in front of him, for his request.

'Go on!' he quietly instructed Addams.

'As you know, I've been having some very successful talks with the British about getting an agreement signed up on the grounds of offering them a ceasefire. There seems to be a lot of distrust about this in the Army Council, which I totally understand and respect due to the break down in ceasefires that have passed our way before. But, and this is a big but, there's a new fella on the scene, Andy Blayre.'

'Leader of the opposition?' Murray asked.

'The very one', Addams confirmed, before helping himself to a drink of water. Murray clenched his eyebrows as he was trying to work out where this was leading.

'Tim, I'm willing to put everything on the table and everything I stand for, that two major things are going to happen. And we have to be ready when these things come our way, and we must embrace them when they do. Firstly, the Conservatives will lose the next election, leaving the pathway clear for Andy Blayre, and secondly, this man and all the men around him, are going to do their utmost to be rid of the conflict of Northern Ireland.'

'What kind of men has he around him?' Murray asked.

'You know Paddy Scott from Crossmaglen?' Addams asked.

'Yes.'

'His niece, Claire Scott is planned for a position in government if Blayre wins. She once publicly stated that there was no need for the British to have any presence in South Armagh, because there is only one community in South Armagh, a Catholic community.'

Murray held his hand up to stop Addams from speaking.

'Garry, if you want me to go to the Army Council with this, you know full well they'll back you up. We are also fully aware of the tension between Europe and the British at the moment. Germany are talking of funding a European inquiry into Bloody Sunday themselves. The British are worried at the moment, and Hayward seems to be putting tension on the puppet strings to the Loyalists. We can all see that.'

He then leaned forward on his chair in the exact same manner as Addams had done before, and asked:

'Come on, Garry. What's the real reason you've asked to see me?'

'I'm worried that there's going to be trouble from the inside.'

'From within the movement? Why?'

Addams looked at the floor for a brief moment. Then he continued as he looked at Murray in his left eye without looking away once:

'When things have got out of hand before with the IRA, I've never shown an interest in names, you know that', Addams stated.

'I know', Murray agreed and acknowledged.

'Tim, I ask the same of you now.'

Murray stayed focused on him for a moment and then turned to look at the table, and then looked back at him before replying, 'Okay.'

'One of our members in the South has been involved in the setting up of an operation to catch Tony Dwyer in London. He's been talking with the IRA's Southern Division, and helping to set the whole operation up.'

'We know of the operation. We originally set up an operation in South Armagh to catch Dwyer, but we lost a couple of good lads who were being watched and got picked up when we sent them to London to find the arsehole.'

Handling A Mistake

'The problem with the way the operation has been set up by the Southern Division, Tim, is they're working with the British to catch Dwyer.'

Murray's face dropped into a face of disbelief, a face of anger and a face of distrust. That distrust wasn't directed at Addams, it wasn't directed at Sinn Féin, it was directed at the Southern Division. Addams saw this and quickly tried to interrupt Murray's thoughts.

'Tim, although I knew nothing of our man's actions, I take full responsibility for his actions. The buck stops here with me.'

'Why?' Murray asked, clearly pointing at how this could have happened.

'Our fella was trying to show the British that we were

genuine about our commitment to peace. The problem is, Tim, I have to go with it now, that's the position I'm in. But none of us can afford a split within the movement because of it.'

Addams leaned forward in his chair, only this time he was looking down on Murray as he spoke.

'It's a mistake, Tim, a bad mistake. But it is a mistake we can build on. No one needs to die on our side because of it.'

Murray looked at Addams for a moment, and then stood up and walked over to the window. He looked out at the quiet street below him and then turned to face Addams, who hadn't moved from his chair.

'I remember once', Murray began, 'we set up this trap for a British SMP (Six Man Patrol) on the Newry Road, just outside of Crossmaglen. It was a retaliation attack to a murder by the British on two innocent young men.

'The two lads were driving through town on their way to work, their van's engine back fired and a Brit opened fire on the van killing the pair of them. One of the lads was only fifteen, and neither had any connection with the movement.

'Anyway, the SMP walked straight into our trap, only twelve hours after the van was shot up. Two of the British fuckers backed away from the car we left at the side of the road as bait, and I pressed the button that set off the car behind them.'

A big smile grew across Murray's face, at the delight of the picture in his mind.

'One of the soldiers further back, was on fire as a result of the explosion. I watched that fucker run the half mile back to town as the flames burned into his stomach. I just wanted that bastard to suffer. To suffer for those two innocent lads, going to work and minding their own business. But when he got to town, some stupid fucker invited him into his house, where he was thrown into the bath and water thrown on him.'

He paused, thinking of the actions that followed. He himself had to visit this house owner on his own, with a baseball bat.

'That happened eight years ago, and that house owner still

now walks with a limp.'

Addams made no response, he could only sit and listen.

'I can't tolerate anyone dealing with the Brits, no matter what the reason is, you know that. I'll make sure you get the backing you need from the council, but don't ask me not to react to it in the way I see fit. That's the position I'm in.'

Addams just stood up, to show that this meeting was concluded.

'I can't argue with that, Tim. I respect that, but just try and remember my position, hey. I can't afford for the British to discover that the Council have been weakened before a ceasefire takes place.'

'They won't know a thing, Garry, I give you my word.'

'Thanks for your time, Tim', Addams told him as he put his jacket back on.

'How are your Pigs these days?'

'Ah you know yourself, they pay their own way.'

27

COMPLICATIONS

Allan sat in his car in Battersea Park, watching the entrance of the car park in which he was parked. Fifty yards to his left was another car with two men sitting in the front on full view. They were Allan's back up, out in the open to prevent any trouble from the outset.

Smoking a cigarette while listening to the smooth classics on Classic FM, Allan thought about the events that had unfolded today. He had no reason to question Brooks about his actions taken on missions before, but he didn't feel comfortable with the blatant shooting down of an IRA member on the streets of London, especially in the current situation. He tried to understand the reasons, the viewpoints, the aims and results Brooks would have gained from this. But he also knew only too well the reaction of the IRA's Army Council, Sinn Féin and, most importantly for the short term, Ten Downing Street.

A Tense Meeting

His thoughts were broken by the car coming through the entrance. The Ford Fiesta approached him at a slow pace. This gave him enough time to check the Auto .25 hand gun strapped to the underside of his steering wheel column. The car pulled up just in front of his own. The engine cut out and a figure emerged from the driver's door. O'Shea, and looking a picture of anger.

'The beautiful prelude to Bach's suite No.1, in G major.'

The voice on the radio interrupted.

The music had been that soothing that Allan had forgotten that it was on, until the announcer invaded his train of thought on what his actions should be in these coming moments. O'Shea opened the passenger door of Allan's car keeping his eyes fixed on the two men he knew were back up in the other car. After a few moments of watching the other car, he turned to Allan.

'Right, fucking talk!' He demanded.

'Where did you get the car?' Allan asked.

'Fuck the car. Talk!'

'He'd worked with Dwyer on the Church Street bombing', Allan immediately answered.

'How in God's name did you lot find out?'

'We didn't. Brooks and Dillon found him. They couldn't afford for him to blow the lid on the operation, so Brooks set it up to make it look like the police had found him.'

'And the two that were lifted?' O'Shea asked.

'Brooks and Dillon.'

'Dear fucking God!' O'Shea said as he looked across the car park. 'This could end up in a fucking gang war if we're not careful.'

Allan sat thinking about the statement O'Shea had just made.

'Maybe that's it', Allan said.

'What do you mean?'

'Dwyer thinks we've got to two of his people.'

'Or had two of his people' O'Shea concluded. 'And you can be as sure as I am about my arse pointing south, that two bodies are going to show up dead within the next couple of hours.'

'Why?' Allan asked.

O'Shea looked at Allan in disbelief at the stupid question, before answering it.

'Dwyer thinks he's got two traitors in his camp. He won't find them, but he has to make an example of whoever he suspects. Where the fuck are Dillon and Brooks now?' O'Shea asked.

'I don't know', Allan replied.

A Serious Situation

O'Shea just gave a little laugh to himself before opening the door to get out, but then quickly declined, closed it, and then turned to Allan.

'Can I give you some advice. I'd bring your man in at the earliest opportunity.'

'What about Dillon?' Allan asked, intrigued more than concerned for her.

'Dillon knows what she's dealing with, your man doesn't. When this thing kicks off, he won't stand a chance.'

'What do you mean?' Allan asked.

O'Shea stared at the second car for a brief moment, as he knew that the information he was about to pass on, would shock the pants off Allan.

'The IRA's Army Council know about the mission, they just don't know that we've got a couple of Brits on board', O'Shea informed Allan, much to his astonishment.

'But...'

'You were told that the IRA wanted your help?'

'Yes', Allan acknowledged.

'IRA, Southern Division are more than likely in front of the IRA's full Army Council at this very moment, and there will be hell to pay when they find out that they've turned to the Brits for help.'

Allan's body turned ice cold with fear. Five minutes ago, all he had to worry about was the Prime Minister panicking about finding out that the mission was still going on behind his back.

'Jesus Christ!' Allan shouted as he flew open his car door and jumped out. 'You wait until now to tell me this! What in fuck's name were you and that bitch thinking?'

'She doesn't know', O'Shea said as he followed the same actions as Allan, before he realised the shame in his statement.

'She doesn't know?' Allan said in disbelief as he held his hand up at the second car whose driver already had his hand

214

out of the window, and the safety catch of his Colt .45 hand gun undone, ready to shoot.

Allan knew the seriousness of this whole situation and decided that it was best that the two of them be alone. He motioned the second car to drive away and leave them, and quickly gave a thumbs up as thanks to their quick reaction.

'Forget Dillon for the moment. My concern is that the Army Council may decide to get over here and sort things out for themselves.'

'How the fuck do you people think. You're telling me that the IRA might decide to come over and try to take the fucking lot of us on. And Dillon knows fuck all about this. Do you not give a shit what happens to her.'

Something Personal

Allan was so wound up he didn't even realise he was shouting. He didn't even realise that somewhere, in his heart, he suddenly found himself worried for Dillon's life.

'Calm down!' O'Shea started. 'Believe it or not, she's a lot smarter than you think. She'll slip out a back door somewhere when she gets wind of it, but your guy won't have a clue. He'll be getting his bollocks blow-torched before he realises what's going on.'

'Why?' Allan asked. All of sudden he was very calm, so O'Shea couldn't make out where the question was directed.

'Why what?'

'Why didn't she know. Were you scared she'd back out or, worse still, tell the IRA's Army Council', Allan asked as he stepped a little closer. 'Or is it something else?'

'What do you mean?'

O'Shea started to feel uncomfortable with the questions coming at him. Allan looked at O'Shea's face long and hard as if he was trying to read something.

'It's out of your hands isn't it', he concluded.

'What are you talking about?' O'Shea was on the back foot, and Allan knew it.

'You really don't give a fuck what happens to her, do you? And even if you did, you don't get a say in it, do you? It's out of your hands.'

'Of course I give a fuck for her, you bastard', O'Shea shouted back.

Allan walked away from him as he replied:

'No you don't, you don't give a shit for her.'

O'Shea lunged at Allan and threw him to the floor. Allan tried to fight back but it was no good. O'Shea had overpowered him. As he turned Allan around and brought him closer to his own face, tears began to show within his eyes, as he himself started to shout. 'Of course I care.'

'Don't give me that. You'd be persuading me to get them both out, if you cared.'

'I do fucking care, you bastard!' O'Shea was spitting the words at him. He was completely weakened.

'Why do you care then, give me one good reason why you care!'

O'Shea panicked and punched Allan twice in the face, but Allan knew he had struck a nerve, and that was more powerful than the pain he was enduring.

'Come on you fucking prick, why do you care?' Allan shouted at him.

O'Shea looked at Allan long and hard before he answered the question.

'Because I think she's my daughter.'

Silence..........

The air could be felt and heard blowing between them. The two of them didn't move, although they started to look away from each other. Allan was shocked. He was dumbfounded. If only he could go back to just worrying about the PM. Why didn't he call this mission off when he had the chance.

O'Shea let the dumbfounded Allan drop to the floor.

'Of course I care', O'Shea repeated as he walked back to Allan's car.

Allan just watched him walk back to the car.

28

DROPPING THE GUARD

James Moore was sitting at his desk in the main area, in Hayes, the following morning. He was watching the two monitors in front of him. No volume came from either screen. The only sound that could be heard was that of his spoon, stirring the tea in his mug on the table. The screen on the left was showing the video footage of Warwick running around the pub, waving his gun around like a lunatic, while the screen on the right showed Warwick fast asleep upstairs in the room where O'Shea had laid his head down for an hour last night.

Warwick had a two inch wide bandage wrapped around his head, covering the cut at the roof of his nose. On his removal from the hospital last night, the cut opened up once again, causing the nurses at the hospital to be concerned for his welfare. Warwick shouldn't have been moved last night, but in Allan's position he had the last word over anyone. Even anyone in the emergency services.

Warwick was asleep on arrival at this secret location last night and hadn't woken up yet. James had a doctor in to check on him. The doctor confirmed that the drugs he'd received at the hospital mixed with the exhaustion his body was suffering had got the better of him. Allan had left strict instructions with James for Warwick to be monitored, but not woken up. Not until he was ready to interview him.

Strange Coincidence

James pressed **STOP** on the video as he turned to type some instructions onto his computer keyboard. He had been going through Warwick's files all morning on the computer and one piece of information seemed to be standing out among the record of unsolved cases that Warwick had worked on:

Bank Robberies, Feb -April (Of Last Year).

It explained how Warwick had come very close to catching a gang of robbers as they held up a bank in New Southgate, London.

These robbers were responsible for many robberies in London, but this was the first one to take place in North London and Warwick was the first person who had almost foiled the robbers. It was only due to the lack of back-up from his station that the robbers weren't arrested. This should have automatically put him into the position of head of investigation on this very case but, due to the loss of his wife and son, he was taken off the case.

James focused on the line at the top of his screen:

Robbery of Midland Bank, New Southgate, London: 23rd April.

James then picked up the page next to the keyboard, and looked at the information at the head of the page:

Death of Helen Warwick and Jonathan Warwick, Enfield, London: 23rd April.

'Now if that's not a fucking coincidence, do you mind telling me what is?' he said to his mug of tea as he raised it to his lips.

He opened the file that had been delivered to him only an hour before. It was the autopsy report on Helen and Jonathan Warwick. The report was hand written. James had highlighted and numbered certain parts of the report that he felt he had to read again:

1. *Never in my twenty eight years in forensics, have I had such a job to put a name to two bodies. The remains that were laid out before me on the slab this morning, resembled that of a display from the London Dungeons,*

218

the only difference being that these remains were that of a mother and her son, innocently killed in what can only be described as a freak car accident.

2. The explosion, caused by the nature of the car crash, had reached these two victims on impact.

3. Jonathan (The Son) has been successfully identified by dental records.

4. Helen's head (The Mother) seemed to be at the core of the explosion, so dental records were of no use. Luckily for us, her left hand didn't lose it's outer skin.

5. By finger prints, Helen has been identified.

6. Signed: Stan Percival.

James closed the file, placed it back on the desk and looked at the screen that displayed Warwick asleep in bed.

'If there is such a place as hell, I'm sure you've been there', James whispered.

He knew as he sat there looking at the screen that Brooks would be the best person to look at all this information. He'd piece it all together somehow.

A Time for Rest

Dillon woke up in the passenger seat of the car to the sound of the traffic around her as Brooks made his way along the bank of the Thames through the early morning London traffic.

'Jesus, I've been asleep all night', she said.

'I know', Brooks told her.

When they were smuggled out of Hennessy's house last night, Dillon was told by Brooks to wait in the car once they were at Kilburn police station, while he was being interviewed by the police. Thinking he'd only be about twenty minutes to half an hour, Dillon closed her eyes in an attempt to get a quick sleep as she knew, once Dwyer got hold of the news that the police had lifted two people out of Hennessy's place, all hell would break loose and then there would be little time for sleep.

It was in her training long ago. Get any sleep you can,

219

because a time may come when you will have to go without.

'How long did the interview go on for?' she asked him.

'Three bloody hours', Brooks cursed. 'All they're bloody worried about is how bad the police are going to look for letting us go.'

Dillon was opening and closing her mouth to try and get some air to the bad taste she was experiencing. She knew that there was only one cure for that as she opened her packet of B&H, extracted a cigarette and lit it. Brooks looked at her in amazement at her action.

'You've only just woken up.'

'So fucking what?' she barked back at him.

Brooks pulled the car off the road and drove into a car park at the rear of a block of apartments on the bank of the river Thames. He then drove the car into his allocated parking space.

'Where are we?' Dillon asked.

'My place. I think we could both do with a bit of a rest, don't you think?' Brooks asked of her.

As Dillon looked across the Thames water she felt strange in many ways at this moment in time. She watched all the cars, taxis, bicycles and buses rushing along the road at the far side of the water. Everyone rushing to their place of work to start another week in the rat race. Yet here she was at a stranger's house, ready for a bit of a rest. If she were to ask a member of the British if they would like to take a rest in her house, that meant she would eventually kill them, as they would always know her address. Still, she knew that once Dwyer was captured, Brooks would be attempting to be rid of her, as she would of him. Permanently.

'Yeah, Okay', she agreed, as she opened her door to get out.

Once inside the front door of his first floor apartment, Brooks pressed the code into the alarm system's keypad and then turned to Dillon.

'Welcome to my place', he said to her.

Dillon was impressed at how tidy the open area was. Once

inside the front door, she arrived straight into the lounge area. The open area was painted yellow with red squares appearing in no set pattern and the ceiling was light blue. Dillon liked the decor. She thought it was very seventies. A framed film poster hung from the wall to the left hand side of the door. A man in a white boiler suit and bowler hat, holding a knife, was smiling under the words, "A Clockwork Orange." A wide screen television and stereo system with a large record collection underneath it, occupied the left hand side of the room while an open kitchen area occupied the right. Straight in front were the floor to ceiling windows and the clear view of London Bridge outside.

'How often does your cleaner come in?' she asked.

'I don't have a cleaner', Brooks replied as he removed his coat and threw it on the chair.

Dillon really liked the place. It felt really relaxing.

Making Oneself 'At Home'

'Look, help yourself to tea, coffee or a beer. If you don't mind, I'm going to get my head down for an hour?' he asked her as he kicked off his shoes.

'No, you fire away. I'm fine here', Dillon replied as she walked around the room, still admiring the decor.

They both stood still for a moment and looked at each other without saying a word. He was desperate for a rest and was about to leave an IRA member free to sit in his own front room. Free to roam around his home.

She felt she was going to be sitting in this Brit's front room like a lame duck.

Amongst these thoughts there seemed to be an air of relaxation. A relaxation that was dangerous, considering the circumstances.

Still, they looked at each other and both began to smile as if one knew what the other was thinking.

'You need the sleep, go on', Dillon broke the moment.

'Okay. Call me in an hour', he requested as he smiled back.

'No problem.'

Dillon took her coat off, stretched her body and decided that a cup of coffee was just what she needed. As she made her way over to the open kitchen area, she noticed a box of tools and a reel of cable on the floor behind the door. Beside it she noticed the break in the plaster work around the twin socket outlet on the wall. Brooks had obviously been doing a little DIY. Dillon half closed her eyes as she stopped to think for a moment. She lifted her coat up and pulled the gun from her pocket. The useless unusable handgun that Brooks had given her, was her only weapon at the moment. She placed the weapon back in the coat pocket and made her way over to the box of tools to examine it. A reel of 2.5mm twin and earth cable. Also in the box was an industrial torch and an old light switch. She stood up and turned to look at the entrance to the corridor where Brooks had just disappeared.

No sound. Good.

She walked over to the kitchen, opened the top cupboard, then another and then another.

'Bingo', she said to herself as she grabbed a bag of unopened icing sugar. Then she turned and walked across the open front room quietly to the open window.

'Bingo', she again said to herself as she eyed all the fresh compost in the flower bed on the balcony.

'Bingo fucking bingo', she almost sang as she walked back over to the box of tools. She removed a pair of side cutters, a pair of plyers and a screwdriver, and went to work like the true professional she was.

29

A JESUS CHRIST POSE

The wind blew hard across the courtyard of Murray's border farm complex in south Armagh, as Séamus Kelly slowly walked from his car to the side entrance of the old cow house. For some reason, out of the blue, he suddenly started to wonder what would happen, if the council knew of how the mission in London had been set up. If they had any idea at all, if they had the slightest notion of British involvement, there would be no way he would walk away from the meeting this morning in one piece. No way.

Terrifying Thoughts

'Jesus Christ', he said to himself as he stopped walking and turned back to look at his car. He then turned his head back in the direction of where he was walking and stared at the side entrance to the cow house. He took his packet of Carrols from his pocket, flipped open the lid, extracted one and placed it in his mouth before lighting it. His hands started to shake with fear at the thought of how the Army Council would react if they knew and it started to play on his mind. His body went cold from the inside.

'Do they know? Could they know? How would they know? How would they find out? '

'No', he told himself convincingly, as he was sure that there was no way anyone would tell the council. He had made sure the mission was completely sound proof.

Tim Clery of Sinn Féin, South Tipperary, would be risking his life, if he told anyone of the mission that he and Southern Division IRA had set up with the British in London. If he told anyone else within Sinn Féin about the mission, surely he'd know that it would get back to the IRA Army Council. Sinn

Féin was only too aware of the council's feelings on politicians trying to intervene in the real struggle that takes place on the front lines.

'No' he once again told himself as the shaking in his hands calmed down. He slowly started to walk again to the side entrance of the cow house. He threw the cigarette into a puddle of water that had gathered from last night's rain.

Once inside, Kelly stepped into the slim corridor at the rear of the milking cubicles. The corridor was wet and dim, with light only coming in from the milking cubicles along the right hand side of the corridor. He knew he was to turn left and enter cubicle number six, the cubicle reserved for the Southern Division. Just before he took his steps, he turned to look at the metal red doors that led to cubicles one, two and three. He knew only too well that to enter one of those cubicles by accident meant a bullet in your head there and then. They were reserved for the main council. The three main heads who had never set eyes on each other and, in return, no one had ever set eyes on them, unless to face them for one's own execution.

Kelly had been present at "Tout Executions" before. He'd watched as men were dragged from their cubicles and made to stand in front of the three main heads. You always had a clear view of anyone standing before the council. You could see the fear in their eyes as they saw the three faces of the army council. That was a sure sign that their time was up. Slowly it would be, as "Tout Executions" were always slow. That way, it was more effective to the victims and more effective in the warning to the witnesses.

Kelly had stood before the three main cubicles before, but their area was in darkness. They knew his face but, like many, he didn't know theirs. His hands once again started to shake. He walked along past the next two doors into cubicle six and sat down on the stool that was placed in the middle of the six foot squared area.

The centre of the cow house was lit by three flood lights that hung unevenly from the ceiling by chains. There was obviously a leak somewhere on the roof, as you could see the water dripping in the light's beam.

A Time For Prayer

As he sat down he heard a voice coughing from one of the first three cubicles. He looked up over the concrete wall to his right and saw the trail of tobacco smoke coming from one of the main council. He then looked over the wall to his left.

No mist? No one in the next cubicle? How strange!

He then looked across the front area to his left to see if there was any mist coming from cubicle eight. Nothing!

As he looked down at the ground a sudden coldness came over him. There were no cars in the courtyard.... He looked up at the ceiling to his right, only this time he lifted himself up a little. The lights were on in the first three cubicles.

An execution?

'Oh shit!' he said to himself, as he quickly stood up from his stool, causing it to fall backwards in his panic.

Realisation set in. He'd been set up. He was here on his own.

'Oh shit', he once again told himself.

'SIT DOWN YOU WEE FUCKING SCUM BAG!' a voice shouted at him from behind.

Kelly knew that voice only too well. He turned to see the "Undertaker" standing in the doorway to the cubicle. His big six foot two inch frame filled the doorway so much he had to tilt his head forward a little so as not to bang his head on the brick frame work.

The barrel of the SMG was facing Kelly's stomach. The Undertaker's thick heavy eyebrows were as bushy and as big as his moustache. This made his face impossible to read. In situations like this it was as stern and as hard as an iron gate. What made it even harder to read was the light reflecting off the bald patch at the roof of his head.

Kelly was frozen to the spot. He was sure now that this was a set up. His boss knew this was a set up. That's why he had sent him.

'You fucking bastard!' Kelly's mind was saying, as he pictured the face of John Fitzpatrick asking him to come to this meeting this morning.

'I said sit the fuck down!' the Undertaker whispered.

Kelly's hands were shaking crazily. This was making it hard for him to pick up the stool, but he did so and sat down, facing the Undertaker.

'Turn around and face the front!' he was again instructed.

'Okay', Kelly said as he raised his shaking hands in defence, before turning himself around on the old stool.

Times before, Kelly had often wondered if the first words he had ever spoken as a child were the words to the prayer, 'Hail Mary.' It is often the first prayer learnt by Catholic children. It is the prayer that asks for help from the mother of God. Mary, the virgin mother of God. As a child, Kelly's family were very religious but, deep down inside, he wasn't. Yet he could recite the words of the 'Hail Mary' backwards, and had done so on many an occasion for a bet.

Now, seated with his back to the Undertaker, he was ready to recite Our Lady's prayer in the correct manner, as he now wanted her help. It was the first time in decades that he had turned to her for help. He closed his eyes as he began.

'Hail Mary, full of.....'

The Undertaker smashed the handle of the SMG into the back of Kelly's head, which caused him to fall from the stool and into a heap on the floor.

A Painful Reality

When Kelly's eyelids finally opened, the nerves above his eyes were the first things to greet him, as they gave off a pain from the light that invaded his now comfortable dark vision. His natural reaction was to cover his eyes with his hands. But as he tried to lift his hands up a great pain shot up both of his arms. He quickly turned his head to look at his left hand but he couldn't focus correctly. He tried to lift his hand up but it wouldn't move. He could feel a coldness down the back of his body from the top of his head to the back of his heels.

The floor? He was lying down. He was lying down with his arms spread out beside him. He turned again to look at his left hand but his vision was still blurred. He could see a little patch of red, but nothing else. He could feel a pain in his palms which was getting worse by the second. He tried to lift his feet but then a greater pain shot up both of his legs.

'AAAARRHH, FUCKING HELL!' he shouted.

In that split second, his body naturally tried to lift his arms up at the same time. The pain coming up from his legs was met in his stomach by the pain travelling along his arms, which caused him to be sick. He vomited all over himself.

'Go on you wee fucking bastard. Eat it back up, because that's about as good as it's going to fucking get', the Undertaker shouted into his face, before standing back up to kick Kelly in the ribs.

'OH JESUS CHRIST', Kelly screamed out from the pain.

As the Undertaker stood over Kelly, he took a cuban cigar from his pocket. The cigar was approximately eight inches long and twenty millimetres in diameter. It came, with a box of fifty, from America in the latest batch of donations.

As he finally got the recommended red end on the cigar, he took a lungful and leant down to blow the smoke into Kelly's face before speaking.

'The pain you are feeling in your hands right now is from two six inch nails that have been driven through your hands with a hammer into the ground you are lying on. The pain in your feet is from a nine inch nail.'

'OH JESUS CHRIST!' Kelly cried.

'When you do meet the angels in heaven, I suggest you thank them for the fact that you were out cold when we drove the nails in', the Undertaker whispered.

'Okay, that's enough', the voice of Tim Murray calmly told the Undertaker.

A Death Wish

Kelly started to cry to himself. He just wanted to die. He just wanted to be killed. But he knew it wasn't going to be that easy.

Murray was standing about six feet away from where Kelly's feet were nailed into the ground. He was chewing loudly on the piece of gum in his mouth that had lost it's taste about five minutes ago. He had a bad habit of chewing gum loudly when an execution was taking place.

'Tell us everything there is to know about the mission in London and I'll give you my word, Séamus, we'll make it quick. No cutting off of the legs or bollock burning. I give you my word that it will just be a bullet to the head', Murray told him as he walked around the crucified body on the floor of the old cow house.

As Kelly watched Murray walk around him, he heard that voice coughing again, as it had done when he first walked into the cow house earlier. Whoever was behind that cough had sealed Kelly's fate today. That voice would have aired its approval for this execution to take place today.

'What do you want to know?' Kelly cried as his vision became clear again. He saw the old face of Murray looking back at him with disgust. Then Murray turned away to nod at the Undertaker.

The Undertaker then took a Browning .47 from his pocket, placed the gun's barrel over Kelly's left knee cap and began to laugh as he spoke.

'You're an awful fucking whore, Kelly. Because, believe you me, this is only fucking foreplay.'

The second Kelly heard the gun shot, the pain drove through his leg and up the spine to his back, producing complete incontinence.

'OH DEAR GOD!' Kelly screamed out, before crying uncontrollably. Every time he moved any part of his body a new pain would cancel the old one out, but only for a moment. The warmth of the blood on his left knee cap was cancelled out by the warmth of the urine on his right.

Questions And Answers

'PLEASE JUST FUCKING SHOOT ME. PLEASE!' he once again screamed.

'NOT UNTIL YOU FUCKING TALK, THAT'S THE DEAL', Murray shouted, although he hated shouting. He regarded shouting as an action of one who couldn't keep his cool. He looked down at the ground to help re-compose himself, before looking back at Kelly in the eye as he calmly continued.

'You talk, then I'll kill you, I promise', Murray told him before beginning his line of questioning.

'Who's on the mission in London? Who's working with the British?'

'Dermott O'Shea and Sinéad Dillon.' Kelly just about managed to get the words out.

'Who set the mission up?' a voice shouted out from one of the first three cubicles.

Kelly turned his head to the right in the direction of where the voice was coming from. The three cubicles were now in darkness. Would he not get the opportunity to look at his killers' faces? They may not have a gun in their hand but they were sure as hell calling every shot.

'Just myself and O'Shea', Kelly lied.

The undertaker placed the barrel of the gun over Kelly's right knee cap. Kelly looked at the Undertaker, but the smoke from his cigar and the flood lights, shining off his head, made it hard to see his face, but Kelly could just make out the smile on his face as the Undertaker unclicked the gun's safety catch, and then slowly motioned the gun up the inside of Kelly's right leg. As the gun moved around the groin area, it changed direction and moved back down the leg past the knee cap and down to the right foot.

'Did your Ma not teach you manners? It's rude to lie', the Undertaker said, as the barrel stopped over the top of the big toe on Kelly's right foot.

Kelly's voice seemed to be singing in flat monotone as the tears poured down his face. He was awaiting this new pain to join his body. The Undertaker turned and looked Kelly in the eye, before speaking with a lilt of a laugh in his voice.

'Jesus Christ, this is going to hurt.'

'YOU PSYCHO FUCKING BASTARD', Kelly screamed as the gun shot deafened everyone present.

The functions of Kelly's body seemed to be running themselves independently to his brain. Before he had a chance to scream out from the pain in his foot, he once again was sick all over himself. It happened so quick that he didn't even have the chance to raise his head up and the strong juices from his mouth made their way into his left eye.

'OH DEAR GOD, PLEASE JUST FUCKING KILL ME!' he screamed.

'Like I said before. You talk, then I'll kill you', Murray calmly responded.

Kelly started to panic, as he didn't feel he had the strength to carry on talking. If his mind went numb, they'd burn him alive, he was sure of it.

He once saw a Tout bite his own tongue off before he had the chance to tell the Council what they wanted to hear. They cut the Tout's body with a stanley knife from head to toe, poured petrol all over him and set him alight as he began to have a massive heart attack.

Kelly stopped crying for a moment as he coughed and spat some sick from his mouth. It won't be long. He just had to tell them everything. Then they'd kill him.

'I don't think I'm going to able to talk for much longer', he pleaded in Murray's direction. Murray stared straight back at him, as he could see by looking at Kelly's blood shot eyes he was only going to last two or three more minutes.

'Okay', Murray said as he crouched down beside Kelly. 'This is your last chance, otherwise we'll leave the cow house and let the Undertaker here do some real damage to you. Let's do a quick Q & A.'

'Thank you', Kelly cried with a little relief.

'Who set the mission up?'

'Tim Clery of Sinn Féin, South Tipp, John Fitzpatrick and myself', Kelly said as the thought of being free from this pain gave him such hope. As he concentrated so hard on the questions it took his mind away from the pain of his foot, but not that of the left kneecap. His arms had now become completely numb as the blood flowed from them at such a rapid rate that the gutter of the cow house could be heard constantly dripping.

'Who had the idea of working with the Brits?' Murray asked, still crouched beside him.

'Tim and myself', Kelly replied as a drop of blood poured down his cheek from his left eye.

Murray knew time was ticking away.

'Why O'Shea?'

'Because we didn't want to lose anyone good on this mission. O'Shea is expendable. He shit on the movement before, remember?'

The pain couldn't be heard in Kelly's voice for this brief moment. His brain was starting to shut down. It had quickly become overpowered by the pain breaking down the body's defences.

Murray could see he only had a minute or so.

'Why Dillon?'

Kelly gave out a little cough of pain as the nerves in his kneecap were still fighting to stay alive.

'Why Dillon?' Murray asked again.

Kelly turned to look at Murray in the eye.

'O'Shea turned on the movement at a time when it needed to pull together. For that, we wanted to use him and then kill him.' Kelly coughed again before continuing.

'It just seemed like a nice touch, to throw his daughter into the equation as well.'

The look of surprise on Murray's face was clear to see.

'Sinéad Dillon is O'Shea's daughter?'

Kelly smiled for the first time today, and for the last time in his life.

231

'Check the medical records! John Fitzpatrick has them.'
Murray stood up and looked at Kelly, still in shock from the revelation. Kelly still had a smile on his face as he whispered his last words.

'I'll see you in hell Tim. Shall I tell your folks you said hello?'

'Fuck you!' Murray whispered as he calmly took the gun from the Undertaker.

'And fuck you too', Kelly quietly replied.
Murray stayed true to his word and shot Kelly clean between his eyes.

30

THE AFTERMATH

As Murray handed the gun back to the Undertaker he turned and stood still with his back to Kelly's dead body, staring at the ground.

'Get this mess cleaned up', he ordered. 'Dispose of the body, and have no more said about it. I want no one in the movement to know of what happened here today. There's no lesson to be learned from what has taken place. Do you understand?'

'No problem', the Undertaker replied with a lung full of cigar smoke.

'Good!' Murray replied as he walked over towards the three dark cubicles of the main Council. For some reason, Murray declined from switching the lights back on to their spaces.

Next Item on The Agenda

'Gentlemen, you have some decisions to make and those decisions lie squarely with yourselves. Like the Chief of Staff, I will make no attempt to influence what decision you make, but let me at least tell you of a plan I have that may be of some beneficial use to your job.'

As he talked he paced the ground up and down in front of their cubicles looking down at the floor. He had his arms folded and his face was scrunched up, as he was deep in thought.

'As you know, we need a break from the war. A break to re-group and get our act together. The Brits want a ceasefire. So let's give them one.'

'Hold on', a voice called out from cubicle two.

Murray held his hand up. 'Let me finish', he asked, as he

turned and looked across at the Undertaker who was standing still, watching Murray walk up and down. He wouldn't clean up the mess of Kelly's body until this meeting was complete. Murray was glad of that, as the silence helped him think a lot more clearly. For that, he gave a smile of appreciation to the Undertaker who simply nodded back.

'The Unionists won't be able to handle a ceasefire. Clinton and the American government will be falling over themselves to keep us to a ceasefire. John Hayward and the Unionists will fuck the whole thing up in no time at all.'

Murray stopped walking and turned to look at each of the cubicles slowly, one at a time, before continuing.

'And, believe you me, when that time comes, I'll give those fuckers in London the biggest fucking surprise they've ever known.'

He turned and walked over to a wall that had different switches and isolators on it. He pressed a switch that activated a flood light at the far end of the cow house.

There stood the result of Murray's latest project. A blue car-transporter lorry. It sat neatly amongst the neglected bales of hay with the flood light's reflection shining off the few shiny areas the transporter possessed. It raised a couple of gasps of astonishment from the Army Council.

Murray had a lump in his throat from the pride he felt at his guests' reaction.

'This thing will hold 3000 pounds of explosives', he broke the silence.

'What kind?' cubicle one asked.

'Ammonium nitrate fertiliser mixed with icing sugar', Murray replied.

The Undertaker walked over to the side of the transporter and rubbed his left hand up and down the welding work that he was so proud of.

'If all three of you decide to go with the idea, then in return for your vote of confidence I will clear up this mess in London. You have my word on it. But I must have three votes, and no less, on this.'

Murray looked at the body of Kelly as he completed his request.

'You have the vote of One', the voice said from cubicle one.

'You have the vote of Three', the voice agreed from cubicle three.

'What of Tim Clery?' cubicle two asked.

'I regard him as part of the mess in London. He will be silenced', Murray informed him.

'Who will you send to London?' cubicle two again asked.

Murray turned to look at the Undertaker who, in return, stopped admiring his work on the lorry and stood to attention for Murray.

'I will send my very best. I will send the Undertaker.'

The cow house was in complete silence for a brief moment as the Undertaker stood, like the proudest soldier ever known, for his Commandant.

'In that case you have the vote of Two.'

A smile grew across Murray's face as he nodded his head in the council's direction.

'You have made a great decision today, Council. I will not let you down.'

The Undertaker took the lighter from his pocket and re-lit his cuban cigar.

0044 For England

Dillon sat looking at Martin Brooks' record collection with her head leaning sideways, reading the titles of the albums.

'Mia Rosefeld?' she said to herself in amazement, as she hadn't heard this record for years. She took the record from the collection and sat admiring the cover.

"*Live In London, 74*", the big white letters read across the top of the album's cover. The blurred picture of the beautiful Irish Mia Rosefeld, singing into her hand held microphone, brought back so many memories of Dillon's mother singing from the kitchen on a Sunday afternoon as she prepared dinner just for the two of them. That thought stayed with her for a moment as she pictured the scene in her mind. Her mother telling her to turn the volume up on the eight track machine when a certain song came on.

She took the second record from the double album's cover, held the twelve inches of ceramic wax up to the light, blew the little bit of dust from it, and placed it neatly on the turn table.

She didn't think for one moment that it was unusual for Brooks to own a record by the famous Irish folk singer of the Seventies. Mia Rosefeld had sold over seven hundred and fifty thousand copies of her 'Live In London, 74' album, before retiring from the music industry in 1975. The English regarded it as a great swansong for Mia Rosefeld, when her biggest selling single, '0044 For England', mentioned their country in the title and in the song's chorus. Little did the English realise that Mia Rosefeld wasn't singing for the love of England.

As the crackles eventually stopped, a crowd of voices could be heard clapping and cheering from the speakers. Then the beautiful sound of an acoustic guitar, playing a string of soft open chords, sent a spirit across the room that Dillon hadn't felt in years. She lifted her hands to her cheeks to calm her feelings down. She didn't want to cry. Not here. Not now. Not behind enemy lines.

But what a beautiful sound! The sound of free music! The sound of freedom! Yet beneath the sound of freedom was a message of loneliness. The sound of someone having to live under racial tension.

More cheers could be heard as the keyboards joined in with the guitar. Eventually the bass guitar and the drums slowly blended into the background as the hairs rose on Dillon's neck from the sounds that were bringing back such happy memories. For a moment she could get the smell of the food drifting in from her mother's kitchen. For a moment she could feel the warmth coming in from the open fire that she was tending to, at her mother's request. For a moment she

could hear her mother's beautiful sweet voice singing along
with Mia Rosefeld in those opening verse.

> *Far beyond a mountain,*
> *Far beyond a dream.*
> *Far beyond a river,*
> *Far beyond a scream.*

More cheers came from the right hand speaker.

> *Beneath a wave lies a flame of wonder,*
> *Beneath rain of tears.*
> *Far beyond the rain and thunder,*
> *Far beyond our fears.*

Now the cheers erupted from both speakers as Mia lifted her
voice for the chorus.

> *Double O forty-four for England.*
> *I know that you can make me smile.*
> *Double O forty-four for England,*
> *I wish that you would make me smile.*
> *So make me smile.*

A tear had found its escape route from Dillon's left eye and
rolled down her cheek as she pictured her mother dancing
around the kitchen in one of her hippy dresses, while singing
the words note for note.

> *Far beyond a voice is calling,*
> *And the echo's caught.*
> *Now there is no pain and suffering,*
> *Just a happiness is bought.*

Dillon was unaware of the fact that Brooks was standing
in the doorway behind her. He couldn't sleep, but he was

pleased to hear his Mia Rosefeld album being played. He didn't want to frighten Dillon, so he let out a little warning cough. On the sound of his voice, Dillon wiped the tear from her cheek as she turned to face him.

'Did I wake you?' she asked.

'No. It's hard to sleep when you know that all the action could kick off at any second', Brooks replied.

'True enough', Dillon agreed. 'The shit will hit the fan when Dwyer tries to find two touts in his own organisation.'

> *It's far beyond a mountain,*
> *It's far beyond a dream.*
> *It's far beyond the reasons,*
> *To why we all must dream.*

Brooks walked into the room, sat down at the far end of the main couch and picked up the record's cover to look at the track listing on the back. He didn't notice the small offcut of 2.5mm cable that Dillon had carelessly left on the coffee table.

'Double O forty-four for England', he began. 'What made you pick this song?' he asked.

'This was my mother's favourite song. As a young girl I absolutely hated it, but now I seem to hum it to myself at least once or twice every day.' As she spoke she leaned forward to pick up her coffee from the table and, at the same time, she calmly removed the offcut of cable.

Again the crowd cheered from both speakers as Mia Rosefeld sang the chorus of her swansong for the last time in her career.

> *Double O forty-four for England.*
> *I know that you can make me smile.*
> *Double O forty-four for England,*
> *I know that you can make me smile,*
> *So make me smile.*

Prying into Her Past

Brooks placed the record's cover back against the other records and then looked at her for a brief moment. He noticed that, in the time she was seated there listening to Mia Rosefeld, her defences seemed to have dropped a little. She looked vulnerable for the first time since he had met her. Music had a funny way of doing that to people. If he was to pry into Dillon's past, now was his chance.

'Did your father have a favourite tune.'

On his question, Dillon looked straight back at him with a sharp stare in her eye, but Brooks quickly looked away and carried on. He didn't look at her as he spoke.

'My father was into classical music and as a child I absolutely hated classical music. But, now that I'm a little older, I find I hate it even more. I find that I hate the bloody thought of classical music, let alone the sound of it', he said while looking out of the main window at London Bridge.

Dillon began laughing at his statement, but Brooks had a serious look on his face.

'Even now, the thought of it is bloody well winding me up.' He lifted his feet up on to the small coffee table in front of him, showing he felt relaxed, but that look was still on his face, much to Dillon's amusement. He looked at her as he continued.

'I can understand the relaxing nice tunes you have in certain films, but it's that weird going around the houses crap that I can never........ and will never..... and never bloody want to.......... get my head around.'

Their conversation stopped for the short time.

'That's music', Dillon declared while the crowd cheered their approval as the song continued.

'Bloody right and all', Brooks agreed as he decided to pluck up the courage to try again.

'So anyway, what sort of music did your father listen to?'

Dillon was looking at the speaker as she answered.

'I've never met my father. I've never known who he is. It

was always just my mother and myself.' She looked down at the floor as the lines on her face appeared from the thinking she was doing. 'I don't know if he is alive or dead. My mother made it her aim in life to protect me from knowing. She felt I would be in danger if I knew.'

'And here you are, safe and well, serving for the IRA', Brooks joked.

They both burst out laughing from the statement for, as serious and as true as it was, to say it out loud just sounded so funny.

'Is your father still alive?' she asked.

Brooks was just about to answer when his door bell rang. He jumped to his feet and pulled his hand gun from his waist. He put his finger to his lip to warn Dillon to stay quiet. As he approached the door he unclicked the safety catch from his gun and looked through the eye hole. On looking through the hole, he released the gun's safety catch and opened the door.

'Hello Sir', he welcomed Allan as he walked into the apartment, followed by O'Shea.

Allan just nodded at Dillon out of courtesy and then turned to Brooks.

'We need to talk in private', Allan said as he walked over to the kitchen area.

'Oh don't mind us, will you', O'Shea commented as he stood beside Dillon.

Brooks and Dillon looked at each other as realisation kicked in. They shouldn't feel relaxed around each other. It's not right.

31

TOOLS FOR THE TRADE

The air was cold around the streets of Hackney that morning as the wind was carrying the fallen leaves of the few trees Hackney possessed into the morning air. Some of these leaves rattled off the windows of a Hackney warehouse that was under refurbishment works, along with an adjacent industrial park.

Veterans in Waiting

Two men were strapped to two chairs in the centre of the warehouse. Their mouths were taped up with industrial silver tape which was wrapped around the head twice, and their hands were tied to the arms of the chair with rope, as were their legs. The chairs were fixed to the ground with galvanised angle brackets. These two men weren't going anywhere.

The two men were Tommy Skinner and Frank Clarke. Both were members of the IRA's Fifth Brigade. Tommy and Frank were warned many months ago about the excessive gambling that they were getting up to late in the evenings. Frank had actually been caught gambling IRA fund money in a casino in Luton, while Tommy had drawn attention to himself within the brigade for shooting a fellow card player in a game one night. Both had been brought before Dwyer and warned by him personally, while he held a chainsaw in his hands, that if they were ever caught gambling again, he'd "cut their fucking bollocks off."

Tommy and Frank were both in their early sixties. They had given so much of their lives to the IRA's fight both in Ireland and on mainland Britain. The only problem with that was that, since Dwyer had taken over the Fifth Brigade nearly six years ago, they had had to fend for themselves financially. Regarded as too old to work on building sites and too old to carry out missions for the movement, they were now treated as a couple "go fors" by the brigade's top men. But in their prime, they were fine soldiers. Tommy was one of the greatest snipers in his day but, due to the abuse he had thrown at his own body through alcohol, his shaky hands had changed all of that.

Both Tommy and Frank were totally unaware of the incident that had taken place at Liam Hennessy's place last night, as they were at a card game in Camden Town. The other thing that they were unaware of, was the fact that they were the only two members of the Fifth Brigade who weren't anywhere to be seen last night. They were unaccounted for. As far as they were aware, or as far as they thought, they had just been rumbled again for gambling.

The warehouse was situated two floors above the building site in Hackney. The main contractor on the building site was O'Connel Building Contractors Ltd.. The warehouse had been part of the main contract, but the Fifth Brigade were allowed access to the warehouse whenever needed. After a phone call was put through to the site office this morning, the warehouse was shut off to the workers as the warning signs were posted up at all entrances to it. "**KEEP OUT!! ASBESTOS!! KEEP OUT!! ASBESTOS!!**" No one else was in the warehouse.

Five hooded men had strapped Tommy and Frank to the chairs almost an hour ago. They were the same five hooded men who had pulled them from their beds that morning, beat them from the van to the warehouse and left them to think about what was coming to them. They left them strapped to the two chairs in only their blooded long johns to protect them from the cold.

Frank and Tommy may have been old but, by God, they were tough. Neither one of them let out a scream, a word or a tear from the small beating they took as they were dragged into the warehouse. For they had carried out the very same task in their youth.

As they sat there for an hour, thinking over what was to

become of them and how they had been caught gambling again, they didn't shed a tear. They took it like real men.

The 'Madman' Arriveth!

Both of them jumped when the door in front of them flew open at the far end of the warehouse. Dwyer slowly walked into the warehouse followed by Peter O'Connel. Dwyer had a pleasing smile on his face as he eyed the two men before him.

'Good morning, Gentlemen', he greeted them as he walked over to a workbench full of tools, that had obviously been abandoned this morning in the asbestos panic.

He stopped walking, turned to look at Frank and Tommy again and shouted:

'I SAID, GOOD MORNING!'

His voice echoed through the warehouse. Peter O'Connel wanted to tell Dwyer to keep his voice down so as not to attract attention from anyone on the building site below. But he thought it better to keep quiet.

The veins in Dwyer's red face came through in the madness of his features. He had that look in his eye, that look of evil playfulness. Tommy and Frank looked at him, completely defenceless. They couldn't even utter a sound, the tape was that tight on their faces. Suddenly Dwyer was calm again.

'Very well. Fucking suit yourselves.'

When he got to the bench he removed his black bomber jacket and placed it on a stack of milk crates beside him. He rubbed his hands together as his eyes viewed all the tools scattered across the table in front of him, and a smile grew across his face until he laughed to himself.

O'Connel looked behind him at the open door, pulled a tissue from his pocket with his shaking hands and wiped the sweat from his brow. He then walked over and closed the door. As he closed it he closed his eyes in the hope that this madness would soon be over.

'Jesus Christ', his shaky voice spoke to himself.

Testing' The Tools

Dwyer picked up a terminal screwdriver from the bench and held it up to view the sharpness of its head.

'Ah, the old terminal screwdriver!' he announced with delight. 'Used for the termination of screws on electrical appliances and accessories, or can be used for making a small pilot hole in wood.'

He cleared a little area of the bench free of dust and began to make a pilot hole with the screw driver by turning the handle clockwise and pressing the head of the driver into the bench.

'This wood seems to be a trifle tough', he said to no one in particular as he lifted the screw driver up into the air and rammed it into the bench.

The head was now in the bench.

'There, that's better', he calmly acknowledged with a smile.

After he pulled the driver out of the work bench, he walked over to Tommy very slowly as he began to talk.

'There's no point in asking where you two old farts were last night, as I think I have a pretty good idea. So you may as well all just sit back and watch me enjoy myself.'

O'Connel started to shake with fear. He couldn't look up at what was going on, for he had known Tommy and Frank for years. He knew that they weren't a couple of Touts. No way. But, then again, who was he to argue with Dwyer? Who was anyone to argue with Dwyer? Frank was looking at O'Connel, wanting to look him in the eye.

Dwyer placed his left hand on Tommy's shoulder.

'I was wondering. Which do you think is tougher? A sixty year old bone or a lump of wood?'

Tommy's eyes pierced into Dwyer's. Dwyer replied with a smile, and then lifted his right hand up in the air with the head of the terminal screwdriver facing downwards, and rammed it into Tommy's shoulder.

Tommy's voice could be heard screaming out from behind the tape. It sounded like a scream from beneath a pillow.

Dwyer laughed and then leaned closer to inspect the screw driver's handle sticking out of Tommy's shoulder. Blood was squirting out from below the handle like a fountain.

'Fuck me. I didn't expect that to go all the way in up to the handle', he said with an air of astonishment. He then looked Tommy in the face. 'Did you?'
Five inches of the screwdrivers neck, was buried in Tommy's shoulder. Tommy's eyes were now filled with tears. Dwyer had succeeded in breaking him.

'No, I didn't think you did', Dwyer replied with a smile. 'But', he said, raising his finger up to his face, 'I wonder if I can break the bone from the inside. What do you think?'
Tommy's scream got a little louder, but not loud enough to attract any attention from outside of the warehouse. Dwyer turned and looked at O'Connel.

'What do you think, Peter? Want a bet?' he shouted to him.

A Mad Misunderstanding?
O'Connel looked up. He had tears in his eyes. What had he become part of? This wasn't the way the IRA handle their people. They execute Touts, yes, without question and rightly so. But only when they have been proven guilty and not beforehand. This now was madness.

'Whatever', O'Connel replied with his shameful shaky voice.
Dwyer reached into his pocket and pulled out a five pound note, walked back over to the bench and slammed it down as hard as he rammed the screw driver into it only moments before.

'There you go. Five fucking pounds says I can break that fucking Tout's shoulder blade from the inside with the driver, Okay?' Dwyer shouted in O'Connel's direction, who was still staring at the ground.

Tommy and Frank looked at each other and both could read each other's mind ringing question.
'Did he just say Tout?'

'I said Okay?' Dwyer repeated in O'Connel's direction. O'Connel looked up with his watered, shamed eyes and replied, 'Okay.'

Dwyer could see the shame that O'Connel was experiencing and that just made the whole thing even more enjoyable for him.

As Dwyer walked back over to Tommy he looked over at Frank.

'Sorry, Frank, I would let you in on the bet too, but you quit gambling, remember?

He didn't even hesitate as he grabbed the screw driver handle and pulled on it as hard as he could. Again Tommy screamed out and again it became louder. Frank just looked on in shock. He knew that his treatment would be worse. He knew Dwyer was only just getting warmed up.

'He thinks we're fucking Touts!'

Something snapped in Tommy's shoulder and Dwyer fell backwards holding onto the screw driver's handle. The blood shot up from Tommy's shoulder as if it was being fed from a garden hose that was turned up to full, and poured into Tommy's face, which loosened the tape around his mouth, freeing him to scream. And scream he did, as the whole warehouse was filled with the voice of a man in great pain.

O'Connel panicked as Tommy did so. He feared that the workers below would hear Tommy screaming. O'Connel took the Browning .57 with silencer attached, from his inside pocket and shot Tommy three times in the stomach.

Now Frank started to scream but, like Tommy before, it just sounded like a scream from beneath a pillow.

'What the fuck have I done?' O'Connel's shaky voice whispered to himself as the tears rolled down his face. 'What the fuck have I done?'

'Can you believe the handle snapped off!' Dwyer said calmly, as he stood up behind O'Connel. Then he started to laugh as he spoke. 'I can't fucking believe the handle broke. It's obviously cheap foreign shit.'

He then threw the handle across the floor behind him and walked back over to the bench. He picked up the five pound note and walked back over to O'Connel who was still staring at Tommy's dead body. Dwyer placed the five pound note in O'Connel's top pocket and walked back over to the bench. O'Connel didn't even notice what Dwyer had done.

'Ah, the 25mm auger drill bit. The bladed spiral that drills a perfect hole in wooden joists for pipework or cable', Dwyer announced with delight. He then placed the drill bit into the battery drill that had been abandoned on the work bench. He pulled on the drill's trigger. The sound of the drill's electric motor spinning brought a smile to his face. As he turned around and looked at Frank his face went deadly serious.

'I wonder how a 25mm auger drill bit will get on with a sixty year old knee cap.'

'Please God help me. For I'm no fucking Tout.'

32

REMOVING MASKS

Allan stood looking at Dillon and O'Shea who were both out on the balcony of Martin Brooks' apartment. They went outside soon after he and O'Shea arrived earlier.

'This whole operation has been set up without the go-ahead from the main IRA Army Council', Allan told Brooks as he took a sip from the glass of Jack Daniels which he had helped himself to when he arrived.

Open Secret

'I know', Brooks replied.

Allan looked at him surprised. 'How long have you known?'

'Dillon let something slip last night when we were talking in the warehouse. '

Brooks looked at the floor, as he was thinking about what Dillon had said to him when they were sitting in the car at the Hayes warehouse last night. Then it came to him.

'She mentioned something about West Belfast blowing London clean out of the water, if they knew what was really going on.'

He then glanced back at Allan who looked like he had a face that was turning to rage.

'And it didn't cross your mind to fucking tell me?' Allan shouted. He quickly looked over to the window, as he had forgotten about Dillon and O'Shea for that small moment. They didn't look back in. They obviously didn't hear him.

'I have to honestly say that no, it didn't cross my mind to tell you, because what difference does it make?' Brooks asked as he took a sip from his cup of earl grey tea.

Allan's face calmed down as he looked Brooks in the eye.

'Martin, you're the best at what you do, there is no

question about it. But this is getting out of hand. We're fucking with the wrong people here.'

He then stepped a little closer to Brooks as he continued.

'Even the best can get in over their heads. I can't afford for you to be involved in this fucking mess when the IRA army council decide to join in on the fun and games.'

'So what are you saying? That you want me to pull out of the mission? A mission that has killed one of the IRA's fifth brigade, and has got Tony Dwyer thinking he has two informers in his camp, all within twenty four hours.'

Brooks looked over to the window and, seeing that O'Shea and Dillon weren't looking in, he continued.

'I'm sorry Sir, but I've got a job to complete and until that's done, I'm not going anywhere.'

'What about the girl?' Allan asked.

'Once the job's complete, I'll kill her', Brooks stated with no emotion in his voice whatsoever.

Allan just looked down at the floor. He didn't like Dillon one little bit. But after the revelation of what O'Shea had told him in the park earlier, and the fact that she would be killed once this mission was complete, made Allan feel that he couldn't help but feel sorry for her.

'Very well', he acknowledged.

Mixed Feelings

Dillon was leaning on the railings of the balcony as O'Shea sat at the balcony table, playing with his cigarette packet as he spoke to her.

'You do know the Council will send someone now, don't you?'

'Yeah, I know', she softly replied, still looking at London Bridge.

'Why?' he simply asked her as he stopped playing with the packet and lit a cigarette.

'Why what?' she asked, still with her back to him, and still in a soft voice that had a manner about it, A manner that

249

made O'Shea feel that she didn't want to talk, and it made him feel that she couldn't be bothered to talk.

'The Watchmaker. Why kill him?' O'Shea asked as he blew a line of smoke into the cold London air.

'It wasn't planned. Things just went a different way to what I hoped', she told him, still with her back to him.

A moment of silence passed as Dillon carried on admiring London's famous bridge. O'Shea sat at the table with his head facing the ground, smoking his cigarette as he listened to the Thames water drifting below them. He opened his mouth to ask her the question that was playing on his mind, but then he closed it again, declining to ask.

But he had to ask.

'When are you planning on departing from the mission?' his nervous voice asked of her. Dillon turned around to look at him. She had a smile on her face but it wasn't one of friendliness. It was one of knowing. Knowing that she was right about something. Knowing that she was right all along.

Nothing Simple

'I fucking knew it', she declared as she walked from the balcony.

'Knew what?' he asked.

She started to shake her head from the thoughts of disgust that she felt for this man.

'I can't for the life of me understand why Kelly picked you for this mission. Now that you can make a run for it with your money, you're just going to get the fuck out of here, aren't you, and leave me to complete the job?'

'Sinéad, it's not that simple', he began.

'Oh yes it is, you fucking scab.'

'Look, just shut up for a minute and hear me out', he said as he stood up to confront her.

'Go on then, let's fucking hear it!' she demanded as she walked over to the table to help herself to one of his cigarettes.

'There's a Leisure Centre around the corner from the Dominion Theatre on the Tottenham Court Road called Harry Fords.' He took a key from his inside pocket and placed it on the table.

'What's this?' she asked, looking at the key.

'There's no use for me on this mission any more, Sinéad. I've helped these bastards pin Dwyer down in a photograph. They've got no use for me now. The first chance they get, they'll kill me. The first chance I get, I'm gone.'

Dillon looked at him with some confusion in her face.

'How did you manage to spot Dwyer in a photo, when you've never seen him before?'

O'Shea looked at the floor, then back to Dillon.

'Pure luck, I guess.'

Dillon looked at the key and read the number engraved into it. *231.*

'On the first floor of Harry Fords there is a unisex changing room. In locker **231** there is fifteen thousand pounds in Irish. If I don't make it to that locker within the next twenty four hours, it's yours.'

'How do you know that I won't help myself to it, as soon as we leave here?'

'I trust you', O'Shea replied.

'Bollocks!' Dillon replied.

'Sinéad, there's something you should know', O'Shea began as he knew that this moment now would be the best and maybe the last chance he would ever get to tell her what he knew or at least what he thought he knew, about their relationship.

'Sinéad, listen to me....'

The door to the balcony swung open as Brooks spoke to Dillon.

'We've got to go. There's a Detective Warwick that we've got to interview over at Hayes. This could be the lead we've been looking for.'

'Okay, let's go', Dillon replied as she placed the key in her pocket and brushed past O'Shea.

33

AN ADDICTION

Dwyer threw the bloody battery drill back onto the work bench in front of him as he wiped the blood from his eyes. His upper body was absolutely soaked with Frank's blood and sprinkled with parts of his flesh. He was amazed at the fight that Frank's body gave to stay alive. For as fit as Frank was for his age, no heart on earth, no matter how young or old, can stand up to having a 25mm auger drill spinning at high speed, tearing through the middle of its veins.

He gave a little laugh to himself as he thought about the execution he had just carried out.

'Christ, those auger drills are something else, Peter, don't you think?'

A Sickening Sight

Peter O'Connel stood shaking as he viewed the bloody mess of Frank before him. No butcher's shop, doing business today in London, would have a mess on their floor like the one in his warehouse now.

Dwyer didn't have to look at O'Connel to sense what was going through his mind. The stony silence was enough. Dwyer hadn't enough time to worry about the acts he had just carried out. The job in hand was always more important than that of the job already done.

'Peter get a grip of yourself!' Dwyer ordered casually as he removed his bloody T-shirt and threw it over to the two dead bodies. 'Don't you feel an ounce of guilt for a pair of fucking touts like Tommy and Frank.'

O'Connel looked over at Dwyer as the fuelling anger raged through his eyes and into his mouth.

'How can you be so sure it was Tommy and Frank at

Hennessy's last night?' his shaking voice whispered with demand.

'Where else were they then?' Dwyer casually asked as he slowly walked over towards O'Connel. 'They weren't out gambling again, were they, Peter? Your men didn't disobey an order of mine to stop gambling, did they?'

Dwyer stopped walking when he came within a foot of O'Connel, and then leaned forward until their noses were only an inch apart.

'Please don't tell me I've just executed two innocent men because you, their boss, couldn't keep them in order?'

Dwyer had a great gift at turning a situation around like this. He could go from being the guilty to inflicting the guilt. And he did so now with O'connel.

The tears filled up in O'Connel's eyes as he looked at Dwyer and then turned to look back at the two bloody bodies on the floor. He started to think about the situation. Was it he who had let these two loyal IRA soldiers down? Was he responsible? If he'd paid a little more attention to what Tommy and Frank were getting up to these days, would they now still be alive?

'Surely they wouldn't turn to touting', O'Connel thought. 'Surely not.'

Dwyer knew only too well that Tommy and Frank weren't the touts he was looking for, but he needed to send a shock wave through the Fifth Brigade. He also wanted to get his next mission on the go, as he felt it might be his last. If it was to be his last mission, he needed it to go off with complete success. There could be no bigger insult to his life than for his last mission to go wrong. *If* it were to be his last.

He didn't seem to blink in the short time he was standing face to face with O'Connel.

'Do I need to take my business elsewhere, Peter?'

O'Connel couldn't find the words to speak, as he felt he wanted to be sick. All he could muster was a shake of his head.

'Very well, Peter', Dwyer said as he turned slowly to view

the two bloody bodies heaped on the floor.

'Get this mess cleaned up!' he calmly ordered, and then walked away towards the end of the warehouse where he would wash himself in the small temporary washroom.

O'Connel could do nothing more, for the moment, but to stand and stare at the bloody mess he now felt he had caused.

Once inside the washroom Dwyer took his packet of cigarettes from his back pocket, removed one and ignited it, then placed the packet and lighter beside the sink and stood for a moment in silence looking at the floor. He exhaled a lung full of smoke across his chest, before raising his head to look up at the open ceiling above him. He then placed the cigarette on a dry surface close to the sink. He then proceeded to remove all of his lower clothing right down to, and including, his boxer shorts. The blood hadn't soaked through to his skin, but he felt he needed a wash. He also needed this moment to himself, as he needed to asses his situation.

A Surfeit of Terror

He viewed his reflection staring back at him. He may have had short grey cropped hair, but he looked good for his forty five years. His face didn't seem to be scarred by the lines of worry that a man of his age should have.

As he stood looking at himself in the mirror, he started to think over the addiction that had kept him going all these years until now. His addiction of terror.

As he viewed his reflection, he stared hard at the face that expressed the terror behind it. Terror that had politicians up and down the country condemning his actions to win the votes of the people. Terror that had parents fearing his actions to protect the lives of their innocent. Terror that had people like Peter O'Connel welcoming his actions (except for the executions he'd personally attended) to earn him an income beyond his wildest imagination.

But the terror that had entertained Tony Dwyer's life for so long, had all become a bore. Tony Dwyer had been addicted to this madness for as long as he could remember.

At the young age of five he had tortured the lives of his neighbours' pets until he became a complete professional at the task. Neighbours didn't think butter could melt in young Tony Dwyer's mouth. They would have found it hard to believe that he'd tied a firework to the tail of their cat before igniting it. As Dwyer grew up, he found new victims. People. People's lives were only objects for his enjoyment and his enjoyment was destruction.

It was like a dream come true six years ago, when the IRA gave him full control of their Fifth Brigade. Prior to this he had just been a freelance terrorist and a good one at that. Although he took contracts from many organisations, he had no political preferences. He'd help the National Front burn community centres one week and then stand shoulder to shoulder with black people in Brixton the next, throwing bricks at the police. On 17th May 1974, he helped set up four car bombs in Dublin for the Ulster Defence Association which was a Protestant movement opposed to the IRA. The bombs went off without warning, killing twenty two people. Six months later, on the 21st November, he aided the IRA on their bombing campaign in Birmingham, England, which killed nineteen people and injured one hundred and eighty two. Anarchy. Chaos. Destruction. Violence. Murder. Killing. Tony Dwyer loved every blood soaked second of it. Until now. Now he was completely bored of the whole thing, and he had become bored with life in general.

People To Meet

He picked up the cigarette and took in a lungful, before exhaling it over his reflection in the mirror. He had one more job to do and then he would meet up with Billy Hopkirk. Like he promised. He would also get to meet the one person he ever cared for in this world, apart from Billy Hopkirk. Mary, his niece.

Mary had died two years ago from cancer. His sister's only

child. His sister moved away to Australia soon after Mary's death. He had no love for his sister whatsoever, but he loved Mary. She seemed to have the only innocence he'd ever seen in this world. Her death was the only death that ever had an impact on Dwyer.

He took another lungful of smoke as a smile grew across his face at the thought of someone else.

'And what of you my friend, Detective Thomas Warwick? Where the fuck are you?'

Warwick was someone Dwyer would love to meet again. Before he headed off into the next world.

34

THE MADNESS OF UNFOLDING EVENTS

When Warwick opened his eyes, he yawned for a short moment and then sat upright in the bed. He looked around the room in confusion. He had no recollection of being in this room before.

'Where the hell am I?' he asked himself.

'In the shit, and lots of it, my friend', Allan's voice replied to him from the corner of the room.

Warwick swung around to look in the direction from which this voice that had frightened him, came.

'Who the fuck are you?' Warwick asked, as he knew that Allan wasn't a doctor or a nurse from the way he was dressed. Allan pulled a Colt hand gun from his pocket and pointed it at Warwick.

'Put your dressing gown on. We've breakfast for you downstairs', Allan informed him.

Warwick didn't seem troubled by the sight of the gun.

'Where am I?' he simply asked.

Allan let out a sigh.

'Look, I'm not in the mood for this shit, okay? You've had a nice long sleep and I've had fuck all sleep. Get your fucking dressing gown on and get downstairs!'

A Familiar Strangeness
Warwick was now getting use to the madness of unfolding events. After what he had been through in the last sixty hours, nothing was surprising him anymore. He'd just woken up in a strange room, in a strange place, and had a strange man pointing a gun at him. Strange was becoming familiar. Slowly and reluctantly he did as he was told and put on the dressing gown.

Meanwhile downstairs, James Moore was just coming to the end of his briefing to Brooks, Dillon and O'Shea on the information that he had obtained on Warwick. Brooks and Dillon were seated by one of the desks that had the only active computer working that morning. O'Shea was sitting over at the big main table, smoking a cigarette with his cup of tea, watching and listening to James talking.

James walked over to the active computer, leaned forward on the desk and pressed a button on the keyboard and a date flashed across the top of the screen.

23rd April.

'Now if that is not a fucking coincidence, do you mind telling me what is?'

Brooks eyes flinched at James and then he shook his head before asking of him:

'What's with the swearing?'

James looked taken aback by the question. 'What do you mean?' He asked.

'You have just produced a great report on this Warwick and then you ruin it by cursing at the end of your briefing', Brooks pointed out.

James looked over at O'Shea who, ignoring the situation, just took a sip of his tea. He then looked at Dillon who gave a smile to herself before looking down at the floor. He felt a little embarrassed by Brooks's question. He flinched his eyes back at him, as he couldn't believe what Brooks was saying to him. He'd put a lot of time into this report and all Brooks could do was moan about his cursing.

'Are you fucking serious?' James asked. For James listened to Peter Allan swearing all day long. Surely if Allan, being the boss, could swear all day, so could James.

'Allan swears all the time', he pointed out.

'And obviously too much around you. The day you take over as director of Section 13, you can swear at me as much as you like. Until then, curb it!' Brooks told him before looking back down at the report on the desk in front of him.

He didn't notice as James sat down, looking tired and dumbfounded from Brooks' comments. Dillon put her hand over her mouth to stop herself being seen smiling.

Brooks picked up the report to read a couple of lines and then placed the report back down and then picked up the autopsy report. After a short moment he placed that down and turned to Dillon.

'Let me do all the talking. This could take a couple of hours', he told her before turning to James. 'Get Warwick's breakfast for him!'

'No fucking problem', James replied.

Ice Cold Evil

Dwyer was sitting by the sink in his blood-drenched jeans in the Hackney warehouse when O'Connel walked into the room, carrying a sports bag containing Dwyer's change of clothes. He placed the bag in the middle of the room and turned to walk out.

'Is everything ready?' Dwyer asked O'Connel, stopping him in his tracks.

'Yeah. The package is in a brief case next door', O'Connel replied with an air of disapproval.

'What time is it set to go off?' Dwyer asked as he jumped down from the sink.

'Five o'clock. The middle of rush hour', O'Connel replied.

'Five o'clock, middle of Piccadilly Circus, and just in time to catch everyone on their way home', Dwyer announced with satisfaction. 'Perfect.'

Dwyer whistled a tune as he opened the bag and took out a jumper. He pulled it on over his head as he walked out of the door. O'Connel walked over to the sink, filled it up with ice cold water and washed his face. He was still in shock from the execution of Tommy and Frank.

'When will I be rid of this fucking madness?' he asked his reflection looking back at him from the mirror above the sink. Dwyer walked back in with the case and placed it on the surface below the mirror.

'What's the number?' he asked O'Connel, looking at the combination locks below the brief cases catches.

'Two, two, three and two, two, four', O'Connel replied as he dried his face with the towel that hung from the back of the door.

Dwyer had a big smile on his face as he viewed the bomb that he himself designed for the Fifth Brigade's bomb assemblers to put together.

'Five bags of semtex, wired to three PP9 batteries via a timeclock, which also had a parallel circuit wired to an override switch', Dwyer explained as he ran his fingers across the great workmanship of the device.

O'Connel looked at Dwyer with a confused look on his face.

'Why the override switch?'

Dwyer just smiled as he turned to face O'Connel.

'In case I have to manually set off the device in an emergency condition.'

O'Connel felt himself go ice cold at the thought of it as he watched Dwyer unlatch the plastic cover to the override switch.

Dwyer smiled that evil smile as he turned to O'Connel.

'That gives me, the carrier, full control.'

'Dear God help us', O'Connel thought.

35

JIG-SAW PIECES

Warwick didn't eat much of the microwaved breakfast that had been placed in front of him. The scrambled eggs were like rubber, the bacon was cold and "that sausage", he mumbled, "resembles something that may have fallen out of a donkey's backside". When he pierced one of the tinned tomatoes with his knife, the cold juice squirted across his dressing gown. He pushed the plate away in disgust.

After James had taken the breakfast away, Warwick sat drinking his coffee, watching the figures of Allan, Brooks, Dillon and O'Shea who were seated over at the main table, out of ear shot.

'Where the hell am I?' Warwick thought. 'How in God's name am I going to get the fuck out of here and back out on the road?'

He helped himself to a cigarette from the packet of Silk Cut that James Moore had left on the table in front of him. After lighting it, he inhaled his first lungful of smoke and then started to focus his mind on what was important to him right now.

'Jacobs, you piece of shit. Where the hell are you?'

Brooks stood up from the main table and looked over to where Warwick was sitting.

'Oh well, here we go', Brooks said as he stepped away from the main table.

'Sizing' Each Other Up

Warwick eyed Brooks up and down as he slowly walked over. He guessed that Brooks was a few years younger than himself. He noticed the healthy glow Brooks had about him. A face that had obviously been tanned many times before, as

261

the ageing lines around the eyes were hard to notice. It was only the small shades of grey at the side of his head that gave any indication away to his age. His clothes were clean. Clean blue jeans, clean red checkered shirt and clean boots. Warwick hated that in a man. Clean boots? Boots should be dirty, as they are designed to get dirty. Toilet paper isn't designed to always stay clean, eventually it gets dirty. It's the same thing.

Warwick had become so defensive in the last sixty hours that he naturally hunted for any physical weaknesses he could see in this stranger coming towards him. If Warwick had to take this stranger on in a "one to one" fight, could he do it?

'Yeah. I could take this prick on', Warwick told himself.

'How was your breakfast?' Brooks asked him.

'It was shit', Warwick replied as he blew an unwelcoming cloud of smoke into the path of Brooks.

Brooks gave a smile to himself. Not only did he have the attitude of Dillon to contend with, he now had the whole new personality of Warwick to entertain him as well.

Dillon now stood up and walked over towards Warwick. She instantly liked Warwick's attitude. She also liked his rough looks.

Warwick may have had plenty of sleep last night but he still looked as rough as hell to everyone present. The cut above his nose looked raw. Yet Dillon was attracted to Warwick's roughness. He looked like he'd lived. She knew what he had been through in his last year, with the loss of his family. She'd read the file that James Moore had put together. To her Warwick had the face of a survivor.

She sat down at the end of the table, which brought her at a distance of about three feet between Brooks and Warwick. Brooks looked like a young man in front of Warwick. His blue eyes and shiny healthy skin made Warwick look old, rough and tired. But the way Dillon saw this picture was completely different. Brooks looked like a little boy in front of a real man who has lived, survived, and is still living.

Warwick had looked Dillon over from head to toe as she walked over to the table. He agreed with himself that this young lady was beautiful. She had a figure that would send any man's brain into a fantasy of events, if time permitted. But right now for Warwick, time was against him.

'But, by Christ, she's a fine looking woman', Warwick told himself.

O'Shea stayed at the main table as Allan sat down at one of the desks just off to the right of where Warwick, Dillon and Brooks were now sitting. James Moore didn't come back into the main area. He stayed in the kitchen.

'You're probably wondering where you are and who we are?' Brooks started.

Warwick turned to Dillon.

'Give the guy a fucking medal', he joked.

Dillon smiled back at him as he stayed looking at her eyes until Brooks broke the moment.

'I'm Martin Brooks of Section 13 and this is Sinéad Dillon.'

'Of?' Warwick asked, still looking at the bright green eyes of Dillon.

Dillon looked back over at Brooks for a signal as to whether she should say anything yet. Brooks shook his head slightly. She turned back to face Warwick. She really liked this knackered old looking man.

The One Quarry

'Detective Warwick', she began with the softest tone that Brooks had heard her use in the short time he had spent with her.

'Call me Tom', Warwick told her.

'Tom, Mr. Brooks needs to ask you some questions about a man we are trying to trace. After a while it will become apparent which organisation I work for', she told him, before helping herself to one of the Silk Cut cigarettes.

Warwick turned to look at Brooks and then asked him a

question.

'So what the hell is Section 13?'

'It's a section from the Ministry of Defence', Brooks replied.

Warwick closed his eyes for a moment and rubbed his eye lids.

'What the fuck does the Ministry of Defence want with me?' he asked himself.

Then he opened his eyes, startled by a thought in his head. The thought of Jacobs. He took another pull on the cigarette, turned to Brooks and asked.

'Are you after the same fucker that I'm after?'

'Who are you looking for?' Brooks asked him.

'A bastard called Jacobs.'

Brooks stood up and walked back over to the main table.

Warwick turned to Dillon and apologised, 'I'm sorry for my bad language, you'll have to excuse me.'

'Jesus, don't fucking worry about it. You should hear me go when I get pissed off. I can sound like a right fucking gobshite', she softly replied, to which Warwick smiled.

Brooks picked up a photograph and brought it back over and placed it in front of Warwick. It was the picture of Warwick and Jacobs talking at Stansted airport.

'Is that the guy you call Jacobs?' Brooks asked him.

'Yeah', Warwick answered, but he had a confused look on his face. How the hell did they get a picture of him and Jacobs together?

'Why? What do you call him?' he then asked.

There was a moment of silence, as Dillon blew a cloud of smoke across the table. It accidentally went in Brooks' direction. Brooks let out a cough before answering the question.

'That is Tony Dwyer, leader of the IRA's Fifth Brigade.'

Warwick scrunched his eyes in disbelief as he looked back at Brooks.

'Fuck me?' Warwick announced in astonishment.

'Not while there's stray dogs on the street, I'm not', Brooks replied.

36

PEOPLE TO BE SILENCED

Tim Clery stepped out from his front door and took in a lungful of clean fresh Tipperary air. He then turned his head back inside the open doorway.

'Are you still meeting me for a drink later?' he shouted up the hallway to his wife Maureen who was in the kitchen washing the dishes left over from breakfast.

'Yeah. Will you ring me about half an hour before you're ready, and I'll come into town to meet you.'

'Okay, no problem', he replied as he shut the front door and walked away in the direction of his car, thinking about the Sinn Féin meeting that was due to take place that afternoon.

He stopped halfway across the driveway to move his five year old boy's play tractor. Seán was always leaving the red plastic tractor abandoned on the driveway when his mother called him in for dinner.

'I'll end up driving over this thing one day', O'Leary said to himself as he lifted it up with his right hand and placed it on the lawn. 'Then there'll be tears.'

A Cigar Like Any Other

Then he stopped for a moment and stared at the ground. Something was on the ground that shouldn't be there. His face was a picture of confusion as he bent down to pick up the object.

A cigar butt. He lifted the brown cigar butt up close to his eyes and examined it for a moment.

'Who do I know that smokes cigars?' he asked himself. Then he held the butt close to his nose and smelt it. He didn't recognise the strong scented smell.

'Thrown from the window of a car, I'd say', he concluded as

he threw the cigar butt into the ditch in front of him and walked over to the car.

'Bet you it was a Kilkenny car too.' (Kilkenny being the next and nearest county).

He took his keys from his pocket and unlocked the driver's door and placed his hand under the handle.

The house front door opened at the same time and Maureen shouted out to him before she even appeared on the doorstep.

'Tim, mind Seán's tractor, won't you!'

Tim was just about to reply when he lifted up the door handle at the same time.

Maureen walked through the doorway just in time to witness the top half of her husband's body flying through the air and over the ditch. The explosion was deafening. Blood splashed upon the driveway as if it had been tipped from a bucket in the sky. The top half of Clery's body landed in the adjacent field before his legs and waist fell over on the driveway.

The Undertaker looked into his rear-view mirror, smiling at the smoke coming from Clery's driveway. His face went serious again as he turned down the sound of The Doors playing on the car stereo and rolled down the window. Then the smile was back on his face again, brought on by the sound of his achievement. The sound of Maureen Clery, screaming at the top of her voice, acknowledged that Tim Clery had been silenced. He unclicked the top of his Zippo lighter and created the satisfied red end on his new Cuban cigar. He blew the smoke out of the open window as the smile on his face looked like it could stay there indefinitely. As he started the car up and pulled away from the field entrance out onto the N76, he turned up the sounds of Jim Morrison and The Doors.

He had a plane to catch from Cork Airport in two hours. His first call in London would be to Liam Hennessy's old job. O'Connels Building Contractors Ltd. Tim "Tough" Murray and the Undertaker weren't stupid. They knew that the shooting of Liam Hennessy had to be a direct result of the mission that was being carried out in London. So the best place to start would be with Hennessy.

Looking For Action

The Undertaker was looking forward to some field action again. Since becoming Murray's right hand man, moments of action had become few and far between. It was all meetings and executions. No real action. He was looking forward to sticking a bullet in that "stupid bastard" O'Shea.

How could someone be so stupid and so naive to think that they could try and persuade Sinn Féin to condemn the actions of the IRA's South Armagh brigade for the Enniskillen bomb six years ago?

'Jesus Christ?' he laughed out loud at the thought of it.

'And that's for you, you fucking whore', he told the open road in front of him.

By God, the Undertaker was looking forward to meeting Dillon again. He always felt and had always said that it was dangerous to have a woman so high up in the ranks of the IRA. He felt now, like he'd felt in front of Murray a few hours ago, that he had finally proved his point. The Undertaker was old fashioned and set in his ways. He never liked Dillon's cockiness.

He knew the council rated her higher than himself at one stage, due to the rate of successful snipe shots she'd carried out on one of her stays in West Belfast.

'She's a woman, and there's no place for women in the ranks of the IRA', he justified as he shook his head with the smile disappearing from his face.

He was now looking forward to killing both Dillon and O'Shea. If he could take a couple of the "British bastards" along the way as well, all the better.

37

MORE JIG-SAW PIECES

Warwick helped himself to another cigarette as Brooks wrote out something on a piece of paper in front of him. He then turned the piece of paper around and placed it in front of Warwick.

The Fateful Day

"23rd April", the piece of paper read.

'Ring any bells?' Brooks asked him

'Of course it rings a bell, you stupid fucking wanker!' Warwick shouted across the table. How was he going to forget the day his wife and son died.

'I suggest you get to the fucking point', Warwick spat with anger.

'I'm not talking about Helen and Jonathan', Brooks told him. 'Think!'

Warwick stared a long hard look into Brooks as he took a long hard pull on the cigarette. He turned to look at Dillon. She was looking at him with that waiting squint in her eyes. If it wasn't for that innocent looking squint in her eyes, Warwick would have tipped the table over Brooks's head, broken one of the legs off and rammed it up his arse.

Brooks realised now that, with the time it was taking Warwick to think about the other events that had taken place on 23rd April, Warwick wasn't the sharpest tool in the box. Brooks would have to guide him through the motions.

'23rd April. You came very close to catching the robbers who raided the Midland Bank in New Southgate', Brooks reminded him.

'That's right', Warwick remembered as he stared at the ground thinking back on that day. 'I was looking at

photographs, when I ....when I received the phone
call.'

'What photographs?' Dillon asked.

'I was tipped off about the robbery. I sat waiting for the
robbers to come out of the bank. One of the bastards saw me,
went to shoot me but made a run for it instead. I got a
photograph of the robbers driving away. I got a clear fucking
view of the one who was going to shoot me. I was trying to get
a match on the computer.'

Brooks stared at Warwick for a moment.

'Did you get a match?' Allan asked.

'I didn't get that far. I was interrupted by the phone call',
Warwick replied staring at the floor.

He didn't have to say what the phone call was about. The fact
he called it the phone call was enough. A phone call would
have been questionable, but this was the phone call. The call
that changed the rest of his life.

As Brooks stared at Warwick, he wondered if Warwick was
prepared to accept what he was about to be told. Was he ready
to understand what he had got himself involved in?

Brooks waved a cloud of smoke away from his face as he
began.

'We have reason to believe that a robbery took place at
Barclays bank in Enfield on Saturday morning prior to the
bomb going off. I take it you know about the bomb?'

'Yeah, I heard', Warwick pretended with indifference.

We also believe that these were the same people that carried
out the robbery in New Southgate on 23rd April.'

Warwick took another long drag on his cigarette.

'And Jacobs?' he asked.

'Dwyer', Brooks corrected him.

'And Dwyer?'

'Dwyer's behind all of this, that much we know.'

Warwick was looking at Brooks in astonishment.

'The IRA?' Warwick asked as his brain was obviously
trying to catch up on all of the information.

'The IRA', Brooks acknowledged.

'Bloody hell', Warwick announced as he stubbed out his cigarette in the ash tray in front of him before taking a fresh one from the packet and lighting it. After doing so he turned to Dillon.

'IRA?' he asked.

'IRA' Dillon acknowledged as Warwick still didn't catch on, or ask, who Dillon was working for and no one thought of telling him.

Everyone sat in silence to let Warwick absorb the information he was hearing. Brooks now moved the ashtray to one side as he felt the annoying smoke was drifting into his face. He waited for Warwick to look at him before he continued.

'We've seen security footage of you and Dwyer at Stansted airport. We saw the confrontation you had with Dwyer and the way you got away with his bag of cash. Ninety four thousand pounds, to be precise.'

'Where's the bag?' Warwick asked with sudden urgency.

'With forensics. I'm afraid you've lost that my friend.'

'Oh shit!' Warwick shouted as he slammed the table with his hand.

'You didn't expect us to let you walk away with a hundred grand, did you?'

'I couldn't give a fuck for the money, you prick. It's something else that was in the bag', Warwick shouted at him.

'The gun?' Brooks asked, referring to the one that was in the bag.

The Little Black Book

Warwick's eyes lit up. 'My jacket, where's my jacket?' he asked.

'Here', Allan announced as he held it up, from the bag of clothes he was given at the hospital.

'There should be a little black book in the inside pocket', Warwick announced as he remembered the little book that was in the bag.

Allan placed his cigarette down in the ashtray in front of him. Brooks stared on in disbelief. He was the only person present who wasn't smoking. If it wasn't for the intense nature of this interview, he would have complained.

'Here it is', Allan announced as he stood up and walked over to Warwick, handing him the book. Brooks looked over his shoulder to where O'Shea was seated. O'Shea was just stubbing out a cigarette. Brooks shook his head in disbelief and then smelt the sleeve of his shirt. It stank of smoke. He decided that he would bin the shirt when he got home. Disgusting bloody habit, he thought.

Warwick opened Dwyer's black book to the first page. Then he looked at Brooks.

'O'Connels Building Contractors Limited', Warwick said as he handed the book to Brooks. 'If we are to find Jacobs.'

'Dwyer', Brooks once again corrected him.

'If we are to find Dwyer, then we need to talk to O'Connels.'

Suddenly the door swung open from the kitchen.

'We've got two bodies', James announced. 'Two Irish builders in their sixties.'

Brooks looked over to Dillon.

'Bingo!'

'Bingo, fucking bingo!' she replied as she killed her cigarette and stood up.

'Martin, get over there straight away and take Dillon and Warwick with you', Allan began as he stood up before looking over at the quiet O'Shea. 'You can travel with myself and James', he instructed.

'Whoop de fucking doo', O'Shea replied as he blew a lungful of smoke towards Brooks.

38

ON THE QUEEN'S HIGHWAY

The rain had stopped now for the day as the road began to dry, and the sun tried to shine its way through the passing clouds. Every few minutes the sun would gain its success in shining brightly and then minutes of dullness would follow as the sun would sit behind the clouds again, waiting for its next break. This constant weather change caused the temperature to frequently rise and fall, which made the air become a little humid. The sensible drivers on the M11 motorway became a little cautious about their speed and their braking distances, as the humid air can turn a wet road into a dangerous sliding surface.

A Careful Cabbie

One taxi driver drove his cab towards the M25 at a steady pace of sixty five miles per hour with caution of the road's condition. He was also cautious about the passenger he had in the back of his cab.

Ted had been a taxi driver since he was twenty six and stayed as one for the next twenty five years. He was indeed a good driver and, most importantly, he was a sensible one. At intervals of watching the other cars around him he'd glance in his rear-view mirror at the strange man he had just picked up back at Stansted Airport. The passenger hadn't said a word in the ten minutes he had been seated in the back of the taxi. The big six foot two man said only two words when he got into the cab at Stansted. "Enfield, London." It was hard to pick up an accent from only two words. Since then the passenger sat there in silence, stroking his big thick moustache.

Ted had met some strange characters in his twenty five years of driving. He knew that some people who travelled on their own, wanted the company as well as the lift. For those Ted would make small talk or get into a deep conversation with them, depending on the customer's wishes. Others just wanted peace and quiet with little fuss.

A Sullen Passenger

Ted couldn't assess the kind of customer he had in the back of his cab at the moment because, for some strange reason, something didn't feel right about this man. He couldn't put his finger on what it was he didn't like, but he didn't feel comfortable about this man.

Every now and again the man would stare back at Ted when he was looking in his rear view mirror, forcing Ted to look away.

When the passenger was looking out of the window, Ted could see the lines of sweat across the baldness of the man's head.

'It's not the slightest bit warm in here', Ted thought.

Ted had air conditioning installed in his cab a few months ago which made the air in the cab almost perfect, as was the temperature. Yet this strange man was still sweating in the back of the cab. Something just didn't feel right, but Ted didn't want the thought of this passenger in the back of his cab to interfere with his concentration on the road. He decided to ignore his passenger.

Ted had a clean record of driving and a clean record of communication and tidiness. No one smoked in his cab and he always made sure there was no litter on the floor, before he would pick up a punter. He took great pride in his taxi. Not once in his career had a passenger taken down his ID number which was always on display at the front of the cab, and reported him for bad manners, bad driving or annoyance.

As Ted pulled out across the middle lane of the motorway, he heard a clipping sound from within the cab. He didn't recognise the sound or where it had come from, which made him feel uncomfortable. Then he could smell the smoke. He looked into his rear-view mirror to see the passenger sitting in a cloud of smoke, closing the top of his Zippo lighter.

'Sir, this is a non-smoking taxi', Ted informed him.

The passenger didn't reply, he just simply blew a line of smoke in Ted's direction.

'Hey! there's a sign in front of you!' Ted told him as his anger showed from the tone of his voice.

The passenger leaned forward in his seat and asked in his thick heavy Irish accent,

'Is that fucking so?' And with that, he placed his hand through the open separating window, holding a big thick cigar, and stubbed it out into the seat beside Ted. The smell of burning plastic instantly filled the cab.

'RIGHT YOU BASTARD!' Ted shouted in anger as he turned the steering wheel left, taking the taxi across the slow lane and into the hard shoulder.

The passenger just laughed out loud as his body was thrown across the back seat as the cab skidded to a halt on the hard shoulder. Ted was fuming. The hole in the front seat had now grown to approximately seven inches in diameter as the plastic burned even more with the breeze blowing in from the open side window.

Ted flung his door open and walked around the front of the taxi towards the back passenger door. He kicked some loose gravel on the road across the hard shoulder in anger. He didn't care how big this passenger was, for no one had the right to vandalise his pride and joy.

'I'll rip his fucking bollocks off!' Ted cursed as he went to open the back passenger door. Just as he lifted the handle up, the door flung open, catching him square in the face. His nose took the full weight of the door.

Ted's vision was the first thing to go, before his brain acknowleged the pain he was about to endure. His instant reaction was to hold on to his nose that now had blood pouring out from it like running water from an open tap. Now the pain kicked in as he fell backwards towards the ground screaming.

'AAARRRRRRHHHHHH!!!!!!!!!!!!'

Before his body had a chance to hit the ground, the passenger grabbed Ted by his jumper and heaved him back up onto his feet.

'I'll smoke where I fucking well want to!' the passenger told him in his heavy Irish accent.

A Present From Cork

Before Ted could say or do anything, the passenger pulled a sharp object from his back pocket and stabbed Ted twice in the stomach and once again in the heart. He then pushed him down in the ditch at the side of the road. It happened so quickly, Ted didn't even have the chance to scream out or fight back. Before he knew what was happening, he was holding on to the knife that was causing the stinging sensation around his heart, as the hill bumped around his body.

The Undertaker closed the back passenger door of the taxi with his foot, walked around the front to the driver's door, and re-lit his Cuban cigar before getting in behind the wheel.

'Welcome to England', he said to himself as he adjusted the car seat to allow his long legs some comfort.

Ted was lying at the bottom of the muddy hill, holding on to the letter opener that had punctured the life out of him. A letter opener that bore the words, *Cork Airport, Ireland.*

He heard the wheels spinning from above the ditch as the gravel fell upon him in his dying moments.

A Claustrophobic Feeling

Brooks had battled through the mid afternoon traffic with impatience, as he was desperate to get to the location where the two bodies were found in White Hart Lane. His journey had brought him past the *BOOKS Inc* shop in Charing Cross Road where yesterday's bomb had exploded. Another so-called victory for Tony Dwyer and the IRA's Fifth Brigade.

Brooks gave a thought to the man who had died outside the shop on Denmark street, while holding onto his daughter.

'Another life wasted, and one mentally scarred for life. And all for politics and cash', he thought.

He also thought that no journey on earth could be worse than travelling through London in the mid afternoon traffic in humid conditions, mixed with the stuffy London smog, and two smokers puffing away to their heart's content in his car, when all he wanted was some fresh clean air. He was now getting especially annoyed with Dillon as he pulled the car over outside the Burger King bar at her request.

'Why didn't you go to the toilet before we left?' he asked out of frustration, as he really wanted to get to White Hart Lane as soon as possible to investigate the two bodies.

'Can't the lady take a piss without going through the third degree?' Warwick asked from the back seat.

'What lady are you talking about?' Brooks asked, not needing Warwick's attitude on top of everything else.

'Fuck off, you prick!' Dillon replied to Brooks as she leaned across him to take the keys out of the ignition, much to his surprise.

'What do you want them for?' he asked.

'I need my bag from the boot', she informed him as she opened the door to get out.

Brooks was just about to ask why she needed her sports bag to go to the toilet, but decided he didn't want to know.

'Hurry up!' he shouted as he looked at the clock in front of him. He wanted to be at White Hart Lane before three o'clock, like he told Allan. It was now ten to three. He'd be late.

Dillon threw the keys back to Brooks through his open window as she walked towards the Burger King.

'Where the hell is she going now?' Brooks asked Warwick as he watched her walk straight past the Burger King towards a Leisure Centre on the corner, called "Harry Fords".

'Jesus Christ, give her a break, will you!' Warwick replied as he lit another cigarette.

'Oh great', Brooks sighed at the new cloud of smoke that filled the car as he opened his window.

As Dillon walked towards the steps of the entrance to the Leisure Centre she pulled from her pocket the key that O'Shea had given her earlier, and once again looked at the number engraved on it. *231*

Unrelated Thoughts

Brooks and Warwick sat in silence for a couple of minutes as they both watched the London people walking up and down the path beside them.

People window shopping, for clothes or gifts.
People window shopping, for somewhere to sleep.
People making money.
People begging for money.
People high and mighty.
People high on smack.
People drinking coffee from a posh cardboard cup.
People drinking Tenants Pilsner from the can.
People on their lunch.
People out to lunch.
People smelling of perfume and aftershave.
People smelling of piss.
People living and people dying.
All London people.

As he watched the London people walking up and down the footpath, as did Warwick, he found he didn't really know what to say to him. He could tell, just by looking at Warwick earlier, that his bad luck had made him as tough as concrete and as hard as nails. For, as much as Brooks and Dillon were worlds apart, he could relate to her a little because they both worked for organisations that gave them orders, and they followed them without question. But Warwick? He was a loner who'd just had a long run of bad luck, and was in a mess that he shouldn't have been anywhere near.

Finding Focus

'He thinks I've still got the money', Warwick broke the silence.

It came out of nowhere. Warwick hadn't been watching the people walking up and down the footpath at all. He'd just been resting his eyes as he sat there thinking about the mess he was in. Maybe Warwick was in a mess, but he was focused.

'Maybe he's not that stupid after all. For I didn't give that a second thought', Brooks thought to himself.

'I know he's meant to be fighting for the fucking IRA or whatever', Warwick began, waving his hand across the air in front of his face as he said the letters, IRA, showing that he didn't care for them one way or another. He'd obviously had more than enough to worry about in his lifetime, let alone other people's wars.

'At the end of the day all he's about is the fucking money. You think they robbed this bank on Saturday before they bombed it, for whatever cause or fucking bullshit they told everyone, but at the end of the day it's just about the fucking money, isn't it?'

Brooks had to hide a smile to himself as he listened to Warwick talking. He wished that Dillon was here to listen to this. To Brooks, Warwick's ignorance of the IRA had such spirit to it, it was beautiful.

'And all the bullshit that he gave me about Helen and Jonathan.' Warwick stopped for a moment as his eyes went red, as if he was about to cry from the anger.

'That fucker gave me a beating and gave me enough fucking rope to hang myself. Yet the only time he dropped his fucking guard was when I took the bag of money away from him at the airport', Warwick whispered, as dimples began to show in his chin.

Was the big tough man about to cry?

No.

'All he's about is the fucking money', Warwick concluded as the spit sprayed from his lips, due to his anger towards

Dwyer. He took a hard pull on his cigarette as Brooks opened his window a little further and thought about something that Warwick had just said.

'What did Dwyer say about Helen and Jonathan', Brooks asked with curiosity.

Warwick looked at Brooks, narrowing his eyes, as he had to think about what Dwyer had said to him.

'It's not so much what the bastard said, it's the fact that he knew they were dead. How the fuck would he know that?' he asked Brooks.

'Well he only had to look at a newspaper to find out, didn't he?' Brooks replied after a little thought.

'But it wasn't in any newspaper. The Police force kept it out of the news for some reason. They never told me why, but they did. So how did he know?'

Brooks didn't reply, as he felt a new twist had been added to the puzzle. He looked over to the busy footpath as he thought

'Why did the Police force keep it out of the news about Warwick's wife and son? Why would the news of their deaths be a threat to the Police force? When Warwick was in the middle of his bereavement, it wouldn't cross his mind to ask why.'

For where Warwick's mind shone with honesty and simplicity, Brooks's shone with intelligence.

'He's just about the fucking money, nothing more and nothing less. Don't you agree?' Warwick asked him.

Brooks didn't reply as he sat there staring into space thinking about something.

'Don't you agree?' Warwick asked again.

'Can I have a look at that book again?' Brooks asked him, referring to the one that Warwick had found in Dwyer's bag. Warwick took it from his inside pocket and handed it to Brooks.

Brooks opened it, looked at the first page that bore Dwyer's hand writing, before turning to the next page. Then he looked out of the window again in deep thought.

'Sergeant Davis', Brooks said, after a few moments of

silence. 'I take it you know Sergeant Davis?'

'Yeah, I know the prick', Warwick confirmed as he opened his window to throw out his finished cigarette.

'He was in the Moon Under Water pub on Saturday night before you showed up. He was in there talking to Dwyer', Brooks told him as he handed the book back to Warwick with the second page opened.

Warwick looked at the page as he suddenly realised what Brooks was getting at.

    Mr. Davis, 4k cash.

It was there in blue and white. Warwick's face turned to anger.

'I knew there was something not right about that fucking wanker.'

Dillon opened the passenger door and sat back down in the seat.

'Better?' Warwick asked from the back seat as his mood quickly changed in her presence.

'Much better, thank you for asking', Dillon replied as she threw the sports bag down between her legs.

'He still doesn't know that she's IRA', Brooks thought, as he could sense a little chemistry between them in the way they talked to each other.

It didn't bother him that Dillon had taken a shine to Warwick, because he knew he'd eventually have to kill her. He wasn't sure at the moment as to whether he would do the same with Warwick, but he was damn sure that he would have to kill her.

'Well I'm pleased to hear that', Warwick answered to her reply, with a yawn. As he did so he felt the cold sore that had developed on his lower lip. His body started to feel weak. On top of all his injuries he was starting to feel really run down and stressed out.

How much more was his body willing to take?

How much more was his mind able to handle?

'I wonder if she wears a G-String?' he thought as he looked at Dillon's reflection in the rearview mirror.

39

THE HAVOC OF A FOX

Brooks drove across the other side of White Hart Lane as the sun made it's way through the clouds, making it suddenly warm in the car. Both Dillon and Warwick opened their windows, much to Brooks' approval, so the car could receive some fresh air. He drove the car up to the gate of a huge wasteland beside an electrical distributors which seemed to be the only building on this stretch of the road. A police car that was blocking the entrance, pulled out of Brooks' way as he was waved through by a policeman when he showed his M.o.D. badge.

Shut Mouths

Once inside the boundaries of the wasteland, he drove in the direction of where Peter Allan stood leaning on the bonnet of his car, sarcastically looking at his watch as he watched Brooks' car approaching him. Brooks turned to Dillon as he stopped his car about ten metres in front of Allan's.

'You know the score by now, I take it?'

'Keep my mouth shut in case anyone hears my accent', Dillon confirmed with annoyance.

'And what am I expected to do?' Warwick asked from the back seat.

'Exactly the same', Brooks replied before opening the door to greet Allan.

'Fucking great', Warwick commented. The truth was, he was thankful for the rest and a bit of time to himself with the beautiful Dillon.

O'Shea was seated in the passenger seat of Allan's car as he watched Brooks get out. He looked at Dillon. She looked back at him with disgust and then turned away. He punched the dashboard in anger. This was meant to be his mission to run. That was how the IRA's Southern Division had set it up. He was to run the operation, with Dillon carrying out the ground duties only. But she now seemed to be closer with the Brits than she was with O'Shea.

'You stupid little fucking bitch!' O'Shea said through his gritted teeth as he looked over at Dillon who was looking down at something in her lap.

'If only you knew the truth about me.'

He thought back to when they were standing on the balcony of Brooks' place that morning. Back to the moment of when he was going to tell her that he thought that there was a strong chance that he may be her father.

'If only you knew', he said as he looked down at his own lap.

He had great plans for this operation and he had great plans for himself and Dillon. But it didn't take long for those British bastards to hijack the whole operation.

'You're late!' Allan commented.

'Where's James?' Brooks asked, ignoring Allan's comment as he noticed O'Shea sitting alone in the car.

'I decided it best if he stayed back at base in case we need some quick info', Allan replied.

Death in A Tent

'Fair enough. What have we got then?' Brooks asked.

'Two men, early sixties, brutally murdered about two hours ago', Allan informed him as he took a sip from the plastic cup in his hand that was filled with black coffee, no sugar.

'An execution, do you think?' Brooks asked as he looked around the wasteland, remembering that once it had a busy clothes factory working upon it, which shut in the recession of the late eighties.

There were six police cars parked in the middle and three others blocking each entrance to the area.

'Oh, no doubt about it', Allan confirmed as he walked towards a white large tent in the middle of the wasteland, followed by Brooks.

As Brooks followed him, he wondered why there were always so many policemen required at a murder scene. Surely their job was the prevention of wrongdoing and protection of the law. Yet in the middle of this wasteland he counted nine police cars, twice as many policemen, and six plain clothes officers who were doing nothing more than stretching their legs from their break at the station office. Four uniformed officers stood talking and joking while drinking from their plastic cups within feet of the white tent.

'Why?' Brooks thought, shaking his head in disgust as he walked past them, and he made damn sure they heard him tut. It silenced them, for they knew of his importance.

The tent was about ten feet high and fifteen feet wide, with an opening at the back away from the main road behind them. As Brooks approached the tent he could smell the death that was calling out to him from within those white soft walls. It wasn't a smell of decomposed bodies, it was a strange, cold, almost herbal smell of nothingness. In truth, it was his brain preparing him for the view of death. It was something that he had become so used to in his job. But anyone who deals with death in one way or another on an almost daily basis, knows that the brain refuses to become immune to death. If it doesn't cause the body to become sick or go into a state of shock, it will play with the mind's remaining senses. And, with smell being the strongest, it becomes the brain's obvious choice of guard. Nature has taught the brain to fear death. For death is not a normal everyday occurrence, no matter whether you're a doctor, a funeral director or a murderer.

Brooks always considered himself to have a good hold on death, but his brain secretly feared it.

'Some kids that were coming over here to play football, found the bodies', Allan informed him as they turned the corner of the tent towards the entrance.

'Have they been interviewed yet?' Brooks asked as he took in a deep breath of the almost herbal air, preparing himself for the sight of death.

'Yeah, they're down at the local station now with their guardians.'

Brooks went ice cold with the view that confronted him when he looked up from the ground. The ground within the tent was dark red. Blood.

Before they could go too far into the tent, they had to put on plastic gloves and plastic covers for their shoes. There were four people from forensics inside the tent, going over every inch within the white soft walls. They looked like space cadets in their white disposable overalls. One was taking picture after picture of every inch within the tent. Every piece of the ground had to be brushed over with a fine tooth comb.

Set To Go Off

Two bodies, uncovered, were laid out on the ground behind a fairly new red Ford Escort van.

'Have forensics moved the bodies already?' Brooks asked feeling annoyed, not so much at the fact that he thought the bodies were found in the back of the van but from the fact that his brain was instructing him to feel like that.

It was another way of protecting itself from death.

'No. Nothing has been moved. The bodies were dumped behind the van, attached to a trip wire', Allan told Brooks as he walked around the left hand side of the bodies to where a fishing line lay on the floor.

Brooks made his way around the other side of the bodies, ignoring them for the moment, to peer underneath the back bumper where Allan was pointing. He was weary of all the blood on the floor below him but, so far, refused to look closely at the bodies until he could take everything in around him. He carefully crouched down and looked under the bumper of the van to see a lump of plasticine the size of his fist, with a red wire coming out of the left hand side and a black wire coming out of the right. Adjacent to it was a PP9 battery which was taped to an old light switch. Brooks had a confused look on his face as he looked back up at Allan.

'Set to go off on discovery of the bodies', Allan confirmed. 'Luckily, the line broke from the device.'

'With only enough Semtex to blow the van', Brooks responded as he finally looked at the naked body nearest to him. It was Frank's body.

Allan was looking at Brooks with a confused look on his face.

'Are you sure?' he asked, trying to figure out why there would only be enough explosives to burn the van.

Brooks didn't reply as he studied the body. He noticed the clear shaped hole in the victim's left knee cap.

'A drill?' he thought.

He then noticed the two bullet holes in the large stomach.

'Dwyer wanted the bodies to be found', Brooks said as he looked back to the hole in the knee cap. 'The explosion would have only burned the bodies, it wouldn't have destroyed them. We still would have seen this', he said as he took a pencil from his top pocket and poked the end of it through the hole in the knee cap without even touching the sides.

'He wanted us to find these bodies. To him this is a work of art. This was definitely done with a drill.'

Brooks then looked away from the knee cap to the other body. Tommy's body. In noticing the dried blood that resembled a picture of a red stream that once pumped from the body's shoulder, he asked: 'What's with the shoulder?'

'Found half a screwdriver in there apparently', Allan replied.

'A screwdriver. A drill. How much more of the building trade connection is he trying to give us?' Brooks asked no one in particular as he looked back at the drilled out knee cap.

Allan looked at the van as he thought over everything Brooks was telling him.

'There must be something in the van then. He didn't have time to clean it down properly, that's why the fucker was

trying to torch it', Allan declared as he made his way over to
the forensics man who was standing at the passenger side of
the van, writing on his clip board.

Important Normal Things

'What was found inside the van?' he asked as the forensics
man looked up at him.

The man was in his early sixties. He had been in his trade all
his working life. There was no urgency about him, especially
compared to that of Allan. He slowly removed his glasses,
coughed to clear his throat, and then began in his polite
accent and at his own polite pace.

'Well, on the human tissue connection side of things, we
are quite fortunate to have encountered a variety of
findings..........'

'Right, hold on a fucking second!' Allan rudely interrupted
him. 'Normal. What normal things did you find?'

The man paused for a moment, looked back at Allan with
disgust at his attitude, placed his glasses back on again and
looked back at his clipboard. His politeness disappeared as he
read quickly from the top of his page.

'The dashboard contains fifteen different types of
fingerprints, the ashtray was packed and a plastic bag on the
floor was full of rubbish.'

'What about the glove compartment?' Allan asked.

'Collection notes.' As the man said it, he lifted a clear
plastic bag from the bonnet and handed it to Allan.

Allan ripped the bag open with impatience and looked at the
first of the three pink collection notes. They were from an
electrical wholesaler in Wood Green. Allan looked at the top
left hand side of the note.

O'Connel Building Contractors Ltd..

'YES, FUCKING YES!' Allan shouted as he removed his plastic
shoe covers and gloves. 'Come on Martin!'

Allan walked out of the entrance before Brooks had a chance

to say anything. Brooks ran out after him, removing his plastic shoe covers and throwing them down next to Allan's.

'What have you got?' he asked of Allan as he removed the gloves.

Allan didn't turn around as he spoke to Brooks, he just kept walking to his car. He held the pink slips up and said:

'Collection notes for O'Connels Building Contractors. I can nail that fucker straight away.'

He was delighted at his finding of the collection notes. 'I'll sink the son of a bitch.'

'Who?' Brooks asked out of frustration to Allan's impatience to slow down and explain himself properly.

'O'Connel, that's who.'

'And what about Dwyer?' Brooks asked as he finally caught up with Allan enough to be walking beside him.

Brooks was now getting annoyed with the whole situation as he snatched the slips from Allan. This stopped Allan in his tracks. Brooks looked at the order number in the top right hand side.

B/17649/1007

Brooks began to smile as he took his mobile phone from his pocket. He tapped two buttons before holding the phone to his ear. As he waited patiently for someone to answer the ringing tone at the other end, he looked at Allan who now looked as if he had been quickly knocked off track. Brooks gave him a look that was almost sympathetic. He felt that he had suddenly taken the light from Allan's discovery.

'We all know about O'Connels, and after we've found Dwyer, we'll deal with it. But, right now, we want Dwyer, remember.' Brooks held the pink slip up and pointed to the order number.

B/17649/1007

'The B at the front refers to the order pad that the number has been lifted from. The next five numbers are the actual order number.'

He allowed a moment of silence to pass between them before

he got to the point.

'Those last four digits are a job number. If we can trace where that job is, we'll find out where this van came from. Then we'll have the place where Dwyer carried out the execution.'

Recognition of Style

'How can you be so sure that it was Dwyer that carried out the execution?' Allan asked, as he felt Brooks was going a little too fast for him.

'There's too much detail for it to be anyone else. The drill? The screwdriver? Too much work went into those executions for it to be someone else within the Fifth Brigade. Someone else would have just shot them and dumped them. Dwyer executed them in style. He carried out the executions because he's the one trying to prove a point to the rest of the brigade.' He leaned forward a little closer to Allan as he held the slip between them.

'And he doesn't know that we have this slip, remember. So we now have the upper hand.'

Allan was motionless as he looked at Brooks. Brooks turned away as he spoke into his mobile phone.

'James, I need you to run a check on an account for me. The company is O'Connel Building Contractors Ltd.'

Allan's smile disappeared as he looked at the excitement on the face of Brooks.

'I don't like the sound of this', Allan told himself, as he could sense a Brooks idea coming on.

'This mission shouldn't be happening', he quietly reminded himself as he thought of the Prime Minister for a brief moment.

He looked over to his own car where O'Shea was still sitting in the passenger seat. He then looked over to Brooks' car, noticing Dillon seated in the passenger seat smoking, and Warwick asleep in the back. As he looked at all three of them he felt himself go a little cold on the inside.

'They will all have to be eliminated once this mission is complete', he thought as he looked over to the boot of his car, thinking about the item he had stored away in the back.

He should have handed the item over to forensics instead of holding onto it.

Brooks closed the flip on his mobile phone.

'James is going to get back to me with the information', he announced with delight.

Allan looked out to the main road, rubbing his chin, knowing that he may regret showing Brooks the item he had in the back of his car. But if Brooks was going to go the whole way with this mission, it was sure to come in useful.

'I've got something to show you', Allan slowly informed him.

40

THE EVIL WITHIN AND WITHOUT

Dwyer sat by the open window of O'Connell's office in Muswell Hill, North London, resting his feet on the desk in front of him, smiling with a contented look on his face. It had been an hour since they had dumped the two bodies in White Hart Lane and, with everything else that was taking place at the moment, that made him happy. It was one less thing for him to worry about.

Exhilaration

Dwyer loved the hours that passed before a bombing and, with this one being so special, it made the passing hours even more enjoyable. O'Connel was sitting in the main chair at his desk, smoking and watching the contented Dwyer.

'Don't you feel the slightest bit nervous?' O'Connel asked, as he couldn't understand the relaxation of a man who was about to carry a bomb into the heart of London.

'I feel great', Dwyer replied as he took a sip of whiskey from the glass that he cradled in his right hand.

'Why?' O'Connel asked with a frown of confusion.

Dwyer looked away from the open window to O'Connel as he began to speak.

'I'm about to change people's lives forever. People I know and people I don't.'

O'Connel knew full well who Dwyer meant by saying people he knew. He meant O'Connel. For he was getting rich off the back of Dwyer's mayhem. He also meant the IRA's Fifth Brigade. Dwyer studied the colour of the whiskey as he gave his thoughts to the IRA.

'I'm about to tighten the fist of the resistance in Northern Ireland.'

He stopped briefly to down the last of the whiskey from his

glass as he thought about the cause for which he was about to kill. It wasn't a cause he particularly believed in one way or another, but it was a cause that fascinated him all the same.

'The Englishman travels far and wide', Dwyer continued, 'to make business by exporting shit and importing the best. But everywhere he goes, he is asked about the embarrassment of Northern Ireland. America would love to put a sail on Ireland and bring it across the Atlantic, not to make it American but to protect it from his friend, the Englishman. Because the Englishman treats Northern Ireland like it's bastard child.'

Universal Guilt

He placed his glass on the table to allow himself a small cough and a smile before continuing.

'And what of the people I don't know?' he asked out loud as he looked back out of the window.

'Why can't we spare them? Why can't we give a warning on this one?' O'Connel asked as he felt he had seen enough killing for one day.

'Why should we do that?' Dwyer asked with that tone that indicated that he wanted to debate the issue.

'Because we're killing the innocent', O'Connel tried to reason.

'INNOCENT? WHAT FUCKING INNOCENT?' Dwyer turned to look at O'Connel again as he shouted, causing the veins to bulge around his forehead.

'There's no such thing as fucking innocence. If people wish to turn their backs on a political situation that they don't understand, then they arc just as guilty for fuelling the situation's resistance. For their ignorance only makes the British propaganda machine even stronger.'

Dwyer leaned forward in his chair as he looked at O'Connel and smiled.

'And for that they will die.'

O'Connel wiped the sweat from his brow as Dwyer leaned

forward in his chair.

'Don't insult my intelligence by expecting me to pity the weak and stupid that consider themselves to be innocent. They only class themselves as innocent to hide their own shame and stupidity. They are just as fucking guilty as I am.' Dwyer leaned back in his chair as he looked out of the window again.

'It's a wonder that ordinary people don't carry a suicide note around with them in their pocket for the amount of ignorance they possess.'

Dwyer took his packet of Marlboro Lights from his pocket as he stared out of the window, thinking about the innocent. O'Connel said nothing as they both sat in silence, letting the minutes pass between them.

'Fuck 'em', Dwyer concluded as he stood up. 'Right, let's get going. We'll head back to Hackney to pick up the case and then I'll take the train to Piccadilly.'

Dwyer lit his cigarette as he headed for the door. O'Connel didn't move for the moment as he sat there thinking over the speech that Dwyer had just given about ordinary people. He hated the hours that passed before a bombing. He hated the guilt he had to endure, if anyone innocent was ever caught in the blast. But there was to be no warning on this one. Killing was the object of this mission. A mission he was financing.

'Come on!' Dwyer called back to him from the other side of the door.

The Sense of Smell

Warwick opened his eyes from the short nap that his mind was thankful for. As he opened them he was aware of two things. Firstly he was aware of the herbal smell that filled the car and, secondly, he felt really cold. He looked up to see Dillon sitting sideways in the passenger seat with the door open and her legs hanging out. He looked out of the window to see that the sun was once again trapped by the passing clouds. Suddenly he found this herbal smell making him think of his wife Helen in the way that he did two nights ago in the toilets at the service station.

He closed his eyes and thought about the days when he and Helen were just dating. Helen was a hippy chick who loved the music of The Doors, Mamas & The Papas, Jimi Hendrix and The Grateful Dead. His own music was the likes of Zakk Zombie, The Sex Pistols, Discharge and The Clash. All bands that he had seen in their prime. He'd seen Zakk Zombie seven times, right up to his last tour of 1978. The only hippy music he liked was that of Zakk Zombie from his Toby James days. Helen's music was filled with love, peace and happiness. His music was anarchy, rage, blood, sweat and honesty. Oh and Zakk Zombie.

Warwick preferred to sit with a couple of beers, listening to the sounds of Zakk Zombie, before moving on to some whiskey with The Sex Pistols and Discharge. But when Helen was around, it was The Carpenters and Dolly Parton. Before they took on their roles of parenthood, Helen would smoke marijuana while chilling out in front of the television, or reading a book while listening to her music.

He opened his eyes as he now recognised the smell. Marijuana. That sweet herbal smell brought back the voice of Karen Carpenter singing through her nose, asking the postman to hang on a second.

A Sense of Relaxation

Warwick smiled as he looked at Dillon smoking the roll up. It was the one she had prepared for herself yesterday. The thoughts of Helen left him now as he found himself looking at Dillon in a way he hadn't looked at another woman in years. He found her to be beautiful and sexy.

'Are you going to share that thing or are you going to keep it to yourself?' he asked, surprising her.

She was surprised by two things. Firstly by the fact that he was now awake and secondly at how, being a policeman, he was willing to have a puff on what the ignorant public regard as the "killer weed". She turned around and looked at him with a surprised look on her face. Then she handed the roll up to him.

'Knock yourself out!' she told him.

'I will, thanks.'

Dillon had a great big smile on her face as she sat there, watching Warwick inhale the illegal susbstance.

As Warwick felt the heat of the smoke fill his lungs he looked back at Dillon to see her red glazed eyes smiling back at him. For the first time in days his heart slowed down, giving him the great sensation of relaxation. A smile seemed to grow upon his face without his control, as the skin beneath his eyes felt like it was moving up to say hello to the lines upon his forehead. His cheeks were beginning to hurt already, as he seemed to be pulling a smile that his face would have thought impossible to do six months ago.

'Fucking hell!' he laughed.

'Easy, tiger', Dillon said to him. 'Take it nice and easy .... and pass that thing back here ... okay.'

'No problem', he said as he took one more puff from it and passed it back to Dillon. As he sat there for a moment smiling, looking over to Allan and Brooks, who were still standing in the middle of the wasteland, he asked Dillon the question.

'So, you never did tell me, which organisation do you work for?'

Truth, The Leveller

Dillon took three more pulls on the roll up before throwing the dead end of it away into a puddle of water a couple of feet away.

The smile that she wore disappeared. She took the packet of cigarettes from her pocket and extracted one. She always needed a cigarette after smoking some good marijuanna. It seemed to level things out for her. As she did so, Warwick did the same before opening his door and resting his feet upon the ground of the wasteland.

'The Provisional Irish Republican Army, Southern Division', she finally answered him.

There she said it. She finally said it. But she wished she hadn't.

She never thought she'd see the day that she'd be ashamed to say it. Warwick seemed to be the only person that she had met on this mission that she found to be on her level. And now she felt that was gone.

The moment passed in silence before she turned around to see Warwick staring at the ground speechless.

'Well, say something, even if it's bollocks', she said with an air of frustration.

She clearly wasn't going to get to enjoy any buzz from the marijuanna, as this situation was clearly putting a stop to that. Well, at least for a little while anyway. Then the delayed relaxation would kick in.

'Well, what do you want me to say?' he asked her, raising his shoulders up to show he wasn't able to answer the fact that she worked for the IRA, one way or another.

'Do you want me to praise you or condemn you?' he inquired with a look on his face that clearly stated that he didn't seem to care one way or another. And it wasn't the marijuana doing this because that had quickly worn off him. Although he still felt relaxed, he knew exactly what he was saying. From two puffs of the roll up his buzz quickly went, but the relaxation stayed intact as his body openly welcomed that feeling.

'If I sit here and try to condemn you, then you're just going to go into a big fucking speech of how you're protecting your Emerald Isle and all that shit and, believe you me, I'm not interested'

Dillon wanted to scream back at him but couldn't help but admire his honesty. The tone of his voice was strong but not overpowering. It made the listener want to listen. It wasn't a voice of dictation. It was a voice of truth.

'I leave all the political bullshit arguments to the likes of him', Warwick said, pointing over his shoulder with his thumb to where Brooks was still standing with Allan.

'I'm sure you have a great argument and bloody good reasons for doing what you do. But, believe you me, not one bit of it is of any fucking interest to me', he said with genuine friendliness.

Dillon sat in silence as she realised that she was in the presence of a person that had a lot more important things in his life to worry about than the situation in Northern Ireland.

'Why are you after Dwyer?' he asked.

Dillon paused for a moment before she answered. She felt she needed her answer to be as unpolitical as possible.

'He's been carrying out a bombing campaign that the IRA have never agreed to, and they want it stopped', she replied as she blew the smoke from her lungs over the red end of her cigarette.

Warwick looked at her, admiring her beauty. He stayed looking at her until she turned to look at him.

'You didn't answer my question', he pointed out to her. 'Why are you after Dwyer?' he asked, fixing his eyes on hers until she had to look away.

The Truth of An Answer

Dillon looked at the ground thinking of how she would word her answer. How could she word her answer? How could she say she hated the British. How could she say she hated the fact that some British bastard was bombing London and taking money for it that should be going to the IRA. For that was what she truly felt. But how could she put that into words. She turned to look at him, almost helpless. She needed some time before she could answer.

'Why are you after Dwyer?' she asked, trying to buy some time.

Warwick took in a good lungful of smoke as he looked at the ground in front of him. He stayed still for the next minute. His face was scrunched up with concentration. How could he explain to a beautiful terrorist his motive for wanting to find Dwyer. He went to speak and then paused for a moment longer before he began his explanation.

'Some years ago, when I was making a bollocks of my front garden with the lawn mower, my young boy gave me the fright of my life. He was playing with his toys on a playmat on the driveway. My wife was at work, so I was doing my chores as well as minding the young one. He never strayed out onto the pavement or near the road because he knew I'd shout at him with my awful bellowed bloody voice. I never once hit Jonathan but by Christ I'd shout at him, if I thought he was going to do something where he might hurt himself.'

Warwick paused for a moment as he took a pull on his cigarette and looked across the wasteland in front of him. He played over the events of that day in his mind before he transferred it into words.

'Like a fool I mowed over my electrical extension lead which caused the fuse to trip in the house fuseboard. I went back inside the house to the socket outlet and removed the plug; then I went to the electrical fuseboard and reset the trip switch. As soon as that was taken care of, I went back outside to   check   on   Jonathan......................to   find that.............................he was gone from his playmat.'

Dillon was hanging on to his every word. Warwick was staring at a stone on the ground in front of him, with a frown on his face.

'I ran back inside to check downstairs; I ran back out to the footpath; I looked out on the road and I ran back upstairs to check if my two year old boy had made it up a fucking flight of stairs in less than twenty seconds behind my back. I even checked the back garden, even though the back door to the garden was locked. My brain went absolutely mental; I ran like mad to the shops at the end of my road to see if a two year old boy had walked along the footpath by himself.'

He stopped for a smoke and then focussed his eyes on the same stone again.

'My brain didn't think about the fact that maybe someone had taken him from the driveway while I was messing around with the electrics indoors. My brain refused to let that thought enter my head.'

He looked up at her for a couple of seconds.

'I just kept looking, to occupy my mind to stay away from the thought that, maybe, some sick fucker might have my boy.'

He looked back down again.

'But after five minutes that all changed. I could almost picture some sick fucking bastard driving down the road with my boy rolling around in his dark car boot. Driving him away to some seedy fucking room somewhere to do some sick inhuman fucking things to an innocent young boy.'

This was it for Warwick. He was relaxed but a tear began to fall down his cheek. Dimples were scattered around his chin. He wasn't shedding tears without good reason. These were tears of hate.

'My mind was filled with some sick fucking visions, I can tell you.'

Dillon now looked at the ground, trying to understand what Warwick must have been going through that day.

'Finally I heard him crying in my garage. I'd left the door wide open and he'd walked in there, looking for me.'

A Social Sickness

Warwick flicked his finished cigarette out into the cold wind.

'To find him was the greatest relief I've ever known. But I couldn't get those visions out of my head. I even had to go and speak to a fucking shrink about it afterwards. And do you know what she told me?'

Dillon didn't get the opportunity to have a guess.

'If parents lose their children when they're shopping, or in a crowd, or at a park............. it is a natural reaction after five minutes of looking.......................... to picture them being hurt by some sick fucking bastard.'

He looked at Dillon.

'That's the kind of sick fucking piece of shit of a world that we live in. If you can't find your child after five minutes, there's a good chance that a pervert is having a fucking field day with them somewhere.'

Dillon went pale with that thought alone.

'How the fuck can you..... or him..........' Again he pointed over his shoulder with his thumb at Brooks. '......................expect me to give a fuck about the IRA, Northern Ireland, bank robberies and bombs, when our own society is completely overrun by sick fuckers?'

Dillon looked back at him for a moment with that helpless look on her face, as she really didn't know what to say. Warwick wiped the tear that had quietly made its way down his cheek, before he continued.

'Last Friday I was called to a restaurant in Southgate, to investigate a suicide. A twelve year old boy, called Billy Hopkirk had taken his own life in the middle of a packed restaurant.'

He looked at Dillon as he continued.

'Your friend and mine, Dwyer, was sitting with Billy Hopkirk until two minutes before it happened. He left the restaurant without paying the bill, obviously knowing full well what young Billy was going to do.'

Warwick raised his hand to the roof of his nose to examine the cut that Dwyer had inflicted upon him on Saturday. As he did so, he looked back down at the stone that had somehow helped him to concentrate.

'Dwyer also knows something about the death of my wife Helen and my son Jonathan and I want to know what that is. And I also want to know how he helped Billy Hopkirk commit suicide.'

He raised his hands up in the air, composing a look of non interest as he turned to Dillon.

'You will have to excuse my fucking ignorance, but I couldn't give a flying fucking shit about the money that

Dwyer's stealing from banks or the IRA, and I don't give a shit for the IRA or their so-called fucking struggle.'

He looked out across the open wasteland.

'I just find the fact that a normal parent has to endure the thought that some sick fucking pervert could be with their child after five minutes of them being missing, a little more important than cash and politics.'

Dillon was going to interrupt him with her viewpoint but decided against it and allowed him to continue.

'Dwyer played a part in the death of Billy Hopkirk's innocence and I'm going to find out why. And I'm going to find out what he knows about my family .... even if it kills me.'

41

FINDING ENTRANCES AND EXITS

The Undertaker sat in his car which was parked just off the Muswell Hill Circus. He was eating a bacon sandwich which he'd obtained from Old Joe's Cafe around the corner. Upon making his way back to the taxi from Old Joe's, he found himself trying to assess his impression of this North London town. On noticing all the litter blowing around the street, and the smell of urine that came from a doorway he had to walk past, he summed it all up in four simple words. 'What a shit hole!'

An Electrical Undertaker!

After finishing his sandwich he took his half smoked Cuban cigar from the ash tray and re-lit it. As he did so he watched Dwyer and O'Connel leave O'Connels Building Contractors office from across the road. Of course, he wasn't aware that he had just seen the one and only Tony Dwyer, otherwise he would have put a bullet in his head there and then and saved himself the bother of trying to find Dillon and O'Shea. For he was sure the Brits would dispose of those two once Dwyer had been taken care of. He also wasn't aware of the fact that he had just seen Peter O'Connel.

After watching the two men get into the red Escort van and drive off in the direction of Muswell Hill Circus, he stepped out of the taxi, made his way across the road, and around to the back of the building.

The Undertaker's entrance to the storage area of the office was an easy one. When O'Connel had the burglar alarm system installed to his premises he paid more attention to the computers and files in his office than he did to the plant and materials he kept stored out the back. The Undertaker only had to pick the lock to get inside the store area and, now he was inside, all he had to do was locate the riser cupboard, find the alarm panel and override the infer-red sensors that overlooked O'Connel's offices.

Alarm panels were a hobby of the Undertaker. He knew how to override the tamper switch on about ninety five percent of the ones sold and installed in the UK and Northern Ireland. It was a hobby he'd picked up in his old day job as an electrician.

As he stood in the middle of the store room he admired the ladders, drills, bricks, the box of electrical accessories and generators that were scattered around the stores. He had a frown on his face as he looked at the box of electrical accessories.

'Now that's a strange stock to be holding for your average building contractor.'

He lightly laughed to himself as he took his zippo lighter out from his pocket and lit his half smoked Cuban cigar. He noticed the door to the riser cupboard of the building in the corner of the storage area. He then noticed the lock on the door. He let out a laugh and a lungful of smoke at the same time as he took a flick knife from his inside pocket and flicked out the thin shiny blade.

'Bingo!' he proclaimed as he took in a lungful of Cuban smoke before preparing to do his work on the door.

Men With A Mission

Brooks made his way back over to his car as Allan's car pulled out onto White Hart Lane away from the wasteland. He was thinking about the news that James had just phoned him back with. A building site in Hackney and the job number refers to the refurbishment work taking place at the site's main warehouse.

'It's showtime!' he said to himself as he neared the car.

Warwick looked up at Brooks and noticed the sports bag he was carrying. It looked like the one he had taken from Dwyer at Stansted Airport on Saturday.

'The lying son of a bitch!' Warwick proclaimed on seeing the bag and thinking about what Allan had said to him back at the base in Hayes.

Allan had obviously held onto the bag of money instead of handing it over to forensics like he said he had done.

'Look, whatever you think, this is our key to getting to Dwyer', Brooks reasoned.

'Hey, I'm not fucking stupid. I can fucking well see that.' Warwick was so angry he banged his head off his car door's frame as he leapt out to stand up in front of Brooks.

'I don't give a fucking shit for that money inside. All I'm interested in is using it to get to that wanker as well. That's all I've been interested in from the fucking start.'

Warwick rubbed the top of his head, giving himself a chance to calm down a little bit as he continued talking, but in a reasoning manner.

'I just hate being fucking lied to, that's all. That's bullshit!'

Brooks said nothing for a moment as he stood there looking at the tired beaten face of Warwick. He watched Warwick rubbing his head from the clumsy knock it took as he stood up from the car.

What would he do with Warwick when this mission was complete? How would be able to kill such an honest man who had experienced more hardship than anyone else he had ever known?

Brooks looked at Dillon for a moment and, on noticing her blood shot eyes, he asked 'Are you tired?'

'A little', she acknowledged, trying to hide the little buzz she was now feeling from the marijuana.

He then turned to look at Warwick who was looking over at the same stone he was admiring earlier.

Brooks asked him the question to which he needed the answer. An answer that could take this mission to its finale.

'Are you ready to face Dwyer?'

Warwick looked back at him as hate moved around his eyes.

Then he slowly nodded his head as he kept his eyes on those of Brooks.

Dillon stood up out of the car on hearing Brooks say it.

'What?' she asked.

'I think we've got him. I've got an address of a warehouse in Hackney and I know he was there today, but I'm not sure if he's there at the moment. But even if he isn't, we're another step closer to him.'

'Well I'm ready when you are', Warwick replied to Brooks' original question.

'Good', Brooks acknowledged with a smile before looking back at Dillon. 'Let's go. I'll fill you both in a little more on the way.'

The Plans of Mice and Men

Not a word had been uttered between O'Shea and Allan since they had left White Hart Lane. There was just the sound of the engine humming and a lot of smoking going on and that was mainly on Allan's part. O'Shea was feeling even more despondent now with this whole situation and this farce of a mission. He'd had enough. The mission hadn't gone as he'd planned and he knew, because of that, that his contribution to it had been small.

'I've got to make a break from this whole miserable shitty fucking thing', he thought.

He knew that he had left it too late to speak to Dillon. But he felt sure that, with her being the best there was at her job, she could survive. If he could also survive the mission as well, then there was a slim chance that he could make amends with her another time somewhere.

'A slim chance was better than no chance', he thought.

'Where have Sinéad and Brooks gone?' he asked of the quiet Allan.

Allan turned to look at him with a surprised look on his face. He looked back at the road in front of him and then back to O'Shea.

'Are you fucking serious?' he asked.

'What do you mean?' O'Shea asked, surprised at Allan's reaction. Allan's eyebrows rose up in such a manner that his forehead's skin hadn't been that scrunched up for years as he reacted to O'Shea's questioned answer with rage.

'You know full fucking well what I mean. Why do you suddenly care for their whereabouts?'

O'Shea said nothing for the moment as he looked out at the Camden High Road that disappeared beneath his feet. Then he realised what Allan was annoyed about. Allan had clearly got the impression that O'Shea didn't care for the person whom he had tentatively declared to be his daughter back at their meeting in Battersea Park.

'Take it easy', O'Shea thought. 'Explain yourself.'

'Look, I still believe everything I said to you earlier about Dillon. But she'll survive this mess one way or another. Believe you me, she's the best.'

Allan pulled the car over to the kerb in such an angry manner that his front nearside wheel banged onto the pavement and then back down again with such a thud that it felt like the bottom of the car had also bumped the high pavement. Allan didn't seem to care for the car, that much was obvious. Any other driver would have got straight out to check for any damage. He also didn't turn off the engine. He just pulled up the handbrake without the aid of its button. He turned to O'Shea with a face that was red, raged, ready to let rip and pissed off with impatience.

'Well, we'll find out how fucking good she really is', Allan began as he found himself suddenly changing his tune about Dillon.

For he didn't give a damn for Dillon now, as he was sick to death of working with his Irish counterparts. He had also been deceiving his Prime Minister by not aborting this mission when he was told to do so. Well he knew now that Brooks could end this whole thing within the hour.

Before he continued talking he turned the key in his ignition, one more turn, which caused a bleeping sound to happen somewhere in the car. Then the bleeping stopped. O'Shea's eyes tightened as he tried to work out where that bleeping sound had come from. But he didn't take his eyes off those of Allan's.

'Brooks, Dillon and Warwick are on their way to see Dwyer. We've discovered his whereabouts and we did it before your IRA scum did.'

Allan's face smiled a pleasant smile as he moved a little closer for O'Shea to be able to smell his nicotined stale breath.

'And we'll be finished with the likes of Dwyer, Dillon and yourself before this day is over. That much I believe'

The Sword of Damocles

O'Shea felt his life was suddenly threatened and it was threatened in the short term.

'Open the glove compartment in front of you!' Allan instructed him.

O'Shea stayed absolutely still for the next minute as he didn't take his eyes off Allan. Then, slowly, he raised his right hand up to the handle of the glove box. As he opened it the same bleeping sound happened again. He went ice cold with the view that confronted him from the glove box. Two shiny silver gun barrels, both an inch in diameter, faced him. Each gun contained a small red flashing light which sat at the top of each barrel.

'Oh shit!' He now confirmed his earlier sense of trouble and danger.

He just wasn't quite prepared for the grave danger that now faced him.

'You've just set off the relay that is connected to your door's handle. If you try to make a break for it, you'll end up shooting yourself. And before you think about any of the other doors in the car, they're all connected to the same relay as well.'

O'Shea looked at the two barrels that faced him. Allan took great delight in continuing.

'When you opened the glove compartment, not only did you set off the relay but you also set off those barrels' homing devices. They'll follow you around this car until you open a door and set off the relay.'

The homing device was obviously wired to the red flashing lights.

Allan broke into a laugh and then suddenly stopped.

'Each car belonging to Section 13 contains a device like this to prevent intruders getting away with any vital information.'

'What's wrong with a normal burglar alarm, you sick bastard?' O'Shea asked, now feeling frightened for the first time in years.

Allan let out a small laugh again.

'We don't fuck about at Section 13, Mr.O'Shea. And we don't allow our organisation to get into a mess, like the IRA did, with Dwyer.'

As Allan said it he turned around in his chair, let the hand brake off, and pulled back out onto the Camden High Road. O'Shea sat in silence looking at the two barrels in front of him.

'And as for Dillon, she'll be dead within the hour', Allan added.

Out of The "IN" Tray

The Undertaker sat in the main chair of Peter O'Connel's office in Muswell Hill, North London, feeling satisfied with his work on the alarm system. The rest of the building was still alarmed, but Peter O'Connel's office was clear, thanks to the Undertaker's work on the alarm panel. He gazed at the open door of the safe, that was also locked when he arrived at this destination.

'Another easy break in', he silently congratulated himself, as he thought of the ease with which he opened the electrically locked door.

'Will people ever learn?'

He spun the chair around to face the picture on the wall. The picture was of Peter O'Connel standing outside these very offices. He raised the gun he had just taken from the safe. A shiny classic Smith 58 with bullets and silencer attachment. He screwed on the silencer and pointed the barrel's end at the head of O'Connel in the picture.

As he pulled the trigger, the gun gave out a clean sounding thud. The picture exploded.

'Who was your friend, I wonder? the Undertaker questioned, knowing now that he had seen Peter O'Connel earlier.

He placed the gun down on the desk in front of him and took all the papers from Peter O'Connel's "IN" tray. He picked out the large brown envelope that bore the word, **TIMESHEETS**. He ripped open the envelope and flicked through the sheets which were in alphabetical order. He stopped at Liam Henessy's and took it out. He looked at the job location column, then smiled to himself.

Job No. 1007. Hackney.
Warehouse refurb.
Radner Road. Hackney.

He then blew out a cloud of Cuban smoke.
'Hackney here I come.'

A Cage of Terror

Allan pulled the car over to the pavement beside the closed Camden Market stalls in North London and turned the engine off. They were at the rear of Camden Market, which was closed today. Hence the quietness of the area. The road had no houses, just lock-ups and garages covered in graffiti street art.

'What's going on?' O'Shea asked as he looked around at the quiet road that bore no life whatsoever.

'I'm off, as this mission's over. Not that you've been much

bloody use.'

As Allan said it, he pulled on the handle of his door. O'Shea lifted his hands up in a panic as he went to scream but declined once he saw Allan's door open. The barrels didn't fire. They were sitting perfectly still, looking at him with their flashing red lights.

O'Shea turned to look at Allan with a questioning look on his face.

'The relay will only go off if the homing device picks you up opening the door, opening a window, or if a door is opened from the outside', Allan informed him.

'Goodbye Mr. O'Shea. It's been a pleasure killing you', Allan farewelled as he got out of the car.

'You fucking bastard', O'Shea cursed as Allan closed the door behind him, smiling, as he was taking great pleasure in killing O'Shea in such a slow tormenting manner.

O'Shea sat in disbelief of the situation he now found himself in. His heart was racing. He wanted to kick the dashboard in anger. But he knew only too well that he had to be careful, as the chances were that the homing device contained an anti-tamper mechanism which would trigger the relay if the dashboard was kicked. He just placed his hands on top of his head and pulled at two lumps of his hair in anger at himself.

'Why in fuck's name didn't I make a run for it before now? Why the hell did I leave it too late? Look what it's all come down to!'

He started to sweat as he moved from side to side, watching the two barrels also moving from side to side, following him.

'You fucking bastard!' he once again said, thinking of the now departed Allan.

'How in fuck's name am I going to get out of here? How the fuck am I going to get out of here alive?' his panicking mind thought.

He was physically shaking so much that his vision was getting distorted, as his body was on the verge of having a fit.

His body wasn't young anymore. He had to think. He couldn't get anyone to open the car from the outside and the handles were connected to the relay on the inside, so he was in a life threatening catch 22 situation.

He was starting to sweat even more now, so he took off his jacket to try and relieve himself of the unwanted heat that he was now feeling. He looked up the road in the direction that Allan had just walked, but he was now long gone.

He needed to stop his shaking and calm down.

He took out his cigarettes and lit one, as he decided that time was still on his side and he also had to calm down and just think this whole thing through. He pulled his jumper out away from his body and back in again a few times to try and fan himself a little. On the last pull of the jumper he pulled it to the right a little and the gun's barrels moved in the same direction. The movement of the barrels made him jump.

'THAT'S IT, I'M FUCKING DEAD!' he shouted with such a panic that a tear ran down his face.

He hadn't felt panic like this since the early hours of August 9th, 1971, when the British bastard soldiers of Northern Ireland were chasing him down the alleyways of Ballymurphy.

He ran like mad that night. He ran like crazy because his life, like so many others that night, depended on it. The British wanted blood that night and they didn't give a damn if it was IRA blood or not. As long as it was Irish blood, they'd be satisfied.

Mind And Matter

He now couldn't run from death. He just had to sit there and stare death in the face, wondering why the gun's barrels had suddenly moved when his body was stationary.

'Why did it move? Why suddenly move? I didn't go anywhere.'

Then a thought crossed his mind as he laid the cigarette in

the ashtray. He pulled his jumper slowly to the right. The barrels followed his movement. He then pulled his jumper to the left. Again the barrels followed his movement. He began to smile.

'Well I'll be fucking damned to hell', he laughed a little.

Very slowly he removed the jumper, making sure that he leaned towards the centre of the car, so as not to confuse the homing device that he was making a move for the door. As he pulled the jumper off over his head he could hear the barrels moving up and down in time with his movements.

Now was the test. He placed the jumper in the driver's seat and sat back in his own. Now the barrels faced the driver's seat.

'You thick fucking homing device!' O'Shea laughed.

For as great as the idea was for such an anti-intruder weapon, it's homing device was old. It only picked up the material on O'Shea's jumper, for that was the first thing it saw in the passenger seat when he opened the glove compartment earlier.

O'Shea quickly leaned across the driver's seat, wrapped the sleeve of the jumper around the handle of the door and leaned back in his own seat looking at the barrels. They were now facing the driver's door.

As he pulled on the other sleeve of his jumper, the barrels let out two shots each into the driver's door. O'Shea then opened his own door. Nothing. The red lights had stopped flashing. He was free.

As he smiled, another tear ran down his cheek. He'd survived the mission.

'You lucky bastard, Dermott!' he told himself. 'You stupid lucky bloody bastard!'

Faxes And Guns

Brooks pulled his car over in Baker Street, next to the entrance of an old deserted industrial estate. Baker Street itself was a quiet road with no buildings or houses. It used to be a route to the old Baker Industrial estate. It was two streets away from Radner Road.

Brooks looked at his watch while Dillon and Warwick sat in silence, waiting for the go-ahead from Brooks.

'15.50 hours', he acknowledged to himself. 'And today's bomb hasn't gone off yet.'

He turned to Dillon, but kept his eyes moving around the perimeter of the car.

'Can you open the glove compartment, please?' he asked her.

Dillon's eyes frowned as she looked back at him.

'Sorry, have your fucking hands fallen off or something?'

Brooks looked at her with an annoyed look on his face.

'This isn't bloody playtime anymore darling. If you want to carry on with that cavalier Irish attitude, I'd much rather you'd bugger off now and leave myself and Detective Warwick here to complete the mission.'

'Let's calm down a little bit, people, shall we!' Warwick intervened.

'Jesus Christ! Chill out a bit, will you', she instructed Brooks.

As she said it she reached her left hand up to the glove compartment's handle and turned it clockwise. She let the door of the compartment drop open in shock, as the buzzing noise from inside the glove box made her jump. She couldn't believe what she was looking at. Why would someone have such a device in their glove box?

Brooks laughed at her reaction.

'A bloody fax machine?' she asked.

As she opened the glove box a fax was being transmitted from James Moore at the base in Hayes at that precise second. The screeching noise of the fax machine had made her jump.

She now realised that she had to get herself on guard, as the marijuana had relaxed her a little too much. She'd opened that glove box without even thinking. Anything could have been in there.

'What's the fax?' Warwick asked from the back seat.

'One is a map of this area and the other is a sketch of the Warehouse where I think Dwyer is. These are from the Resident Engineer's files', Brooks announced as he handed the map to Warwick.

Warwick smiled in amazement.

'How the hell did you manage to get hold of them so quickly?'

'Our James Moore can get hold of anything you want. He's a bloody genius, but I just wish he didn't swear so much.'

Again Warwick smiled at Brooks' simplicity. Warwick always found "Gentlemen" to be simple people.

Dillon and Warwick followed Brooks in getting out of the car and walking around to the back of the vehicle. Warwick looked at Dillon with a frown in not knowing what was going on. Dillon replied by shrugging her shoulders, showing that she didn't know either. Brooks opened the boot of the car and turned to Warwick.

'You'll need a gun, I take it?' he asked.

'Most definitely', Warwick agreed.

'Same here', Dillon added, 'but one that fucking works this time.'

Brooks smiled as he took three identical Kilmer 46 hand guns from the first aid box next to the car's spare wheel.

All three hand guns had attached silencers. The Kilmer 46 hand gun was a little larger than your average hand gun, due to the extra fire power that it possessed. The Kilmer 46 also contained double the amount of bullets that your average six shooter had.

Brooks closed the boot and placed the three guns on the car's metal work.

'You can pick first', Brooks proudly announced as he turned to look at Dillon.

Dillon picked the middle Kilmer 46, unclipped the bullet compartment which was located in the handle of the gun. On seeing the twelve tightly packed bullets, she turned and smiled at Brooks. Brooks returned the smile. She then turned away from him, extended her arm out with the gun facing the ground, and fired a single bullet into the pavement. Upon pulling the wide, finger comfort trigger, the Kilmer 46 let out a thud, only as loud as a lazy hand clap. The pavement stared back up at her with its new perfect smoking hole. She smiled. She now felt safe and secure.

'Now that's what I call a girl's best friend. A fair sized, loaded weapon', she claimed as she gave Warwick a slow sexy wink of her left eye.

'Nothing makes me happier. I'll take this one, thank you', she informed them both.

Warwick smiled back at her as he found her actions so sexy. He'd never been one for independent women or a woman who tries to equal a man. His wife Helen, in her time on earth, was a lady. Dillon was a woman, and a damn fine sexy one at that, as any man would agree on the way she smiled with the comfort of her new found friend. The loaded handgun.

'Well, how do you want to do this then? I mean, fair enough, we've got the drawings but how do you want to play it with Dwyer, if he is there?' Warwick asked.

Brooks took the bag of money from the back seat of the car and then walked back around to the other two and handed the bag to Warwick as he explained.

'Like you said before, he's only about the money.'

Warwick said nothing for a moment as he stared at the ground thinking.

Dillon said nothing, as she was now content with the loaded gun in her back pocket. As well as feeling a little stoned, she decided that it was best to say nothing for the moment.

'If I walk in there with ninety four thousand pounds in fucking cash, I very much doubt that he'll want to have a little chat about it. Do you?'

Warwick opened the boot of the car, then unzipped the bag and tipped the cash into the car. As he closed the boot he gave a cheeky smile to Brooks.

'I'll give the fucking bastard something to talk about.'

He then zipped up the empty bag and walked off in the direction of Radner Road, followed by Brooks and Dillon.

42

IN THE CORRIDORS OF POWER

John Hayward walked the corridor to the Cabinet conference room very slowly and in silence. He was about to face his Cabinet. Something he wasn't looking forward to doing. Something that he hadn't been looking forward to doing for the last three days. Waiting for him was a room full of people who should be working together as a Government but, in reality, would step on each other to take their own career a little further.

This present Government was re-elected in the last General Election. It was the first time that John Hayward was voted in as Prime Minister by the British public. Prior to this General Election John Hayward was only Prime Minister, because he had replaced Maggie Thornbird, after she resigned due to her position being challenged by Michael Hornby for the Conservative leadership. Now John Hayward was Prime Minister because the British people wanted him to be.

A Cabinet In Crisis

Now was his chance to be the great leader. Now was his chance to take Britain to an economical high, with Europe being his gateway to success. Five months after being elected by the British public his Government was responsible for the English Pound toppling out of the European Rate Mechanism, costing Britain billions upon billions of pounds to repair. Even to this day repair is being made by the British tax payer.

The past year will go down as an 'Annus Horribilis' in British economic history. Twelve months ago to the day, for unexplained reasons, the pound's rate was falling rapidly. Someone, somewhere, had dumped a load of English currency onto the market, making it almost worthless. All Britain could do was buy it's own money back at someone else's price. This was to become Britain's financial darkest hour. Some accused the pro-European countries of trying to enforce a single currency by tactic. Others blamed the Germans.

Germany's interest rates are decided by the German Bundesbank which is independent of the German government. Twelve months ago Bundesbank decided that the well being of Germany was more important than that of the ERM and, with the deutschmark being the German currency and also being the benchmark of the European Rate Mechanism, caused the necessary mayhem for Britain to be forced out of the ERM.

Britain needed help that day. No country in Europe leapt to her defence and the Americans were too busy that day pumping their Dollars elsewhere. How embarrassing! How expensive! How could a Government be so incompetent to allow themselves to be suspended from the European Rate Mechanism? Something that John Hayward's predecessor, Maggie Thornbird, had taken this country into only two years previously after years of hard work to do so. John Hayward decided that he would resign that day, were it not that a phone call from his sister, Pat, convinced him otherwise.

Norman Lanson, the Chancellor of the Exchequer at the time, seemed to shoulder the blame for his Government's embarrassment over Black Wednesday and was replaced by Kenneth Foot at the Cabinet reshuffle.

This new Cabinet also had little time for the way the Northern Ireland situation was being handled at the moment. This year started off with the Sinn Féin leader, Garry Addams, being given an "Authorised Limited Duration" Visa to the USA from Bill Clinton, the President of the United States of America. Then in March the IRA announced a three day cease fire to facilitate talks between Britain and Sinn Féin. The cabinet felt that they were being dictated to by terrorists.

They were.

The Cabinet today, wanted to talk about this middle of the road Tory who was now leading the New Labour party. Andy Blayre had only been in the position of leadership of the New Labour party a few weeks and already he had the national press wrapped around his little finger. This present government looked old and tired. Andy Blayre looked young, handsome and healthy.

A Corridor Conference

John Hayward was accompanied on his walk by Sir Patrick Maynard, the Northern Ireland secretary, and Richard Howard, the Home Secretary. Also present, and walking a few steps ahead of the party, was Sir John Primark.

'This isn't making things easy for the police force', Richard Howard broke the silence, talking of the embarrassment caused by the release of Brooks and Dillon from the incident at Liam Hennessy's house in Kilburn last night.

The party stopped walking, due to the Prime Minister stopping. He turned to look at Howard.

'What?' he asked with annoyance.

Richard Howard went red with embarrassment as the tense party all looked at him.

'This whole farce in Kilburn has made it look as if the police let two key witnesses go free. And we're all aware, that this was an M.o.D operation.'

Howard looked at Sir John when he said it. Sir John just smiled back, as he didn't care for the Home Secretary or the police force. As far as he was concerned, his business was far more important than that of the Home Secretary. And the business of Section 13 was even more important than his own. He just stood there, looking at Howard with that "I don't give a shit" smile on his face.

Hayward turned away from Howard and walked to the window. He took his glasses from his nose and rubbed his eyes, trying to rid his head of the ache that seemed to be constantly with him these days. So much seemed to rest on his shoulders. So much he had to prove when the public voted for him. But now his time was weighed up between the bickering of his Cabinet and those, like Howard, who were more interested in trying to prove that his job was being well served, instead of pulling together with the rest of the Cabinet like a team. A team leading a country. Or at least, trying to.

Then he thought of Peter Allan.

'Where the hell are you Peter?'

He wanted to know what the hell was going on. Why were terrorists being shot on the streets of London, if the mission had been aborted? He knew that was a Section 13 killing. You could smell it a mile out. If anyone on the cabinet had the slightest notion that such a mission was being carried out, they'd tear him to pieces like savage dogs.

'You will have to shoulder the burden of the embarrassment, Michael, for the situation of Northern Ireland is more important at this moment than that of the police force's reputation', John Hayward informed him.

Northern Ireland was more important to him. He knew this government wasn't going to make it to another election. He also knew the next government would demand a higher income tax to repair the damage of his Government's mistakes of *'Annus Horribilis'*. He needed to be remembered for one thing. And that one thing was to be a start to peace in Northern Ireland.

'Why should that be, Prime Minister?' Howard interrupted his thoughts. 'Why should the reputation of the Home Front suffer for that of the situation in Northern Ireland and for the actions of the M.o.D.? Why?'

Hayward was just about to give Howard the same answer he had given a moment ago, when Peter Allan's voice came out of nowhere.

'Because Section 13 of the M.o.D. has discovered direct links between the IRA and the police force in the last forty eight hours. That's the fucking why!' he shouted.

Hayward let out a sigh of relief as Allan walked through the middle of the party.

'There is a Sergeant Davis of Enfield Police Station in Chase Farm Hospital at this very moment. He was caught in the explosion that happened there last night and his condition is critical. Chances are he'll never walk again.'

Allan walked closer to Howard and turned to look at him as he continued.

'And I hope the dirty fucker never does walk again, to be honest with you. For he was involved with the IRA's brigade that performed the bombing on Saturday morning in Enfield.'

Howard went white with shock.

'I suggest you deal with the embarrassment of the police force, Home Secretary.'

By calling Howard by his title, Allan knew only too well that it would make him more defensive of his own position.

'I'm quite sure, with the Prime Minister's permission of course', Allan stopped briefly to look at Hayward and then back to Howard, 'that Section 13 of the M.o.D. will make sure that the Davis situation is taken care of, if you would be so kind as to do your best to dampen the flames within the cabinet, about the two arrests last night.'

Howard looked at the floor as he weighed the whole thing up.

'Direct links between the IRA and the Metropolitan Police? Dear God!' he thought.

How could he ever walk away from his job with any pride, if something like this got into the hands of the public, let alone the cabinet.

'Consider it done', he said as he raised his head and looked at Sir John.

Sir John was looking back at Howard with a great big smile on his face. Allan turned to Hayward.

'We need to talk right away!' he told him.

Hayward looked at him for a moment and then turned to Howard.

'You will represent me today at the cabinet meeting', he told him.

'But, Prime Minister, the Cabinet has waited for three days to speak to you.'

'Michael, for once will you do as your leader tells you!'
His words were harsh and his stare was cold.

'Right, lets go to the Churchill Room', Hayward announced as he led the way for Allan and Sir John to follow.

'I suggest we bring Sir John up to date with the latest information on our mission, Peter.'
Hayward couldn't have Sir John knowing that Allan had ignored the order to cease the mission so he played along as if everything was normal. Allan wasn't sure as to whether he should be pleased or not. But he decided that he too would play along as if the order was never given.

'This sounds like trouble', Sir John Primark commented, as he knew that if he was to be informed about the details of a Section 13 operation, something wasn't right. The Prime Minister was obviously uncomfortable about something.

Howard turned and walked slowly towards the room of savage dogs that waited for him in the cabinet conference room.

43

WALLS WON'T TELL!

The warehouse had been cleared of all the mess of the earlier execution by the Fifth Brigade's cleaners. The Fifth Brigade cleaners were the best at what they did. Other firms around London had used the same cleaners to clear up after gang executions, dog fights, cock fights and information extraction sessions. The gangs that had used the cleaners, knew that they were IRA but turned a blind eye because they knew that these people were the police forensics' worst nightmare. Had they set up the device on the red van containing the bodies of Tommy and Frank, it would have blown the whole of the wasteland all over White Hart Lane.

They were the best at what they did. Not a trace of blood could be found on the floor of the warehouse and the bench that was covered with tools earlier, was now empty. All that sat on it now was the open briefcase containing the device.

A Final Strike

Dwyer took his cigarettes from his pocket, extracted one and ignited it. He then blew an air of smoke out across the space above his head and stretched his arms out at the same time as he rewarded himself with a smile. For the time was getting closer for him to take his new device into the heart of London and wreck some ignorant, innocent lives.

And amongst those lives, would be his own. Then he would be with Billy Hopkirk again as he had promised. He looked out at the now clear blue sky through the dusty window and smiled with satisfaction. The device that sat in the open briefcase in front of him, contained enough explosives to impact a grave measure of damage on the heart of London. He would make sure it's device activated in Picadilly Circus.

Deep in the heart of tourism.

'What a beautiful day for destruction!' he declared to himself. 'What a beautiful, beautiful day!'

As he said it, Peter O'Connel walked back in through the open double doorway, wiping the sweat from his forehead with one of his white cotton handkerchiefs. Dwyer turned around to face him, as O'Connel walked across the open area.

'Well?' he asked, looking at the nervous looking O'Connel.

'Nothing', O'Connel replied with his shaky voice. He did indeed look incredibly nervous.

'What?' Dwyer asked in disbelief.

O'Connel stopped walking as he looked at Dwyer in disbelief at having to explain himself as his voice was filled with rage.

'I've checked the local radio stations, I've checked the TV, I've checked the word on the fucking street, I've checked every fucking thing there is to fucking check and no one has seen or heard a single fucking word about the police finding Tommy and Frank's fucking bodies!!! OKAY??'

As his voice had got louder and louder, ripping through the air of the warehouse, his face was turning red with rage. Spit dribbled down his chin. Water spilled from his eyes, not from crying but from the pure pressure his body had forced upon his own face. If ever he should have a heart attack or a nervous breakdown, now was the time.

Dwyer just stood there smiling at O'Connel.

'Jesus Christ! I was only asking', Dwyer said with an air of enjoyment in his voice that showed how entertaining he found it to see O'Connel losing his head.

A Local Dispute

Below the warehouse was the building site where the refurbishment works were taking place for the "New Baker Industrial Park". Fifteen years ago, the park had moved to this new location from the Baker Street two roads away. The new industrial park was two hundred metres squared, with the warehouse sitting neatly at the north western side of the southern entrance. All the original buildings, which had been badly erected in a rushed contract fifteen years ago, had become badly damaged in the October, 1988, storms, where roof tiles had been blown away and the discovery of the park's poor flooding defences was made. Controversy had surrounded the Industrial Park, due to the original one in Baker Street still being able to withstand the forementioned storms and flooding. But, for some strange reason, public fury at the council's public spending was ignored and the New Baker Industrial Park was to undergo a fifteen million pound face lift.

The public had failed to see something that would have surely fanned the fire of controversy even more. The company which had carried out the work fifteen years ago, was the same company that were carrying out the work of refurbishment. O'Connel Building Contractors Ltd. Fifteen years ago that was not the name on the building site's gate, because the work had been sub-contracted out to them by a larger contractor of that time.

For all the scandal that surrounded the project, what with the old park sitting unused two roads away and all the public spending that had been wasted on the new park, O'Connel Building Contractors Ltd. found the project to be a little goldmine.

A Grim Gateway

Warwick was walking ahead of the other two, looking at the entrance to the building site which was located at the other side of the road from them. As he stopped, Brooks walked on a few steps past him to get a closer look at the two signs above the entrances gate.

New Baker Industrial Park.
Undergoing Refurbishment Work .
Due to Re-open January 1995.
Main Contractor.
O'Connel Building Contractors,

Muswell Hill, London.

323

He then looked at the smaller sign on the gate itself.

All Visitors must report to the site office!!!!!!

'Well?' Dillon asked as she threw a finished cigarette into the gutter and looked in Brooks' direction.

Warwick was also looking at him.

Brooks looked up and down the street, noticing the three other red vans identical to the one that was found in White Hart Lane. As he looked at the furthest van from him, trying to read it's registration plate, he suddenly realised the tiredness in his own eyes. He hadn't slept for two days now. He could feel the other two looking at him, waiting for his answer. He looked up the road towards his left, away from them, as he mindfully cursed himself for not getting a couple of hours' sleep this morning back at his flat.

'You bloody fool, Martin!'

He had to be on his guard. Not just with Dwyer but with Dillon as well. He had to make sure that he took care of this whole mission today and that included taking care of Dillon, permanently.

He didn't dislike Dillon but he knew he had to take care of her for two reasons. Firstly, if the job was to be completed correctly, she had to be silenced. And secondly, most importantly, he didn't know what she was thinking? What had the IRA told her to do on completion of the job? Was she thinking in the exact same way that he was? There was no doubt about it, she had to be dealt with. He decided in the car journey here that he would leave Warwick be. At least for the moment anyway.

'I should have got some sleep. I need to be sharp today.'

'We go in!' he declared as he walked across the street, followed by the other two.

Warwick allowed enough distance to be made between Brooks and himself so he could have a quiet word with Dillon.

'Is your head clear yet?' he asked of the her.

If anyone else had asked her that question, knowing that she may be a little stoned, she would have told them to "piss off", in the forbidding manner that she possessed. She couldn't stand people probing her about her use of marijuana. But she could see that Warwick wasn't about to lecture her, as he just seemed a little concerned that she might not be a hundred percent on the ball. She could see where he was coming from.

'I'm fine', she assured him.

Then she looked at the back of Brooks' head and smiled.

'I'm ready for the bastard.'

'Same here', Warwick replied as he looked down at the empty bag he was carrying. Indeed he was ready to face Dwyer. Or Jacobs as he had first known him.

For Warwick wanted answers.

Warwick wanted his blood.

44

BEHIND CLOSED DOORS

Sir John Primark said absolutely nothing throughout Peter Allan's briefing as he sat motionless with his legs crossed and his hands clasped together in front of his mouth. This disguised any reaction he had to the fact that Section 13 had undertaken and were at this very moment carrying out an operation with members of the IRA.

The fire burned brightly in front of him as he looked at the Prime Minister's private collection of Jack Higgins books that sat in alphabetical order of story titles upon the shelf beneath the large picture of the Oval stadium. The Oval is home to the Surrey cricket team and is two miles from the house where John Hayward grew up. Hayward often watched cricket there as a child, away from the hustle and bustle of his Peckham surroundings. The large picture which was taken from a helicopter above the stadium, always made the Prime Minister happy for both the memories of his childhood and the fact that it is the home of his first love of sport, cricket.

An Uncomfortable Briefing

Sir John Primark listened to every word that was being said by Allan and would simply nod every now and again to acknowledge that he understood everything so far. Upon completion of the briefing, a few minutes passed in silence before Sir John stood up and walked over to the sideboard to help himself to a large whiskey from the Prime Minister's very own private Jamesons collection.

John Hayward and Peter Allan said nothing, as they knew that they had to give Sir John the opportunity to digest everything he had been told. Allan was thinking the exact same thing as Hayward.

'What's Sir John thinking?

'How's he going to react to this bizarre situation under the current climax of bombings by the IRA's Fifth Brigade?'

'Do you think Martin Brooks can pull it off, Peter? Sir John suddenly asked.

Allan was a little taken aback by the direct unexpected question but answered it all the same.

'Yes, I believe he can.'

'Then that's good enough for me. What of the two terrorists?' Sir John casually enquired of Dillon and O'Shea, as he took a mouthful of whiskey and washed it around the front of his mouth.

'One has been eliminated already and I am confident that the other will be taken care of within the hour, as will be the entire mission.'

'Really?'

It was John Hayward who now asked the question.

Allan turned to look at John Hayward as he continued.

'Section 13 has been successful in locating where Tony Dwyer was this afternoon. And it was all thanks to the fact that the Kilburn Police Station seemed to have let two of Liam Hennessy's associates go free last night.'

Sir John walked back over to where he was sitting earlier and asked Allan another question as he sat down.

'Who were the two people that the police let go last night?'

'One of the IRA, who is working with Martin Brooks, and Brooks himself', Allan confirmed as John Hayward stood up and walked over to the sideboard to help himself to a large whiskey.

He now started to feel nervous as he thought about the situation he was now in. His cabinet were downstairs, waiting for him to answer the questions that they had been brewing up for three days, and yet here he was upstairs discussing the details of an operation that was being carried out with active members of the IRA.

'I'm still trying to connect Tony Dwyer with the release of

the two associates in Kilburn?' Hayward asked with a look of annoyance on his face.

'Dwyer thought that he had two traitors in his camp. And to keep the Fifth Brigade intact, he had to find the traitors and make an example of them.'

Allan now stood up, as the Prime Minister sat down, and made his way over to the sideboard and helped himself to a large whiskey. As he poured the whiskey he continued.

'Dwyer executed two men that he thought were the traitors, and he left so many clues around their bodies that our man in the field could trace where Dwyer was this afternoon before Police forensics could sort out what blood type the victims were.'

Sir John had a great big smile on his face when Allan turned around and looked at him.

'Brooks again, I take it?' Sir John asked, knowing that it would have taken some brains to achieve such a feat.

'Yes it was. Martin Brooks, Section 13's finest', Allan proclaimed with pride as he continued. 'He'll have this operation closed today, giving the IRA a chance to take control of their activities to allow the British government to sit down with Sinn Féin and work out a plan for peace.'

'And at some bloody price', Hayward added as he could feel his heart racing within his skin.

He took his glasses from his face and placed them on the table in front of him.

What the hell was he playing at? Giving the IRA chances? Planning to sit down with what many of his cabinet viewed as the IRA's excuse for a political party to talk about peace? And all at a great price of his name being attached to an operation that took place between the British Secret Service and active members of the IRA.

Sir John looked at the Prime Minister, knowing that he was looking and feeling uncomfortable about the whole situation.

'What's your problem?' Sir John casually asked of the

uncomfortable looking Hayward.

Hayward looked up at Sir John with a look as if there was constant flow of thought going through his mind. He looked at the table in front of him, took his glasses from the table and placed them back on his face and then he looked back to the fire.

A *Question of Belonging*

'So what happens when I sit down to talk of peace with Sinn Féin? What happens to the Loyalist movement of Northern Ireland? What happens to the people who fight to keep the roads of Northern Ireland, the property of Her Majesty's Highway? What happens to those British people?'

'BRITISH PEOPLE?' Sir John asked aloud. 'Don't insult me as a proud British person by throwing me into the same category as those fucking pricks!'

As he said it, he slammed his empty glass on the table and stood up. He gave the Prime Minister the look of a person who had been greatly insulted and was about to return that insult through an answer.

'Look at you', he began by pointing to the Prime Minister.

'Peckham boy done good. Peckham, the place that the black people are associated with. A part of London that is rich in the Jamaican culture, rich in the African culture, has a great Irish community and has an Asian community that seems to grow stronger by the minute.'

Hayward looked at him with a face that was edging Sir John to get to the point. And fast. For he was proud of the fact that he had grown up in the multi-cultural area of Peckham. For he'd opposed the view points of Enoch Powell's "Rivers Of Blood" speech in 1967 where Powell, a member of the then Conservative shadow cabinet, warned the country of the dangers of immigration. Many of the Conservative party at the time backed Powell. But John Hayward didn't, due to his upbringing in the beautiful multi-cultural area of Peckham. He stood up to Powell's views within the Conservative party and to much criticism at the time. And he won.

Sir John continued his attack on the Loyalists of Northern Ireland, after giving Hayward enough time to think about his own multi-cultural childhood background.

'How British do you think the Loyalists of Northern Ireland are? They can't even live with the Irish. In their part of the United Kingdom you can't even get a job if you have the wrong religion. You can't even drink in certain bars if you are not of the right nationality.'

Sir John leaned on the back of the chair where he sat only moments ago, with both hands as he continued.

'Imagine how those so-called British people would react, if Black people or Asian people applied for a job in their territory. How far do you think those multi-cultural people would get?'

Sir John then stood straight with an air of pride as he completed his attack.

'Being British isn't about terrorising other cultures with fear, no matter who they are. Being British takes a lot of beating by any country. For we welcome the hand of friendship from any culture that cares to live in our homeland because we have the power to do so.

'In my opinion, the Loyalists of Northern Ireland may as well sleep with the National Front's racists of England, because neither of them have a clue about what it takes to act British.'

Sir John didn't have to say any more as he walked back to the Jamesons collection and poured himself another healthy measure of whiskey. Allan didn't need to say any more. If that little speech didn't knock Hayward's head into place, then nothing would. And it obviously did, as Hayward turned to Allan.

'How long before we'll know when the operation is complete?' he asked, as he was anxious to see this god-forsaken mission come to an end.

'I'm confident that this operation will be wrapped up

within the hour', Allan replied.

'How can you be so confident?' Hayward inquired.

On enjoying another mouthful of the sharp taste of Jamesons, Sir John replied to the Prime Minister's question.

'Because Martin Brooks is our man in the field and he is the best agent Section 13 has.'

Relief of Monotony

Once inside the gates of the site, Brooks, Dillon and Warwick found themselves standing in a wooden, 8ft high by 3ft wide by 12ft long corridor. It was part of a small temporary hut that was attached to the gate that bore the sign "Site Entrance Building" on the left hand wall. It was a deceiving little hut, as you wouldn't know it was there from the outside until you tried to gain entry to the site.

There was a window to the right hand side of the gate, which you had to walk past to gain entry to the site. On the other side of the window was a man in his late fifties who was known on site as "Paul The Gate Man". He had the face of a heavy drinker. His cheeks were rose red below the bags that were so layered that they covered the bottom half of his eyes. His hair was the same shade of grey as that of his moustache.

'Yes Sir?' he politely asked in his old husky English cockney voice that sounded rough, due to the fact that it had to endure the smoke of sixty cigarettes a day.

He was always glad to see some new faces as his job could become quite boring at times, just waiting for someone new to walk into the Site Entrance Building.

'Yes, we're here to see Peter O'Connel of O'Connel Building Contractors Limited', Brooks replied as he was just about to take his M.o.D. badge from his pocket to show to the gate man.

'I take it this is for the commotion that took place in the main warehouse this morning', Paul replied as any opportunity to have a bit of chat or a chin wag with a stranger was a golden one.

He was, of course, referring to the so called discovery of asbestos in the main warehouse that had caused the electricians and carpenters to come to a stand still, due to the site manager having to make the decision to close the warehouse until further notice.

'You know what it's like', Paul continued. 'Some daft prat discovers something that looks a little like asbestos and everyone's got to stop work and wait for you lot to show up.'

This was a decision that didn't go down too well, as those workers in the warehouse were all sub-contractors to O'Connels Building Contractors who were working on a fixed price. They weren't being paid to wait around for the asbestos to be given the all clear or to be taken away.

Brooks now declined to remove his badge from his pocket as he let the gate-man continue chatting.

'The sparkies and chippies (electricians & carpenters), have been sitting in the canteen all day, waiting for you lot to turn up. I take it you're here for the asbestos?' Paul enquired, as he handed Brooks an A4 sheet of paper and a pen.

'I'll need your names, please mate', he explained.

'Yes, that is correct. We are here to investigate the condition of the main warehouse', Brooks casually lied as he wrote his name on the sheet of paper and also wrote in the column that asked for the company name,

Section 13

Warwick now spoke up.

'Have you got some hard hats we could borrow, please mate, as I've left ours back in the motor.'

As he took the pen and sheet from Brooks he was looking at the sign on the door in front of him that stated,

Hard hats and boots must be worn on site at all times.
O'Connel Building Contractors Ltd..

'Yeah, no problem, squire', Paul replied as he passed three red hard hats to Brooks through the window.

'I take it you're all wearing toe protectors?' he asked.

'Oh absolutely', Dillon spoke up.

'Good', he said, followed by a small cough, as he turned to point at the door at the end of the corridor.

'Right through the door and straight across the site in front of you. The entrance to the warehouse is at the rear of it. It's a huge ramp, you can't miss it as it's big enough to drive a car up there. Ok?'

'No problems, thank you very much', Brooks replied.

'My pleasure', Paul said as the three visitors now walked past his window and made their way to the end of the wooden corridor.

As he watched the cute arse of Dillon's walk past his window, he almost dribbled from his mouth. Beautiful women were a sight for sore eyes for people working on building sites. As she closed the door behind her, Paul could still picture her in his mind, dreaming of what it would be like to have her to himself in his little smoky cabin for half an hour.

'I bet she bangs like the door of an outside shithouse on a windy night', he told himself.

45

MOVING IN ON THE DEN

Dillon was now feeling very sharp. The relaxation of the marijuana had actually paid off, as did the sleep she'd got last night in Brooks' car. Her body was now ready for action, and her mind was now alert after the brain had been given the opportunity to relax. The relaxation of marijuana is considered harmless as long as it doesn't interfere with such activities as driving, using machinery, working at heights or, as in Dillon's case, preparing to kill a "British bastard".

An Armed Posse

She had the Kilmar 46 tucked into the front waist of her jeans, concealed by her jumper. She could pull the gun out from that location, unclick its safety catch and shoot it in less then two seconds. She was ready for action.

Warwick felt indifferent now, as he knew his time had come to face the man he'd been trying to track down for two days. The activities of the last forty eight hours had prepared him for this moment.

In the last forty eight hours he'd stolen a hundred thousand pounds in cash from one of the IRA's main bosses. He'd also killed a Jamaican man, stormed into a pub waving his gun around like a lunatic, killed a pub manager, put himself in hospital by almost killing himself in a car accident, and now found himself working with the British Secret Service. All brought about from the suicide of Billy Hopkirk.

'Fucking amazing!' he thought to himself in his own mind as he contemplated the situation he was in.

Yet his nerves didn't come into the equation. He too, like Dillon, felt better for the rest he had earlier in the back of Brooks' car in White Hart Lane. His brain was a little more relaxed which again, like Dillon, was thanks to the small puff of marijuana he'd had.

He had the Kilmar 46 in his right hand, buried in his pocket ready for action. As he walked across the main open area of the site in front of Dillon and following Brooks, he was rubbing his finger up and down its trigger.

Brooks walked along, looking around at his surroundings. As he admired all the new ground work that had taken place to improve the foundations on which the new warehouses would be built, he wondered why Dwyer hadn't disposed of the two bodies in a pool of concrete out here, instead of dumping them on the wasteland in White Hart Lane.

Was it an act that was purposely carried out so the bodies would be found, or was it a stupid mistake? Brooks found it hard to believe that it could be a stupid mistake, as he too had heard of the fantastic work that the Fifth Brigade's cleaning section could perform. Whether or not it was a mistake, it was definitely an act carried out by Dwyer himself, as the Brigade's cleaning section wouldn't have made such a stupid error.

As he walked along, he noticed how quiet the site was. He looked down at his watch. 16:05. As he looked over to the green site offices that were off in the distance to his left, he kept thinking of what the IRA would have told Dillon to do at the final moments of this mission. As he looked at the skips and the canteen that sat behind the skips, he actually could feel his nerves waking up. He could feel a little twist in his stomach. He saw the workers that the gateman had spoken of before, watching him from the canteen window, hoping that he could give the all clear on the asbestos.

'For they can't go near the warehouse until they have been given the all clear', he thought.

He suddenly stopped in his tracks, causing the other two to also stop.

'What?' Warwick asked of the frozen Brooks.

Brooks looked back over at the eyes that were watching him

from the canteen.

'They can't go back to the warehouse until they have been given the all clear.'

Warwick and Dillon looked over to the canteen and then back to Brooks as he continued.

'That bloody warehouse has been off limits all day.'

It didn't take long for the other two to understand what it was that Brooks was driving at.

'A perfect fucking place to hold an execution, wouldn't you know', Dillon acknowledged.

They all looked at the warehouse in front of them.

'This is it lads. This is definitely fucking it', Dillon concluded.

Paul the gatemen felt bored already, and it was only two minutes ago that he was chatting to his three new visitors. As he took one of his Superking cigarettes from his packet and set light to the end of it, he picked his two way radio up off the table in front of him and pressed the talk button on the left.

'Peter O'Connel call back! Peter O'Connel call back!' he spoke into the microphoned section.

He took in a good lungful of the cheap tobacco and blew it out of the open window.

'Peter receiving', the radio crackled.

'Just to let you know, Peter, the asbestos people are here. I've sent them around to you at the warehouse.'

There was a moment of silence as Paul sat there waiting for Peter's response. He was just about to repeat his statement, but decided that he really needed another hit of the cheap English tobacco first.

'Okay, Paul, thanks. I'll be waiting for them!'

Reception At The Den

Peter O'Connel looked across the warehouse to where Dwyer was having another wash in the temporary toilets.

'What fucking asbestos people?' he said to himself as he

took a Smith and Wesson from his inside pocket and checked to make sure the chamber was full.

The call to cease work over the discovery of asbestos was a hoax on his part. It gave Dwyer the time he needed with Tommy and Frank and also gave the Brigade's Cleaning Section time. He was going to inform the workers that they could carry on working, now that the Cleaning Section had done their work.

'So who in fuck's name would be calling to check on the asbestos?'

He knew the workers wouldn't call anyone in, as it could have an effect on their daywork claims if they did so. They weren't that stupid. He looked up again as Dwyer started to whistle a tune to himself from within the plasterboard walls of the toilet. Should he tell Dwyer of the new visitors?

'No. I've seen enough torturing for one day.'

'I'll be back in a minute!' he shouted across to Dwyer.

'Yeah, whatever', Dwyer shouted back out to him.

As they rounded the corner to the back of the warehouse, they saw the ramp that Paul the gate man had spoken of. It was a concrete ramp, twenty feet long, that turned left at the top into the big double green doors of the warehouse. Brooks looked down at the ground, noticing that the gravel of the ramp had been brushed recently, as the clean underside of dust was showing.

'The Cleaning Section are a little too clean', he thought.

Dillon could hear the running water of the stream that was situated behind the ramp. She walked away from the other two to try and get a view of the stream at the rear of the ramp, but it was no good. The view of the stream was blocked by the overgrowth of grass and weeds. She felt the urge to check, as she didn't feel comfortable with standing in front of a camouflaged area. She removed the gun from her waist as she walked towards the overgrowth.

'Back in a second', she told the other two as she walked away.

Brooks ignored her as he crouched down to investigate the gravel. Warwick simply nodded to her and then took his cigarettes from his pocket and extracted one. He then placed the empty sports bag on the ground.

'What you looking at?' Warwick asked of Brooks as he lit the end of his cigarette.

'This gravel has just been turned over', Brooks answered. Warwick said no more as he looked to his left at the open doorway to the bottom section of the warehouse. He too felt the urge to investigate his surroundings, but didn't feel the need to prepare the Kilmar 46 for attack, as he could see it was completely bare inside. With the walls being fresh white, it was easy to see it was empty.

The floor of the warehouse was laminated cheap wood, indicating that the place was obviously being groomed for a showroom of some kind. Warwick walked towards the wall on his left, noticing that the walls had recently been painted. He turned around, taking another pull on his cigarette as he went to place his right hand around the Kilmar 46 in his pocket. As he was doing so, he was walking towards the open doorway. As he stepped outside, the view he encountered was one that made him wish he had taken his Kilmar 46 out in preparation.

'Make one more move, and I'll blow his fucking head off!' The man standing over Brooks, holding the Smith & Wesson to his head, informed Warwick in his Irish accent.

'Take your right hand out of your pocket very slowly!' As O'Connel ordered Warwick to do so he unclicked the safety catch on his own gun, showing Warwick that he meant business. For a brief moment, as Warwick lifted his left hand up to take another pull on his cigarette, he played with the idea of shooting him. Brooks would most certainly be shot dead but there was a good chance that Warwick could fire a bullet into the Irish man's throat before he had time to turn his body around and shoot back. More silence followed before Warwick rejected the idea as he slowly removed his right hand from his pocket. He made the move so slowly that he had time to lift his left hand up once more so he could enjoy another lungful of smoke.

Warwick looked at O'Connel with disgust, as he hated people who threatened him or anyone with a gun. He always considered it to be an action of the cowardly weak. He would have had a little more respect for his opponent if he at least had made an attempt to hit him in the back of the head with the butt of the gun when he wasn't looking. At least that would have been physical. Warwick had threatened many people many times with his fists, but never with a gun. Even when he held his gun to the back of the Jamaican man's head two nights ago, it was not as a threat, it was as defence. For he was the hunted, creeping up on the hunter.

As Brooks looked up, he wondered what had made Warwick reject the idea of shooting the Irishman, and looking after his own interest in this mission. If he was standing in Warwick's shoes, he wouldn't have hesitated for a second. He would have shot the armed man, causing his associate to be also shot.

What had made Warwick reject the idea of shooting him? What had made Warwick disarm himself? The sound of a Kilmar 46 unclicking its double safety catch answered those very questions.

'Drop the fucking gun!' Dillon ordered him as she placed the barrel of the gun on the rear of O'Connel's head.

O'Connel did as he was told without hesitation, as Brooks caught the Smith & Wesson, and re-applied its safety catch. Warwick immediately lunged at O'Connel, head butting him square in the roof of his nose, causing the cut on his own nose to re open. O'Connel fell backwards over Brooks.

Brooks stood up and away from the situation, allowing Warwick to pick O'Connel up by the scruff of his neck and drag him into the bottom warehouse. Dillon kept her eyes and the Kilmar 46 moving all around them to see if anyone had noticed the commotion. She was confident that there was no one around to witness what was taking place.

As Brooks picked up the sports bag and walked into the warehouse he found himself to be a little shaken at being caught off guard like that. He was alive, thanks to the decision of Warwick not to shoot O'Connel when he had the chance.

Warwick kicked O'Connel twice in the stomach, before lifting him up against the wall and punching him twice in the genitals.

'You're not so big now are ya, you fucking wanker!' He then slammed O'Connel's face down into the bone of his knee.

As O'Connel fell to the ground like a sack of potatoes, Warwick spat at him as he had no remorse at all for this coward of a man. He then removed the gun from his right pocket, unclicked the safety catch and then, for the first time in his life, placed the barrel of the gun in his victim's mouth. O'Connel should have been out cold from the beating that Warwick had just inflicted on him, but instead, he was shaking like mad with fear.

'Name?' Warwick asked as he took the barrel from O'Connel's mouth, allowing him to speak.

'O'Connel. Peter O'Connel.'

'I've got one fucking question, O'Connel', Warwick whispered, 'and I want one fucking answer. Is that piece of shit, Dwyer, upstairs?'

O'Connel had tears running down his face. The fear of being shot was stronger than the pain he was feeling in his body.

He nodded his head.

Dillon couldn't believe the beating that Warwick had given O'Connel as she found herself to be breathing a little heavier than normal. It wasn't because she was out of breath, it was because she found it quite arousing to see Warwick throw this wanker's blood all over the wall where it belonged.

'Jesus Christ! Peter O'Connel', she thought.

'Will you talk to us about the activities of the IRA's Fifth Brigade?' Brooks asked him.

O'Connel again nodded as he found himself thankful for a

chance to live, as he didn't want another beating from Warwick.

Dillon's face dropped. Trust Brooks to break the moment. She would have preferred to have seen Warwick finish him off.

'Let's go!' Brooks said to Warwick, before turning to Dillon.

'Wait here and watch him!' he told her as he pointed back to O'Connel, half expecting her to argue about it. For he was sure the IRA would have told her that she was to be the one that put the bullet in Dwyer's head, not the British.

But she didn't argue as she simply nodded and replied:

'No problem.'

Brooks was surprised and pleased at her response.

'Great!' he announced.

'Great!' she acknowledged.

Going In For the Kill

As Brooks followed Warwick out of the door, he removed his own Kilmar 46 from his pocket and double clicked the chamber's loading section before placing it in the back waist of his jeans. He then took O'Connel's Smith & Wesson from his front waist and handed it to Warwick.

'Take this and conceal the Kilmar 46, in case he asks you to toss your piece.'

'Good idea', Warwick acknowledged as he placed the Kilmar 46 in the back waist of his jeans.

'Listen, thanks for not shooting him back there when you had the chance. I thought I was finished there for a moment', Brooks thanked him.

'To receive such a fucking welcome, proved to me that Dwyer's here. So I couldn't have him or anyone hear the gun shots', Warwick told him.

'But your gun had a silencer', Brooks quizzed.

'I know. But his didn't.'

Brooks went cold as Warwick was frank with him. He thought Warwick was stupid at first to disarm himself.

How wrong can you be?

'Well, we can't both go walking in the front door with our fucking dicks in our hands. How do you want to do this?' Warwick asked.

Brooks thought back to the direction in which his back was facing when O'Connel crept up on him.

'He came at me from behind. So there must be a fire route around the west side of the building. I'll enter that way. You take the front door!'

'That suits me fine', Warwick announced as he walked away from Brooks and up the ramp, holding the Smith & Wesson ready in his right hand and the sports bag in his left.

46

DUTY RATHER THAN REVENGE

O'Connel was kneeling with his hands on his head and his eyes looking down at the ground as Dillon had instructed him to do only moments ago. Throughout her instructions he didn't look at Dillon once, as he didn't have the opportunity. Had he done so, he would have recognised her face from the meeting she had with Tony Dwyer eighteen months ago. It was the meeting that she had spoken about to O'Shea in the car on Saturday.

Peter O'Connel was at the very meeting that was meant to take place between Tim Holleran and herself. Instead, Tony Dwyer and O'Connel turned up. That meeting ended with Dillon being held down by O'Connel as Dwyer sliced an eight inch long cut along the skin protecting her left rib cage, with a carpet fitter's stanley knife. O'Connel could recognise that her accent was Irish but with the amount of informers that the British Service is rumoured to contain, he didn't give it another thought that he would know of her.

Dillon didn't know that the man that held her down eighteen months ago, was Peter O'Connel. The man who threatened to rape her, if she didn't keep still, while Dwyer scarred her skin with his warning to the IRA of West Belfast. It was a warning. Because to scar a member of the IRA, showed you meant business. But to scar a female member of the IRA in such a manner showed that you didn't give a shit either. If she knew that the man who threatened to rape her eighteen months ago was Peter O'Connel, she would have undertaken this mission on her own without O'Shea or the British.

Scars Reopened

As Dillon stood behind O'Connel she started to play that meeting over in her mind. It took place in the boiler house below a Catholic secondary school in Crouch End, North London, eighteen months earlier.

Whilst sitting beside the six foot squared boiler control panel where Tim Holleran told her to wait for him, so that he could give her the funds that she had come over from Ireland to collect, she was jumped from behind by O'Connel. He wrapped his arm around her neck and pulled her over the back of the chair. She tried to sink her teeth into his arm but it was no good, as he had tucked his forearm right in under her chin. O'Connel had a tight grip on her left hand as she tried to free her neck from his hold with her right. She put up such a struggle in the fight to defend herself that she knocked herself unconscious as she accidentally banged her head off the boiler control panel.

When she woke up twenty minutes later she found herself tied to the chair which was now situated in the middle of the boiler room. In the struggle with O'Connel earlier they managed to damage the thermostat control on the wall which was the reason why the main heating pumps were now working at full peak. This accounted for the amount of sweat that was dripping off her when she awoke. Her mouth wasn't gagged yet, as she had to explain what it was that she had met Tim Holleran for.

When Dwyer told her that Tim Holleran was now dead and that there was no way he was going to give a penny to the IRA headquarters, he informed her that she would have to take a scar back with her to prove that he meant business. She started to kick and scream as O'Connel held the chair still by applying pressure to her. She spat and she screamed.

'Keep that fucking bitch still!' Dwyer instructed O'Connel.

'Keep still for fuck sake. It'll be over before you know it', O'Connel told her as he tried to apply some plumbers lagging tape to her mouth.

But she shook her head and wiggled her body, making the job hard for the pair of them.

It was when she started to scream again that the panic set in again for O'Connel, as the school was actually in session when all of this commotion was happening in the boiler house. O'Connel lost his temper as he slapped her across the face. Dillon stopped screaming as she spat at him and cursed.

'You fucking bastard!'

O'Connel grabbed the bottom part of her V neck sweater and ripped it open, revealing her soft white laced bra. Dillon went silent as the real fear went through her.

'If you don't shut your fucking mouth, I'll give you something to really fucking scream about!' O'Connel declared, as he unbuckled his belt and dropped his zip to show her that he meant what he saying. Dillon said nothing for the moment as a tear ran down her face. The fear of being sexually interfered with grabbed a hold of her as the dark reality set in. Her heart was pounding like mad as she could feel the sweat of her face dripping into her bra.

'Oh please God help me! Jesus Christ help me! Don't kill me off like this!'

Dwyer took the tape from O'Connel and applied a piece to her mouth. He then pulled her sweater back together and placed a piece of tape over the rip on it, which covered her breasts back up. As strange as the situation was, it was the gentleman thing to do. It wasn't what Dillon was expecting him to do but she felt blessed that he did.

Dwyer then turned to O'Connel and slapped him hard across the face.

'I suggest you take a cold fucking shower when we're finished here, you fucking prick! There is going to be no interfering of that kind with this fine soldier. She is merely carrying out her duty and for that I respect her. She's not a fucking criminal!'

He then turned back to her.

345

'And for that, I will only do what I have to do. Nothing more, I promise. Please accept my apologies for him.' He pointed to O'Connel over his shoulder.

'But you have to understand my situation here. IRA headquarters have to learn that when they gave me control of the Fifth Brigade, that meant complete control. I have to give a message to the IRA headquarters. Surely you can see that, can't you?'

Dwyer let the moments pass by in peace, to let her come to grips with the action he had to undertake. She knew why he was going to scar her. She could see that he had to do what he had to do. If he wanted complete control of the Fifth Brigade, she would have to bear the scar to prove it.

She looked at the floor and then back to Dwyer as she nodded her head, giving him the OK to continue. He took the yellow stanley knife from his back pocket as O'Connel held her shoulders back. Dwyer went to work.

Back To The Present

Dillon let out a big sigh, as she knew she had to concentrate on the job at hand. The past was in the past where it belonged. Not here in the now and present. But she couldn't shift that thought from her mind.

'This dirty old bastard actually threatened to rape me once.'

She didn't care for the scar that Dwyer gave her, for scars came with the job. But rape, that's different.

'Get to the job at hand Sinéad, for Christ's sake!' she reminded herself.

'Don't let this situation become personal!'

She let a moment pass before she began her questioning.

'So you're willing to talk about everything to do with the Fifth Brigade, are you?' she asked him.

'Everything', his shaky voice replied.

'Everything?'

'Absolutely', he again acknowledged, feeling relieved that

Warwick was now out of the room.

Dillon waited a moment before she continued.

'I'm going to ask you some questions to which I only want yes or no answers.'

'Okay', he replied.

'Can you give us names and addresses of all the members of the IRA's Fifth Brigade?'

'Yes'

'Can you give me the names of any persons that have carried messages to the headquarters in West Belfast?'

He paused for a moment. This proved to Dillon that he was telling her the truth as if she were a British agent.

'Yes, I can give you names of people we have dealt with.'

He emphasised the words "dealt with".

"Dealt with". That meant people like Dillon.

'Jesus Christ, he's going to tout on everyone. He'll turn the whole of the Fifth Brigade over to the British scum along with anyone who has dealt with them.'

As she unclicked the safety catch of the Kilmar 46 she recited one of the paragraphs of the oath that she swore when she signed up for the cause of the IRA ten years ago. The IRA oath was a modernisation of the original proclamation made by the Provisional Government of the Irish Republic to the people of Ireland in 1921.

'Our founders placed the cause of the Irish Republic under the protection of the most high God whose blessing we will always invoke upon our arms and we will always pray that no one who serves that cause, will dishonour it by cowardice, inhumanity or rapine.'

O'Connel's face dropped as he suddenly realised he was in the presence of an active IRA member. He went to speak but paused for a moment. He quickly decided that he could try and talk his way out of this mess. But he didn't get a chance, as Dillon continued.

'And it seems to me that you fit the description of all three dishonours. Which means that you are way beyond the help of prayer, you fucking touting piece of selfish shit!'

As the Kilmar 46 gave out its thud, O'Connel's blood splattered across the clean white walls, shooting out from the neck that once held the head above his body. What was left of his head fell across the floor as it watched its own body go into a headless spasm.

Dillon watched the headless body jump around into a violent fit, at times lifting itself a good two feet off the ground. She walked over to O'Connel's head and kicked it across the ground away from the now dead, still body. She had to admit it, she was impressed by the power of the Kilmar 46.

As she walked away to the open doorway she smiled to herself, as she felt proud of what she had just done. She'd just killed O'Connel before he had the chance to tout on the London division of the IRA. She didn't kill him out of revenge for the threat he gave to her eighteen months ago, she did it in the line of duty. She always killed to achieve, not in revenge. She had just killed in the line of duty for the cause. She was now again a fully active member of the IRA, ready for her next target.

'Come and get it you British piece of shit!'

47

CLOSING IN

Warwick opened the small door to the left of the large garage door and slowly stepped inside the warehouse. As he did so, he cautiously closed the door behind him. There was no one waiting on the other side of the door for him, as he'd expected. He looked around as he unclicked the safety catch on the Smith & Wesson.

The smell of the cut wood took him back to the time he attempted to do the work on his own fitted kitchen two years ago. Helen used to moan at him about his lack of enthusiasm in home improvement. He would always give her the same reply.

'Is it not bad enough having to do a day's work let alone come home to do some more?'

The boxes of drawers and cupboard fronts still lay in the corner of his now bachelor kitchen.

Music In The Den

As he moved slowly along to his right hand side of the warehouse he could hear the sound of a voice humming in the distance. He stood perfectly still as he tried to locate where the sound was coming from. He could trace it to the plaster board walls at the far end of the warehouse from him, on the east side of the warehouse. It was the temporary toilet area where Dwyer was washing himself.

Dwyer was humming the tune of a song that Warwick knew only too well. When Dwyer started to sing, Warwick recognised his voice.

She sings hollow words of regret,
She sings of times she can't forget.
Holding her own,
Because she's never been shown,

The right way to bereave.
She brings back things you can't retrieve.

'Why the fuck is this piece of shit singing a Zakk Zombie song?' Warwick thought.

He knew now it was Dwyer as he continued humming the tune of the song.

The marijuana had obviously long worn off Warwick by now, as his right hand started to shake. The confidence he possessed earlier, when he beat the hell out of O'Connel, had now disappeared. He held his right hand out in front of him with the Smith & Wesson being his defence. He now had to lift up his left hand to support it after placing the sports bag on the floor. Then as the humming voice seemed to be nearing the opening of the toilet, Warwick's hands shook even more. What would he say to Dwyer once he confronted him again? He had longed for this moment over the past forty eight hours. To be face to face with the man who knew the answers to the questions that were spinning around his head was a nerve twisting feeling.

As the humming came even closer he found himself giving a quick thought to Helen and Jonathan. Would he be with them soon? Would Dwyer finish him off here and now? For Warwick knew he was a small pawn in a big game.

'How in fuck's name did I end up in this situation?'

The humming got closer.

'How the fuck am I going to keep my nerve?'

The humming was as clear as if the walls were no longer blocking the freedom of the musical sound.

'Oh sweet Jesus Christ!'

Then he appeared. Dressed in a casual brown suit, shirt and tie. Tony Dwyer walked slowly out of the open doorway.

Brooks made it to the top of the metal fire escape route at the east side of the building. He had the Kilmar 46 at the ready in his right hand. Luckily the fire exit door was still ajar from O'Connel's earlier exit. He decided he'd wait a few moments before he entered the warehouse. He felt he had to give Warwick the opportunity to talk to Dwyer first, because he didn't feel that there was a need to rush. For, as far as he was concerned, Dillon was still downstairs with O'Connel.

Hunter And Prey

Tony Dwyer stepped out of the toilets and walked across to the briefcase which was situated on the window to south of the warehouse. Warwick was standing on the north side. Dwyer didn't notice him as he walked out. Warwick's heart was pounding like mad. He could feel it pounding up through his throat. It was a wonder that he didn't get sick on the spot.

'GET A GRIP FOR FUCKS SAKE! GET A FUCKING GRIP!' his thoughts were shouting at him.

A bead of sweat dropped from his forehead and into his left eye, causing him to blink from the irritation. He took his left hand from the gun and wiped his eye to relieve himself of the annoyance. But his right hand was shaking even more now in the presence of the man who had given him such a beating on Saturday.

It was at this stage that Warwick could have cursed the people who had designed this model of the Smith & Wesson. This model had been designed to take four different sizes of bullets, with the largest size being for the hunter who needs that extra power and is willing to pay the extra cash needed for that power. O'Connel obviously had gone for the cheap bullets. As the sound of them shaking in the over sized chamber of the gun had made enough noise to grab the attention of Dwyer.

Dwyer turned around and looked north in the direction of the noise as a smile grew upon his face from seeing Warwick. He broke out into a genuine welcoming laugh.

'Detective Tom Warwick, how the devil are you?'

48

FACE TO FACE WITH A FOX

Dillon made it to the top of the ramp on the west side of the building that Warwick had walked up earlier. Like Brooks, she had her Kilmar 46 at the ready in her right hand. She paused outside the large green doors, unsure as to whether she should enter the building or not. She didn't know what could be going on in there. She knew that Brooks would be over on the east side of the building, as she heard Warwick and Brooks talking outside the bottom warehouse earlier.

'Come on, Sinéad, are we going in or what?' she asked herself.

Then a sound made her mind up for her. When she heard the sound of a voice talking she put her left ear up to the big green left hand door to listen.

The Epic Encounter

Dwyer's facial expression was like that of a young innocent child seeing the line of presents that the man with the long white beard had left for him on Christmas morning.

'How in the Lord's name did you find me?' he asked Warwick.

Now the gun shook even more in front of Warwick as the sound of Dwyer's voice sent his brain into a defenceless spasm.

'Just.... just........ good de....detective work, I'd say', Warwick's nervous voice replied.

Dwyer laughed a little more and then suddenly stopped before becoming very serious.

'Bullshit. You're a shit detective and you know it.'

Although Warwick was armed and Dwyer wasn't, Dwyer still possessed the upper hand here. It didn't matter that Warwick had the back up of Dillon and Brooks. Dwyer had information that Warwick was willing to die for and Dwyer knew it.

Warwick had the sports bag with him that he had taken from Dwyer on Saturday at the airport but little did Warwick know that Dwyer didn't care for the bag of money anymore. For at this darkest hour money was the last thing on Dwyer's mind. Warwick lowered the gun, as he felt it was showing his weakness, not his strength.

'If I'm such a shit detective, then how the hell did I track you down, hey?' he asked.

Dwyer tilted his head a little as he thought about the question for a moment.

'You must have got help from somewhere.'

Warwick looked at the ground as he pulled his cigarettes from his pocket and extracted one.

He needed to calm down.

'Why can't you just accept the fact that I've found you?' Warwick asked.

'Because you are shit and you have always been shit and you will always be shit!'

'FUCK YOU!' Warwick shouted as he lifted the gun back up again.

Dwyer smiled back at Warwick.

'So what is it you're planning to do with that?' Dwyer asked, as he pointed at the shaking gun in Warwick's right hand.

'I'll shoot you're fucking brains out if you don't shut the fuck up!'

Dwyer just laughed as he looked on at the gun that jumped around in front of him.

'Would you like me to dance around? Would that help?'

Warwick lowered the gun as he took his lighter from his pocket and produced a red end on his cigarette. He gazed down at the ground for a moment as his mind seemed to forget about Brooks and Dillon. He felt as if it was just the two of them for that peaceful moment.

'So why did you let Billy Hopkirk go through with the

suicide?' Warwick asked as he blew out a cloud of smoke.
Dwyer looked back at Warwick with a face that suddenly revealed a thousand thoughts. And yet, he looked at a loss to answer the question. Warwick couldn't believe that Dwyer didn't answer the question with his obviously natural cockiness. Had Warwick hit a soft spot?

'Come on Dwyer, tell me about young Billy.'
Dwyer looked up in shock.

'How did you know my name?' he asked.
Warwick had only known Dwyer as Jacobs up to now.

'How the hell did you find out who I was?'

'Like I said before, it was just good detective work', Warwick replied.

'Bullshit, Tom! I know you only too well. You are not a good detective.'
Warwick looked back at Dwyer with no expression. He didn't want to give anything away now as he suddenly felt he had something on his opponent.

Touching Nerves

'Who's Mary?' Warwick asked with coolness.
Dwyer's face turned to hate in the blink of an eye.

'What's that got to do with anything?' Dwyer asked through gritted teeth.

'My God, I've hit a nerve here, I've almost struck gold I think', Warwick thought.
He knew he had shaken Dwyer with the mention of that name but he couldn't figure out how or why.

'Come on, Dwyer, who the fuck is she?' Warwick taunted, for he knew now that he would have to really rattle Dwyer's cage if he wanted answers.

'Come on, Dwyer, tell me all about her.'

'Fuck you!' Dwyer spat as he went to reach into his inside pocket.
Before his left hand could open the one attached button of his casual brown blazer, Warwick had the Smith & Wesson held

out in front of him, pointing at Dwyer. He unclicked the safety catch and clicked it again to show he meant business.

His hand was as steady as a rock. Dwyer stopped in his tracks. Warwick's confidence was back with him and it was back in full swing. Maybe the marijuana had popped back up for one last buzz before it disappeared forever.

'Remove your jacket slowly!' he ordered Dwyer.

Dwyer slowly moved his arms until he was holding his hands out on either side of his body. He then placed a hand over each of his shoulders as he slipped the jacket off and let it fall to the floor. He now stepped away from the jacket, smiling, and turned around to show he held no gun anywhere else. When he had turned his full three hundred and sixty degrees, he bore that cheeky smile that he had when he saw Warwick first standing there at the north end of the warehouse.

'And wipe that stupid fucking grin off your face!' Warwick added.

'Or else?' Dwyer still smiled.

Warwick said nothing. What could he say? What could he do? For he needed answers and Dwyer knew this only too well.

'Exactly. You're going to do nothing at all because you want to know what I know about Helen and Jonathan', Dwyer smirked.

'Who is Mary?' Warwick coldly asked as he tried to ignore Dwyer's comments.

'Do you know what I know about them?'

'Who is Mary?' Warwick's chin was showing dimples as he could feel the tables reversing as his hand began to shake at the mere mention of his departed wife and son.

'Do you want to know what I did on the twenty third of April?' Dwyer inquired.

Warwick again lowered the gun, as he knew now that Dwyer had once again obtained the upper hand.

'Who is Mary?' Warwick whispered as he looked at the ground and took another pull on his cigarette before throwing it to the ground.

'I was very busy that morning doing a little job in New Southgate. You may remember, as you were there', Dwyer began, referring to the bank robbery at the Midland bank.

Warwick wasn't shocked by the revelation that Dwyer was involved in the robbery, as Brooks had worked this out already and informed Warwick of it this morning back at Hayes.

'I prevented one of my colleagues from shooting you in your car across the road from the bank.'

As Dwyer was talking he walked over to the south window to retrieve his packet of Marlboro lights and lighter. As he did so Warwick was looking down at the ground, playing that moment over again in his head.

One of the hooded men raised his shotgun in Warwick's direction but, for some unknown reason, one of the other hooded men stepped in front of him, preventing him from doing so.

Dwyer. The man who saved Warwick's life that day. Warwick looked up at Dwyer as he thought about this.

'Why?' he asked. 'Why did you let me go?'

Getting Answers

As Dwyer blew out a cloud of smoke from his first intake of Marlboro Light, he gave his explanation.

'We had just completed a successful tour of London's banks, and we were untouched. No one came close to catching us until that morning in New Southgate. We walked out that morning with two hundred and seventy three pounds in cash. The last thing I needed was the death of pig, to fuck it all up.' Dwyer now shook his head as he played those moments outside the bank to himself.

'I stopped you from being shot and yet, you still wouldn't let things be, would you? You took a photograph of one of my men as we were getting away.'

'How the fuck did you know that?' Warwick asked in astonishment. Then it came to him.

'Sergeant Davis!'

Dwyer gave out a little laugh.

'It does pay to know the right people in the right places.'

Dwyer laughed a little more as he took another pull on his cigarette.

'Anyway. Word had it that your little tip off from Mark Gerald could have become my worst nightmare. So you had to be stopped. And you were.'

Again Warwick thought of how close he was to identifying that face in the picture. When he looked up at Dwyer, he saw that cheeky face staring back at him.

Dwyer shook his head once more.

'Do you know what the strange thing is about all this? You know yourself that you're a shit detective. Your record of solved cases is pathetic. The nearest you came to succeeding at something was catching me that morning in New Southgate, and that was only because of your help from Mark Gerald.'

Dwyer's face turned to ice as he thought about how disposable he considered Warwick to be.

Warwick looked back at Dwyer with the look of an innocent child waiting for the bad news. Although he didn't know the details of the bad news, he knew it was coming.

'If you hadn't taken that picture, Helen and Jonathan would still be alive now.'

Warwick unclicked the safety catch of the Smith & Wesson.

'The Fifth Brigade came to a decision that day to silence you. But obviously with our connections within the police force, we were warned that there would be no toleration of shootings or killings of fellow pigs.'

Dwyer stopped, to take another lungful of the Marlboro Light.

'The funny thing was, they never mentioned spouses. So that's where we decided to hit you.'

Dwyer smiled for a moment, as he felt pleased with himself at having the time to tell Warwick all this before he headed off on his last mission.

'You received a phone call that evening from Sergeant Davis telling you that your wife and child were involved in a massive car accident where the explosion was so great that their bodies were burnt to pieces on impact.'

That was exactly what Warwick was told on the phone that evening.

'We installed a newly developed remote control steering device on your wife's car that day and waited for her to drive to her sister's house before we activated the remote control system on it from two cars away.'

Dwyer tilted his head sideways with pleasure.

'I actually drove Helen's car into the garage on Lancaster Road, into the petrol pumps and activated the bomb that was installed in the boot of her car that day and watched her and Jonathan fry like a pair of fried Kentucky chickens.'

Warwick raised the gun up and shot Dwyer in the left shoulder. The gun shot echoed through the warehouse. Dwyer spun one hundred and eighty degrees and then fell to the floor, holding on to his bloody shoulder.

Warwick walked straight over to him and kicked Dwyer's hand away from the shoulder and then sank the heel of his shoe into the wound.

'You fucking bastard!' Warwick cried as he kept digging his heel in until the amount of blood falling across the floor, trebled.

Throughout this ordeal Dwyer didn't scream, cry or murmur. He just took the beating and shooting like a man. Warwick walked away from Dwyer as he sobbed like a little child.

Brooks opened the door and rushed straight inside when he heard the gun shot. He ran to the plaster board wall in front of him which was the rear of the temporary toilet on the west side of the warehouse. Dillon also opened her door but didn't move inside. She peered around the frame of the door and had a clear view of everything that was going on.

'So why the fuck didn't you take me?' Warwick asked of Dwyer.

'Because....'

Dwyer was in pain from the beating on his shoulder.

'Because that would have been too easy and too messy.' Dwyer managed to stand up as he continued.

'There would have been a major investigation if you were killed. All the cases you were working on, would have been handed over to someone else. So someone else would have got the photograph and the information of the robberies, which would have spelt disaster for me.'

He walked to the window and used its ledge as support.

'But instead, you took six months off work, no one went near your unsolved cases, because there are so many of them, and the Fifth Brigade was in the clear.'

The warehouse was in silence now for the next few minutes until Warwick took the Kilmar 46 from his back waist and removed its silencer.

49

REVELATIONS

The blood had now spread out to an area of approximately four squared metres, and counting.
A couple of rats were milling around the doorway, sizing up O'Connels head to see if it was worth the risk of a closer investigation, as the smell was very inviting.

'Peter O'Connel call back! Peter O'Connel Call back!' A voice called from the radio that was still attached to the belt on Peter O'Connel's jeans.

'Peter O'Connel call back! Peter O'Connel call back!' Paul the Gateman requested as he spoke into his radio.
He then turned back to face his new visitor.

'I don't understand why he ain't answering, mate, as I know he's with the asbestos people at the moment.'
Paul then placed his radio back on the table and turned away from the window as he took a hard hat from the large box behind the door. As he did so he informed his new visitor of one of the site rules.

'Oh, and by the way, mate, it's a non smoking site. So you'll have to put that big cigar of yours out before go through the door!'
As Paul turned back to the open window he found himself staring down the silencer of a classic Smith 58.

'What the fuck is it with you British people and your non-smoking rules?' the Undertaker asked.
The sound of Paul's brains splashing off the ceiling drowned out the thud of the gun.

Watching From the Wings
Brooks made his way around to the south side of the plaster boarded toilet area, and along to the east side of the warehouse. Then he saw Dwyer.

Dwyer was still hanging onto the ledge of the window on the southside of the warehouse for support. Brooks could tell by the way Dwyer was supporting himself that he was the one who had been shot. He felt pleased that it was Warwick who was still alive, but also felt as if he was being cheated. He knew that Dwyer was responsible for killing three fellow field agents of Section 13 in the past. And now when Brooks could see Dwyer for the first time in the flesh, it made him realise that he wanted to bring this man in alive.

'Imagine the reward for Peter Allan and Section 13, if I could bring Dwyer in and put him on trial for his actions.' Neither he nor Peter Allan had ever given this any thought before because they thought it was going to be a task in itself to find Dwyer and kill him. But now that Brooks saw Dwyer in the flesh, he wanted to bring him in alive.

'And put the bastard on trial', he thought.

Dillon didn't move from her position. She stayed on the other side of the door at the east entrance, glancing her head around the corner every now and again.

'Who is Mary?' Warwick asked again as he lifted both hands up.

The unsilenced Kilmar 46, was poised next to the Smith & Wesson, ready for the attack. Warwick now seemed to have abandoned the idea of teasing Dwyer with the empty money bag. For the news of Helen and Jonathan's death took him over like a wild spirit. Hate was fighting to get out of his every pore. He just wanted to kill Dwyer and have done with this whole bloody mess. His stomach turned over, which caused him to bring up some vomit. He spat it out in three mouthfuls onto the ground while keeping his eyes on Dwyer. He coughed up some more sour lumps as his mind kept playing a vision of his wife and son burning in the car that night in the petrol garage.

Burning with helplessness.
Burning with violence.
Burning with innocence.
Burning because of his ignorance.

He should have taken heed that day outside the bank and not taken that photograph. He should have acccepted the warning when one of the robbers was going to shoot him.

Dwyer now looked across the ledge to the briefcase. He knew now that his last mission's location would have to be moved from Picadilly Circus to the Hackney warehouse. The case was open and the override switch was on display, waiting to be activated. He knew he would be with Mary soon, just as he had promised Billy Hopkirk on Friday night.

'Mary and Billy.'

The Awaited Answer

Dwyer's thoughts were with those two people now. He decided to tell Warwick about Mary and about Billy Hopkirk.

'I suppose I owe this useless piece of shit that much', he thought.

He then grabbed a greasy old cloth that was on the ledge and placed it on his shoulder to stop the cold air from causing the irritation he was feeling.

'Mary was my niece.'

He stopped to let out a groan from the pain he was now feeling in his shoulder as it tried to adjust itself to the new temperature.

'She died two years ago from cancer.'

He stopped briefly to help himself to a comforting cigarette, from the packet on the ledge.

It took a minute to perform the task with one hand.

Warwick said nothing as he knew he would have to listen to Dwyer talk about the things that had led him to this point in his life. The questions possessed him about this Mary and Billy Hopkirk.

'Then I'll kill this no good piece of shit', he thought.

Finally Dwyer's task with the cigarette was complete.

'She was only twelve years old.'

After blowing out an ring of smoke, it seemed that the tobacco was the perfect medication for his shoulder.

'Mary was a loner. Her mother, my sister, was a useless piece of shit. Through her pregnancy she smoked and drank and, before you knew it, she was a fucking junkie on cocaine.' Dwyer looked at the ground as he thought of the poor upbringing Mary underwent until he stepped in.

'So she came to live with me.'

He paused to think upon the memories of that perfect little girl.

'What a chilled out, perfect little girl she was. Every parent talks about how great their child is, but Mary was something else.

And Mary wasn't even mine, remember', Dwyer added. 'Anyway, like I said, the cancer got the better of her. It started in the bones of her right arm and spread throughout the rest of her body within months.'

The air could be heard brushing between Dwyer and Warwick as it passed between the open doors on the east and west sides of the warehouse.

'She passed away. But only after I looked after her for two years. Between her mother stealing to pay for her fucking habit and the health service being unable to cure the cancer Mary suffered, I did everything I could to comfort her. I was the only person in her world of loneliness. Her last three months were quiet ones.

'Confined to a bed with nothing to do but read books and watch television, her life slipped away from her.'

Dwyer stopped again to scrunch his face in defeat to the pain his shoulder was now developing, which was brought on from the acid of the grease on the dirty rag.

'Because of her useless whore of a mother, Mary didn't receive much schooling. And as you know only too well, with schooling comes friends. Because of her lack of schooling there was a serious lack of friends in Mary's life. So she died a loner.'

Dwyer seemed to look for some understanding in the loneliness Mary must have felt in her last darkened days.

'She once wished for a friend on her twelfth birthday, three days before she passed away. She didn't wish for a friend for comfort. It was only so that she could pass on her toys and her rocking horse to someone else. That was all she wished for.'
He then looked back up at Warwick.
'That, my friend, is true innocence. Pure and fucking simple.'
He flicked the ash from his cigarette and inhaled some more of the required tobacco smoke.
'Anyway, two years later, I had to go underground for a while because of a Section 13 in the British Secret Service, who were a bit pissed off at me for three executions I'd carried out on their agents six years ago. It seems that one of their agents was doing a little ground work on me.'
Dwyer had to stop himself for a moment because he didn't think that Warwick would know anything about his connections with the IRA. He looked up at Warwick as he quickly fobbed him off with an explanation. But Warwick knew only too well what Dwyer was mixed up in.
'Let's just say that the British Secret Service didn't appreciate where some of the money was going.'
Brooks went cold as Dwyer said it.
'How the bloody hell did he find that out?' he thought.
Brooks had been doing a little studying of Dwyer's handy work a few months ago. Dwyer had an insider working for him before, but Section 13 found the traitor.
'There must be another insider!'
That made Brooks' mind up for him once and for all. He had to bring him in alive.
'So I went undercover, as you know already, as a private tutor.'
Dwyer had to stop for a moment after throwing his half smoked cigarette to the ground so he could free his hand to turn the soaked rag around on his shoulder.
'That was when I met up with Billy Hopkirk. A young boy in need of private tuition. A young boy in need of a way in life.

Because his father had committed suicide himself three years ago. It seems his father went into a state of depression when he developed arthritis in both hands, causing him to become unavailable to work any more. He was a professional piano tuner. A man who loved his work.'

Warwick had read the file on William Hopkirk two days ago. He knew the man's history.

'Billy was also a loner. He didn't understand the other kids at his school. He couldn't get into the innocence of growing up. The death of his father had taken that away from him.'

Dwyer looked at the ground with a face of deep thinking. Thinking that caused his eyes to water.

'He reminded me of Mary in so many ways. He too had an illness. The illness of having those visions of his father, hanging from a wooden beam in his garage, tattooed on his brain.'

Warwick thought back to the pictures he had on his desk on Saturday morning, of William Hopkirk's body slumped across the table.

'Billy loved his father. He told me he wanted to be just like him. That was the main thing that made his mother panic. Having a young son who envied someone who'd killed himself. Isn't it bad enough that kids envy these stupid fucking spoilt pop stars that kill themselves on drug and drink binges. Imagine a boy who envied a father who'd killed himself.'

A Twisted Theology

'You knew full well he was going to kill himself, you bastard', Warwick spat with anger.

Dwyer smiled back at him. Warwick's words came with a level of anger.

'You walked out of the restaurant that night without paying for the bill because you knew what was going to happen.'

Dwyer started to laugh.

'Of course I knew what was going to happen. I encouraged

him to do it. If it wasn't for me, he wouldn't have done it.'

'WHY?' Warwick shouted.

'BECAUSE HE WANTED TO BE JUST LIKE HIS FATHER', Dwyer shouted back before he stopped to lower his voice as he continued.

'And, like I said before, Mary never had any friends in this fucked up shitty world.'

Warwick's eyebrows rose up, as the penny suddenly dropped for him. The pieces came together in his own mind. He thought of those last words that Billy Hopkirk said before he pulled the trigger on Friday night.

'I'm off to see Mary.'

Warwick looked at Dwyer with disbelief. His eyebrows formed a frown as he tried to understand the sick thinking that he thought that Dwyer must possess.

'You encouraged young Billy to kill himself so that he could be a friend of Mary's?'

Dwyer smiled again as he thought about it.

'Thou shalt not kill!' Dwyer quoted one of the ten commandments.

'And that includes killing yourself, for fuck's sake', Warwick added as he tried to understand the madness of it all. How would Billy have made it to see Mary, if he had broken that commandment?

Warwick had a face of confusion that accompanied the words coming from his own mouth. Dwyer gave a slight laugh of satisfaction as he continued.

'Mary made it to heaven because she was pure and innocent. Billy also made it to heaven because he was pure and innocent. It was not his fault that he took a life. I encouraged him to do what he did.'

'You sick bastard!' Warwick could feel the vomit rising again in his throat.

'Billy won't have to answer before God on the actions he committed to take his own life.'

'You sick son of a bitch!'

Small segments of sick spilled from the side of Warwick's mouth. He held onto his stomach with his right hand whilst also keeping hold of the Smith & Wesson.

'Only I will have to answer for those actions when my time comes.'

'You twisted fucking areshole!'

With Warwick's words came spits of sick across the ground in front of him. His head began to ache in such a way that he thought it would suddenly explode.

'I know Mary will now be sharing time with her new friends.'

Warwick closed his eyes as he knew the two names that Dwyer was about to say.

'Billy Hopkirk ....and Jonathan Warwick.'

Warwick raised his hands up again, pointed the guns at Dwyer and unclicked the safety catches on both guns.

50

TO KILL OR NOT TO KILL?

Brooks jumped out from behind the plaster board walls, his Kilmar 46 ready in his right hand, but not pointing up. It was just at his side, ready at a moment's notice.

'Hold it Warwick, hold it there!' he demanded, holding his left hand out with his palm on show.

Dwyer smiled at the sight of his new guest. Warwick looked across with his eyes only to Brooks.

Different Reasons To Kill

Dillon unclicked the safety catch on her Kilmar 46 as she stepped inside the east door and raised the gun up, pointing it in Brooks' direction.

'Fuck off Brooks, this is not your call', she ordered him.

Brooks looked back at Dillon with a startled reaction, as he foolishly thought she was still in the lower warehouse watching O'Connel.

'I suggest you back the fuck off and let Detective Warwick finish the business he has come here today to complete.'

The pupils in her eyes, were at their smallest. She was ready to kill or be killed. She knew that Warwick was dying to put a couple of bullets in Dwyer and there was no way that she was going to stand in his way. Because, if he didn't do it, she would. But she knew only too well by the way Brooks jumped out to prevent Warwick from shooting Dwyer, that he wanted Dwyer alive. And as far as Dillon was concerned, there was no way that was going to happen. Not today. Not while she was alive. She had to kill all links between the IRA's Fifth Brigade and the British. That was why she was here.

Dwyer was amazed at the appearance of Dillon. He remembered his first encounter with Dillon eighteen months ago. He knew that she was here to kill him. His thoughts were unaffected by his shoulder's injury.

'The IRA headquarters obviously want me dead.'

'If you kill him, he'll get exactly what he wants.'

Brooks couldn't believe what he was saying. But he had to reason with Warwick if he was to keep Dwyer alive.

'What do you mean?' Warwick asked as he kept his focus and both handguns on Dwyer.

'Shut up Brooks!' Dillon interrupted. 'You haven't a fucking clue what you're talking about.'

Brooks kept his eyes on Dillon and she kept hers on him. He had to wait for his opportunity. He had to stare her out until his moment would arrive.

Dillon could feel the air brushing past her towards Brooks. She blinked. He blinked. Then she made a silly mistake. Brooks' moment had now arrived. In the split second, when Dillon's eyes moved to look at Warwick, Brooks' right hand was up, his Kilmar's safety catch unclicked in the process and it's barrel's end was facing Dillon. Brooks was sure that he had achieved the movement in record time. 0.8 of a second.

The view of events from the ceiling of the warehouse, must have resembled something out of a New York gangster story. Dwyer on the south, holding on to his wounded shoulder. While Warwick pointed two guns at him from the north. Dillon on the east, pointing her gun at Brooks on the west, who in return had his gun facing her.

'Put the gun down, Dillon!' Brooks ordered.

'Fuck you!'

'PUT THE BLOODY GUN DOWN!' he shouted his demand.

'FUCK YOU!' she shouted back.

Warwick's head was pounding like mad, but he had to shout to grab Brooks' attention.

'WHAT DO YOU MEAN?' he shouted, referring to Brooks' earlier statement.

Brooks looked at Warwick with the caution of Dillon's finger rubbing against the metal of her gun's trigger.

'I knew I shouldn't have given that bitch a gun!' he thought as he turned some of his attention to Warwick.

'If you kill him, then he has a strong chance of being with Mary. If you shoot him, he will become the victim. He then will have the opportunity of answering to God. You'll be giving him everything he wants.'

Dwyer smiled as he looked at Brooks.

'So you are the Martin Brooks. Section 13's most secret agent', Dwyer concluded with a smile.

Brooks ignored his comment as he continued to work on Warwick.

'This dirt bag believes that, if he is killed or is killed in action with others, he makes it to heaven. If you leave him be, then I can make the son of a bitch die, a lonely old man in prison, many years from now.'

'Tom, he hasn't a fucking clue about what he is talking about', Dillon interjected.

'SHUT UP!' Brooks shouted back at her.

Ready To Die

Dwyer began to laugh as he looked around the warehouse at his three guests. Brooks turned away from Warwick to look at Dwyer laughing while keeping his gun pointing at Dillon. Although she had her gun still pointing at Brooks, she, too, turned to look at Dwyer.

'Look at the three of you!' Dwyer interrupted his own laugh. 'Warwick, you only came this far by taking a tip from your mate Mark Gerald six months ago. But I have to admit, I'm impressed that you have made it here today and you clearly have the upper hand. But I refuse to believe that it was done from your own doing.'

Dwyer was, of course, right and Warwick knew it. He was here by luck, both good and bad. He was here because he stupidly nearly killed himself in a car accident.

'And Sinéad Dillon. One of the finest soldiers I had the pleasure of dealing with before, when we met eighteen months ago. Of everyone here I have respect for you. You will make sure I am killed because that is what the IRA headquarters have asked you to do.'

Dwyer then looked to the west side of the warehouse to Brooks.

'Martin Brooks of Section 13. This is a great pleasure.'

Dwyer slowly moved towards the briefcase on the ledge. He had to get to that override switch. Warwick was the only one with the guns facing him. If he could get to the trigger before Warwick shot him, he could blow the warehouse sky high. What a way to go.

Although Warwick had the two guns facing him, his watered eyes were facing the ground in front of him. And Dwyer was using that as an opportunity to edge his way to the briefcase as he continued talking to Brooks.

'Section 13, the most secret of departments within the M.o.D. And yet I was successful in getting to your fellow agents.'

'Only by using an insider', Brooks reminded him.

'Like yourself you mean?' Dwyer asked.

Brooks froze in puzzlement at Dwyer's comment.

'Oh come now Mr. Brooks. Are you trying to tell me that you got here today by your own detection. You found me because Dillon here helped you. The IRA helped you find me, because you're too shit to do it on your own.'

'That damned bloody insider', Brooks cursed.

'I knew the IRA would come and track me down, with you on board. That's why my last mission will be a success.'

Dwyer began to laugh again.

Dillon realised what he was doing when she saw the case on the ledge.

'Oh shit, he's got the bomb, Warwick, he's got the bomb there!'

Problem Solved

Warwick's eyes raised up to see Dwyer's left hand drop the bloody rag and reach out to the override switch. Dillon went to shout at Warwick to shoot Dwyer, but Warwick didn't need to be told as the deafening shots exploded from the guns in front of him.

Warwick's mind was running on hate as his body quickly adjusted to the kick-back given off from the power of the Kilmar 46 as he fired bullet after bullet into Dwyer. Dwyer's arms were outstretched as the first of the bullets pushed him away from the briefcase.

No sooner were Dwyer's stomach muscles flying from the open wounds inflicted upon him, than his body was trying to fall to the ground. But every impact from a new powerful bullet would lift him back onto his feet. The window of the south wall was soon covered with Dwyer's insides. Dwyer was exploding everywhere. Warwick raised the gun up a few inches and fired three shots at Dwyer's head, which was enough to make it explode from the shoulders. The power in the Kilmar 46 was having the greatest effect.

Brooks and Dillon were in limbo for that brief moment as they both turned to look at each other, realising that the mission was now almost complete. Dillon wore a smile as she pulled the trigger. Brooks had no smile when he pulled his. He had that concentrated, determined look that was almost his signature face when he'd killed people before.

Warwick tossed the Smith & Wesson to the floor when its empty chamber kept clicking in his right hand. And yet he kept firing bullet after bullet from the Kilmar 46 into the bloody tissued mess that was left of Dwyer.

51

THE ENCORE

Brooks held onto his stomach as the bullet entered his gut. The immediate pain was incredible as it spread out amongst the nerves of his body in seconds. Urine flowed from him uncontrollably. He dropped the gun from his hand as he fell forward to the ground, listening to Warwick on his killing spree. Listening to the bullets fire across the area in front of him from the gun he himself had supplied to Warwick earlier.

Brooks had fallen onto his knees, still holding on to his stomach. He couldn't believe he had been hit. He couldn't believe he had been shot down by Dillon. But he was sure he had shot her. Yet he didn't have the energy to look up and see. As he fell forward his body went numb. His mind began to close down into darkness. His mission was complete as his head met the ground in front of him at full speed and with the full weight of his upper body. His mind and body were now eternally shut down. Mission over.

Aftermath of Madness

Dillon looked down at her own stomach. She was in total shock. She was sure Brooks' gun fired off at the same time as hers but it was hard to tell with Warwick firing every one of the twelve bullets from his Kilmar 46 into Dwyer, one at a time. Then the firing was over. Dillon moved her left hand all over her middle body, checking for blood. She moved forward, to check that her legs and feet were OK.

'Jesus Christ, Sinéad, you are one lucky bitch', she told herself.

Her bullet had landed in Brooks a fraction of a second before he pulled on his trigger. The bullet from his gun had landed on the framework of the door behind her.

Warwick fell to his knees as he threw the Kilmar 46 to the ground in front of him. He had killed Dwyer. He had blown his body to pieces. As he looked at the carnage of the south side of the warehouse he couldn't work out if Dwyer's body was lying on its front or its back. He had used the power of the Kilmar 46 to its maximum.

He then turned to look at Brooks. He was lying face down, a pool of blood growing on the ground around him. He then turned to look at Dillon. She was still standing there inside the doorway on the east side. Warwick was glad that she had survived the madness of events. He smiled at her. She smiled back. Warwick closed his eyes for a brief moment as he let the welcomed silence wash over him. He was alive. Dillon was alive.

It was unfortunate that Brooks was not alive, but Warwick found no reason to mourn his death, as he felt he hadn't trusted Brooks in the first place. How was he to know that Brooks wouldn't have tried to be rid of him when the mission was complete. He opened his eyes to see Dillon's beautiful smile looking back at him. In the madness of events he'd found himself growing very fond of her in some strange unexplained way.

He couldn't understand how this feeling could be with him now, after what he had just been through. Maybe it was because she had been through it with him as well. At this moment in time this beautiful sexy woman standing before him was the only other person he had any trust for. He was so pleased to see her standing there, holding her Kilmar 46, smiling at him.

The Undertaker Calleth

Then her smile disappeared. A frown grew on her face. Warwick began to frown, as he couldn't understand why she had changed her beautiful smile. Then the blood dripped from the side of her mouth. She shook her head as the blood began to pour from her mouth at a rapid rate. She fell forward onto her face without breaking the fall. As she did so, Warwick could see the shadow of a figure approaching the east doorway.

His senses took over his feelings with amazing quickness as he ran to the east wall on his left in line with the door.

The Undertaker stopped at Dillon's body as he walked through the open east door. He crouched down to retrieve the knife he'd thrown into her back. It was a cold way to kill her, but he didn't give a damn. As far as he was concerned, that was the best way to attack. Catch them from behind.

'A person stabbed in the back is a person who has left himself wide open', he said as he wiped the blood from his knife into her hair.

When he stood back up he took his zippo lighter from his pocket and relit his cigar. He was just about to look behind him when he noticed the bloody mess at the southside of the warehouse.

'That figures!' he casually observed as he wondered about the numerous gunshots he heard on his way across the site below.

He walked a little closer to the remains of the body, blowing puffs of cuban smoke in his trail.

Warwick breathed slowly and quietly as he watched the intruder walk towards the remains of Dwyer. He couldn't move from where he was without being heard. He was a sitting duck. He would be dead as soon as this intruder turned around and saw him.

'I'll be dead in fucking seconds. I'm a fucking dead man.'
The Undertaker started to turn his body around very slowly, towards the east wall, but not his head.

'This is it.'
The Undertaker paused for a moment............................
'This is fucking it!'
.... and then turned around completely to face Warwick.

'OH FUCKING SHIT' Warwick loudly announced as the

Undertaker eyed him up and down.

The Undertaker was so taken in by his new prey, that he didn't hear the safety catch unclick on the Kilmar 46 in Dillon's hand. It only took three shots from the powerful handgun to lift the Undertaker's body off the ground and clean through the bloody-splattered south window.

As she fired the third shot the gun fell limply from her hands. She turned her head in Warwick's direction to make sure he was safe. On seeing him standing there, she simply smiled that beautiful smile. Her last action complete. Her last action was to save Warwick. Her eyes closed. A smile was the last thing to grace her face. It was the expression she was to die with. The beautiful smile of Dillon.

Too Late

Warwick ran over to her but it was too late. She was gone. This most gorgeous woman was gone. The woman he felt something so strong for was gone. He wanted to cry but he felt that there was nothing left in him to cry. How much more could a man lose in one day.

He suddenly felt cold and alone standing over to her slumped body. He stood in front of her for a brief moment, trying to figure out what he would do now without her and Brooks. When he crouched down to take her Kilmar 46 from her hand, he noticed that there was a dust sheet in front of him beside the door. He took the sheet and slowly placed it over Dillon's body. Before he covered her head he crouched down to kiss her smiling face.

'Sleep tight!' he whispered and then covered it up.

He then walked over to Brooks' body and retrieved the car keys from his jacket pocket. As he did so he could hear the distant wailing of police sirens. He walked over to the open bloody window ledge, crushing the remains of Dwyer under his feet as he did so. He could see the police cars driving towards the building site from two roads away. Someone had obviously reported the gun shots.

He turned and made a quick move for the open door on the west side of the warehouse. Just before he was about to run past the boxed-off toilet area, he turned to look at the blanket in front of the east door.

'What a fucking shame!' he declared.

He and Dillon could have had something very special. Something very special indeed. He then turned and fled via the metal staircase of the fire escape on the west side. He was over the east wall below the warehouse before the police drove through the entrance of the building site. No one saw him make his way across the abandoned playground beside the site.

Four minutes later the police drove through the east door of the warehouse and over Dillon's body on their heroic, careless entrance.

52

.... AND THEN THERE WAS ONE

O'Shea thought about Dillon as he slowly walked up the steps of Harry Fords Leisure Centre. He'd been watching the entrance of the centre from the cafe across the road, waiting to see if she'd show up. He took the elevator to the first floor and made his way along the corridor to the unisex changing room. He took the keys from his pocket as he stood in front of locker 231.

'Why the hell didn't I speak to Dillon at Brooks' place. I was nearly killed today. Had that happened, I would have died without ever having the chance to tell her the truth.'
A father, longing to tell his daughter that they were true blood, opened the door of locker 231.

When the door opened his facial expression dropped as he saw the light switch click itself on from the adjusted coat hanger fixed to the back of the locker door. This sent an electric current down the 2.5mm cable from the industrial torch battery to the tightly compact icing sugar. Dillon's plan had worked a treat.

As the explosion tore O'Shea's head into a thousand pieces, the Irish bank notes blew into the air like confetti at a celebrated wedding. Along with fifteen thousand pounds in Irish punts went the bloody brains of O'Shea.

Leaving Things Behind

Warwick got into the car, with ease. There were people out on the street, watching the commotion going on in the next street, as the police sealed off the area. Neighbours were talking to each other for the first time in years. It always takes a disaster to make British people talk to each other. There is an old myth, claiming that British people pull together in times of trouble. It's not true at all. Disasters are just a great opportunity to catch up on gossip.

Warwick was that calm and cool about everything that no one paid him any attention. He had no blood on him apart from the dried blood above his nose. When he pulled the door behind him he took his cigarettes from his pocket. He was just about to extract one when he declined.

'I've smoked more than enough for one day', he decided.

He threw the packet onto the dashboard as he placed both hands on the steering wheel, and placed his head on its centre framework.

Helen, Jonathan, Dwyer, Martin Brooks, Billy Hopkirk, Mary and Sinéad .... Sinéad Dillon. All gone. Gone to the next world while Warwick had to carry on in this empty excuse for a life.

'Fuck it!' he whispered as a tear that had somehow survived his earlier emptiness, dropped from his cheek and onto the black plastic of the wheel.

He thought of the white dust sheet he'd left behind him in front of the east door. The body of Dillon. The living body he would have given anything to make love to.

'She was beautiful!'

There was something there between Warwick and Dillon. It was something that had sparked between them at the Hayes base this morning when they first met. But it was something that died with her as she saved his life.

'FUCK IT!' Warwick shouted as he started up the engine.

Just as he did so he could hear the sound of a mobile phone ringing from the driver's door compartment. He frowned as he reached his right hand down and lifted up the ringing phone.

The Starkness of Truth

John Hayward was now getting anxious as the hour had passed by ten minutes ago. He sat there, like Sir John and Allan, waiting for Martin Brooks to answer his phone.

'Come on!' Hayward impatiently urged the telephone

monitor in front of him.

'He may have left his phone in the car', Sir John commented.

Allan said nothing as he stared at the monitor. An hour had elapsed ten minutes ago. Brooks should have rung in by now. Allan was starting to feel a little nervous now.

What if it all went wrong? What if he failed now in front of Sir John and the Prime minister? Then the ringing stopped.

'Hello?' The voice from the monitor asked. The line was a little crackled, so Allan didn't recognise the voice.

'Martin?' Allan asked.

'No, it's Warwick.'

Hayward and Sir John looked at each other with confusion. Allan closed his eyes as he feared the worst.

'Where's Brooks?' Sir John asked the monitor.

There was a moment of silence as the realisation of Section 13's most secret and dangerous operation came to a close.

'IRA killed him', Warwick announced. 'And they killed him in fucking style!'

Then the line went dead as the dialling tone cut in.

John Hayward stood up from his chair very quickly. He then took a strong mint from the packet in his trouser pocket with his shaky left hand and proceeded to close the top button of his shirt. Sir John watched him do this with a look of disgust on his face. He knew what was coming.

After straightening his tie, he took his jacket from the back of his chair.

'You know the procedure, Peter,...........', Hayward began.

'You spineless fucking bastard!' Sir John called the Prime Minister, who in return ignored him.

'You will have to shoulder the burden of any embarrassment, should this ever become public. You know the "Secrets Act", Peter, you know what you signed up for and you know what you are being paid for.'

Peter Allan placed his elbows on the table in front of him and placed his hands over his face, as he knew what the future held for him. Hope. The hope of not being caught out, that he had operated with the IRA and had a top British Secret Agent killed because of it. And the Prime Minister knew nothing at all about the operation. That was how Section 13 had been set up. That was how it was going to be.

As John Hayward opened the door he stopped for a brief moment and looked at the ground.

'My cabinet are waiting for me, Gentlemen, I will have to leave you, I'm afraid.'

'Fuck you!' Sir John whispered as he placed a comforting hand on Allan's shoulder.

'Good day to you, Sir John', Hayward departed as he closed the door behind him. He didn't even acknowledge Allan at the end.

Warwick opened the driver's window and dropped the mobile phone out on to the road. He then placed the Kilmar 46 in the glove compartment before placing the gearstick in first gear. He then drove away, never to be seen again, with ninety four thousand pounds in cash still in the boot of the car.

OTHER TITLES
by
RED LION PRESS

A STRANGE BLESSING (James McAuley, 1997).
Living With Mental Handicap in Ireland.
Ten personal accounts of the joys, the fears, the challenges, the disappointments and the rewards of experiencing and confronting mental disabilities.

FENNESSY"S FIELD (Enda McEvoy, 1998).
A century of hurling history at St. Kieran's College Kilkenny.
The traditions, the triumphs, the trainers, the tactics and the teams behind Ireland's most respected hurling nursery.

WALLS OF SILENCE (Annie Ryan, 1999).
A sad disturbing account of the hidden squalor, neglect and injustice silently suffered by patients and staff of our mental hospitals throughout this century and of the failure of successive governments to respect the rights of these helpless citizens.

THEMES IN KILKENNY'S HISTORY (2000).
A selection of lectures from the NUI Maynooth-Radio Kilkenny Academic Lecture series.

MENTAL HEALTH NURSING IN IRELAND (Hanora Henry and Richard Deady, 2001).
An overview of the many factors both directly and indirectly influencing the shape of psychiatric nursing in Ireland today.

Red Lion Press. "Woodpark", Great Oak,
Callan, Co. Kilkenny, Ireland.
Tel.: (00353) 056 25162. 086 369 4683.
e mail: redlionpress@elivefree.net